The Havana Treatment

Selected Stories 2001-2014

By Peter Devine

Cover Image Credit: Peter Devine

authorHOUSE®

AuthorHouse™
1663 Liberty Drive
Bloomington, IN 47403
www.authorhouse.com
Phone: 1 (800) 839-8640

Published by AuthorHouse   08/12/2015

ISBN: 978-1-5049-0593-0 (sc)
ISBN: 978-1-5049-0592-3 (e)

Print information available on the last page.

To my wife, who keeps my faith alive, my dreams intact, and my libido active.

And with thanks to FSK for her untiring support and feisty editing services.

Table of Contents

Preface

"The only unions which are always legitimate are those which are ordained by true passion."

Henri Stendahl

"The two sexes mutually corrupt and improve each other."

Mary Wollstonecraft

"The soul should always stand ajar, ready to welcome the ecstatic experience."

Emily Dickinson

"Have I caught thee, my heavenly jewel? Why, now let me die, for I have lived long enough."

William Shakespeare

Part I

Communion

"There was no hesitation, nothing held back. We were not particularly imaginative lovers. Youth has neither time nor inclination for imagination in lovemaking. An erect penis, a blooming clitoris, and plenty of natural lubricants – that's how youth's garden grows."

Communion

First Date

In the time before there was Time, there was a time to call and ask her for a date.

"Morgana?"

"Oh, hi."

"This is Paul."

"I know who this is."

"You do? I mean, you knew?"

"Well, when I heard your voice, Silly."

Silly, you bet. As silly as a boy can be. Silly when he hears your name spoken. Silly when he catches a glimpse of you in the hall with your books under your arm, lost in conversation. Silly when he spies your mother's car, the car he has committed to memory in great detail, sitting at the curb in front of the building after the sixth period bell has rung. Silly as he watches you slide in the passenger door, and sick at heart, in a silly way, as he watches you drive off on Friday afternoon knowing that he will not see you again until Monday mid-morning.

If there were world enough and time, he could calculate her thoughts, know her whims, predict her responses, and avoid putting himself at risk. Instead, driven by forces he only dimly comprehends, one fine Thursday night, closing his mother's bedroom door, he simply dials the number. He has a feeling in his chest of dread mixed with anticipation. Together they add up to numbness. His breathing is so shallow it seems to have stopped altogether.

Now, on the other end of the line, she waits. For the moment, at least, he has her undivided attention. It's not a welcome burden. Perhaps she is bored with him already. Surely she will be in time. Lamely he saunters forth. "I was looking for you after fifth period, but I guess I missed you."

"Mrs. Boyd kept me after class. To talk about my lab project. Can you believe it?"

"Your lab project?" he urges. And thankfully she surges to meet him with a stream-of-consciousness monologue about her school career, peppered with random gossip and candid observations about mutual acquaintances. He listens as she talks, straining through the telephone line to more keenly assess the form and substance of her, get a sense of her home life, her dreams, her desires, her pet peeves, her strongest alliances, her greatest weaknesses. Mostly he allows himself to be drenched in the torrent of *her-ness*. She goes on with little prompting, and after a minute and a half, maybe two, it occurs to him that he is smarter than she is. Smarter in school, that is. Which counts for something. It gives him the insane courage to look for his opening and plunge ahead.

"I was wondering if we could go out sometime. You know. A movie or something."

"I'd love to." God, straight to his heart like a cannonball. He tries to regroup. He's not done yet. "How about next Friday?"

"Oh God, I'll have to check with my mom. My uncle's coming into town and we're supposed to do a big dinner thing, but I'm not sure when." In saying this last part, her voice drops into a conspiratorial register which brings him a sense of pure pleasure, pure dangerous pleasure. "Wait just a sec."

He flops back on his mother's bed and holding the receiver in his hand, senses the tingle of anticipation that courses though his body. He begins to hum *Begin the Beguine* to himself, one of those old beloved standards from his parents' generation. Calling on that old Artie Shaw magic to deliver his prize.

"I'm back." *Her-ness* blossoms in his brain.

"You're back."

"S'okay. We can go."

In years to come, he would think of this moment as his first experience with a mind-altering substance: *Her-ness*.

After a week in which he has done his best to steer clear of her in school, not wanting to seem overly familiar nor give her the chance to pull him aside in the hallway and whisper hurriedly, "You know, I can't really go out this Friday after all, but call me another time, I'd love to get together," he spends Friday afternoon painstakingly cleaning his mother's car. Through the week he has borne the glorious burden of Her with him practically every waking moment. Her-in-him has made him sharper in class, wittier in conversation, more amenable to his mother and his younger brother, less inclined to do homework, more apt to daydream. He has painstakingly buttressed his worthiness by mentally rehearsing a number of humorous family anecdotes he can insert to keep the evening fun and light. He knows from the clothing she wears, the home in which she lives, her father's profession (airline pilot), that with this date he is reaching beyond his boundaries. His parents are divorced alcoholics, his clothing serviceable but outdated, his purse lean, his social connections both at school and in town virtually nil. He has no business dating a girl who is being groomed practically as a debutante, and the thought of what has prompted her to say yes (not only yes, but that phrase which is by now hard-wired into his very being, "I'd love to") is not only a consideration of endless intrigue, but is also the one thing that attacks him with relentless assurances that this date will not occur, there will be a phone call, there will be a cancellation, even now her parents are reconsidering and realizing the grievous error they have made in putting their daughter in the hands (or in the car, at least) of a certifiable social reprobate.

He picks his clothing with care. Over and over again. Looking for just the right level of *savoir-faire* and creature comfort. Making a statement that is really about concealment. A clever disguise in plain sight. Only after he wears himself out with this exercise does he resignedly settle on a pair of gabardine pants and a short-sleeved button-up shirt that are about as undemonstrative as one can imagine. His statement will be: I have no statement to make. He will carry the evening on his wits alone.

Once he is standing on the broad front porch of her house about to ring the doorbell, he discovers that he is, after all, quite witless. He pushes the bell and hears a chime sound faintly within. He listens in an abstract sense for the footsteps that will snatch him from his state of suspended animation and return him to the world of sentient beings, of thinking, feeling, and acting. He has managed to drive the car to her parent's sprawling manse on Military Road, gone through the wrought-iron gates, negotiated the gravel driveway, mounted the steps, crossed the porch, and rung the bell, all without appreciable effort, or even any sense of doing anything. Somehow, here he is. Somehow, he knows nothing, has nothing to say. He's not exactly a victim, but not quite innocent either.

"You must be Paul." Her mother has come to the door. She's fully turned out in a thoroughly practical yet trim-fitting dress, high heels, and faint lipstick. She has a touch of steel in her hair and a fixed grin in place. (At this hour on a Friday night, Paul's mother is already in her robe and slippers sipping vodka from an orange juice can.) She stands back and with a practiced gesture bids him enter.

"Morgana tells us that you're probably the best student in her class," her mother says, leading the way through well-appointed rooms into the den, where there's a television humming.

"I try to keep my grades up," he says. It's the simple truth, and that's all he can muster at the moment.

"Make yourself comfortable, Paul. Can I get you a Coca-Cola? She'll be down in a minute."

"A Coke would be fine." He could care less about a Coke, but he wants to give the woman something to do --

something for her trouble. He perches on the edge of the couch, looking at but not seeing the television. He scans his surroundings, but doesn't retain much of that investigation either. Mother shows up with a tumbler of Coke and ice cubes, which he gratefully accepts. Mother then disappears again.

"Hey." She announces herself. He hasn't seen her enter. His face breaks out in a grin. Happy and relieved, and also speechless, he stands up to greet her. She's a castaway's vision in a peach-colored outfit, with a sweater over her shoulders and a bow in her hair. As she draws closer, the smell of her perfume immediately intoxicates him. He's in a state of narcosis, with his own heartbeat drumming in his ears, and insane, impracticable thoughts skirting the perimeters of his consciousness.

"You're a knockout," he says gallantly from his place in the clouds. It's a phrase from his parents' era. His mother, before her marriage to a seafaring man, had lived in Greenwich Village, New York City. The phrase should have some currency still, even in the South.

"Aren't you sweet?" she says, and hits him with a practiced widening of the eyes. A pure debutante move. "Mama, we're on our way, okay?"

Mother returns briefly. "Paul, it was lovely to meet you. You kids have a good time." And then, to her daughter, "Honey, not too late. You know Uncle Bill will be getting in early."

Morgana kisses her mother's cheek distractedly. "I know, Mama. And you don't need to wait up."

"Drive carefully, Paul," Mother says.

Not until they are halfway back to town, with Morgana thankfully going on about her Biology classes, does Paul return to his senses enough to realize that his date is not wearing one of the frilly dresses she favors for school, but has on instead a comparatively tight skirt. She rides with her legs curled under her on the bench seat of his mother's Edsel, the skirt tucked demurely just above her knees. The curve of her thigh and the animated features of her face softly lit by the dashboard's glow give him such a sense of fullness that he slows the car to a stately 35 miles per hour, just to prolong the moment. He senses that it is a moment not soon to be repeated, if ever.

"Have you heard anything I've been saying?"

He catches himself. "I've heard most of it," he assures her.

"It's okay. My dad tells me I have a tendency to rattle on." She laughs. He chances a glance at her, and she is looking directly at him. *Her-ness* pours into him, and he grips the steering wheel. "You're sweet, you know that?" Her perfume mingles with his skin and fills his senses. He drives doggedly on.

As he had promised, they go to the movie. A movie with Doris Day and Rock Hudson. Doris is such a winning personality, she can't help but make the night memorable, that's Paul's thinking. In the darkness of the theater, he tries to interpret Morgana's body language as she settles in next to him. They share popcorn. She holds the bag for both of them, and when she leans in his direction, their shoulders are briefly welded together and her hand slides across his forearm in an arc of electric bliss. Once in a while he steals a glance at her face, and is surprised to see that she has donned glasses. In the blue-moon glare of the darkened theater her short black hair frames her face and leaves her shorn of all artifice, a vision of pure ageless innocence, a girl and her dreams. Her face suddenly looks like her mother's. He swears to himself to protect her and deliver her from all enemies, foreign and domestic. He longs to hold her and caress her. Another part of him longs to bite her and shake her. They finish the popcorn, and her hand falls on his upper arm and lingers there. Time, and the movie, grind to a dead halt. The back of his neck prickles and he senses that he may be perspiring. *Good God, Doris, can you please get on with it*, he prays. Then it is over, and they are forced to recover their senses and turn out into the street like the innocents they pretend to be.

"How about we stop in at the Hill?" he asks her. It's the

burger and shake dispensary and teen after-hours hangout at the crossroads of rural roads 190 and 63 on the eastern edge of town. It'll be on the way home for her.

He goes inside (there is no curb service) for the coke floats, and brings them back to the car. He observes that in his absence, she has touched up her makeup, her lipstick is darker than before.

"You know, I've always wondered why you didn't go out for the cheerleading squad," he says. An oblique way of complimenting her sex appeal.

"Grades," she says, sucking on her straw. "Mom was always afraid my grades would suffer."

"I could help you with your homework," he says. "It's really just a question of boning up before tests."

She regards him evenly across the rim of her cup. "Plus those cheerleader outfits. I think ours are atrocious."

"Not on you they wouldn't be." After all he's been through tonight, he's feeling wrung-out and reckless. Relaxed at last. Plunging ahead without a plan or a design of any sort. Just to plunge.

She's sitting with her shoes off, her back against the door, her legs drawn up, and she extends one leg and prods him briefly on his thigh with her toes. "It's really just a question of boning up before tests," she mocks. "If you've got brains, that is."

He reflexively has to stop himself from catching and holding her bare foot. "Like you don't," he mocks back.

"Not the way you do." she says. Paul dimly realizes that both she and her mother have gone out of their way to compliment him on his academic accomplishments, but not until this moment has he realized that doing well on multiple choice tests might at times earn a fellow a girl's bare foot snuggled against him. He makes a mental note, and underlines it twice.

"I'd rather be pole vaulting," he says truthfully. Last spring he had taken two gold medals and a silver in regional track meets, a singular achievement that seems not to have registered at all with the desirable females in his class.

Instead, he's the Homework King.

"I know about your pole vaulting, mister," she says, and grins. "I've seen you at practices."

"You have?" He's unabashedly bathing in the stream of *her-ness* that's coming his way, not knowing how long it will last or whether he'll ever be invited to immerse himself in it again.

She looks over his shoulder and her eyes widen. She emits a muted girlish screech. Paul turns and sees a couple approaching the car. He rolls down the window. "Oh, lookit *y'all*," Morgana says. He dimly recognizes the couple, a pair whom he cannot recall ever seeing together. Maybe they are first-time daters, just like he and Morgana. It bodes well.

Briefly they exchange pleasantries, little whoops and sorties of humor. Friday night blowing-off-steam conversation. After taking up what seems like too much time that should belong exclusively to him and Morgana, the couple excuse themselves and drift away. At least the news of Paul's dating this sensuous creature the world calls Morgana will be published abroad at school. He'll have that going for him.

The evening is winding down. After they leave the Hill, there are only two choices left. He either drives her home, or they go somewhere and park. Parking, he knows, is a pastime reserved for couples who are going steady, or for dates with girls who have a certain reputation. Since he and his Morgana fall into neither of those categories, he dutifully bends his route along Military Road towards her house. It's after 10:30, and if there is to be any deviation from the schedule, it will have to be her idea. Frankly, he's worn out. The fact that she has returned her bare foot to a place against his thigh is not so much an invitation to mischief as an affirmation of something good, something comfortable about him. A trophy with which he will be content.

Thorough the wrought-iron gates they go, and he eases the car up the drive and stops below the porch. What he does then requires the kind of stupid courage, of desperate heroism, that he does not instinctively possess. He turns off the motor and the lights, reaches impulsively down and, gripping her foot lightly with both hands, tugs gently until he pops one of her toes. She giggles and he pops another one. He pops all five.

"Come here, Silly," she says, and drawing her leg back underneath her she leans across in his direction. He catches a glimpse of the tops of her breasts as she comes in, and then he is enveloped by the perfumed heat of her. Her mouth primly goes against his own. Her lips are cold from the Coke float. Her tongue, pointed and polite, flicks briefly against his teeth, unlocking his jaw. His tongue edges forth to meet it. There is a sudden surprising intake of her breath, and he thinks he detects a low hum of pleasure in the back of her throat. She places a hand against the back of his head and works her lips against his while with her other hand she lifts his hand and presses it to the top of her thigh with sudden fervor. There is a surge in her breathing, almost a sigh, and she pulls her face away briefly and regards him. She has taken charge. "Kiss me some more," she tells him.

Suddenly it's like driving a car, or shooting a basketball. He's got the hang of it. Adroitly he explores the inside of her mouth with his tongue, and even hums with her when she sounds deep in her throat. Even though it's only been going on for a minute or so, it seems likes he's been here before, been here forever, locked at the lips with arguably the most desirable girl in his class. He permits his hand to grip her thigh gently, and wander, unguided, higher and closer to the Forbidden City. Beyond the background noise of her perfume, he can taste and smell her room, her homework, her endless phone conversations, her television-watching, her bath soap, her girl-ness, her personhood. Under his hand she stirs restively, and her breasts press against his forearm. With a mild shock, he realizes that she apparently has an appetite for this sort of thing. She's getting *all carried away,* as his mother would say. Something in him is triggered by this realization, and he feels an impulse that seems foolhardy but undeniably right. Heroic, even.

With his hands he quiets her, and with a last lingering

inhalation, he uncouples their clinging mouths. Her eyes are momentarily unseeing, she seems to have lost her bearings as she leans back against the seat. Gently he brushes strands of damp hair from her forehead, and leans across and plants a chaste kiss at the corner of her mouth. He removes his hand from her leg, and grins crazily, happily, contentedly. "I meant what I said about the homework," he tells her.

Communion

It's funny how time passes.

Fast or slow, I mean. Sometimes it goes so slow it seems to double back on itself and come to a dead halt, years later. Or maybe what actually happens is that it races ahead, so far ahead, that it travels clear out of sight, leaving you standing there like the last man at the last bus stop in the world, with no idea whether there'll ever be another bus coming along.

Out of time. Caught up in time. Ahead of your time. Timeless.

It's funny. How time passes.

I was in Portugal last year. On business. Well, mostly business. I take pictures for a living. Wow, you say. How neat. You're thinking of yourself in an exotic location, snapping photos of any and every thing that catches your fancy. It's not really like that. I take photos for travel publications, and when I'm on assignment, it's very targeted work. Hotels, attractions, and historic places mostly. Nothing too artistic or creative. Nothing that's going to place too much of a strain on the imagination of the reader who's casually flipping through the pages, or scanning the website, trying to get comfortable with a vacation destination. It's a job, is what I'm saying. And like most any job, it loses a lot of its luster once you're inside it for awhile. Portugal never loses its luster, though. So I had that going for me.

I was in a rented car about thirty miles south of Oporto. Off the beaten track. Or at least off National Highway Five.

I'd had to leave the track to get photos of a monastery that had recently been converted into an *auberge* - a hostel. It was on a hillside above a narrow valley. Twelve rooms only, but each room with a valley overlook. An ancient orchard in front of the property. The orchard was being cleared and spruced up. New trellises had been installed, and flagstones were being laid to form a patio. Here, guests would be able to take tea in the morning, or drink their Port wine in the evening, looking out over the valley. One of the women who was working at cutting away the overgrowth and the tangle of wild vines gave me such a smile that I offered to take her picture. She was round-cheeked and heavy-set, had a shawl tied around her shoulders, and she smiled resolutely, with a gap in her teeth, when I took the photo. I pressed the review button, and when she saw herself, she smiled up at me with a kind of ironic smile, as though the two of us were looking at a photo of a third person who neither of us knew very well. I patted her shoulder. *"Obrigado, obrigado,"* she said earnestly contentedly, and I went on back down the path toward my car, leaving her to her work.

Maybe it was a bend in the road, or the way the light struck a copse of trees ahead, but I suddenly found myself thinking about my first wife. We had honeymooned in Portugal. Had probably come down this very road. We were young, we were hitchhiking, the fact is, we weren't even married yet. I'd been living in Europe for a year, and then she joined me after her college graduation. We'd gotten together in Barcelona in the heady month of September, and after three days of romping each other in the room of the pension overlooking the *Ramblas*, we set out straightaway to peruse the Iberian Peninsula. First we took the train over to Madrid, then up to Salamanca, after which we relied on hitchhiking, crossing the border at Fuentes de Orono, which, as border crossings go, was benign and lovely in the autumn light. Once into Portugal, we slowed the pace and stuck to back roads, in no particularly hurry to get anywhere. Which, in itself, is kind of a treasured talisman from youth. Once you're past fifty, spending even fifteen minutes without being in a particular hurry is a rarity indeed. And hitchhiking on the back roads of Portugal in the Sixties was a pretty good remedy against getting yourself into a hurry-up state. As hitchhikers, you were naturally at the dispensation of the drivers, and the secondary roads in those days were narrow and only sporadically maintained, wonderfully medieval in nature. They were traveled principally by farmers, peddlers, trades-people, and the occasional retired military man. The motorists that came your way were seldom traveling more than 20 or 30 kilometers further along, and it was, in most cases, going to take them the better part of an hour to do that. But we were each twenty-one years old, and it was the month of September. And it was Portugal. You do the math

Generally by late afternoon or early evening, we would begin to consider our night's lodging. We'd inquire of the drivers. Or scan the roadside structures as we rolled though (or occasionally walked through) towns along the route. Lodging was not difficult to come by, even in the small towns -- another medieval trait. Oftentimes it was just a run-down older building with two or three sparsely furnished rooms for travelers. Occasionally it was a little more grand -- an actual *pension*, with a reception desk, an inner courtyard, a second story. Perhaps a small dining room for *el desayuno*, along with a *patrona* who attended you solicitously, while a couple of dogs tucked up behind her skirt watched you with guarded skepticism. Since most of the guests were overnight travelers, as were we, there was little time or incentive to become overly familiar with either the people or the surroundings. When we arrived at the door we would ask whether there were any rooms available. *"Hay habitaciones?"*

Pushing her dogs back out of the way, the aging crone would take us down a hallway, or through a courtyard, and swing open the door of a room. An old iron bed, sagging noticeably in the middle, with a thin coverlet. A nightstand with a metal pitcher on it. On one of the walls, an image of the Virgin, or the Sacred Heart. The floor of ancient tile. Overhead, a bare 40 watt bulb operated by a chain. A small writing table that seemed to have resided there peacefully since the Middle Ages. And a single window (we always insisted on a window, and seldom were disappointed) looking, if we were lucky, onto a garden, or a patio. The toilet was seldom in the room itself, but in the better establishments you might have your own toilet attached. Even as we took in what we knew would be our night's lodging, even as we delighted that it was located several blocks above the main street, away from the traffic, with a pleasant view of the valley stretching away to the west (I always went immediately to the window to examine the view), we would inquire about the price. As a formality. *"Treinta-cinco escudos,"* she would say, in a perfectly flat take it or leave it tone of voice. Somewhere in the neighborhood of a dollar and a half. Inexpensive, but on our traveling budget, not inconsequential. Toilet in the room, a bonus. *"Esta bien,"* I would tell her. We would sling our knapsacks onto the creaking bed, and while Karen paid her visit to the toilet, I would briefly discuss with the *patrona* where dinner fare might be obtained at the appropriate hour, and which, if any, local legends or heroes the village might boast or publish. Then she would move away down the hall and leave Karen and me to ourselves and our imaginations.

As I mentioned, at this point in time we were not yet married. We could not know for a certainty that later we would marry, and remain in that state for 22 years, with the union producing three fine and handsome sons and terminating in a not-unfriendlydivorce. Of all this we were blissfully unaware. What we had was our imaginations, our shared enthusiasms, a couple of healthy libidos, and, for the time, an untrammeled future. The world waited to see what we would do, the way it customarily will for youth. And when the world is waiting, that is a sense of power indeed. Power that, to youth, seems a natural attendant, like the old woman's dogs, to come at one's bidding, or to lie in wait at your command. And though we lived out of knapsacks, Karen never failed to present herself as attractively, and as undoubtedly female, as she could. I dressed simply but conservatively in worn familiar trousers and unremarkable shirts. Iberia in these times was not yet awakened from its medieval slumber, and there was still great respect for personal etiquette, good manners, and common courtesy. So, groomed, courteous, and completely sensible, we would saunter forth to seek victuals as the September sun bled its life away into the hills above the valley.

Later, back in our small aerie, alone together again, together after a year's separation, and together without any thought or consideration of ever being in any state other than together, we would fall to the evening's sweet work. I would mount her wonderful blonde body, she would spread her legs wide, and it would be a case of the old in-and-out until our hungers were abated. Looking back on that small room above the valley, I listen across the years for sounds she may have made. I try to remember the look in her eyes, the set of her lips, to recall the sense of her shapely legs encircling me as she took me in. She received me in an absolute Catholic sense, as a dispensation, as something ordained by heaven and ultimately intended for the betterment of the both of us. There was no hesitation, nothing held back. We were not particularly imaginative lovers. Youth has neither time nor inclination for imagination in lovemaking. An erect penis, a blooming clitoris, and plenty of natural lubricants – that's how youth's garden grows.

Well, the years intervened, as years will. The dispensation ended. The lack of imagination became a fatal disease. But none of these things rendered that little room, and others like it through which we passed, less holy. As in medieval times, we would awaken early in the morning and often engage in serendipitous morning sex before showering, dressing, and preparing to push off. Only the occasional stains of our issue on the sheets would reveal our secrets, and after we had gone our way and the *patrona* entered the room and removed the sheets from the bed, she would know, and understand. As in medieval times, she understood our dispensation, and the communion that we had taken. And she would remember her own communion, now years past, and cross herself reflexively.

And somewhere, out on the highway, or a secondary road, Karen and I would be in the sun, laughing, eating grapes, and already becoming hungry for communion again.

Sentimental Journey

A big crackin' sky, his grandfather would have called it. And it was a big crackin' sky. Of course it may have seemed like such a big crackin' sky because Lordsburg was such a small crackin' town. Lost in the vast expanse of the southwest New Mexico plateau, it was not much more than a street with a drugstore, a couple of gas stations, and an old hotel. Bridey had spent the night on a bench in front of the Conoco station and was relieved not to have been rousted. With the newly-emptied POW camp nearby, he could easily have been mistaken for an escaped internee, he looked half Italian anyway. Even with his uniform on, which didn't hang on his slender frame that way it had when he'd mustered out, he probably had a misplaced look about him. Sitting on the bench he had tried to mentally rehearse a story that he could give the MP's or the Hidalgo County Sheriff's department if they picked him up. He would need a story too, because if he told them the real one, he'd end up in stir before you could say twenty-three skidoo. *My mother got tired of me sitting on the front porch all day drinking Early Times and Coke, she was worried that my mind wasn't right since I got mustered out back in July, so she clipped out and sent in an entry form with my name on it, and we won first prize and now I'm riding the Sunset Limited out to Los Angeles to meet the dancer Eleanor Powell, who is my mother's favorite actress. That's right, all expenses paid.* Yep, a story like that would really go over well. Even if he had been serving in an MP unit in

Belgium at the end of the war, they'd run him in PDQ with a story like that. But somehow they had overlooked him and as dawn broke in the chill air, he thought briefly about his grandfather because of that big crackin' sky of Lordsburg.

The railroad tracks lay just one block south of Main St. and after the sun had cleared the mountains in the east, Bridey picked up his satchel and walked that way. He would've spent the night in the station itself, except that it was locked from sundown to sunup, again because of the proximity of the POW camp. He didn't mind being out-of-doors, anyway. He'd gotten a ride down the evening before with Bill Beedle who ran a hot-shot service, and the anticipation of riding the famous train out to Los Angeles had made the night pass quickly. His mother had been more impressed that he was. "Loss Angeleeze," she exclaimed, rolling the name on her tongue. "Your dad and I were going to go once. We never made it."

"There's a lot of places you never made it, Ma," Bridey told her. Since his dad had gotten himself killed under a farm combine she hadn't been more than 15 miles out of Silver City. And that had been ten years ago.

For the train ride Bridey was going to wear his dress uniform. His mother came into his room as he was packing. "This is for once you get out there," she said. Over her arm she carried his father's cream-colored sport coat. It was in a plastic bag. Bridey had seen him wear it only a time or two. With his broad shoulders and his ruddy outdoor complexion, on him the coat had looked like a million dollars. Bridey had the same complexion, but not quite the shoulders. He slipped it on. It hung well enough. "You look like that Tyrone Power," his mother said. She teared up.

"I'll need a tie," he told her.

Now the station was open. It was high-ceilinged room with some worn-out benches and at one end a small counter where passengers could buy tickets. Over the counter was a large clock. The hands read ten minutes to seven. Behind the counter was a man with wire-rimmed spectacles and a green eye shade, just like in those old western movies.

Bridey was the only passenger in evidence. He parked his satchel near one of the benches and approached the counter. "What time does the Limited come through?" he asked.

"Schedule says 7:11," the man said without looking up from his paperwork. Bridey wondered what kind of paperwork could keep a man busy at this hour in Lordsburg.

"Fellow get a cup of coffee?"

"If you're a passenger, there'll be coffee on board," the man said. He raised his head and looked at Bridey, his eyes flicking across the decorations on Bridey's tunic. He reached down and brought up a thermos from under the counter. "Or you can grab you one of those cups over yonder."

Bridey took a ceramic cup from a tray under the window facing the tracks and brought it over to where the man waited. Unscrewing the lid of the thermos, he poured the cup half full of steaming, good-smelling java. "Got some sugar back here, no cream," he said.

"This is fine," Bridey said. It was only the two of them in the quiet station. "Appreciate it."

"That'll get you down the road, Sergeant."

Bridey went over and sat down on one of the worn black benches. He held the cup in his hands and let the heat work its way into his palms. "You wasn't out at the camp here at one time?" the man asked. He had gone back to his paperwork. It was an idle inquiry.

"First time in Lordsburg," Bridey said. "Last POW camp I seen was in Belgium."

"Is that right," said the stationmaster. At one time the Lordsburg camp had held upwards of 5,000 German and Italian POW's, which wasn't much compared to the numbers they'd managed in Belgium. But Eyeshade was once again immersed in his paperwork, and after a minute Bridey took his coffee cup and went out the front door of the station onto the narrow trackside platform. The high desert morning was clear as a bell with an unbroken cupola of early blue stretching overhead. The coffee was warming going down and the stiffness of sleeping on the bench was beginning to work its way out of Bridey's frame. Los Angeles, here I come, he thought. And for the first time, his arrival on America's Pacific shore seemed to be a real event.

He had just drained the last of his cup when he detected a shift in the atmosphere to the East. A low hum accompanied by a movement in the air signaled the approach of the train, which then sounded its air-horn, a sound as suddenly exhilarating as a Tommy Dorsey trombone section. Peering down the tracks Bridey caught sight of the big locomotive coming on. He watched for a long moment as it gained mass and substance, and then went back into the station for his grip. "Appreciate your hospitality," he said to the stationmaster, replacing the coffee mug on the tray where he had found it.

"Looks like we'll get you out of here right on time," the man with the wire-rimmed spectacles said. Above his head the clock marked five minutes after seven. Bridey went back outside as the locomotive came rolling past, the big firebox like a living, breathing thing. The train slowed and ground to a halt while Bridey watched. A conductor swung down from the silver Pullman car and looked up and down the track. A moment later a gent in a fedora and a blue suit came down and stood beside him and then they both waited, looking expectantly back at the car. A third man now appeared, this one with a large camera around his neck. He came down to the platform and took up a position looking back at the train, his camera at the ready. Bridey picked up his satchel and walked toward the men. As he approached, Fedora held up a cautionary hand. "Just give us a moment, pal, if you don't mind. We've got the lady coming down."

Bridey stopped in his tracks and joined the three men in waiting. Directly a young woman appeared at the top of the steps. The conductor stood close and offered her his hand while the photographer snapped away. The girl had dark blonde hair down to her shoulders and wore high heels and white gloves and a dark red suit over a white blouse. On her head she had a pillbox hat and she smiled broadly at the conductor. She shimmered with the unmistakable air of a celebrity of some sort, and Bridey watched from afar as she stepped onto the platform, her faced wreathed in a wonderful welcoming smile, the kind you can usually turn on and off if you're good at it as most celebrities are. The photographer shot her from one angle and then another but always with the train in the background. Fedora meanwhile had gone back onto the train and now reappeared carrying in his hand a stand or a post of some sort. Following the photographer's instructions, he walked over and placed the stand in front of the station windows. Bridey could now see that the stand had a clock affixed to the top of it, a clock with a white face and black hour and minute hands. Once he had the clock in the position that the photographer wanted Fedora beckoned for the blonde to come and stand where the clock was visible over her shoulder as the photographer lined up his shot. Bridey could not imagine the purpose of this activity, particularly in a place like Lordsburg so early in the morning. But looking at the blonde he had to acknowledge that she appeared to be a classy girl and would likely not have gotten involved with a scheme that was idle or foolish. Giving it no further thought, he picked up his satchel and was about to make his way up the steps to the Pullman when he heard a voice calling over his shoulder: "Hey pal! Excuse me. Soldier. Hey!" He turned and saw that he himself was the object of Fedora's call. The blue-suited fellow approached him and solicitously touched Bridey at the elbow. "D'you think I could get you to step over here with us for a moment for a souvenir photo with the lady? Just take a moment." Up close the fellow had the insincerely sincere look of a fellow who sold expensive items for a living. He was well-shaved and his shirt was clean and pressed. "Whatta ya say, sport?" And he gently drew on Bridey's elbow until the two of them were moving in the direction of the clock and the girl and the photographer. "What'd you say your name was, soldier?" Fedora asked him as they moved.

"Brisco. Sergeant Bridey A. Brisco. Third United States Army." He realized it wouldn't mean much to Fedora, but it was the most impressive credential he could summon at the moment.

"Terrific. Sergeant, this is Miss Doris Day, she sings with the Les Brown Orchestra, and we're out here to honor the troops as they arrive back home." Bridey found himself wondering briefly which troops they were honoring on the nearly empty station platform in Lordsburg before he found himself momentarily face-to-face with the blonde, who beamed in his direction. Fedora relieved him of his satchel and pivoted him so that he and the blonde stood side-by-side facing the photographer, who clicked away, moved for a different angle, and clicked away some more. At one point Bridey looked at the blonde. "Eyes this way, Sergeant, if you don't mind," the photographer said. He clicked away some more, and then was done. "Thank you, Sergeant," Fedora said, and handed him back his satchel before moving in to take the blonde by the elbow and steer her in the direction of the train.

"Appreciate your help, soldier," said the photographer as he collected the stand with the clock on the top. On closer inspection Bridey could see that the face and hands of the clock were not real, but were painted to represent 7:00. Gathering it under his arm, he toted it back toward the train. The conductor stood at the bottom of the Pullman stairs. "Board!" he shouted in his conductor voice, and up the stairs Bridey went. At the top of the stairs he turned right and went about halfway down the length of the nearly-empty Pullman car before he tucked his satchel into the overhead rack, removed his jacket and placed it on the aisle seat and slid into the window seat on the platform side. Almost at once the train began moving, and very shortly the Lordsburg platform had disappeared from view and they were gathering speed as they rolled out into the vastness of the New Mexican desert.

Being aboard a train and feeling the rhythm of the car clipping over the rail joints caused Bridey to reminisce – his last journey by train had been three months ago, after he had mustered out in New Jersey and ridden home, a two and a half day journey which marked the passing of an era for

Bridey. Like so many others, his life had been consumed by the war. For three years and nine months his every waking activity had been monitored and managed by the United States Army, and while he had done his best to reserve some identity for himself, in the end it had all belonged to the Army, and the Army had molded him into a species of man that was an implement of its will, and the will of the Army, the all-powerful force around which his life was centered, was as mysterious, inscrutable, arbitrary, un-knowable and damnable as God Himself. The considerations that had been present in the life of a nineteen-year-old before the Army had called - a car, a girl, a tractor, a job, a friend or two – had been systematically expelled from his waking thoughts to be replaced by considerations of a more mundane and pressing variety: a hot meal, a hot shower, a chance to sleep, a dry pair of socks, a moment of uninterrupted solitude. During the train ride back from the East Coast his mind had been coming to terms with all that, and with the absence of all that, and the thoughts of what would come to replace all that, and even though the train at times had seemed to barely crawl across the vast landscape of his home continent, he hadn't minded the slow passage at all because it was, after all, the end of an era and even at his tender age, he had learned that the passing an era is not something that should be hurried.

"Hi." There was a rustle at his side and he looked up to see the blonde standing in the aisle. "Do you mind if I sit with you for a moment?" She had shed her jacket and the white blouse was buttoned modestly up to her neck. She beamed at him in the toothy way she had displayed on the platform, and then just as suddenly turned down the beam and relaxed her features.

"Hope I'm not disturbing you."

"No ma'am," Bridey said. In his Army years nobody had ever minded disturbing a fellow. In fact, most of the people in his life during those years seemed to extract pleasure out of disturbing him. "No disturbance at all." He gathered his jacket from the seat and held it on his lap while she slid with easy familiarity into the seat and angled her body towards him. She was a drop-dead looker, all right. Bridey had been able to tell that even at a modest distance on the platform.

"Well, I kind of wanted to apologize for the treatment back there on the platform. Those boys are always in such a hurry they sometimes run roughshod over people, and you fellows deserve better than that. I certainly think so anyway." The earnestness in her tone, the resolute beauty of her easy smile, and those captivating eyes gave added weight to her sense of conviction, and Bridey was sure he would be in complete agreement with just about opinion she cared to express. "I'm Doris Mary Ann Kappelhoff, by the way. Cincinnati, Ohio." She had shorn herself of the white gloves of earlier and eagerly held out her hand for Bridey to take. Her grip was sincere, warm and firm.

"Bridey Brisco, ma'am. Silver City, New Mexico."

"Silver City. You don't say. What a positively wonderful name for a town." She beamed at Bridey again, and he realized that she wasn't putting it on. She was a natural-born beamer. "I just love your state. The wide-open spaces and all. Ohio is much more hilly and full of forests and woods. I've always loved the wide-open spaces. And please don't call me ma'am. I'm 23 years old and half the time I'm not sure who I am or where I'm supposed to be, so ma'am doesn't quite fit." She paused, and relaxed her features. "I'm really going on a bit, aren't I? I didn't come up here to bother you. I just wanted to say thanks is all."

"I don't mind, ma'am. Spent the last few years in the company of people who don't talk much, and the sound of your voice is fine by me." He smiled in her direction, but his smile felt awkward and unnatural, not at all like hers. "I guess I'm not sure what the thanks is for is all."

"Well, for helping out with our little project for one thing. I never know what those fellows have in mind, they don't always explain things to me, so I was as surprised as you probably were when they shanghaied you to step into the picture. But I'm sure glad they did." She smiled at Bridey again, and he began to think she might be one of the prettiest girls he'd ever laid eyes on. Since he was momentarily at a loss for words, she went on. "In case you were wondering, we're doing some crazy publicity photos for the song. CBS arranged it, and we tied it in with a trip I made home last month to visit with my mother, who's still back there in good ol' Cincinnati."

"You don't live in Cincinnati anymore? Where do you live?" Bridey was struggling manfully to follow her conversation, but the alluring sight of her lips moving was keeping him distracted.

She laughed, a laugh of genuine good humor. "This girl sort of lives with the band, and I certainly don't mean that the way it sounds. But we're on the road more often than not. Although I do have a tiny apartment in Beverly Hills, which as you may know is out in Los Angeles. I think I slept there a couple of times last month, but I can't always remember. Do you mind very much if I smoke?" And she opened the clutch she was carrying, took out a gold-colored pack of cigarettes and withdrew one, inclining the pack in Bridey's direction. He wasn't usually a smoker, but he wanted what she wanted so he took one. She then rummaged briefly, pulled out a lighter, and lit his first, then her own. Her hand was a little less than steady. "I only smoke when I'm nervous, and the boys discourage my smoking of course, so sometimes I just have to get away from them."

"I'm 23 myself," Bridey offered, wondering briefly what she had to be nervous about. A long draught on the cigarette had calmed his nerves and cleared his mind somewhat, and he was happy to be able to contribute to the conversation.

"No kidding! Tell me your name again and I swear I won't forget it twice." She had settled herself comfortably back in the seat. The smoking seemed to have calmed her as well. She had crossed her legs and the brief glance which Bridey afforded himself revealed a slender well-formed calf that went along perfectly with the rest of her.

"Bridey. Bridey Brisco. And I'll confess I might need to know yours again as well."

"Doris. Doris Mary Ann Kapplehoff. But if it's easier,

my stage name is just plain Doris Day."

"And you travel around with a band?"

"That's right," Doris told him. "The Les Brown Band. I'm the girl singer. I've been with Les for a couple of years now. And glad to have the work, if you want to know the truth. You might have heard us on the radio, although I wouldn't blame you if you hadn't. Out in Los Angeles people sometimes assume that the world revolves around the entertainment industry, but once you get away from all that, you realize that most people are just trying to get on with their lives, more than anything."

"Huh. I guess that describes me all right," Bridey told her, a confession that ordinarily couldn't have been pried out of him, but at the moment came rather easily.

"I can imagine," Doris said. "Most of the service guys I meet are kind of up in the air with their futures and all. Certainly the enlisted men are. You're a sergeant, aren't you?"

"How'd you know that?"

"That how you were introduced to me when I met you." She turned and looked at Bridey with an air of inviting familiarity that he didn't think he'd ever received from any woman before, not even his mother.

"I guess I was distracted by the guy with the clock," Bridey grinned.

"Oh, that." Doris laughed. "It was just a prop for the song. You know: *seven, that's the time we leave, at seven.*" She had lifted her chin and with a coy smile had sung the line in a low, even tone with a kind of sweet accent on the sevens that made Bridey consider the hour in a way in that he had never thought about it before.

"I've heard that before," Bridey said. "That's your song?"

"Well, it's Les's song actually. But I recorded it with the band, yes I did. And to tell the truth, Mr. Bridey, sir, when I made the recording, I was thinking of you."

"You didn't even know me then," Bridey said.

"Well, when I say you I mean all you boys in uniform,

especially the ones who got sent overseas. The name of
the song is *Sentimental Journey.* Would you like to hear it?
I could sing it for you." So saying, Doris extinguished her
cigarette in the small ashtray in the arm of the seat, sat
forward, straightened her spine and cleared her throat, as
earnest and eager to please as a little girl at a recital. "Only
if you really want to hear it," she said, shooting Bridey a
sidelong glance. Bridey nodded without hesitation. She took
a breath and launched into her song in a soft but perfectly
controlled, honey-coated voice. As she sang she enunciated
each word and infused it with unabashed tenderness. When
she mentioned the memories she rolled her eyes as though
sifting through memories of her own. At the mention of
"wild anticipation" she turned in Bridey's direction and he
watched as her eyes adopted a coyness and her lips became
taut and teasing, the tricks of a professional. *"Seven, that's
the time we leave at seven, I'll be waiting up for heaven, countin'
every mile of railroad track that takes me back..."* When she
sang of heaven she made it sound like the place they found
themselves at that very moment, right there on a train
heading west together. As the last low notes escaped her
lips, her eyes welled with tears and she dropped her head.
"Oh golly. I'm sorry, Bridey. It just gets me every time when
I think about what we've all gone through..."

Without thinking, Bridey reached out his hand and
placed it lightly on her forearm. "That's about the most
beautiful song I've ever heard Miss Doris. I'm much obliged
to you." He gave her arm a squeeze and withdrew his
hand. Then she leaned across and placed a sisterly kiss on
his cheek. "No, Bridey, it's I who am obliged to *you.* Now,
if you'll excuse me a moment, I do think I need to visit the
powder room." She excused herself, stood, and moved aft
down the Pullman while Bridey turned his attention to the
window and the lonesome stretches of the New Mexican
prairie that rolled by. The nearness of such a good-looking
girl and her solicitous treatment of him had sent waves of
well-being washing through his soul and for the moment he
was content to linger there, not even trying to make sense of

it all. When he heard the sound of the connecting door of the coach being opened and closed again, and he looked up, his heart sank. Two MP's in their white helmets and carrying white night-sticks were making their way down the aisle with time on their hands and their gazes displaying the unhealthy curiosity that usually spelled trouble for men in uniform. Servicemen called them"Snowballs" because of their telltale white helmets. Bridey turned his attention back to the scenery hoping that they would pass him by, but from the corner of his eye he saw the tip of one of the night-sticks come to rest on the arm of the aisle seat and he knew it was not to be.

"Enjoying the scenery, are you soldier?"

For a long moment Bridey resisted any acknowledgement of this deliberate irony. The night stick was raised briefly and came down insistently on the arm rest. "I got my bag and got my reservation," Bridey responded without looking at the two. The line from Doris's song fit the occasion perfectly.

"How about your paperwork? Guess you got that too."

Reluctantly Bridey looked up at his inquisitors. The one in front had the flat eyes, the wide-set nostrils and the jutting chin of a pugilist, probably a failed pugilist. The other, Bridey noticed briefly, was smaller and younger with a dark countenance and the stone-dead look of a man who beat up women. A perfect pair of rousters they were. Just doing their jobs. Bridey reached into the breast pocket of his uniform blouse and pulled out his driver's license and train ticket and handed them across before he went back to looking out the window, displaying a marked lack of interest in how the snowballs chose to interpret the documents.

There was a brief pause before the smaller man piped up in his high-pitched voice, "These don't look like no discharge papers to me. You better dig some more, pal."

Bridey turned to face the two MP's. Having served in an MP platoon briefly in Belgium after the Germans had surrendered, he understood the need for military law, and understood the unruly nature of enlisted men when they've got walk-around money in their pockets, drink available, and a civilian population which they neither understand nor greatly respect. None of these particulars existed here in peacetime New Mexico, however, and the whole charade of military regimentation had worn thin on his sensibilities. But there was no point in pushing his luck. "Fellows, I mustered out in Bayonne, New Jersey over three months ago. I'm basically a civilian. The war is over. I don't believe there's any law says I have to tote my discharge certificate with me everywhere I go."

At this the big man tapped his night stick on the armrest. "When you're wearing that uniform, as far as we're concerned, you're still military personnel. And you're in Military District IV, which is one of the most sensitive districts in the country with the camps and all. So to answer your question, you'd better stand up and come on out here where we can get a better look at you."

Bridey turned for a last look out the window at the peacetime countryside passing by and considered his options. He knew the liberties that the Snowballs could take with a man in uniform. Heaving him off the train might be the least of the indignities he would suffer. A good working over with the nightsticks on account of General Principles was almost a certainty, simply because he had talked back. This time the nightstick reached out a little further and pointedly probed his upper arm. "Nice and easy, pal. Step on out."

Without looking up, Bridey turned back towards the two of them. He had decided not to comply. In the close confines of the Pullman they'd have a hard time handling him, and he could do some damage before they managed to subdue him. There was no point in it, he knew, but he'd had a bellyful and just wasn't in the mood to play along. He had reached up and actually gripped the offending nightstick when he heard Doris' voice coming up the aisle at a good clip. "Excuse me! Excuse me, fellas. Is there something we can do to help you?"

Bridey looked up in time to see the Snowballs' attention diverted towards the source of the inquiry and he watched as their faces registered momentary confusion at the approach of a beautiful, determined, and possibly bossy young woman. The big man recovered first. "Not really, ma'am. We're just policing the area, keeping the trains free of undesirables and the like…"

"And I'm so glad you are!" Doris was right up near them now and in her high heels was able to look the taller one right in the eye. "And I'm so glad that you won't find any in our car. Will they, sweetheart?" She beamed at Bridey, her most special beam. Bridey did a credible job of beaming back at her. "I'm Doris Day, the singer, from Los Angeles, California, and this is my fiancé, Sergeant Bridey Brisco from Silver City, New Mexico. We've just been to visit his parents to kind of get their blessing, you know. And I'm happy to report that they like me just fine." Under her snug white blouse Doris had a reasonably full and wonderful bosom and she didn't spare the snowballs the full impact of it as she stood proudly erect in front of them.

"You're Doris Day, the singer?" ventured the smaller Snowball. "I read about how you was married and all. I seen photos of you with your hubby."

Doris was chewing gum and she now used it to good effect as she flexed her jaw and cast a stern eye on her interlocutor. "Yeah," she said. "I was married, all right. And then I divorced the crumb-bum. That's a lady's prerogative, I'm sure you know. Now I've found the right guy and we're kind of off here by ourselves, just enjoying the solitude. I've got my publicity agent traveling with me, and I'll be happy to get him in case you fellows have any more questions…"

The Pugilist for one was ready to declare a truce. "You're the gal who sings that song about the sentimental journey on the radio, ain't that right?"

"That's me all right," Doris affirmed, allowing that customary brightness to return to her demeanor. "At the moment, the number one girl singer in the country, believe it or not." As she spoke, Bridey, who had in the meanwhile stood up, watched the eyes of the smaller Snowball, who was less quick to fall into the ploy. He sensed that he was about to be deprived of the right to bend his nightstick across Bridey's temple and he was not happy about it. But that Doris, she had a marvelous ability to tune into her audience. "Either of you fellows been out to L.A?" she asked brightly, innocently, intimately.

The Pugilist grinned shyly. He was a sweetheart after all. "Not as yet. Heard good things about it and all…"

Looking over the shoulder of the Pugilist, Doris put her beam on his partner. "And how about you, Lieutenant?" Shorty was no such a thing, and likely Doris knew it, but upgrading a man's rank when you wanted to flatter him was, during the war at least, another of those women's prerogatives. He was a fucking Corporal, Bridey thought to himself.

"Not yet, no ma'am," responded the alleged Lieutenant. And despite himself, he yielded to Doris with a stiff grin. Short stuff was retiring from the fray.

"Well, I just want to say, when you get there, and I'm sure you will, you go straight over to the Columbia Record Building on La Cienga Boulevard and tell them you're my guests. They'll see to it that you get tickets to the show, with front row seats and dinner after that. And I want to thank you again for the work that you do, helping keep our country free of those undesirables." And so saying, Doris eased herself past the Pugilist and into the seat next to Bridey where she sat herself down, tugging him down beside her, and bussed him affectionately on the cheek. "Now if you'll excuse us, me and my guy are doing a little catching up, so we'll see you again when you get out to Los Angeles." Doris resumed carefree chewing of her gum and dispatched the duo with a last breezy look before she turned back to Bridey with a wink and a grin. After mumbled apologies the two moved away down the aisle. When they were safely out of earshot, her expression changed to one of earnest concern. "The nerve of those two. I saw what they were doing. They were going to arrest you, weren't they?"

"Just doing their job as they see it," Bridey ventured. He saw no point in stirring Doris up further.

"Some job," Doris said. "Harassing our men in uniform."

"They're happiest when they're swinging those nightsticks," Bridey acknowledged, and then out of genuine curiosity changed the subject. "Is it true that you were married?"

"Oh jeepers yes," Doris said. Her mouth turned down at the corners and she sat back in her seat and peered straight ahead, remembering. "A horn player. We were both kids, but he wasn't ready to grow up at all." Then she brightened. "How about you?"

"Well, I guess I kind of grew up in the Army, whether I was ready or not," Bridey said.

"No, Bridey. I meant whether you were married." She looked at him and her eyes were alive with possibilities that Bridey found quietly exhilarating, but which he could not begin to identify.

"Oh, that. No, I'm not, ma'am. I mean, Doris. I need to settle in a little bit before I take that on."

"You're a wise man, Sergeant. The worst of it is, I'm about to take the plunge again. With another musician!"

"I hope he knows how lucky he is," Bridey responded. He didn't think he had ever seen or met a girl that was in a class with this one.

"I hope so too, Bridey. To tell you the truth, I hope he's a little like you. I mean, respectful, not always putting himself first, grateful for the blessings of everyday..." Perhaps abashed at her own sudden intimacy with a man who was after all a complete stranger, Doris looked away from Bridey and busied herself brushing off her skirt.

"Thank you, Miss Doris. And I am grateful. Or at least I try to be." He would have no trouble at all being grateful to wake up in the morning next to a girl like Doris, he knew. "You know, that song you sung for me, I have heard that on the radio. And I can't tell whether it makes me happy or makes me sad."

Doris was nodding. "Would you believe it, it affects me exactly the same way. I mean, happy because its always nice to come back home to a familiar place. And then it's sad when you get there and you find that the place is gone. Or maybe never even existed quite the way you remembered it…"

With sudden clarity Bridey was confronted with the thought of his mother waiting for him in Silver City during those months when he was trooping through Europe getting pounded by German 88's and then when he got home discovering that he had so little of himself left to offer her. Doris was watching him carefully, and seemed to read something there on his face. "I think that's kind of what happened to a lot of us over the last few years, Bridey." And looking past Bridey at the passing landscape she lifted her fingertips in that practiced way a woman has of drawing away the moisture that has gathered in the corners of her eyes.

Unable to resist the urge for physical contact with her, however brief, Bridey reached out and placed his hand on top of Doris' hand where it rested on her knee. He felt the unaccustomed sensation of being the bearer of comfort to a person who was much stronger than he. Or maybe part of him was stronger than he imagined. After just the right number of heartbeats he lifted his hand away.

Doris flicked a glance at her wristwatch. "Golly, I've got to get back to the fellows. We've got some kind of show coming up this evening in Tucson, and I guess we're going to go over it together." Doris paused. "I can't tell you what pleasure it has been to spend time in your company this morning, Sergeant." She looked at him and beamed, but the beam was a little quieter than before, and meant just for him and not for the rest of the world.

"You're not going on to Los Angeles then?"

"Not today, I'm afraid. We're over-nighting in Tuscon. The whole tour is to promote the song, you know, as a kind of welcome-home to the troops. Well," she added, "If anybody knows, you do." And with this, she stood.

"And thanks again for keeping me from getting my head busted," Bridey said. He thought to stand and embrace her, but then thought the better of it. Doris extended her hand and when Bridey took it, she looked down at him intently with only a faint trace of her wonderful girl-next-door smile, squeezed his hand hard, and then turned away and was gone back down the aisle.

Not more than ten minutes later, as Bridey lolled in his seat watching the pasturelands roll by, it occurred to him that while he and Doris had been visiting, the train had left New Mexico and entered Arizona. Measuring their passage against a not-too-distant barbed-wire fence, he calculated the train's speed to be about fifty miles per hour, and glancing at his watch noted that about an hour and ten minutes had elapsed since their departure from Lordsburg. He took pleasure in measuring the coordinates of time against space, and it helped him to focus his mind on his journey. The words of Doris song came back to him: *counting every mile of railroad track that takes me back.* Well, he wasn't going back exactly because it was a route he'd never taken to a place he'd never been, but he sure enough was counting the miles, just like the song said he would.

"Pardon me, Sergeant." Snatched from his reverie Bridey found himself looking up into the debonair countenance of the blue-suited fellow in the fedora who had shanghaied him into the photograph on the station platform back in Lordsburg. Now bareheaded, he was holding out a white business card in Bridey's direction. "Max Rosen. I'm Miss Day's publicist. Do you mind?" He slid into the empty seat beside Bridey, who noted that his demeanor had softened in the last hour or so. He continued to hold out the card, and Bridey realized that he was the intended recipient. He took the card without examining it, and looked at Rosen, who had taken off his suit jacket to reveal a perfectly tailored long-sleeve white shirt with some blue stitching on the breast pocket that Bridey realized represented the wearer's initials. "Miss Day wanted me to be sure to get some contact information from you. She wants you to have a copy of the photograph we took back there in Lordsburg."

"The seven o'clock one, you mean?"

Rosen was briefly baffled at the reference before picking

it up and grinning his practiced business grin, which was, after all, a grin that made you feel comfortable even if you weren't sure where it was taking you. "That's the one. Seven o'clock."

"Just like in the song," Bridey remarked.

"Now you got it, Sergeant. Would you mind jotting down your mailing address for me?" He withdrew a small address book which he offered Bridey, along with a silver-colored fountain pen, two items which Bridey imagined he carried with him as tools of his trade. Bridey declined the offer. "It's just Bridey Brisco, General Delivery, Silver City." Rosen flipped open the book and poised his pen. "Spell that name for me, Sergeant?" Bridey did so and the publicist jotted away, then looked up. "Silver City. That's New Mexico?" Bridey confirmed that it was. It sure was something, he was thinking, that a girl as young as Doris was already so important that she had a guy like this in a monogrammed shirt running around taking care of her business for her. She was some girl, all right.

Rosen folded up the address book and pocketed his pen. "Y'know, Sergeant, Miss Day meets a lot of servicemen in her line of work. But you apparently made quite an impression on her. That card I gave you has my contact information on it. We'll be back out on the coast on Friday. She would really be pleased if you got in touch and we were able to stand you for dinner and a show. You know, just a bit of hometown hospitality. How's that sound?"

"Sounds alright, I guess." Bridey was about to tell the publicist that Doris had made quite an impression on him as well, but then he figured that was for Doris to know, and that she probably did anyway.

Rosen held out his hand and they shook on it. The publicist's handshake was firm and fair. He stood up. "There is one more thing, and I hope you won't mind. Miss Day was curious, but felt it might be inappropriate to ask. While you were over there, did you…I mean, were you, you know…"

"You mean did I serve in a forward area? What you civilians would call a combat area?" Bridey was hesitant to claim any merit for surviving the ugly situation into which Uncle Sam had thrust him. He wasn't one of those "glory-seekers." Still, he felt compelled to answer the inquiry truthfully. "You can tell her that I did, and I appreciate her concern."

Rosen regarded him briefly as if making up his mind about something. Then he brought his fingertips up to his brow and let them linger there for moment before bringing them smartly away, accomplishing just what a salute was designed, in certain instances, to accomplish. "You bet I will, Sergeant. You take care now." And he was off and gone towards the back of the car, or maybe even the next car, wherever his client might be tucked away working on the details of her Tucson show. And Bridey went back to looking out his window at the splendid scene passing by, where the rangeland rolled all the way back to the distant horizon under that big crackin' sky.

Of course Bridey never used the publicist's card, never called his number. How could he? How could he hope that any kind of staged entertainment or formal dinner event could possibly top the sweet serendipity of the encounter with the young singer that had taken place on a train rolling west? Whatever it was that she really felt towards him, whatever kind of sympathetic response he had aroused in her, he had no desire to explore further. It was after all, he reflected, part of her job. When he got back to Silver City, the photograph that Rosen had promised him was waiting, a nice 8 X 10 black and white. While Bridey and Doris were standing shoulder to shoulder on the platform and she was beaming away, it was clear that there was no real connection between them, and Bridey looked just like what he had been: a stand-in, a prop, a warm body in a uniform. He gave it to his mother, who was predictably excited about it. He had no doubts that the brief tears Doris had shed, and the unbounded optimism she displayed were genuine, but the girl was "on stage" most of the time and like she had told him, most people in the entertainment industry assumed that the world revolved around them anyway. Bridey did not want to penetrate that world, nor distract her from her duties to it. While he did cherish the memory of their time together on the train, it was more to protect it than anything that he had he decided not to make the call.

About one thing, however, she had certainly been right. Bridey's future was nothing if not "up in the air," and it didn't have anything to do with the 6,500 foot altitude of Silver City. Neither his trip to the coast nor his meeting with Eleanor Powell (who, for all her lithe charms had none of Doris's girlish appeal) could significantly disturb the equilibrium of solace that had settled in upon him in the waning months of 1945, and back in Silver City in the new year he likewise had failed to come to terms with any new direction or a new spirit that might be counted on to draw him out of a state that his mother gently characterized as "aimless." Bridey didn't argue the point. Over time his drinking sessions on the porch began a little earlier in the day and lasted well beyond sundown. It's one thing to drink whiskey and watch the sun set, and there may be a certain quiet elegance to the act or to the moment, particularly for a Westerner. But to drink the same whiskey until all hours and peer out into the dark on a moonless night, well, that's a different story. When Doris' hit song played on the radio, as it frequently did, Bridey initially listened intently, and remembered the sexy but innocent way she had presented it to him on the train. But by the time the year was ending, he would change the station or turn off the radio when *Sentimental Journey* came on the air.

What eventually stirred Bridey, after he had done a stint at the Sheriff's office, doubled as a ranch hand out at Clive Buell's place, and tried his hand at driving a truck for Bill Beedle, what eventually stirred him was the acquaintance he made with Baldemar Huerta, one of the hands with whom he had ridden at Clive's ranch. Baldemar was a quietly confident and patiently unassuming young man from the state of Sonora, down in Mexico. His English was broken but he spoke it with gusto, and his attitude was resolutely optimistic. His family owned a restaurant in

Hermosillo and he had made his way north into gringoland to save enough money to open a restaurant of his own in the port city of Guayamas. During the war, he told Bridey, the navy had built some new docks in the city and Baldemar was certain that in time, with the beautiful natural harbor and the nearby beaches, it would become a thriving center for tourism. The tales he told of his life in Mexico, of the wealth of the land, the loveliness (and the availability) of the women, the abundance of good tequila, and above all of life in a culture where aimlessness was not considered a liability but a sensible characteristic of sound breeding, appealed to something in Bridey. Thus it was that in the late spring of '48, six months after his mother and died and after the rains had subsided and the weather had faired up, Bridey and Baldy took off together, making their way by train to Tucson and then traveling south by hopping rides on trucks until they reached Guayamas, which was, by Bridey's estimate, about 250 miles south of the U.S. border. In all, the transit had taken them just less than a week. Baldemar had not overstated the case regarding the beauty of Guayamas. Perched on the Gulf of California, it was a shrimping town that was small enough that Bridey became familiar with the layout in just a few days, but large enough so that his anonymity, even as a gringo, was not imperiled. He pitched his GI savings in with Baldemar's grubstake, and the partners were able to secure a nice property just two blocks from the beach in the San Carlos neighborhood. They hired a cook and two hostesses and by September of the year they were open for business, serving a full menu of fish and shrimp plates along with the usual staples of beans, rice, tacos and enchiladas, food that was plenty familiar to Bridey from his upbringing in New Mexico. Bridey gave up on the whiskey and made a staple of beer, which satisfied his craving for alcohol without disabling him by 3:00 in the afternoon. As time passed, the restaurant thrived, Bridey got himself a nice shack-up job with the lovely 17-year-old Ramona, who had been one of their hostesses, and he became something of a fixture in the community, as weathered and distant as a fencepost but still a solid citizen, a good provider, and an agreeable drinking companion. Having eluded the worrisome promises and unrealistic expectations of his own culture, his soul, it seemed, had found a resting place in the predicable rhythms of another.

Several years passed, as peacetime years will do. Periodically Baldemar would travel the 72 kilometers up the line to Hermosillo to reconnoiter the city for vendors offering new products or services they could incorporate into their growing business. (Already they had opened a concession area on the beach where they rented cabanas, sailboats and snorkeling equipment, and offered waterskiing lessons.) Given the nearness of the California beach culture, they were privy to some of the most recent developments, and Bridey had read about a new craze, a glider device that could be towed behind a speedboat and lift the rider into the skies. Deciding to make the trip to Hermosillo in place of his partner, he took Ramona and rode the bus to Hermosillo to seek out an importer who could acquire one of these devices for their beach business.

Ramona, who had been born and raised in Guayamas, loved being part of the bustle and importance of the big city. They stayed in the Valencia Hotel, one of Hermosillo's proudest structures, and dined on steaks at a sidewalk restaurant. Suitably impressed with her man, when they got back to the hotel after dinner Ramona wriggled out of her form-fitting dress, tugged off her underwear, and flopped down seductively on the bed. "Make love to me in this big bed in this fine hotel," she purred. "Come on, Papi, give me something special."

Bridey complied with his girl's request, and while he had never thought of Ramona as any more than a polite indulgence on his part, not a necessity nor an accessory, he felt almost like a married man as she twisted and turned compliantly under him before they both collapsed in satisfied slumber. In the morning, as was his custom, Bridey slipped out of bed early and went out into the freshly-washed streets to smell the undisturbed morning air and seek out a strong cup of coffee. And when he did, he came face-to-face with his past.

At first he didn't recognize her. In the years since he had seen her she had undergone a transformation. Her hair, which he had remembered as shoulder length and more brown than blonde, was now cut close to her head and was platinum in color, framing a face that had lost most of its unschooled Midwestern appeal and now sported the practiced look of a skilled seductress. The beaming smile that she had flashed at Bridey aboard the train was still there, except now it was a smile that was meant not for any one man but developed to mesmerize all men. Still, it was unmistakably hers, and as he stood there on the sidewalk in Hermosillo, the miles and years were peeled away and he was confronted once again with the force of her personality and the fact of her stunning beauty. And as if to drive home the transformation, her artfully crafted plywood form on the marquee of the movie theater was three times life-size and displayed her wearing a shimmering, low-cut, tight-fitting dress that plainly advertised the seductive curves which had been so demurely concealed as she rode next to Bridey on the Limited. The sly, witty, oh-my-gosh girl from Cincinnati had been wholly replaced by a movie star named Doris Day. The man in the street, such as Bridey was, could now only look on in wonder, pay for his ticket if he so chose, and marvel at what God, and Hollywood, had created.

He had not been completely unaware of her career path. He read that she had married another musician and later divorced him, and then married again, a Hollywood producer-type. He knew that her musical career, after yielding a string of popular hits, had led her into films, which had yielded another string of hits. He was glad for her success, and as he looked up at that come-hither face with those laughing eyes and teasing lips, he felt nothing but happy for Doris. Even without her ripe innocence she seemed to represent to him the post-war possibilities he had left behind: the possibilities of homes, babies, jobs, neighborhoods, and the bliss that comes from finding for yourself a fixed place in the universe. The wild anticipation of each new day, and the "mem-ries" one might gather in living it. Maybe it was because that girlish innocence was gone that he found her more appealing than ever.

Bridey was not one to ponder or to brood, but as he stood looking at Doris he found himself wondering for a moment whether he had done the right thing in bailing out, leaving the country and immersing himself in a foreign culture. Things which had seemed simple on the train were not so simple anymore, he knew that much. His "sentimental journey" had carried him right off the map, and for the first time, he doubted he could ever find his way back. Or whether he would ever want to.

After another moment, Bridey pulled his eyes away from the figure in the shimmering dress and crossed the street. A block over he found a small walk-up kiosk where he purchased two *café con leches* to go. He would take them back to the Hotel Valencia where Ramona would just be waking up. She often had an appetite for sex in the morning, and for once Bridey thought he might be happy to indulge her.

Sweating the Big Stuff

Only to a good friend, but also a person who was solidly unsentimental, could Larry offer this confession: "The truth is, I always thought my wife would get me into heaven."

It was December, overcast, pearly grey skies, a bite in the wind. The course was almost abandoned as he stood on the third green while Brad lined up his putt. From a swale near the green a covey of quail rose up out of the bushes, caught the wind, and fell up and away towards the distant tree line. It was after both had putted and were back in the cart that he made his confession.

"I mean, I never kept track of things. Did we need coffee? Was the light bill paid? Had the neighbor's dog done the nasty on our steps? And where in the hell was the belt I wore last week? Come to think of it, where in the hell were the trousers?"

Brad cast a sidelong glance at his golf partner, and turned his face back into the wind. He loved to play golf like this on Christmas Eve. "So you depended on her to keep track of the small stuff," he ventured after a time.

"The small stuff and the big stuff," Larry said. "How do you keep a cat from killing birds? How do you handle a sick dog? How much water do houseplants like? Which picture do you hang over the mantelpiece? And how much Epsom salts do you add to the bathwater to help with a backache?"

"I don't know if that's what I would call big stuff," Brad said. He braked the cart beside number four tee box.

"Well, how about this? You could tune in to the British Open, and without ever seeing the leaderboard, just by watching the way the guys were handling themselves and what they were wearing, she could usually tell you your winner. And even when she didn't nail it exactly, her pick would always be in there fighting at the end. Never played golf in her life. Same with the World Series. She called the winner every time during the years we were together."

A 160-yard par three over the marsh. Brad was pulling his old persimmon three wood from his bag. "Man, sounds like you should have taken her to Vegas."

"I should have taken her somewhere," Larry said. They hit, and rode again.

"So how does all that get you into heaven is what I wonder." The cart swooped down, turning through a dry creek bed, and mounting the other side. They finished their business at the par three and moved on. Next was a par four that was bordered by woods on one side, a creek on the other. Straight out at 200 yards a pair of white oaks, starkly bare against the sky, challenged and invited. After that, the fairway doglegged sharply to the left. The flag was not visible from the tee.

"Well, the thing is, she loved God. She used to accuse him of fucking her over, but she loved him. They had long conversations together. She loved long conversations anyway. I'm sure they talked about everything under the sun. They really hashed it out."

Brad was out of the cart with his driver in his hand, but Larry still sat, feeling suddenly the absence of wind, which was blocked by the trees. "For me, God was kind of like somebody we knew, a friend who lived in another state or something. I was too busy to get with him, but it never worried me, because I knew my wife was in touch."

Brad was ready to hit. He went through his set-up, arms too high and too straight, standing too far from the ball, too many moving parts in his takeaway, swinging hard from the top, cutting sharply across the ball outside-in, a dead-slice swing. With good contact, he might punch his driver

180 yards. But he didn't care about that. He loved the game, and he loved being with his friend.

Larry hit, low and left, and they rode.

"So you kind of left your spiritual arrangements up to your wife?"

"I bet you we all do. Wives are the go-betweens. *'Let me tell you about my guy, God. I've done my best with him. Down deep he's a good and decent man. I know his sins as least as well as you do, and I've forgiven him. So, we're coming in together. How about it?'*

"Especially if God knows that she won't stop bothering Him until He gives you the green light too," Brad said. At this they laughed, cynically and hopefully, as only two men who share the same birthday can laugh. "Oh Jeez," Larry said, wiping his eyes. They had come out of the sheltered area and were back in the wind, heading for Brad's ball.

Brad was out of the cart, peering anxiously at his ball, which had come to rest perilously close to the bank of the creek. "I just feel like showing up at those pearly gates without her is really going to cook my goose," Larry said, more to himself than anybody else.

Home From the War

When he got home from the war, she was not at the airport to meet him. This was a little unsettling. He knew he had no reasonable right to expect that she would know of the hour of his arrival after all, but still it was unsettling, to come home from the war and not be met by the one person for whom you had gone off to fight.

He was light-headed, quite frankly a little dizzy, and unpleasant episodes kept swimming in front of his eyes as he made his way slowly down to the baggage claim area. He had volunteered to go to the war, that was the thing. She had told him he never needed to go, there were plenty of men available who were younger, who were not married, who had nothing better to do with their lives. Let them go, she argued. He didn't argue back. He apologized. Honey, I wish it was that easy he'd told her. I wish I could. It's just something I've got to do, and after that we'll be together. Don't worry about it. Sure, and what if you don't come back she asked. What then? I'm supposed to spend the rest of my life waiting for you? Is that what you want, Mr. Patriotic Citizen? She cried then, and that did worry him. War didn't worry him. It was an inevitable and unavoidable act of God. But when his wife cried, that ate away at him down deep. It was something he didn't think he could fix, and it scared him even more than the thought that some stranger might wish him dead or dismembered, and try his level best to bring that to pass.

The war had begun, as most wars do, with conversation among nations that started out politely as a pack of institutionalized lies, espousing dignity and nobility, then turned ugly and slanderous, and finally became cryptic and coded. Somebody was saying that somebody was saying that war would come, and in this way the population was readied for the inevitable. Still, when he had shown up for induction, there had been a jaunty face put on the adventure, they had stood in long lines in the cold wind, slowly abandoning the pretenses of normalcy for whatever would follow, letting their faces betray them just enough to establish the camaraderie of acknowledged uncertainty. He thought of her then, and of the warm bed he had left behind, and that was the only time that desperation really gripped him, thinking that he would wander through the rest of eternity without ever getting back to her in that warm bed. By the time they had completed the induction process, he was stripped bare and shivering in the cold wind, which is the time-honored way that men are introduced to war. That way they are given to understand that they are starting out with nothing, and so they have virtually nothing to lose. He knew better, they all knew better, but they were willing, even eager, to go along with any philosophy that made the combat to come less frightening to contemplate.

The war had lasted no more than six weeks. The first week they had spent reconnoitering the terrain, with infrequent enemy contacts, getting themselves inoculated to the hardships, learning to think and act as a unit, developing the intuitive skills of survival in a hostile environment. By the third week, enemy contacts were being made on a daily basis, and as individuals they grew accustomed to the fact that in the end they must each lose something of value, that was what the war demanded. So they woke up each morning denying allegiances, avoiding expectations, running from hope or thoughts of home, from anything that would hamper you in a firefight and cause you eventually to die in so many ways whether you were killed or not. By week five, with no end in sight, they were fully engaged and reeling from the daily pounding. They were good fighters then because they no longer cared about anything, their hearts were honestly poisoned towards life, they chose death over life, woke up seeking it, expecting it, some even longing for it. Good fighters. Sex and death, those were the two things they held dear, right to the end. Fuck me, fuck you, fuck death. In the end, war was all about fucking, they learned. The sight, the smell, the feel of fucking and being fucked. Fucked like animals fuck, like the ocean fucks, like the continents and the stars and the insects fuck. He was a fucking organism is what he was, a mutant voyeur with a fucking imagination. As such, it wasn't bad. It wasn't good either. It was war, and they were in it, and they were all truly fucked.

The first indication that the war was winding down was the realization that there simply weren't many people left who could still fight. People were being killed, running away, scurrying into holes and trenches like vermin, and refusing to surface again. *Whores de combat.* Fucked out, fucked up, fucked over. It was with this realization that he first grasped the idea that he might survive the war after all. Then their low-flying troopship crash-landed, and the night was lit up with a violent glare, a lurid light that stripped away every last secret which the darkness had ever harbored. With that, it was over. He was reeling and staggering through the night choking on his tears, drowning in mucus, gulping down his sobs and vomiting on his laughter. Alive. No longer among the living, that's for sure, but damn well alive. Fucking alive, Jack.

He woke up in an aid station, and from there began the necessary processing before he could be sent home. How long this took he could not say. He measured his time by some internal cycles that had nothing to do with the sun or the moon, had nothing to do with anything that he could identify or remember. These cycles were not of his devising, they were oceanic, undulating, like coils. He was shuffling through the mortal coils, feeling disembodied and indifferent. He realized then that he was not even capable of measuring the cycles, but that they were measuring him.

Some ninety days later by the calendar he disembarked from the airplane, and she was not there to meet him, as he guessed she would not be. Returning from earlier journeys he had come up the ramp seeking her out because she never liked to press in close with the eager beavers. Instead she would always stand back among the well-wishers, but directly in line with the jet-way so that he could see her if he looked straight ahead as he came up. Her face was always wreathed in a smile, she would usually have altered or arranged her hair in some particularly fetching or becoming style just for him, and she would usually not move in his direction, but let him come to her as he liked to do, and take her in an embrace that was meant to communicate everything that had transpired in his soul since they had been apart. Moments like that they might as well have been standing on a remote peak, or a secluded beach, so completely indifferent were they to the swirl of humanity around them. But this time she was not there, so he made his way home by public transport.

He was just three or four blocks from the house when he stepped down from the bus and began walking, and at that moment the war caught up with him, and he began to cry. First his eyes became moist, and he developed a lump in his throat. And then, without any warning, the sobs came, sobs that wracked his body so that he had to stop and put down his duffel, and bend over with his hands on his knees in order to keep from falling. After another minute he sank to his knees, and held his face in his hands. Great rivers of tears mixed with mucus from his nostrils flooded into his hands, and his shoulders heaved as though he was never going to catch his breath. He dimly heard voices nearby, but then they went away and he was alone again with only the sound of his own sobs, which were so genuine that they sounded theatrical. After what seemed like a long time, the expulsion subsided, but he did not rise from his knees right away. A glorious lightness had entered into him, his mind seemed capable of infinite expansion, his heart feared no mystery. He realized that he was happier than he had ever been. Thinking that perhaps it had something to do with being on his knees, he remained there until it was nearly dark.

Judy Grows Up

When I was twelve and she was twelve, we became neighbors. I did not trust females then, because I had been instructed by my old man and his friends not to do so. Laugh with them, party with them, kiss them if you want to, marry and divorce them if you must, but do not trust them. Or, more accurately, do not trust the way they make you feel when you are with them. It's a false feeling, they implied, and exposes weakness in a man.

Judy did not expose weakness in me, however. When our lips met, I felt a kind of dazzling strength enter me, a strength that I knew was not mine, but was moving in me and would ultimately cause me to take all the worthwhile steps I would ever take in my life. And that is precisely how it turned out.

But our path was not without its detours. At nights I would tiptoe across the lawn between our houses, and Judy would recite quietly to me from memory through her open jalousie window songs from the Book of Elvis that she thought might prove to be instructive to us. *"Let's think of the future, forget the past. You're not my first love, but dear, you're my last."* Even at the age of twelve, I knew my old man and some of his cronies were missing the boat.

How many nights did I cross the lawn to listen to the sound of Judy quoting from the Book of Elvis while around us the neighbors slept and dreamed? Maybe at first as often as two or three times a week. Later on, not as frequently. But this I can tell you: our whispering trysts went on for years. Long after she moved away, and then I moved away, I never had any hesitation in seeking her out. I found her in college. I found her in Vietnam. I found her afterward, when I was riding the workboats in the Gulf. When I was chain-sawing firewood in the Ozarks. When I was flying down to Buenos Aires, or cruising on the Amazon. I found her when the Democrats ran Congress, and also when the Republicans took over. Through two marriages, a handful of makeshift careers, abroad on three or four continents, and across forty years, I never lost track of Judy. Sometimes the lawn had dew on it, and glistened in the moonlight. Other times, when the moon was dark, and the lone streetlight was on the blink, it was like crossing a dark carpet, with only the faint light coming from Judy's window to guide me. That, and the certain knowledge that she would be waiting there for when I might show up.

Eventually Elvis grew fat and sick, and dropped dead. It didn't matter. Judy had enough material by 1958 to last us a lifetime. She was never lacking for inspiration.

Then recently, things changed. I had gone across to see her, only to discover that she was not in her bedroom, and the jalousie window was closed. I hesitated for a long moment, pondering my next step. Then I rapped faintly with my knuckles on the shutters. My heart flowered in my chest when it was cranked open, only to receive a rude shock when the voice that came forth was not Judy's slightly coy, thoroughly confidential, and wonderfully dulcet tone, but the flat, uninviting sound of her mother's voice. Her mother's voice was tired, aggravated, and utterly lacking in any sense of humor. "Whattayou want?" she asked without interest.

How could she not know what I wanted? "Isn't Judy in?" I tried not to be pushy, but this was a matter between Judy and me, period.

"No she isn't, and I'd advise you not to come looking for her."

Not come looking? "Where is Judy?" This I had to know.

"Judy's right where she belongs, mister. Now why don't you get where you belong?"

I was not going to be lumped in with stray dogs or homeless vagrants. "This is where I belong," I argued unconvincingly. I sounded plaintive. Not like a grown-up at all.

"Not any more you don't. Whyncha grow up? That's what Judy did." And with that dire-sounding pronouncement, the window was cranked shut, leaving me in darkness and silence. After waiting a while, during which time I was more than a little disturbed, I went back across the lawn.

I still don't believe that my old man knew what he was talking about when it came to females. And I don't for a moment believe that business about Judy growing up.

Part II

This World Here Below

"It had of course occurred to Eddie that some day he would probably make a real pass at her, but he was in no hurry. She was licking some unseen romantic wounds, and the wearing of her little halter tops and the tight-fitting shorts that displayed only too well her remarkable assets - well, he didn't take that personal or anything. The girl was a girl all right, even if she was declaring herself off-limits to Eddie because of a philosophical difference regarding dogs."

That Dog Business

That Dog Business

Somewhere a dog was barking.

"Shut the fuck up, Bowser."

She heard his voice come clearly across the way on Saturday morning. Her bedroom was in the back of the house near his patio, and she thought at first the voice belonged to someone else. She stirred and drifted, not wanting to awaken completely. Then, over the hum of her air conditioner, she heard the voice again.

"Bowser. Shut the fuck up!" It was him, she realized. He must be going off the deep end. Then she went back to sleep.

Eddie Dorinda was not universally liked or admired by his neighbors, that was the truth. He could be spontaneously generous, as when he would take elderly Miss Viola to the grocery, to the thrift store, and once even to swim in the river. He always gave the handyman a cold beer when he came to perform some maintenance chore in Eddie's rental house. Gallantry came naturally to him. It was Eddie and his brother (visiting from Manitoba) who chased off a pack of wild dogs after they savaged one of Miss Viola's cats, and later buried the cat with their bare hands in the Peony bed behind her house. He swept the Magnolia leaves from his front yard with regularity, pulled his own and occasionally other's garbage cans back to the curb after the trucks had passed on Tuesdays and Fridays, and was careful never to inconvenience any of his neighbors when he parked his truck. But in spite of these proper and even charitable behaviors, he never seemed to belong in the neighborhood, and one might have the impression (certainly Eddie Dorinda did) that after five years of habitation on the north side of the little white shotgun double he could pull up stakes and leave tomorrow, and never be missed at all.

Not that Eddie minded. He was a loner. Kept to himself. You wouldn't see him drifting across the street on a summer's evening with slices of cold watermelon, or a six-pack of ice-cold Abita Beer to share with a group of neighbors idling on a freshly-mown lawn. He didn't have dinner parties (or if he did, it did not include those living nearby), yard sales, or even sit on his front porch during daylight hours. He came and went, period. From his front door to his truck and back again, keeping the kind of cloistered schedule and single-mindedness of purpose that may not be an inviting way to live, but is certainly an efficient one. Oh, he had invited Miss Viola over one night a couple of years earlier for a small dinner party. The fact that she had gotten sick drunk and collapsed in his bathtub, clutching for the shower curtain and taking it with her as she felt herself going down, well that was certainly not Eddie's doing. The event that had contributed to the polite ostracism which Eddie's neighbors levied against him was not his exactly fault either, but then, a loner does not usually get the benefit of the doubt in matters of social conflict.

It had come from the house next door, where the two nurses lived side-by side in the two halves of a double. One was of Italian descent, a sensual, curvaceous creature with dark curly hair and a mysterious smile. The other was an overweight Jewish Princess named Angela, who had thick glasses, a long nose, and an apologetic air about her. Each kept a dog for protection and companionship. Liana, the Italian, had a beagle named Gino, who was friendly, investigative, and, like most of his breed, dumb as a doorpost. Angela, the JP, had a female Black Lab with a twisted psyche, a snarling mien, and a fervent desire to punish any and all of God's creatures that might chance to cross her path. It was on an Autumn day when, upon exiting her house to walk her Lab, the Jewish Princess lost her grip on the leash. Eddie was walking to his truck at the same time, and the Lab came at him baying like a banshee, lips drawn bag, feet scrabbling on the sidewalk, seventy-five pounds of angry dog meat bent on inflicting lethal damage. Having raised a number of dogs himself, and being no stranger to the pathology of angry, frustrated canines, Eddie took the attack in stride. Though his hands were empty, he squared off, crouched low, drew his own lips back, and returned fire in a voice edged with menace: "Come on, you worthless piece of shit, you fuck with me I'll kick you deader than a doornail." Which is pretty much verbatim.

Thinking better than to pursue her attack in the face of such determined resistance, the Lab veered away and streaked across the street, where providence had placed a friendly neighborhood Terrier who visited Miss Viola's each morning for a scrap or a snack that might be forthcoming. In short order, the Lab had little Pepper dead in her sights and was preparing to pin her against Mrs. Viola's fence and gratuitously tear her throat out. She hadn't counted on the dogged pursuit of Eddie, however, who raced across the street behind her, swearing mightily, to the great consternation of the Lab's owner, who came quickly, her hands fluttering in the air, as Eddie reiterated his intention to dispatch the Lab with a kick to the head that would put the dog out of her "fuckin' misery, once and for all!" Moving fast, he had already positioned himself near the mad dog's head to deliver a kick just as Angela reached her dog. Despite the beast's wretched snarling, she managed to get her arms around the Lab's neck and drag her away from the maligned mutt. As she clipped the leash onto her dog, however, her eyes were fastened on Eddie, and she was plainly aghast as his clearly and forcibly expressed intent of mayhem. Seeing her accusing look, Eddie tried to ameliorate the impact of his words. To a degree.

"Sorry to have to say what I said, but that's a mean dog you've got there, gal. And if she ever goes off on me, or anybody else in the neighborhood, like that again, I will do my best to kill her on the spot."

Well, you can just imagine. It wasn't long before tender-hearted, dog-loving Angela began gently politicking the neighborhood, spreading the word that Eddie was "not an animal-lover," and that he had a peculiar, almost pathological hatred of dogs. Eddie was generally unaware of this development until one morning when he chanced to cross Liana's path as she walked her Beagle. Liana was a breath of loveliness, and her Beagle the essence of sociability, but Eddie could tell that something had changed, at least in the mind of Liana. She angled her body away from him as they chatted, and fixed her eyes somewhere on his shoulder as he recounted to her the events of the week past. He knew she would have gotten the word, and thought he might as well set the record straight.

"That's okay. I understand that you're not a dog lover," she said. She was wearing one of her halter tops, and her shoulders were flawless.

"Not a dog-lover? Liana, I was raised with dogs my whole life. Learned how to take care of 'em before I could ride a bicycle. But a mean dog is mean dog. You don't negotiate with a mean dog." Gino licked his hand and Eddie scratched the top of the dog's head, as always. When Gino attempted to jump up and put his paws on Eddie, Eddie smoothly extended a bent knee, which caught the dog in the chest and obliged him to keep his paws on the ground. (This is the way it is taught in dog obedience schools). If she observed this deft bit of doggie management, Liana made no mention of it, but tugged her dog's leash and sashayed back towards her house, her revised opinion of Eddie evidently confirmed.

No matter. The damage was done. Angela improbably found herself a fiancée some months later, and moved herself and her mean dog out of the neighborhood, but among the other residents Eddie's name was mud. His aloofness was now viewed with suspicion, his comings and goings well-marked by watching eyes. And Liana now pointedly ignored him when they passed on the sidewalk, except when on occasion she gave him one of her Madonna looks, cutting her dark eyes accusingly in his direction. It was ridiculous, is what it was. She had been in Eddie's house, and on Eddie's patio for drinks, her dark curly hair framing her delicate pale oval features as she lingered, laughing lazily over the single glass of wine she permitted herself. On one of his trips abroad, Eddie had brought her back a small gift, a ceramic figurine of a tribal goddess from the Amazon, and she had invited him into her spotless white-on-white living room, where the television droned endlessly. It had of course occurred to Eddie that some day he would probably make a real pass at her, but he was in no hurry. She was licking some unseen romantic wounds, and the wearing of her little halter tops and the tight-fitting shorts that displayed only too well her remarkable assets - well, he didn't take that personal, or anything. The girl was a girl all right, even if she was declaring herself off-limits to Eddie because of a philosophical difference regarding dogs.

In the evenings when Eddie sat on the stoop in back of his house smoking an occasional cigarette, drinking a glass of beer, or reading a book, he would catch a glimpse of Liana slipping out to do her laundry in the small shed behind her house. She moved with an exaggerated slowness, as though daydreaming or in some kind of exquisite pain, and she never turned her head in Eddie's direction though he was plainly visible there. Sometimes late at night, particularly in the summer, she would slip out her back door and sit on her stoop to talk on the phone or smoke the occasional cigarette. Once Eddie caught her peering over in the direction of his patio, only to turn her head away when she realized that he was there in the darkness, partially obscured by the elephant ears that grew so profusely alongside his own stoop. And once, when he was sitting in his truck at the curb prior to leaving for work in the morning, she came by on the sidewalk with her Beagle, and upon becoming aware of Eddie, fastened her eyes straight ahead, a sardonic hardness lingering around her lips, her movements as deliberately soft and feminine as ever. On this occasion, Eddie didn't bother with the charade; he let his eyes linger on her, admiring both her form and her resoluteness at shutting him out of her life. *A woman with that much determination but no better place to put it*, was what he thought.

On the morning of the "Bowser" incident, it was nearly dusk when Liana parked in her driveway, took two bags of groceries from the back of her car, and let herself into her apartment. Gino greeted her with his usual enthusiasm, but for once, she was not in the mood. "I know what you want," she said tiredly, more to herself than to the dog. "Just give me a chance to change my clothes." In her bedroom she shucked her nurse's sea-foam scrubs, slipped into a pair of white shorts and a black halter top, and idly pulled a brush through her lush Italian curls. When she went back into the living room where Gino was waiting expectantly by his leash, which hung from a hook on the back of the door, she became aware of a figure poised outside about to ring her doorbell. In an instant she knew. Apparently he had seen her, because he simply stood there. The doorbell never rang. She went ahead and opened the door, and with some effort looked him right in the eye. It had been nearly a year since she'd lowered the boom on Eddie Dorinda.

"Hello Liana," Eddie said. "About to walk your Gino, I see."

"What brings you over, Eddie?" she asked evenly. Gino had surged ahead and was pressing hard against the wrought-iron security gate, hoping that perhaps Eddie was a leash-bearer.

"I've had it, Liana. I mean, I can't handle the dog business anymore." Eddie returned her steady gaze.

"I love my dog, Eddie."

"Hell, I know you love your dog. He's a fine pooch." Almost as if he knew he was the topic of the conversation, Gino curled his entire body into an exclamation mark of delight and anticipation, his eyes going from Liana to Eddie and back again. He surged against the intervening door, going up on his hind legs with his front paws pressed against the ironwork. Eddie hesitated. "Invite me inside for a moment Liana."

Even as she was uncomplainingly slipping the latch on the gate, Liana felt like she was having an out-of-body experience. She was at a loss to understand her own behavior, but it seemed perfectly acceptable.

Once inside, Eddie stood before her, with Gino, properly knee-trained by Eddie, swirling around his legs while keeping all four feet on the floor. Liana couldn't keep a straight face. "Gino doesn't get much company," she said, grinning a little self-consciously.

"Gino, settle down," Eddie said firmly, and the Beagle backed away and sat, swishing his tail and watching the two of them expectantly. "Liana, I propose that we consolidate our leases and live together as man and wife," Eddie said.

"Is this some kind of a joke?" Liana responded, even though she sensed that it was not.

"Gino's ready right now," Eddie pointed out. "And I've been ready for months. We're just waiting for you."

"I don't even know you that well, Eddie. We've never so much as held hands, and now you think I'm going to be your wife or something? And what do you mean anyway, that you can't handle the dog business?" During this exchange her voice had risen, along with her heartbeat, but she stood her ground, almost within arm's reach of her neighbor. She suddenly became aware of her bare shoulders and her exposed legs.

At this point, in keeping with the spontaneous combustion that was taking over the room, Eddie did something that he hadn't planned on doing. He got on his knees in front of Liana. Gino came off his haunches and began bothering Eddie in an effort to get his tongue on Eddie's face, his arms, anywhere.

"Settle down, pooch," Eddie said tersely from his knees. When Gino went back on his haunches, Eddie turned his eyes on Liana's face. Framed by her curly locks, it was tender, angelic, Italian. She had gained a little weight over the last couple of years, Eddie realized. It looked good for her.

"Liana, I want to sleep where Gino sleeps," Eddie said. "And I want you to touch me the way you touch him. And I want to be the one to lick your face first thing in the morning."

Liana felt herself flush. It was the most ridiculous proposition she'd ever heard. And on top of that, it bothered the hell out of her. "You're crazy, you know that?"

From his position on his knees, Eddie grinned happily. If that was her only objection, they were as good as on their way.

Hold My Hand

I didn't see the doors right away. Not until I was lying on the floor on my back did I notice them above and behind my head. They were swinging doors, not like saloon doors, but full- length gray swinging doors, the kind you push open, and they close again silently of their own accord. My wife sat in a chair above me, concerned and preoccupied with regard to the abdominal pain and the vomiting that had forced me to seek sanctuary in the emergency room of this large downtown hospital at midmorning on a weekday. The doors did not interest her. Her husband's wellbeing was uppermost in her mind. If a man would take a wife for no other reason than this, it would be reason enough.

Emergency or no, there was no sanctuary to be had. Cruel disinterest, callous disregard, and a schedule which permitted no sniveling interruptions – these had been the responses of the admitting personnel in the outer chambers of the ER. Once I took to the floor, however, that policy underwent a rapid transformation.

"Sir. Sir, you'll have to take a seat. Sir!" An earnest Caucasian attendant leaned over me.

"I'd like to help you," I said after a pause. "I really would. But I absolutely cannot bear to be in a sitting position."

"Well, we can't have you on the floor. You have to be seated." He had one eye on me, and the other on nearby patrons of the ER, hoping that I wouldn't trigger an outright rebellion.

"I'm sure you have your rules," I said tiredly, not troubling to hide my distress. There had been precious little sleep the night before, and the beads of sweat on my blessed brow were entirely spontaneous. "But pain has its own rules. Can you dig what I'm saying?" The hipster language was not premeditated, but it seemed to fit the situation.

"Well, look." Another harried glance around the room. "Come on in the back and let us have another look at you."

Bingo.

Of course, I had already been ushered into the back upon my arrival, but the female African-American attendant had granted me no more than a cursory hearing and had maintained an attitude of complete nonchalance and disinterest throughout. I didn't take it as racial. It was simply political. This Caucasian, however, was bound by a different set of politics, and when he pressed my lower abdomen on the right side and I gasped outright, he yielded to honest concern, excused himself, and disappeared behind the swinging doors.

A moment later he came out, this time with an older Caucasian woman who wore scrubs, was in charge of somebody, and had the kind of no-nonsense look about her that is an absolute Godsend when you're at your wit's end. She pinned me with that look of hers while Caucasian Boy described my symptoms. She wasted no time, but gave no indication of being hurried. Together, in medical shorthand, they agreed I was a classic appendicitis presenter. "Bring him," she said, and together the four of us (my wife accompanying) sailed through the swinging doors like Dorothy and her pals on the way to the Emerald City.

Once through those doors, your world changed. On the outside, in the featureless sprawl of the admitting area, you were just another presenter, a whiner, an interruption, a cause for skepticism, maybe even ridicule. But once you were admitted through those doors, you were regarded in an altogether different light. You had become a bona-fide Case, a target upon which the Healing Arts could bring to bear their considerable skill-set. By virtue of your presence, you gained an immediate measure of entitlement. The price of your entitlement was simple: it was pain. The element of pain -- of blustery, swaggering, cruel, devious, remorseless pain -- quickly conjures up the true magnificence and calls forth the compassionate response of the Healing Arts. As they disrobe you and clothe you in a flimsy backless gown and lie you down on a hard metal gurney, your body becomes the very field over which the Arts will do battle with pain, ignorance, fear and superstition. But all that comes later. First, there are the soothing, competent hands that reach out to you and bid you welcome. By whatever torturous route you have come, you have reached the sanctuary, and the RNs' cool, professional touch is the first sign that Everything's Going to Be Alright.

In this case, the hands that first reached out to me belonged to an impossibly good-looking thirty-something nurse in sea-foam scrubs. Her shoulder-length auburn hair with its blonde highlights was pulled sensibly back and casually held, and she had the marvelously cool sexuality of a married woman who can as easily insert a trach tube as stroke the base of her husband's penis and perform either task with complete aplomb. She moved with studied ease through the tight confines of the cubicle. "We're going to insert a drip, Hon," she informed me. God, barely introduced and already we were intimates.

"You bet," I said weakly. By now, the abdominal pain that had gained me entry was sharp and protracted, and I was able to give myself over to this beauty without any reservations whatsoever. She fingered my wrist expertly, turning it over in her hands.

"I'd like to put it in here," she said.

"You can put it in wherever you want," I said, my voice sounding thin as parchment, but full of good humor and honest collaboration. At my response, her laughter trilled like silver water over my hardened sensibilities. Lifting my head I looked for her name tag. Lauren Holland, RN. "Thank you, Lauren," I said. Thank you, you fascinating, lovely, God-fearing, non-judgmental, child-bearing, tongue-flicking, disco-dancing, carpool-driving, life-saving, womanish creature.

I dropped my head and tried to get some rest.

Life came and went over the next several hours. My pain was a constant, however, and distorted my sense of time and place. Snatches of conversation reached me. Nurses' laughter as they worked together, the eternal collaboration of girls. Lying on my back on the hard gurney, I listened to their voices swirling around me, and sensed the shield they had erected around those of us who had gained entrance to their sanctuary. Harm could not reach us here, no more than the harm we had brought with us, and even that was separated and gently herded back out the door.

"Mr. Wilson." I could overhear one of my girls as she addressed a fellow in an adjoining bay. "You told me that the pains started right after you got out of prison. How long ago was that?"

"Dat be las' munt."

"And were you drinking then?"

"Drinkin' some, yes ma'am."

"But you haven't been drinking today?"

"No ma'am. I ain't had nothin' today nor yesterday neither."

They pose questions to all the new entries, and the kinds of questions that they ask are the kind that not your mother, or your wife, or your best friend would necessarily feel comfortable in asking, and if they did, you might not give them a straight answer anyway. But for these women, you're dying to give a straight answer.

"Now sweetie. Are you feeling pain here? How about here? Not really? A little bit, maybe? Do you remember when you smoked the last of your crack?"

A mumbled, unintelligible response.

"Did the swelling start before or after you smoked your last pipe?"

A grunt, a grudging concession.

"Well, I want you to put your head back and just take it easy for a few minutes. I'm going to get the doctor to come take a look at you. Go on, lie back." A rustle of scrubs and one of the girls is off on her mission.

I sense movement at my elbow, and open my eyes to see the earnest gaze of a small brunette I'd admired from afar earlier. "Mr. Cochran? How are you feeling now?" She takes my arm in her cool hands and slips her fingers over my wrist. My betrothed.

"To tell you the truth, feeling like hell." She didn't ask me how I was feeling about her.

She considers me, her fingers still on my wrist. "If it's okay with you, I'd like to give you something for the pain." She seeks my authorization with raised eyebrows.

"You know, I think that would be fine." I try not to break into song.

Later in the afternoon I'm gliding along on the gauzy goodwill of a morphine high when they wheel me upstairs for X-rays. Being wheeled along on your back, headfirst, three feet off the floor, steered by the hand of another, is a wonderful way to travel, albeit a little disorienting. I wince slightly as we bang over the elevator joints. The pain is still there, but it belongs to someone else, like a dog on a leash that happens to be in my hand. Good doggie. Get lost, doggie. I'm a cat lover anyway.

Afterwards I'm back in my cubicle downstairs on my gurney. There's been a shift-change, and some new admissions have slipped in. In the bay next to me is an elderly black gent who's a real sourpuss this afternoon. He sick and tired, and sick and tired of being sick and tired. He's in no mood for the charm, good will, or tender ministrations of our healing Goddesses. They need a blood sample. By the color of their uniforms and the insignias they wear, members of the ER staff are identifiable in the chain of command. The RN's are the only ones with the sea-foam scrubs. Lesser mortals wear trim white uniforms, or burgundy scrubs, or even, in some cases, white lab coats. To draw the blood from my ailing bay-mate, they send in one of the girls in white who looks a lot like an early version of Farah Fawcett. If you do not remember or never saw the early version of Farah, we're talking about a lean, taut, tanned blonde with big eyes, a perfect set of pearly-whites, and an air of accessibility, even vulnerability, that make her seem like your girlfriend from the moment you meet. She wants to please, her mother taught her to please, and she won't be pleased with herself until you're pleased with her.

"Oh, FUCK!" is the first thing that bursts out of Sourpuss's mouth when she probes his forearm for a place to insert her needle. He's been a diabetic for years evidently, and his skin is dried and tough, his veins stringy and on the lam.

"I'm sorry," Farah says, and she really is. She would like nothing more in this moment than to turn loose his arm and spare him additional discomfort.

"Gott-DAMN!" he says when she tries again to locate a landing area. His face is curdled with disgust and condemnation. It's hard for Farah not to take this kind of assault personally. She's standing on the far side of his gurney facing me, and I shoot her an understanding glance. A glance of support. Of comradeship. Of wanting to spoon with her in a quiet room overlooking a remote beach.

"We've got to get this sample, Mr. Palmetto." Another younger female, a wearer of the burgundy, arrives to assist her. My Farah in her starched whites is a vision of cool heat. "I know you're uncomfortable..." And together the ladies launch another probe. What's the point, I wonder. Palmetto has no blood, he's pure piss and vinegar. "Sheeet! What the fuck! You all fuckin' NUTS. Oh Gott-DAMN."

Farah abandons her glide path, and comes to the other side of his gurney. My side. She's close enough for me to breathe her in now. She jostles me slightly as she jockeys for position on Palmetto's arm. Despite her ladylike demeanor and the reticence about her, she has the athletic build of a one-time volleyball player. I take in her aroma. She shoots me a glance for the first time, and I try to smile casually and reassuringly. I don't want to spook her with my naked, unadorned adoration. *"If it doesn't work out with this poor bastard, come over here and work on me. Hell, you can amputate if you want, I won't make a peep."* That's what I'd like to tell her. But I don't. At least I don't hear myself if I do.

Over another string of epithets, she actually manages to get him tied off and get the needle in. It's just as I figured. No blood. Not a trace. Palmetto is cursing blue blazes. Farah nearly has tears in her eyes. She looks at me finally, and her lips twist in an exaggerated grimace, a little-girl look like she'd given her daddy when she was eight and she had attempted something and it hadn't gone right, and she'd promised him with that look that she knew she'd come up short, but she isn't counting herself out, she'll be back, and he'll be proud of her yet. The look, and the intimacy it represents, resonate through the well of my being. When things were at their toughest for the fair-haired maiden, daddy was there for her, and I'm glad, on this occasion at least, that it was me.

The next morning my wife arrives at the top of the hour to visit me. I see her face as she comes around the corner, her eyes alight, looking for her man. I give myself to her wholeheartedly. She holds my hand. It's not the healing handhold of a care-giver Goddess. It's the handhold of a partner. And when you're flat on your back and unable to go home, there is no finer handhold than that.

Government Work

I don't go with prostitutes. Let me make that clear from the outset. It's not my style, never has been. I don't mean I'm afraid of 'em. And I don't condemn 'em. I just don't trade with 'em.

And I'm not going to be one of these jerks who tells you he's never paid for sex. I've paid for sex all my life, for cryin' out loud. Most men do. Maybe not cash. You pay in other ways. A house. A car. A twenty-year job that's a grind. Promises that you doubt you'll ever keep even as you're making them. Visits to the in-laws. Late night conversations in bed when you wish to hell you could just go to sleep. You pay, pal. Only difference is, with a hooker, it's a much simpler transaction, it really is. You want to sample the goods? Show me the money. I mean, how much simpler can it get?

Except that I never knew until later that she was a hooker. A professional party girl. I met her through friends. I got an invitation to stop in for a drink at their apartment just off Magazine Street. When I arrived about seven in the evening, it was just me and the hostess, Karen, and her ex-husband Frankie. Friends of mine for some time. We've partied together. On this occasion, we relaxed and talked for a while, and after maybe half an hour, other people start to drift in. Karen knows lots of people -- she picks up people in bars, at festivals, in art galleries, just because they interest her. When she wants to get to know you, that's what she'll do. Pick you up. So she had invited a few others, it was a Friday night, people were stopping in to wind down from the week. What you'd call a nice gathering.

At first I didn't notice her, this woman. I'm not sure why. She was real easy on the eyes. It had been pretty warm for the last few days, and she was wearing a skirt and a low-cut white sweater, exposing some cleavage. Nice legs. Remnants of a summer tan. Maybe she got it from one of those tanning salons, I don't know. Long hair, black and straight. A smile that was friendly and open. Eyes that took you in. Like I said, I didn't notice her at first, but once I did, we struck up a conversation. She told me she had just gotten back from Vegas, and we talked about the shows and what not. Told me that she paints, that her mother's birthday is coming up and she's painting her a portrait. It wasn't a serious conversation or anything, but we were connecting a little bit. In my experience, if you get a woman talking about her mother, she can tend to open up to you in a hurry. But I've also been a bachelor for long enough to know that conversation over drinks at a get-together doesn't amount to much, and I don't come on to women that way. I did, however, go back to the kitchen to get her a beer at one point, which wasn't unusual, since I needed one for myself. After that we drifted away from one another and kind of fell into conversations with other people.

Understand this. I've got a regular girlfriend, who just happened to be in Memphis visiting her sister for two weeks. We had not had a fight or anything, she just goes to visit her sister every few months, they're real close. So I am not Mr. Man-On-The-Town. Until I got Karen's invitation to stop over, I was on my way to the movies. Perfectly content. And I've got no particular interest in having a private party with some woman I just met. I had told her I was in the security business, and that didn't seem to make much of an impression, why should it? I'm not a very exciting guy, plain and simple. I didn't give it a second thought.

Well, at one point later in the evening, I'm not sure how much later it was, but by then a few people had left,

I'm sitting on the sofa, and there's a spot open beside me, and the brunette in the sweater comes over and sits herself down beside me, and I can tell at a glance that she's been going at the booze pretty regular. She's not messed up or anything, not acting stupid, just quietly getting a little loaded. Her eyes had that carefree glaze. She was smoking a cigarette, which she hadn't been doing earlier. She kind of sizes me up like she's seeing me for the first time. I put that down to her being basically drunk. I don't make a damn thing out of it. Later, I'm coming out of the bathroom and Karen stops me and explains that the people who had brought Sweater Girl to the apartment had left and she was still here and she was pretty loaded, and Karen was getting ready to go to the French Quarter with some of her other guests, and would I mind getting the gal home? So I asked her the logical question, why wouldn't she just go with you and your friends -- what makes you think she wants to go home? I don't think she'd have much fun with us is what Karen says, which to me means she's too fucked up, please just take her off my hands. Since I trust Karen implicitly and we've been friends, good friends, and never romantically involved, I tell her not to be concerned, it's a done deal.

Now before you sit in judgment, understand something: this is New Orleans. Not Cincinnati, not Sacramento, not Dallas. It's a place where people do things, unusual things, things you will never understand or necessarily approve of, all the time, for no reason, and think nothing of it. They eat too much. Drink too much. Dance their asses off and watch the sun come up over the Mississippi. End up in a cab to the airport without ever having slept in a bed. There's not a lot of structure, no use for convention, and not many restrictions either. I can't tell you the number of times I've been in situations that were definitely not spotted in advance. Sometimes I have even been the one who needed to be taken home, although it's usually been the other way around. Hell, I had a small dinner party at my apartment six months ago, and one of the guests passed out fully dressed in the bathtub. She's about seventy years old, and nobody thinks anything of it. One of the other guests walked her home after we got her out of the bathtub. He got the remains of her dinner on his shirt for his trouble. This is just New Orleans, get the picture?

So I've been assigned a mission and I head back to the sofa. I've had a fair amount to drink, but I'm not drunk. Not even impaired. Far from it. I'm dead steady and tremendously efficient. This girl couldn't be with a safer guy.

I start out by telling her that the group is heading for the French Quarter, and that I'm not planning to join in, can I drop her someplace? She puts her hand on my knee and smiles at me very sweetly, and says oh God would you mind? Not a problem, I tell her, and I'll be very candid and confess to you that the way she puts her hand on me and the way she smiles at me give me two thoughts more or less simultaneously: one, that I could probably bang her if I wanted to, and two, that it would probably be a bad idea. And I can't explain why I would think either of these thoughts, but there they are.

I round up her purse from the bedroom, we say our goodbyes, we're leaving together almost like we're a regular couple or something, and nobody makes anything of it. *Bye. Y'all be careful.* Except Karen gives me a grateful look and says something to the girl like, Paul will get you where you're going, and the girl, who had told me her name was Yvonne, says something like, I know he will, and all of a sudden I'm feeling like a kid whose future is being discussed by two adult women.

I walk her around to the passenger side of the car and before I know what's happening, she's got her hand on the back of my head and her tongue in the back of my throat. When I pull back and glimpse her face in the streetlight she suddenly doesn't look so loaded. Sure, I kissed her back. Under the circumstances, as stupid as this may sound, it seemed like the gentlemanly thing to do. In fact, I even say something to her about my being a gentleman, and she says she already knows that, that if I weren't a gentleman, she wouldn't be getting in the car with me in the first place. Is it possible that this was her plan from the beginning? I wish I could answer that.

Once I put the car in motion, I ask her where to? She's got her hand on my thigh, obviously wants to keep me interested. I need to go home, she says. My boys will be wondering where I am. I shoot a look at her, just like she knows I will. Of course, my boys each have four legs and eat food out of a bowl on the floor, she tells me. Tell me how to get there, I say.

We arrive, we park, she puts the lip-lock on me again before we get out of the car, just to make sure I'm going along with the plan. I make no excuses. If she's going to be serving up pie, I'll have me a slice, thanks very much. But if she decides against the pie, and we end up with just coffee, that won't bother me much either.

She lives in big, roomy two-story frame house with wood siding which contains lots of knick-knacks and clutter, plus a piano in the living room. She futzes around at the piano for a bit, kind of serenades me, smokes a cigarette, and eventually comes over to where I'm sitting, slides herself onto my lap, and we do some more making out. She's a decent kisser. She asks me are you going to spend the night? Is that what you want? I ask her. You scare me, she says. That's good, I say. Let's go upstairs.

Cut to the chase. We copulate. Pleasant, but not a barnburner. I suck her titties, which she likes. Watch her face, which she likes. Grab her ass when I'm thrusting, which she likes. Pretty predictable stuff. Except that I'm not wearing a condom or anything. She hasn't asked and I haven't offered. Still, I have no intention of coming until I've gotten an orgasm out of her. That's part of the deal when you make love to a woman, at least it is for me. Always has been. But she makes me stop and pull out, says she needs to go potty. So I wait, lying in the dark on her waterbed with a decent hard-on that isn't going away real soon. Her three dogs are in the next room watching -- they're kept out by one of those folding gates parents use to child-proof certain rooms in the house. I have no idea what's going on in the minds of the pooches as I'm screwing their mommy, but I guess if she's happy, they're happy.

She makes her way back to the bed and lights a cigarette. Looks at the bedside clock. Puts the cigarette in an ashtray and reaches for my cock, wants to make sure I'm still good to go. Not a problem. She spreads her legs and takes me in, makes me bang her hard a couple of times. Look, there's something I need to tell you, she says. Boy, that doesn't sound good, I think, but she's enjoying my cock so much, I don't know what news could possibly be bad news. I really like you, she says. Can you tell?

Bang. Bang. Bang. Sweetheart, I can tell. She's stroking my balls with her fingertips, inviting me to come inside her.

I work for the government, she says. Thrust. Thrust. Thrust. We don't miss a beat.

She grabs me by the ass and digs in with her fingernails. Pulls me deep. And I need your help.

Oh boy oh boy oh boy. How much more of my help can you take? I wonder. As God is my witness, she is liking my cock at that instant. Liking everything about it. Regardless of what came next, I will go to my grave knowing that she was deeply pleased to be getting fucked by me. Is that such a crime, to believe that?

And then she says, next week they're going to assassinate the President.

Which of course, they did. But why in the hell I didn't go ahead and come in her when I had the chance, I'll never understand. I know that's what she wanted.

No Need to Push It

I was with Jayne Mansfield the night she died.

Well, don't let me misstate myself. Not with her in the Biblical sense. Although that wouldn't have been too bad either. But I was at Gus Stevens' Supper Club in Biloxi, Mississippi, where she was appearing. I think she was scheduled to be there most of the week, taking the place of Martha Raye, who had called in sick, resulting in Gus's calling Jayne and asking her to step in as a favor.

In later years, on hearing this, people might have thought, *Jeez, why's a Hollywood star doing a summer night gig in Biloxi, Mississippi, for Christ's sake? She must've been a real bottom feeder by then.* Well, to people that say that, I can only say two things: you never knew Gus's. And you never knew Jayne.

Surprising as it may be to hear it, I can tell you that she had quite an act. She sang a few songs to piano accompaniment: *Funny Valentine. He's Funny That Way. Sunny Side of the Street.* And of course there was *All Of Me*, which she sang as a double entendre while displaying her ample cleavage, as she pretty much did throughout the show. And why not? But let me say this about that: tits are tits. They'll only get you so far. Sooner or later, if you don't have a sense of humor, or some charisma, or some guts, you're stuck with tits and that's that. But Jayne had all of the above. Even if you had never seen her before you saw her show at Gus's, you would know that much about her:

she had all of the above.

Her show lasted about an hour, a good hour I would say. It was a supper club. You had your own table, you had a nice dinner, couple of highballs, and you had your entertainment, of which Gus had the pick of the litter: Tony Bennett played Gus's. Louis Prima and Keeley Smith. Rosemary Clooney. The Ink Spots. You've got to remember, this was the Sixties, and clubs featuring real classy adult entertainment had practically gone into the crapper. You had the Beatles, the Rolling Stones, all the druggies, the long hairs, the heavy metal acts taking over, and outside of Vegas and the coasts, there were damn few places where people of good sense and refined sensibilities could get together. Gus's was one of those places. You came with a date, usually, or you probably went home alone. No swingers at Gus's. Not that I ever condemned swingers. They just weren't my crowd, and they really weren't Gus's crowd, either. And I'm pretty certain they were not Jayne's.

She was doing two shows nightly, as I recall. Nine and eleven, something like that. Naturally I'm at the second show. And I don't have a date, in fact, I didn't even expect to be there, it was kind of a last minute thing. I was driving from Tampa/St. Pete to Dallas, and I pitched camp for the night in Biloxi, which was roughly the halfway point. This was in the days before the interstate, naturally, so it was a pretty good haul, two long days at the wheel. After one of those days, there was nothing like a hot shower, a fresh shirt, a stroll along the beach, and a good dinner. I was expensing everything in those days anyway, so when I saw Gus's, and the showboard out in front featuring Jayne Mansfield, I made a beeline. No coat and no tie, but I'm a respectable-looking guy who blends in real well with a nice crowd, so I was received without any difficulty whatsoever. I'd already wolfed down a couple of burgers earlier, so I take a seat at the bar and order up a double scotch. At the time, I remember thinking, better go easy on the booze there pal if you want to get your early start, but then I'm also thinking, Jayne fucking Mansfield, how great is this. So I order the double and settle in for the show.

You've got to remember, there were a lot of people who thought that Jayne was going to be the next Marilyn Monroe. Well, that worked as long as Marilyn was alive. But when the Kennedy boys snuffed her in '62, all of a sudden it all fell on Jayne, and to my way of thinking, it put a lot of pressure on her to be, or to become, someone who simply could not be replaced. A no-win situation. She couldn't buy a decent script, her management was plainly inferior, and Hollywood just wasn't ready to anoint a new Marilyn. People made comparisons anyway. But Marilyn's whole sad story, that was part of the beauty of her, the fact that she was a foster child who ended up marrying the most popular guy in America and couldn't make it work, couldn't have children, couldn't find happiness, and in the end gets taken out by the President and his cronies, who could possibly top that? Who would want to try, for Christ's sake? This much I can tell you for sure. When Jayne hit the stage at Gus's on that night in June of 1967, there was no ghost of Marilyn in the room. It was all Jayne, and you had to take her for who she was and what she was. If you were willing to do that, trust me, you couldn't help but love her to death. She had absolutely nothing to apologize for, and she knew it.

As I've said, the show lasted about an hour. Her only accompaniment was a pianist. She may have told a joke or two, but mostly it was just singing and flirting. She had one costume change, and I can't remember much about that either, except, as I've said, the lady knew how to put herself together, and she was pretty fabulous looking. I never cared much for the busty blonde type myself, but with Jayne, there was more to her, you could sense it. I think, to be honest with you, that she was a pretty brainy gal. Sharp, you know. Didn't miss much. Aware. And knew how to work a room. Did she ever.

I only drank the one double. After that I backed off a little. After all, I was by myself on a long road trip. I think I may have had one more scotch, but nothing else. At one point, before the show is over, there's a discussion going on at the end of the bar, the end where I'm at. A discussion between Gus, who is clearly recognizable from his picture on the marquee, and another gentleman, who is speaking on Jayne's behalf, and who, as I subsequently come to find out, is her divorce attorney and current boyfriend, Sam Brody. They're talking about transportation. A car. I hear New Orleans mentioned. Jayne is still on stage, but I can overhear their conversation clearly because I'm maybe four feet away. So I gather that after the show, Jayne wants to go to New Orleans, and she needs a ride. I nurse my scotch and think about this. When the two gentlemen finish their conversation, I catch Mr. Brody by the sleeve of his coat as he's moving away.

"I couldn't help but overhear. I'd be happy to drive Miss Mansfield. To New Orleans. Or wherever she needs to go."

He takes me in, kind of sizes me up and down. I don't mind. He doesn't know me from Adam, and I'm butting into his personal affairs. "Who asked you, if you don't mind my asking?" A charming guy he isn't.

"Nobody asked me, and I don't blame you for asking. It's just that you've got a situation, and I'd be happy to help. I'm a big fan."

"You're a fan. Do you know who I am?" He's being a little testy, but as I've said, who could blame him? Guys have been hitting on his girlfriend since she started wearing a bra. Or maybe sooner.

"I'm guessing that you're the man who takes care of Miss Mansfield."

"I take care of her all right. And thanks for your offer. I'll get back to you." And he pushes off.

He's not what I would call rude. Just preoccupied. I would imagine that taking care of a woman like Jayne Mansfield could make you that way.

Not long after that, the show's over. I've finished my drink. I'm ready to settle up. I get the bartender's attention. He brings me my tab, puts it on the bar in front of me. I'm reaching for my wallet when a hand comes over my shoulder and plucks the tab right off the bar. I turn around and it's my new friend, Mr.Brody.

"Come with me a minute, would you, pal? Somebody wants to meet you."

Well, I'm not slow. I know who Somebody is. I follow him. It's the first time I've been up since I first sat down at the bar, and the scotch has me light on my feet and completely at ease. This is turning into quite a night.

We go along the bar, past a curtain, through a door, then another door, and wind up in a very small area, what I guess you could call a dressing room, where Jayne sits in front of a well-lit mirror. She observes us in the mirror as we enter, and she turns to face us once we're inside. My first impression is that she appears smaller in person than she does on the stage. Smaller, softer, quieter. A little tiredness around her eyes I'm thinking. I manage to keep my eyes above her cleavage, which isn't that easy. Oddly enough, I do notice what great legs she's got. Dancer's legs.

"Sammy tells me you're going to New Orleans," she says to me.

"If that's where you need to go, that's where I'm going."

She smiles sweetly but kind of automatically. "Well, I've got my kids with me, you know."

"I've got a big backseat. They could stretch out and sleep."

"Jayne and me would ride in front with you." Sammy has become quite agreeable. But he also wants me to clearly understand the scenario.

"What is it that you do?" Jayne asks me. She has turned back to the mirror, where she watches my face.

"I drive for a living."

They consider this. Jayne smiles at me again.

"How long it take us to get to New Orleans?" Sammy wants to know.

"At this hour, not long. Maybe two and a half hours without pushing it."

"No need to push it," Sammy says. He now has his hand on my elbow, indicating that the interview is over.

"Jayne," I say. I'm old enough to call her Jayne.

She glances at me in the mirror, then turns around to face me again.

"I just wanted to say I think you're not only a beautiful woman, but also one hell of an entertainer. I've always thought so, anyway." I hold out my hand.

She does not take my hand in a traditional handshake, but with her palm down offers hers instead. "That's very kind of you. And thank you for coming to the show." On impulse I lift her hand and very smoothly touch the back of her fingers to my lips.

"Thank you." Then Sammy and I are on our way out of the room and the last thing I see is Jayne's face in the mirror. Her eyes are following me.

Well, you probably know the rest of the story. I was not the one driving the Buick Electra that night. In fact, the car I was driving at the time was a Pontiac Bonneville. Midnight black. Four-fifty-four four-barrel, dual overhead cams. Next to the Bonneville, the Electra was an old lady's church car. But it didn't bother me that they took the Electra. Gus fixed them up. It was a kid from the bar, a cousin or something, who worked for Gus. About 21 years old. Jayne's kids were in the back, with a dog or two. Sammy and Jayne were in the front, just like Sammy wanted. It was the responsible thing to do, I'm sure. On the other hand, if the kids had been asleep in the front seat, everybody would have survived. Well, everybody except the cousin.

The kid was probably not a bad driver. You could argue that it could've happened to anyone.

The road is damn narrow at the Rigolets. I've been over it many a time, both before and after that night. There was no indication that the kid was alcohol-impaired, as they say. The mosquito truck was just a bit of bad luck. That, combined with the eighteen wheeler, double indemnity. But let me just say this about that: you put me behind the wheel with Jayne Mansfield in my car, and I'll guarantee to deliver her safely to any spot on the face of the earth, any day of the week, any month of the year. Over and over again. Double the indemnity, triple it if you want. I'll still get the lady there safe and sound. I knew it that night, I've known it ever since. She'll always be safe with me.

And wherever she is, I think she knows it too.

This World Here Below

I was nineteen that summer. It's not hard to remember nineteen. You're out of school, and unless you're headed for college, which I wasn't, you're coming up with excuses for not yet wanting to become an adult. The last thing you're looking for at that age is to "start acting like an adult."At the age of 19, you're some kind of a freak, that's the truth of it. Especially in a rural Mississippi town like Philadelphia.

Ask me if I gave a damn.

And I'll tell you why. Why I didn't, that is. Give a damn. It's true that I wasn't going to college, at least not right away. And the job I had, working on the maintenance crew at the State Mental Hospital, paid me barely enough to make my rent at the boarding house. I didn't even have a damn car. No car, no prospects, no real education, and stuck in Philadelphia for at least the summer, if not longer. Summer of '64, to be exact.

And none of it bothered me that much.

The reason was Jane Ann Van Sculley.

Jane Ann had decided that she wanted me.

When did she come to this decision? I have no idea. We had gone to school together, and graduated together in the spring of '63. She had never paid me any special attention in school. And Jane Ann, who came from one of the best families in Neshoba County, was the kind of girl who could pick and choose. She wasn't going to date just any fool who might have hungered after her. Philadelphia wasn't a large town or anything, but that's not to say it didn't have society. Families who had been in the county for so many generations, who owned so much land or such and such businesses, who had amassed so many degrees, and who had interests or kinfolk in Atlanta, or New Orleans, or even New York – these kinds of families were society in Philadelphia, even if their children went to high school with the children of white sharecroppers, trailer-park dwellers, people of limited means and baseless dreams, people like myself and my best friend Conway, whose father owned a small body shop next to the Esso Station on South Main. Fellows like us, cut out of common cloth, could sit next to girls like Jane Ann in Geometry class, or across the table from them in the cafeteria, we could even say "hey" to them at football games or school assemblies, but in fact there was a gulf that separated us, and it was there for a good reason. How else are you going to protect polite society from its own baser instincts?

Hell, I never even entertained thoughts of those instincts with a girl like Jane Ann. A hundred and fifty years of breeding, both on her side and mine, had insured that not even the instincts would surface. There was a girl that rode my school bus, I used to jockey for a seat next to her, her name was Joyce, and she was the type that attracted my instincts. She was a good clean girl on the surface, but the way she sat in the seat with her legs crossed and her skirt riding up a little high over those smooth-looking brown knees, and the sidelong glances she gave me spoke of an inner sluttiness, a desire to have acts performed upon her. I used to get a boner on the afternoons I was lucky enough to secure a seat at her side. Even at the age of fifteen Joyce looked like she would get pregnant early and often, that she would probably be slapped by men (and slap them in return), and that she would end up living by herself and watching soap-operas in a tumbledown but clean little cottage nowhere near a lake or a river. My kind of girl. Of course, I never asked her out, but she was the type for whom I was destined, I knew it without ever being told.

Then, in our senior year, the Neshoba County School Board intervened in my destiny. All seniors were assigned to take a six-week course in Communism. That's right, Communism. At this time in our nation's history, it was believed by some that Communism was really On the Move in our country. (Of course, later on I would come to learn that these same people had been saying this ever since the War had ended nearly twenty years earlier). And that the best way to block the spread of Communism (which on the maps they showed us was always portrayed in red, a red stain spreading across the world like a girl's menstrual period might stain her panties) was to make sure that society's future leaders, the high school seniors, understood the threat posed by the Communists, and, even more importantly, knew how to identify and root out this treacherous human tendency. They wanted to take over our United States of America is what it was, and them lying, cheatin' double-dealing, two-faced devious fucks could turn up anywhere. Unless you had some background training and had your wits about you, you were just as liable to innocently buy one of 'em a cup of coffee and let 'em fill your ear with their sedition as you were to rat 'em out and turn 'em in the way you were supposed to.

Well, I wouldn't be exaggerating if I told you that, as seniors, we responded very favorably to the program, on account of the fact that it required cancelling our fifth and sixth period classes, loading us into buses, transporting us 12 miles, depositing us in the pleasant, airy confines of the Mississippi National Guard Armory, and giving us slap-happy seniors, now nearing the end of our long academic incarceration, an hour and forty five minutes of one another's company in a comparatively unstructured environment while listening to a lecture for which there would be no course credit, and hence no need to pay attention in the slightest.

On the first or second day, it so happened that when I slid into one of the folding chairs, I found myself directly behind Miss Van Sculley and her society friends.

That day something about my sense of humor caught her fancy, and it became natural that we found our seats close to one another the next day and every day after than for the duration of the blessed course. When it was over, I couldn't have begun to tell you where to look for a Communist, how to recognize one if you tripped over him, or what to do about it. (The only one who came to mind as a possible candidate was our shop teacher, but I dismissed that thought as quick as I could). But about Jane Ann, I had committed to memory much more: the way the wispy hairs rose off the back of her neck, the way she drew her lips over her teeth when she was about to laugh out loud, the way she unconsciously pumped her powerful legs when she crossed them and was trying to concentrate. After being around her and observing her closely as I did over the span of those six weeks, I came to understand to a greater extent what it was that set her and her kind apart from kids like myself who came from families of lesser means, and meaner lessons. It was the quality of expectation. There were people in Jane Ann's life – mother, father, grandparents likely, probably aunts and uncles – who held expectations for her, and she lived with those expectations every day, lived with them, was sustained and nourished by them, and inevitably gave herself over to them. Her life was in a sense not really her own. That's something that would have bothered me, to feel deprived of my freedom of choice (not that I was capable of making much in the way of informed choices anyhow) but you could tell that Jane Ann had been born into an element that had lived this way for generations, and had learned how to trust those expectations, feel comfortable with them, be embraced by them and shoulder the burden of passing them faithfully on from one generation to the next.

The truth is, Jane Ann made me feel a little like a pauper.

But I wasn't deaf, dumb, or blind. She was still a lovely girl on the cusp of becoming quite a woman, and she knocked me out.

After we graduated, our newfound friendship went on the shelf for a time. I saw her in passing only once or twice that summer, and in the fall, she was off to USM Hattiesburg, while I worked on the maintenance crew at the hospital. In fact, I didn't see her again until March of '64, and then only very briefly. It was in the French Quarter in New Orleans during Mardi Gras. She was with friends, I was with friends, and our respective groups collided with one another, literally, in the patio of Pat O'Brien's. She gave me an unexpectedly exuberant hug, and sagged heavily, warmly against me, with her lips pressed to my ear. "You need to call me, you little so-and-so," she said, and then they were gone back into the street with their Hurricane glasses. As for me, I walked around on a cushion for the rest of the day (only part of the cushion was owing to the Hurricanes), and tried not to get too analytical about the nature of her summons. But no matter how I cut it, there was only one real conclusion I could draw. She was, and had been, secretly in love with me for many months, and, tiring of her collegiate crowd, was longing for the kind of real companionship and honest-to-goodness affection that only I could provide.

Of course I never called her.

Meanwhile, as we approached the summer of '64, there were other, larger concerns creating friction in our lives. Spurred on by the assassination of President Kennedy, and the legislative agenda of his Texas-born successor, the Democratic Party was putting on a big push to register black voters in Mississippi. Teams of young people from progressive states like New York, Pennsylvania, Illinois, and New Jersey were coming to Mississippi to conduct "Freedom Schools," where they coached mostly rural blacks on the ABC's of their voting rights, and the procedures whereby they could exercise those rights.

Now I am a born and bred Southern boy, but believe me when I tell you, that didn't bother me all that much. I knew that the rural blacks whom they were targeting had no interest whatsoever in the voting process, and were made extremely uncomfortable by the attention that came their way as a result of the whole thing. As such, if we had just laid low and let the business run its course, not much would have happened, and our precious southern way of life, or whatever it was, wouldn't have been affected all that much. I personally never even came in contact with the Freedom Workers, or whatever they were calling themselves. It's not like they were all over the county, and the ones that were in the area kept pretty much to themselves, or spent their time in the rural areas with their Negro charges. I had acquaintances who tailgated them on the roads a time or two, and probably shouted some redneck sentiments in their direction. What the hell, they were our age pretty much, and if they would rather chase poor Negroes around Mississippi than hunt pussy back home (some of course suggested than they were chasing Negro pussy anyway), well, that was a strange choice, but in time they'd outgrow it, and we would all be able to get on with our lives pretty much as before.

Unfortunately, not all of us felt that way.

Some of the older men in the community, the ones who felt more keenly the desperation of their dead-end jobs, their bad marriages, their own personal unworthiness – just any kind of burr under the saddle that would not relent – well, they took it upon themselves to harass, oppose, taunt, and generally obstruct this whole process of freedom-schooling the Negroes. I think the crux of their argument, after all the sound and fury died away, could be summed up in a phrase that I heard a dozen times if I heard it at all: "They ain't no better than we are." Not referring to the Negroes, of course, but to the Northern kids. It wasn't strictly racism that prompted the violence that was to follow, there was an ample measure of resentment. It lay in the perception that the ones who were being deliberately schooled in all of this were not the itinerant, shiftless, hopeless Negroes, but the tax-paying, land-owning, law-abiding (in most cases) white citizens of the Great State of Mississippi. And that stung many to the quick. It should have stung me too. But it didn't. And I can tell you why in four words.

Jane Ann Van Sculley.

When a woman of society freely chooses to want you,

as I was convinced that Jane Ann wanted me, you are immunized against the virus of unworthiness, pettiness, even against politically motivated anger and hostility. For a time, anyway.

Things will take their course, I now understand. I can't say I understood it then. Love and hate are powerful forces, maybe the most powerful natural forces in the world, and once they are set in motion, there's no stopping them until they have played out their hand, so to speak. In 1964, when I was nineteen, I had not even a dim understanding of how all this worked. I was a young fellow going through the motions of adulthood, feeling my body, struggling with my natural urges, trying not to panic about the uncertain future. "Love" and "hate" to me were still disembodied notions, like "pride" and "heritage," a couple of other concepts that I heard spoken around town that summer. What I did know was that after I got that phone call, things started to move almost without my even taking an active role, and I couldn't have stopped them if I'd wanted to.

Mary Frances Barnwell was probably Jane Ann's best friend – or at least had been in school. In the three months or so that I'd been at the boarding house, I had never received one call. The phone was in the hallway, not far from my door. I could hear it when it rang, but I never paid it any attention. This time the old man tapped at my door. "Call for you," he said. I came out like a sleepwalker and fished for the dangling receiver

"Percy?"

"That's me. Who's this?"

"It's Mary Frances Barnwell. From school."

"Of course. Long time no talk."

"I know. Iddin' it somethin'? Listen, I'm really callin' cause we're having a get-together at the river this weekend, and Jane Ann asked me if I knew how to get in touch with you to invite you."

"That's real sweet. Tell her I'd love to come, and thanks for askin'."

We made a little more small talk, I got directions, and

politely hung up. And that's all I did. I never went to the fishing camp that weekend (had no car, you may recall), and tried to forget about the whole thing. Two days later, about 5:00 PM on a June evening, they came looking for me. Jane Ann and Mary Frances. At the boarding house. The old man came to my door again. "Couple girls lookin' for you," he reported. I walked to the screen door, and there they were, the two of them, in a four-door dove-grey Pontiac Chieftain with red and white trim. My first thought was, I wonder if their mothers know where they are. I swear to God. I was raised that way.

Well, I was trapped. It didn't take long for them to talk me into getting dressed and coming along. I put on some clean blue jeans and a white tee-shirt, that's all. On my feet I probably had my sneakers. The girls were dressed kind of casual themselves, so I didn't really feel out of place. Well, no more out of place than a fellow's likely to feel when he's riding around in a big gunboat like that with two of the best-looking society girls in his town and he might have $150 to his name. (In his savings account, that is. From his pocket he'll be lucky to pull a fiver.)

Jane Ann had on a sun dress, that I do recall. A pale yellow sun dress. She was riding in the passenger seat, and Mary Frances was driving. I've got no idea what Mary Frances was wearing.

"God, you know I been trying to get together with you," Jane Ann says to me, as if it's the most natural thing in the world.

"I know. I been working a lot," I tell her lamely. "You sure look nice."

"Why, thank you, kind sir." Kind sir? Only a girl with Jane Ann's class could call a fellow something like Kind Sir and not have it sound stupid or condescending. She made it sound like my name. Or a title I had earned. "We're just on the way to get a couple of milkshakes and maybe go for a swim, and we would enjoy your company," she said to me across the seat. She had her long pale arm resting on the back of the seat between us. (Jane Ann was a very fair-skinned girl, and protected her skin against the ravages of the sun years before that became the smart thing to do). She had on red finger nail polish. When I saw the fingernail polish, I remember taking a deep breath and for the first time allowing myself to believe that this was actually happening to me. I caught Mary Frances eying me in the rear-view, and I smiled at her. A genuine, fearless smile. She went back to driving.

They were as good as their word. We actually drove to the Tastee Freeze on Patterson Road and ordered milkshakes. They made it pretty clear it was their treat so I didn't even go through the charade of pulling out my money. We chatted. Well, they chatted, I politely eavesdropped. They talked about parents, school, the town, even briefly about the Freedom Riders. "Oh, one of them stopped me last week to get directions," Jane Ann laughed.

"You don't mean it," Mary Frances said.

"Sure enough. Outside the Woolworth. He was polite as could be. Kind of good-looking, if you like the dark Jewish type. Percy, how many of those boys are down here?"

"I really don't know, Jane Ann. Well, I believe I read that there are something like a hundred of them in the state." I had read no such a thing, but since casual information was about all I had to contribute, I wasn't going to disappoint.

She leaned across the seat then and lightly put her fingers on my knee, as an old trusted friend might. "Does it make you nervous at all, havin' them runnin' around the county incitin' the Negroes an' what not?"

"Not nearly as nervous as just riding around in the car with you," I told her. It was a perfectly candid response, and she rewarded me with a look I have never forgotten. Following which, she actually blushed.

"Oh, you," she said, and grinned at Mary Frances, a very pleased grin.

There was some more riding and some more desultory conversation while we worked on our milkshakes, and before long we had made our way out Rangeline Road, past the old saw mill and into the piney woods that ran along

Broussard's Creek. Pretty soon Mary Frances had actually left the pavement and was gently maneuvering the car along an old logging road towards the creek itself. We had sucked our milkshakes all dry by then, and nobody had much to say. It was quiet and peaceful being under the trees and shielded from the late June sun.

Mary Frances stopped the car and turned off the ignition. "Swimming anyone?" she said.

"You go ahead on. We'll catch up," Jane Ann said.

Dutifully Mary Frances opened her door and got out. She had a tote bag with her. "You got cigarettes?" Jane Ann asked. "Leave us a couple, pretty please."

"Guilty pleasures, hey?" Mary Frances chided.

"Not so guilty." Jane Ann took the cigarettes and placed them in the glove box. "Percy, come up front and sit a while," she instructed, patting the seat beside her.

By the time I had gotten out, come around the car on the passenger side, and slid in next to Jane Ann, we could just see Mary Frances' head and shoulders disappearing from view as she made her way down the bank towards the creek. Jane Ann put her hand on the inside of my thigh like we had been going out for six months. "Kiss me," she instructed.

I obliged. Her kiss was ladylike for the first few seconds, and then it went to businesslike after that. Her fingers tugged delicately at my zipper. For a moment I stopped kissing her and I looked right in her eyes. No, they implied, this was not the time for conversation. We were here for a reason. With her fingers she briefly caressed and teased the bulge in my groin area. Thus assured that I was keeping pace, she pried off her sandals with her toes, and had that sun dress up over her hips before I could even remove my glasses and put them on the dashboard. Then she pulled me towards her again.

Fast forward some forty years. The Old South is dead and gone, long live the Old South. I live there again, but only after many years of restless peregrination, with substantial time spent in New York City, San Francisco,

Austin, Texas and Kansas City, Missouri. I spent enough time away, both physically and culturally, to get a measure of perspective on my adolescent experiences, and on the society that birthed them. The South, with her rhythms and cadences, her kindnesses and her cruelties, her delicacy and her denials – the South, whose regionalism has been so long held in contempt by the rest of the nation even as the rest of the nation borrows from her the things that really matter – conscience, concupiscence, common sense. I don't mind telling you that this is really the first time I've spoken openly of this era of my life, and in particularly of Jane Ann or the Civil Rights Activists. In particular I refer to the events of that long-ago June evening, the evening which Jane Ann Van Sculley chose me to deflower her, which was the same evening that on a sparsely traveled dirt road not three miles from where we had parked, elements of the local Klan waylaid three young men and martyred them in the name of Protecting Our Sacred Heritage. That evening came strongly to mind some weeks ago as a trial unfolded in Philadelphia, Mississippi. Out to exorcise their ancient ghosts, a new generation of Mississippi politicians, with the help of the Federal government and the tacit support of the citizenry, sought a murder conviction in the case. Relatives of the deceased victims were present, evidence was presented, names of men long dead and buried were again heard on people's lips, and the spasm of violence that unfolded on county road sometime between 12:30 and 2:00 AM was again examined. A conviction was obtained, and the chapter was closed. The three martyrs can now presumably rest in peace.

But for the living, neither rest, nor peace can be so ordained by court action. By the time the deputy sheriff and his henchmen, riding in two pickup trucks, had intercepted the station wagon with the two New Yorkers and the unfortunate Mississippi black, Jane Ann, Mary Frances and I had returned from our excursion and had already parted company. I couldn't swear by the clock, but I know it was still daylight, thick dusky daylight, as Jane Ann gathered herself, and used some toilet paper she had brought along for the occasion to clean between her legs. "Oh, mercy," she was saying. Or maybe she only said it once. "Oh, mercy."

"You all right?" I asked her.

She was sitting beside me on the seat again after straddling me during coitus, and she leaned over and kissed me briefly on the lips. "Percy, you're just as sweet as you can be," she commented.

"Glad I could be of service," I told her. If it sounded a little cynical, it was meant to, but she let it go.

"Would you mind to give Mary Frances a shout and let her know we're ready to go?"

So the fact is, we were back within the environs of town by 9:00 PM or thereabouts. They dropped me off at the boarding-house. I was not really surprised that of the two, it was Mary Frances who gave me the sweeter look as we parted company. "You call us now," she said, and Jane Ann chimed in with similar sentiments, without looking in my direction. By the time the first fist smashed into the first New Yorker's head, I was fitfully asleep and lightly dreaming.

Of course, we never called each other, and except for an occasional glimpse of her later that summer, I didn't see Jane Ann again. Early in 1965 I left Mississippi for the first of many extended absences, going to San Francisco and shipping out as on ordinary seaman on a merchant marine vessel bound for Vietnam. That was as far away from Neshoba County as I could hope to get in those days.

Thirty years passed, as thirty years will. Actually, it was closer to thirty-five. I found myself living in New York, but about to take leave of the city to return to Mississippi and spend some time with my uncle, who was in ill health and no longer able to keep up his rambling Acadian-style manse just across the road from the Gulf of Mexico in Ocean Springs. On this particular evening, I went out to a gathering in Queens at the rooftop penthouse of a friend who was a segment producer for National Public Radio. He and his partner were leaving for Europe for two weeks, and this little soiree was to give them a proper send-off. I mixed, I mingled, I knew a few people in the room. Had some drinks and checked out the talent, as they say. At some point I became aware of a not-unattractive fifty-something woman who was engaged in animated conversation with a person on the fringe of a larger group. I happened to be looking her way when she fixed me with a rather pointed gaze over the shoulder of this other person. The next thing I knew, she had detached herself and was making her way towards me. Once she got within hailing distance, her voice was instantly recognizable: "Percy Quinn, as I live and breathe."

"Mary Frances? Are you here in New York, or are you living in a parallel universe?" She sailed into me and we hugged with surprising warmth. Two Mississippians against the world. Or, out in the world -- same thing.

She held me at arm's length. "You're quite the man of the world, Mr. Quinn. And don't deny it. I've read your books."

"Coming from you, Mary Frances, I confess I'm flattered," I told her sincerely. Good God, where is the author that doesn't personally love each and every one of his readers?

We coasted past pleasantries into slightly more substantial inquiries. Career paths. Present cities of domicile. Primary interests in New York. (She lived in Groton, Connecticut with her husband who was some kind of engineer, and they were in New York to visit her daughter, who in fact had invited them to the gathering. Mary Frances had attended, the husband had not.) Then she popped out with it. Since it was our one real link, aside from Mississippi, it had lingered in the air, and I might eventually, certainly after a second scotch, have broached it, but she beat me to the punch. "And I actually still keep in touch with Jane Ann."

"How's Miss Jane Ann?" I asked lightly. "Happy with her life, I trust?" Internally I was bracing myself for something, I didn't know what.

"Oh, she makes a point of it," Mary Frances said, in an off-handed throw-down manner that I positively loved. Jane Ann, it seemed, had married well, divorced, married even better, and owned a string of antique shops in Charleston, or Charlotte, one of those Confederate strongholds. Had a daughter in politics and a son in rehab. Had broken the mold a few times, it seems.

"Well, she damn well broke the mold with me," I acknowledged.

"As her enabler for that little venture of ours, I'm not sure whether I owe you an apology or a pat on the back," Mary Frances said, and I suddenly had the thought that she was a closet liberal parading as a mildly enlightened conservative. My hesitation immediately prompted in her a note of anxiety. "I mean, I know you performed that night, I just never knew whether you resented being set up."

"She told you that I performed?" I was mildly curious at the nature of this girl-talk.

"She didn't have to say anything, believe me. The girl had made up her mind to get laid that summer, and there was nobody from school that she felt she could trust. She'd been taking the pill for about six months and just wasn't going to put it off any longer."

"Hell, what about.....? (Here I named, with as much accuracy as I could, two or three of the society boys in our class, boys who on the surface certainly seemed more likely candidates than me.)

"Oh no, she wasn't going to set herself up for that, the ways those boys gossiped. Lord, they were worse that any of us. She wasn't going to be a notch on somebody's six-shooter. She wanted to have sex, but she wasn't looking for the small-town complications. So I recommended you, if you want to know the truth."

"You recommended me? Mary Frances, you all didn't even know me."

"Look, Mr. Man of the World, you know damn well how in high school people are already displaying their dominant characteristics. And you were a solid character. You kept to yourself, you didn't run with a crowd, you were polite, well-spoken. You treated us girls with respect. In some ways you were ages ahead of the rest of the guys in our class, we all knew that."

I was honestly and momentarily overwhelmed at this perception, and I didn't trouble to hide it. "That is an astounding revelation to me, if you want to know the truth," I said.

"To tell you the honest truth, the summer after that we were hanging out and drinking – we both had serious boyfriends, we were so liberated by then – when your name came up and she wanted me to find you and see if you were up for a repeat, but by then I guess you had left the area."

"Yeah, I was performing a stud service in the Bay Area," I said with what I hoped was a wry grin. I then became aware of a determined approach, and in short order a somewhat matronly and self-contained younger woman who I took to be Mary Frances' daughter was at her elbow. "Mom, we need to be getting back," she said.

"Sweetheart, you've heard me talk about Percy Quinn, the author. How we went to school together and all. This is he. Or, this is him. Percy, my daughter Samantha." What could have been a serendipitous little moment was nipped in the bud by virtue of Daughter's forced greeting and obvious lack of interest in diluting her agenda for one moment to linger with one of Mother's historical artifacts. The two of them soon pushed off, Mary Frances with a faintly apologetic air draped across her shoulders like a shawl. Alone again, I moved over to the bar area, came away with a Dewar's and Seven, and parked myself near a bank of windows that looked over the East river towards Manhattan.

That's when I remembered the blood. It was the first time I could recall ever thinking about it. Even in the immediate aftermath, I couldn't recall remembering it. There had been blood. Both mine and Jane Ann's. In the throes of passion, or perhaps just pain, she had bitten me on the lower lip, and as I stood looking over the East River, one of my favorite rivers in the world, I remembered that I could taste the blood as she carried on about her business, her small exclamations issuing from progressively deeper in her throat. When she pressed herself against me and cupped a breast for me to sample, I could still taste my blood as I politely suckled her engorged nipples, one after the other. "It's okay," she said. "If you want to come in me." To tell the truth, distracted by the blood, wondering where Mary Frances was, and frankly having been thrust into a somewhat violent sexual situation when I would have been satisfied with some slow kisses, ejaculation had not even occurred to me. After that, I rather quickly gathered my forces and made a point of it.

"I didn't come, but it's all right," she said as I began to lose my rigidity and she sagged against me. "I think I'm probably bleeding anyway." She drew back and lifted herself slightly. Reaching over, she opened her purse, tugged out some tissue papers, and mopped briefly between her legs. I watched as the toilet paper became rust-red. She then wadded the paper in a tight ball, rolled down the window, and pitched the ball out into the dusk. "I'm glad somebody came."

"I thought you wanted me to," I said.

"Percy, you're just as sweet as can be," she said then. The tone of voice was that of a dean telling a student that he's made a good effort but his SAT score is not going to get him into Ole Miss.

There had been something else I had tasted as well. Something besides the blood. Something that was in Jane Ann. Or maybe it was on Jane Ann. On her skin. In the pigmentation of her pale skin. I smelled it, or perhaps had tasted it in her mouth or on her nipples as she offered herself up to me. I don't know what it was, but it issued up from someplace inviolate, a sacred place, and not just sacred to people of small-town Mississippi either. On the back of her tongue, where her breath mingled with mine, I detected the aroma of a coal-burning steam engine climbing a long grade: the dry heat and hard work of a slave train. Or a freedom train. In either case, I had the distinct sense of being offered more than mere sex. I was being offered a living sacrifice. Even as she was roughly abandoning her virtue to me, Jane Ann's virtue was enhanced. Here she was, bestowing upon a thirsting young man a foretaste of heaven. And the message I got was: heaven was a rough place. Heaven was bloody and often violent. Too intimate for words, heaven was defined by actions, by brutally direct actions, actions that sometimes caught you off guard and even violated your sense of how things should be. Heaven was not all it was cracked up to be. But it was still heaven. It would always be heaven and men would always die to defend its portals. Or die to enter them.

The Preacher of Philadelphia, he had known that. He had understood Heaven in a way that required no explanation. Or at least required an explanation that he could never have provided. According to testimony at the trial, it was the Preacher who had sent those fellows off on their infamous midnight mission with the heartfelt observation that the two New Yorkers (and the Negro) "need their asses tore up." That meant there would be blood, everybody knew that. Pain and blood. Pain, blood, and likely death. No, not just likely. Preferably. The Preacher had passed a judgment, and because of it, three men would die on that night. If Heaven was in his thoughts (as one would assume it infrequently might be), he was dispatching three souls to its environs in order to have more of the world, this world here below, for himself and his people. I hope it will not be too much of a stretch for me to suggest that, on the same day, Jane Ann had likewise passed a judgment, and that, because of her judgment, something in each of us would die. Not a physical death, no, but the kind of death that one experiences when one gives oneself up to forces that one can never fully comprehend. The kind of a death that ultimately adds meaning to a life. In this world here below.

You, Me, and a Gulf Coast Motel

Let's get away, just you and me.

We can leave on Thursday afternoon, as soon as we get off work. Play hooky all day Friday. Drive straight through. Be there in time to watch the sun set from the balcony of our room.

Or, if not, just work a half day, leave right after lunch on Friday. Still give us a head start on the weekend.

I know you like to be playing (or at least driving someplace where you're going to play) when other people are working, don't you?

C'mon, pack your overnight bag. You won't need much. Couple pair of shorts, halter top or two. Your bathing suit. You know, the striped one. Yeah, the one I like to see you in. (Or see you out of.) I don't mind driving, but we probably ought to take your car. Mine needs to go in the shop, I'll take it over there as soon as we get back. What time do you want to get started?

What'll you tell your daughter? I mean, so she doesn't rat you out to her dad. Jeez, the last thing we need is for him to start some shit. Just tell her you're going with your friend Darleen. You guys used to go off all the time, before she remarried. Call it a girls' weekend at the beach. Wait, your daughter'd probably want to tag along, wouldn't she? Maybe that's not such a good idea.

Screw it. Just tell her the truth. It's not like she doesn't know what we're up to by now. It's not like her dad isn't going to start his shit with her anyway. Let her spend the weekend at your apartment with a bunch of movies. We'll be back Sunday afternoon. Forty-eight hours. Her brother can check in on her

*from time to time. Hell, he might just want to hang out there
with her, invite a couple of friends over. Just so long as they
aren't gang members.*

I've just got to get away with you, get you all to myself.

To get there, we drive east and south. If we're traveling
either east or south, we're getting closer. Marlene has one of
those artist's tablets on her lap, and spends most of the trip
working with chalks. She's drawing a beach and a sunset.
She spends a lot of time working on the sky, layering in
one level of color, and then another. It looks kind of stormy
at first, and then peaceful. Then stormy again. She's got a
couple of seabirds in there. Seabirds in flight, you know,
where you make "V"s, except a little flatter? She's wearing
a skirt, the one she wore to work in the morning, and I'm
watching her bare knees, which are spread just enough to
whet my appetite. I glance at her face and she's actually got
her tongue poking out the corner of her mouth as she tries
to apply just the right touch. Makes me laugh, remembering
a comment I made to her just a few weeks after we had
met. We hadn't been to bed yet, but we both knew we were
heading in that direction. My dog Edie was on her lap, Edie's
a rat terrier, and is quite aggressive about getting to know
people she has decided to trust. She likes to sit on your lap,
put her paws on your chest, and tries to dart her tongue
into your mouth when you're not paying attention. "Hey,"
Marlene says to her. 'What're you doing, you little missy?"

"She wants to get her tongue into you," I explained, and
after a pause, I added, "I kind of know the way she feels."

East and then south. Heading for the Gulf Coast.
Leaving behind a couple of busted marriages, assorted
kids, tangled-up plans, and all the day-to-day baggage that
goes along with unfocused living of two people caught in
the throes of passion. My marriage had ended a couple of
months before we met, hers wound down about six months
later. Our attraction had been pretty much mutual, and
pretty much instantaneous. And pretty much physical. That
didn't make it any less complicated, but it sure gave us each

a good reason to get up in the morning. Or stay up at night.

And it sure gave us a good reason to head for a Gulf Coast motel every now and then.

You can pick out a Gulf Coast motel in any of a number of states, I guess. Florida. Alabama. Mississippi. Louisiana. Texas. Because of my work, I have been in motels in all of those states, but for a getaway romantic weekend, Florida is the one you want, trust me on that. And not because of those famous Florida beaches, either. (As if they aren't reason enough.) Florida is just more upscale, I guess. Got more to do. Got better restaurants. Got nice shops. It's clean, no litter or car-bodies lyin' around. Hardly any vagrants. And got more seaside and waterfront bars, too. In some of those other states, the bars that you find down near the beaches have the same bartenders in them that have been there since they opened. Don't get me wrong, they're friendly people, for the most part. But who wants to be served drinks by your grandfather? Or by a guy who looks like he rode in on a Harley, for cryin' out loud? No, in Florida you're going to get those hard-bodied, bleached-blond guys or gals with the deep tans and brilliant white teeth who can actually make clever conversation, and take at least a passing interest in anything you might care to discuss with them. I guess they see an awful lot of tourists, and they know how to sort 'em out pretty quick. In the case of Marlene and me, who want to hand a camera to 'em and ask 'em to take a shot of us next to the big fiberglass shark that hangs near the front entrance of the bar, there's not much to sort out. They know why we're there. Florida makes a nice living catering to people like us, people on the run, living for today, and willing to pay the price to have a good time at it.

Plus, they can mix any drink in the world, or even suggest a few you never heard of if you're feeling adventurous.

But I'm getting ahead of myself. First we've got to get to the motel. The Sandpiper. What a great name. Sounds like something out of the Fifties. Come to think of it, the motel might have been built in the Fifties, judging from the size and location of it. It's near the beach, and back in the day it might have enjoyed some splendid isolation, but now it's being scrunched in on both sides by the big new Marriotts and the Wyndams, each eight or nine stories high, stretching like aircraft carriers from one end of the horizon to the other. Not our Sandpiper. It's a faded pastel-colored three-story walk-up cement-block building with an ice machine on each floor and every room sporting a little balcony facing the water. Marlene stays in the car while I slip into the office and do the paperwork. The gal in the office is a friendly, efficient college-age blond with a peppy personality, and she has us set up in a jiffy. I grab a couple of those little pamphlets from the rack in front of the registration desk, things to see and do, in case we get ambitious later on. Our room is on the second floor, right in the middle of the building. I park the car, we grab our bags and our cooler, and walk up. It's Friday, it's 5:00 PM, and we're alone together at last. Marlene goes into the bathroom, where she brushes her hair and gives a look at her makeup. I slip in behind her and wrap my arms around her, watching her face in the mirror. She gives me a look and puckers her freshly-touched-up lips. "Hey," I caution her. "Don't go gettin' me all worked up."

"You been worked up since you first laid eyes on me," she says.

And that's no lie.

Part III

Rough Romance

"The mistake I made was in assuming that since she was offering herself as the bait, the trap was her own selfish endeavor, set with the primary purpose of making me beg. I wasn't dissuaded in the least. A man could do worse than to beg a woman like that once in a while."

Secret Agent

Secret Agent

I've had plenty of time to think.

Eleven years of solitary confinement. On top of that, another five years in the general prison population. Of course, I haven't spent all that time thinking. In fact, I've done my best to avoid that pitfall. Thinking is one of the world's most overrated exercises. Where does it lead? What good comes of it? Most of the world's so-called great thoughts were simply casual comments that slipped out over brandy and cigars, or beer and *wurst*. Thinking wears you out, and often leaves you feeling stupid and used-up. If anyone would know that, it would be me. Even while trying to avoid it, I'm sure I've spent more time thinking in the last 16 years that most persons would in a lifetime.

In fact, I much prefer visualizing. Let's face it, prison life limits your freedom of movement, and restricts your choices rather dramatically. But visualization is not bound by these walls, nor can it be monitored by the guards and trustees. Plus, it takes you away, out of your cell, off the block, clear over the wall. To a world of your own choosing. A world populated by people you prefer to be around, doing things you prefer to be doing (even if you've never done them in actual fact.) Visualization is just the ticket, and among the prison population is almost unanimously preferred over thinking. But I will concede that thinking has its place, and it tends to slip in when you're not visualizing.

I'm here – I've been here for 16 years -- because of my

own choices. That's not so difficult to admit. The wisdom of those choices, now that's harder to face. There are two ways you can go about it: one is to rationalize and justify them over and over again until you achieve a state of perfect martyrdom. Martyrdom is a state of being that is invariably lonely, but since you're in prison and you're going to be lonely, you might as well be a martyr.

And the second is: you castigate yourself for those choices and cast yourself upon the mercy of the Almighty and ask forgiveness, and over time become simple-minded, contrite, humble, and broken, thus achieving a kind of practical saintliness.

There you have it: martyr or saint, nothing in between.

Well, I'm in between. It's the hardest place to be, and I've tried for 16 years to find another place, and I always come back to the in-between.

Here's a riddle for you: nuclear secrets and pussy -- what do they have in common? Oh, given a minute or two I'm sure you could come up with a clever answer. I've come up with many of them. For example:

One is a marvel of science, the other is a scientific marvel.

One will blow you up, the other will stand you up.

One produces a chain reaction, the other chains you with a reaction.

One can make a genius out of a fool, the other makes a fool out of a genius.

You need a special code to open either one.

They've each got the world by the balls. (That's my favorite).

Only one cure for either, but nobody's discovered it yet.

You pay for either one, but with the secrets, it's only a one time payment.

Here another one: you can go to prison for either, but at least with the nuclear secrets, you won't dream about it at night. That's not true, incidentally. The dreaming part. The other part is absolutely true, as my 16 years of hard time will testify. Cause and effect: steal nuclear secrets, chase pussy, go to jail. For which? For the stealing, or the chasing?

Well, first for the one, then for the other. That's how it came about in my case.

The cause and the effect were divided by a period of several years, however. First I stole the secrets. After a fashion. After helping to compile the top-secret data, document it, and define policy relevant to it for a period during my seven years at the remote desert facility, I could always argue (and I did) that the secrets were not secrets after all, or should not have been. Naturally, the state of Israel took grave exception to my position, and had no trouble getting a conviction in *absentia* against me after I fled the country. No point in going into the various arguments here. The nature of any state is first and foremost self-preservation, and withheld information, classified documentation, top-secret data is the inevitable result of self-preservation. Nobody would argue that. Whatever so-called humanitarian motives I might have had for making certain features of the state's clandestine program of nuclear weapons development a matter of public knowledge were almost universally despised, openly by those who felt betrayed, and secretly by those who might have benefitted. Overnight, I became a pariah except to those few freethinking journalists and fellow travelers who embraced my boldness, my desperation, my altruism. I was spirited out of the country by friendly interests before I could be arrested, and found myself in Australia, estranged from family, from country, from my profession, given over to a life of safe houses or modest hotel rooms, radio, television and print interviews, and free lunches as certain professionals picked over the carrion of my life, openly lionizing me while secretly searching for clues as to why a man would abandon his sanity for the sake of trying to save a world that wasn't even paying attention.

Then I came to New York. I was hosted by The Committee For Safe Nuclear Policy, or some such, and I was beholden to appear at certain times in certain places and speak of my sins to interested parties (interested in the sinner more than the secrets, I would discover.) Because it was known that the State of Israel had convicted me in *absentia*, and because the government of Israel has the machinery to pull people off the streets of virtually any city in the world, my comings and goings were known to very few people indeed, and the Committee assigned a couple of healthy lads with powerful handguns to accompany me on my rounds, the better to dissuade the *Mossad* from staging one of their little dramas. People who were permitted into my presence were screened, and it was all done very well, with little or no disruption of the public slumber. Generally my needs were well met, except for the needs of a man who feels loneliness, a hunger in his soul for companionship, for understanding, for acceptance, as I did. I kept these needs to myself, and did not allow them to make me careless or overly talkative. I was not in a position to extract concessions from society, and likely would never be again. So when I first met Suzie at a book-signing (where my slim volume was one of the featured items) on lower Fifth Avenue, I was polite, guarded, a gentleman -- all that the situation required. Without prying too much, in our brief conversation that evening I determined that she was 28 (seven years junior to me), unmarried, a book critic by trade, a native of the Great American Midwest, that she smoked and drank rather freely, and that in all likelihood, if the circumstances presented themselves, she would likely make herself sexually available to me at some later date if I were so inclined. (This last was not so surprising, as even moral-minded men who steal nuclear secrets attract a certain type of "groupie," and over the months I had met, and deftly sidestepped, my share.) And so I thought nothing of it. We enjoyed a laugh or two together and went our way, and I was mildly surprised to run smack into her three days later in the lobby of the boutique hotel in the upper 80's where I had been closeted during my sojourn in New York.

"Surely you can't be staying in this building?" I asked her.

"No, they sent me to spy on you," she laughed, and touched my arm playfully.

"Well, they surely know my type," I joked back, but it was true enough. She had her soft blonde hair pulled back into a rather simple arrangement the way America women do, she wore slacks that showed her derriere to great advantage, and a sleeveless blouse that permitted a man to glimpse, in an unguarded moment, the firm nut-brown fruits cosseted there. She could have been in a toothpaste or an automobile advertisement on the television, she gave the impression of impeccable hygiene, unfathomable lightheartedness, and, at the bottom of it all, an unrestrained joy of fucking.

As it turned out, she was, she informed me, on holiday with a friend who lived in the building (a female friend, happily), and was scheduled to leave in two days for the Florida beaches and casinos. She laughed rather easily when we discussed these things and others over a coffee at the hotel coffee shop, and I accepted with little hesitation an invitation to dine that evening with her and her friend at a bistro on the upper West Side. Which we did. Her friend was a bookish sort of girl, very Jewish, accompanied by her fiancé, a rather dour fellow mired in the financial industry, and I actually took the initiative of covertly suggesting that the two of us ditch the other couple during a respite over brandies following the poorly-served and marginally palatable meal. She did not relent at once, but suggested that we stick together "at least until they wear us completely out." Safe to say, at this point I was quite saturated with the idea of wearing out this *shiksa* between the sheets (or on top of them) at the earliest possible opportunity.

It didn't come that night, and the next day she was mysteriously unavailable. I had all but resigned myself to another of those brooding evenings under lock and key when I took a call from her. She spoke low, with a hint of liquor in her voice. (Of course, for the alert male, this is always a sign that he should prepare his boarding party, the prize may presently be taken.) She was at a place called The Living Room on the Upper East Side, she had managed to "ditch her pursuers," and would I care to "come out and play?" My internal radar-scanner was active, however, and as a precaution I alerted Evi in the lobby, who accompanied me, slipped inside the establishment ahead of me, and when I came in the door signaled me from his post near a serving counter in the first parlor. The Living Room was an over-done Victorian after-hours trysting spot, smacking of discretion with its dimly lit alcoves and confidently intimate wait-staff.

I found Suzie in the second parlor, sipping a Cointreau and smoking a filtered cigarette, her blonde locks tumbling fetchingly over one eye. She listed seductively against me when I sat. "This must be the rebel poet in you," I told her, in reference to the whole picture.

She threw back her hair and blew out a long jet of smoke. "I had a poet-boyfriend when I was living in The Village about five years ago. He turned out to be a complete asshole, and he was the last rebel poet that's ever been in me," she pronounced. "Asshole" is such a particularly American term, and is used so effectively by American women. When a good-looking woman uses the term to describe a former paramour to a current prospect, it's a safe bet she's daring the current prospect to prove that he himself is not another of these disreputable failures of manhood. I recall having seen at one New York party a lapel button worn by a fashionable type of woman and it read *One Asshole in My Pants Is Enough*. So very American.

Anyway, I was taken with Suzie, that's the long and short of it. Taken with everything about her on that night: her nonchalance, her blonde beauty (which, as I studied it, was more severe and less compliant that I had originally thought, an observation which only served to further whet my appetite...), her clever conversation, and not the least, her apparent intention to bait a trap into which I would tumble, and tumble hard. The primary mistake I made was in assuming that, since she was the bait, the trap was her own selfish endeavor, set with the primary purpose of making me beg. A man could do worse than to beg a woman like Suzie once in a while.

I didn't, however, get the chance to beg that night. The prize was certainly in the offing, but not yet ready for the proffering. First there had to be unbridled lust, danger, a risk. Suzie was a prize to be sure, and I was pleased that she knew it. "I can't fuck you here," she said conversationally, after she had taken the liberty of resting her hand in the inside of my thigh. "I can barely have a decent conversation with you. You've got your shadows lurking about, and I've got mine."

"Let's go to my place, then," I suggested. "Your shadows won't bother us there."

"Here meaning New York," she countered. "I had something altogether a little more removed in mind." And she smiled up at me playfully.

"Don't say removed unless you mean it." I was getting into the game. I felt at this point like a cross between Arnold Schwarzenegger and Don Johnson -- a bit dashing, a little greasy and completely invulnerable.

"What I have in mind is something like a thirtieth-floor condo in Key Biscayne, where you can see all the way to downtown Havana and still have room service."

"I thought you were going with the Jewish princess."

"I blew her off," Suzie said. "She pissed me off today. Anyway, it's my condo, and I call the shots." She turned to me and gave me a look of bold appraisal. I thought then she was finally going to touch my crotch and close the deal, but her restraint was just as appealing. "Think you can manage a weekend with Suzie in her condo with Suzie calling the shots?"

Well, the rest, as they say in cautionary tales such as this, is history. What prompted me to trust the girl and return quietly to my apartment with Evi only to hastily pack up an overnight bag, slip out of the building alone via the fire escape, drop into the alley in the way I'd seen them do in films, and show up at Newark Airport in a taxi before dawn was that sense of invulnerability to which I alluded earlier -- it wasn't so much that I trusted her as I trusted in the adventure. This was America, after all. By virtue of my training, my inclination, even my profession I was somehow bound to come to America, bound to find an adventure, and bound to follow my instincts when said adventure presented itself. Even with the hindsight of 16 years of cruel self-examination, I can honestly report that it never occurred to me on that fateful evening *not* to go to the airport to meet this Suzie woman and flee with her to the South and to the adventure.

Flee, flew, flight. With her credit card, we were airborne non-stop to Miami by 6:15 AM, sitting cozily in business class, probably looking like quite a handsome couple, she with her well-formed American features, her pert nose, her full upper lip, her wide and expressive eyes and her tousled blonde mane in sharp contrast to my dark Middle-Eastern countenance, my close-cropped hair, my thick, sloping shoulders. "I can see why they'd be attracted to one another," is the thought that might very well have occurred to fellow passengers observing us. We were clearly in heat and heading for the heat, the athletic-looking Jew and his hot-blooded *Shiksa*. For a time she napped and I perused the in-flight magazines (no time for a bookstore in Newark), but I couldn't help but steal glances at her face as she slept, and thinking perhaps how it was similar to the post-coital slumber that I hoped to induce in her within a short time after we reached the promised South Beach condo.

After deplaning, we made our way up the jet-way and she grasped my hand and tugged me towards a lounge that was sparsely inhabited. "I need a smoke and a drink," she said, and she ordered two brandies. "Welcome to Miami," she grinned, and held her glass aloft. I leaned forward and bussed her lightly on the lips. Unlike New York, there was no resistance to my advance. Apparently she had been telling the truth, and our time in Florida's great playground was going to be for just that: playing. She had her smoke, we sipped our brandies, and I left her to her inevitable cell phone calls while I went in search of a toilet.

"Good news," she said when I returned. "My friend Jeremy's picking us up. He'll take us straight to the condo." She leaned forward for a kiss, almost like a bride on her honeymoon, and her tongue briefly flicked out in search of my own. My head reeled at this sudden bounty, and I felt in that moment truly like so many honeymooners must have felt over the years upon arriving in such a place as Florida, and faced with three or four days of irrepressible lovemaking, irresponsible drinking, and irreplaceable memories. In short, in those moments in the airport lounge I was becoming something of a "dope" as Americans would say, a sort of docile, ordinary, manageable fellow whose intelligence, ambition, training and common sense had for the time deserted him. There is something undeniably exhilarating about abandoning yourself to a woman's wiles. Almost as if reading my mind, or the abandonment of it, my lovely blonde creature nuzzled my neck, and brought her fingernails up to trace suggestive patterns on the side of my face. "You ready to play?" she asked me.

In the end, it was over very quickly. No sooner had I turned my back on her to admire the view from the condo's picture window (which was every bit as spectacular as she had advertised) than she invented some errand for herself and slipped out the door, never to return. What returned less than a minute later was the team whose job it was to secure the apartment and subdue, if need be, the subject. There were three of them, big, nimble, athletic lads who liked to hit and made it clear right away that resistance would be a hopeless idea. I'd been had, good and proper, and my little escapade was being prematurely terminated. I'm a scientist, not a warrior, and I humored myself in those moments by assuring myself that it wouldn't stick, that this was America, Miami even, and that not even the *Mossad* could operate here with that kind of impunity. This idea of America as a bulwark of personal freedom comforted me briefly, even though it proved to be an abject falsehood, as least with regard to the situation facing yours truly. The boys had me adequately trundled, sedated, and in motion within minutes of their abrupt entry. That was sixteen years ago this coming September, and the feeling of complete powerlessness that overwhelmed me at that point has stayed with me in one form or another virtually every day since.

Suzie has stayed with me too, in her various forms.

As an Israeli special agent (for so she proved to be). As an American Girl. As an Adult Temptress. As a woman who explored the inside of my mouth with her tongue less than an hour before she stepped out of my life, her mission complete. I've wondered since whether she was simply a footloose party girl who was recruited and trained by the Service, or an educated, trained, and disciplined professional who did a more than passable job portraying a so-called "party girl." I suspect the latter to be the case. Of course, you say to yourself, it doesn't matter in the least -- the result is the same. As a man of substance and pride, moral strength and social rectitude, I was effortlessly led by this woman into the hands of my enemy. I suppose there might be some scant pleasure in believing that I had been bested by a trained professional and not a common whore, but I'd been bested, in my time, by each prior to that fateful evening. Still, in spite of the tale I've recounted here, my memory for the details is rather vague, and I am reasonably certain I would not recognize her today. Her personality, her face, her form have been altered over the years, and the substance of her has become more symbolic than real. Within a month of my incarceration, I knew that I must not permit myself to generate visualizations of my ravishing Suzie in that Miami condo, and I never have. That represents a small victory for me in all of this travesty. After all, she was merely the agent of my demise.

I alone was its author.

Three Rib Plates

"I oughta bang her cracker ass into the middle of next week," Truett said. He was looking across the room at the woman. I didn't care for Truett. He wasn't the kind of fellow I would've chosen to work with. They had sent him over from New Orleans. I had never known a decent professional out of that city.

"Catch you a dose o' the syph is all," Alphonse said. "See how you gone like that."

"I like it fine," Truett responded. "She's country. She knows how to make a man happy. I bet she does."

The woman was sitting on the bed on the other side of the room with her back against the headboard. Eddie and I had picked her up the night before at the club where they'd told us we'd find her. She hadn't wanted to leave with us, at first. Once I made it clear to her that she had no choice, she came along, but she'd been silent and withdrawn ever since. She had on tailored black pants and a nice navy-blue top with spaghetti straps, and was paying no particular attention to Truett. Or maybe she was, just not letting on. Her black hair was parted in the middle and pinned back behind her ears. She had a nice, full body and a turndown mouth like a petulant child. She looked like she might've been hit a time or two in her day. And that she had not hesitated to hit back.

"Truett, why don't you go outside and relieve Eddie," I said to him.

"It ain't my time yet." Like most troublemakers, Truett

knew his rights.

"Go anyway. It's cold outside."

He left the room and went down the hall towards the side entrance of the hotel, walking on the balls of his feet, just looking for trouble. His sneakers made noises on the cheap linoleum. A born punk.

"What time is it, Al?" I wasn't wearing a watch. Typically I don't. You would think I would. The passing of time was a big part of our business.

"Goin' on six," Alphonse said. Al never gave a precise time. "Damn near eight-thirty." "Gettin' to ten." "Seen the last of five." Al liked to dance around time, but didn't care to pin it down.

"Got some hamburgs in the bag if you're hungry," I said to the woman. She hadn't said boo since we'd pulled her in, but she looked like she might have a foreign accent.

"I ate already," she said without lifting her eyes.

"You work at the club? You a dancer?" I was just making conversation. I had an idea what her profession was, all right.

"Not your business, is it?" She sounded like Eastern Europe.

I pondered that. "She a cold one, Doc," Alphonse observed. "Stone cold."

"She might be cold at that. You want a coat? A jacket?" Month of November, and the air was dank and chilling.

She said nothing, so I took off my windbreaker, walked across the room, lifted it over her head where she sat and tucked it around her shoulders. I had on a long sleeve flannel shirt underneath, so I could live without the jacket. I like to layer.

"Got a cigarette?"

"Al probably does."

He did. He took a pack from his shirt pocket, shook one down, lit it, walked over to where she was, and held it out to her at face level. She reached up and took it. "You nigger-lipped it," she said.

"Reckon I did at that, pretty lady." Al was one even-tempered Negro, I'll give him that. Living in Texas, a black man ought to be even tempered, after all.

Footsteps sounded in the hallway and Eddie came into the room. "That's some cold shit out there," he announced. Eddie was small-framed and high-strung, but he was reliable. I'd worked with him before, and I knew he could be trusted. He was good at anticipating.

"Quiet in the street?"

"Just like we like it." Eddie had on his customary ill-fitting black leather jacket. Clothes didn't fit Eddie right. "Hey sister, once we're done here, how about a date, you and me?" He cruised over to the corner of the bed where the woman sat and plunked himself down on the floor near her, all sociable-like. "You could warm me up."

The woman was finishing her cigarette and ignored Eddie's line. Eddie was probably used to that. Eddie reached into his jacket and pulled out a pack of his own, lit up, and inhaled deeply.

Alphonse sat on the windowsill with his back to the window, which had been covered over with cardboard and duck tape. The only light in the room came from an overhead fluorescent. I had been in cheerier places. "How much longer we gone wait, Chief?"

"Till seven maybe. I'll go outside and make a call in a couple of minutes." The fact is, posting Truett in the street by himself had probably not been the smartest move.

"How about you let me walk home now," said the woman. "I live close to here." She didn't lift her eyes.

"Give us just one more hour, Margo, and I'll walk you home myself," I told her. "Then we'll disappear and you'll never see us again."

"I have a sister, Margo. How do you know her?"

I didn't know any sister, and I didn't know any Margo. It was just one of my little tactics, somebody won't give you a name, use any name that comes to mind. Most of the time they'll correct you. Margot was just dumb luck. I used it because it sounded Eastern European. Like Zsa Zsa Gabor.

"I met her overseas, after the war," I said.

"We was just little girls then," the woman said.

"You ain't so little now," Eddie said admiringly.

I felt the air in the room change because the door at the end of the hall had been opened. Then sneakers on the linoleum, and Truett came back in. "There's a black 'n white down at the end of the block," he reported.

"Parked or what?"

"Stopped. Kinda waiting."

So why the fuck wasn't he up there keeping an eye on it was the question. It was a Sunday morning in November, ordinarily not a time when the cops would be exhibiting much curiosity. Of course, after that Friday, there was a lot of curiosity going around.

Al was reading me. "I'll go, Chief." Then he was up and out. He could tell that I didn't want to leave those two crackers in the room with a good-looking white woman and a Negro. Just a bad move, especially in Texas.

With all the smoking going on, the air in the room was getting pretty close. "Truett, see if you can't open that damn window, get some fresh air in here." Any task to keep his mind from wandering.

With his loose-limbed troublemaking gait, Truett went over and without removing his hands from his pockets examined the window. "I can open it all right," he said, turning back and briefly looking around the room. In one corner there was a night table with a metal folding chair. While the rest of us watched in a state of diminished capacity, he retrieved the chair, walked back to the window, and with three good swings managed to crash a sizeable hole in the heavy cardboard and tape construction that covered it. The window had metal sashes, and it didn't yield easily. "Motherfucker's open now," he pronounced.

Somehow I wished at that moment that I was in Los Angeles. Sitting poolside somewhere. During the war I'd used that visualization whenever things got oppressive. Poolside in Los Angeles. I hadn't made it yet, but I could feel it getting closer. In a lounge chair with a good book and a strong drink. And a girl with a nice tan and a moderate overbite lingering nearby.

The door to the room opened and Alphonse stuck his head in. "Chief. Better come right now."

Off we went down the hall. That linoleum. Worse than a farmhouse kitchen in the Midwest. "They's on foot, two of 'em. Coming thisaway."

"They see you?"

"Can't rightly say. Might of."

I pushed through the door and went out onto the sidewalk on the south side of the building. This being Dallas, the cops would have shaken down Alphonse in a heartbeat. Finding his piece would've presented us with a problem.

The two officers were nowhere in sight. At the far end of the block I saw the black and white idling, with the taillights on. Casually I reached into my shirt pocket and took out a pack of Lifesavers, removed one, and slipped it into my mouth. While I worked on it, I used my peripheral vision to scan the surroundings.

We were one block off Commerce Street on the south side. Just to the west of the hotel entrance was a barbeque place. Just to the east was a parking garage. Further along the block was a dry cleaners and laundry. On Sunday morning it was all quiet, no traffic. Across the street was a Negro walking with a bottle of wine in a paper bag. It was a rundown commercial district, and the businesses were closed. The sky being overcast and the air temperature being down in the fifties further suppressed activity. During the week I wouldn't have thought twice about the black and white, but on a Sunday with everything deserted, it made me a little uneasy, especially since I didn't know what had become of the officers that Alphonse had seen. I opened the door just a crack. "I'll stay up here for a while. Better go back and keep those two in line."

I finished my Lifesaver. The cold air on my face felt good after the stuffy room. I didn't particularly care for Dallas. The southern hospitality thing didn't apply, and besides, in the business we were in and the places we frequented, hospitality was in short supply. I was strictly an East Coast guy. I liked the pace and rhythm of the east coast. Sure, the whole area was run down, but it had been through some history, it had earned the right. In my book Chicago was the last outpost of civilization. Once you ventured west of Chicago, it was like a foreign country. And during the war, I had seen my share of foreign countries. Dallas was more like one of those.

Here they came, suddenly, exiting the recessed doorway of a pawnshop three or four doors away. I kept my eyes to the front but observed them as they came. Dallas PD, I assumed. I composed myself, which is something I do well. When they were maybe ten feet from where I stood, I swiveled my head and took them in. "Fellas," I said, just as natural. It's a quiet Sunday morning, we're sharing the sidewalk together. Almost like being in church.

For a moment it seemed like they were going to walk on by, but as they began to disappear from sight over my shoulder, I turned to face them. As a rule, nobody gets behind my back, particularly if they're packing. I wasn't wearing my sunglasses, so they had no trouble seeing my eyes, which was a good thing. I knew how to hold them. "Not much of a morning for sightseeing, is it?"

The shorter of the two spoke up. "You got business in this area, sir?" The "sir" actually was a touch of hospitality. In New Jersey, it would've been "pal" or "bud."

"I wish I did. Afraid I'm just in town for the convention. The one out at the Merchandise Mart."

They had come to a halt between the door and me. I hoped none of the boys would choose to make an appearance.

"You staying at the hotel here?"

"Sure am. I'm from New Jersey. I like the cold air in the morning." These statements were all true. "Anything I can do to help, officers?"

Since Friday the Dallas PD had been a little jumpy. The national media claimed that they were in over their heads. Judging from the two specimens in front of me, there might be some truth in that. Neither of them displayed a high degree of police intuition, or, for that matter, even sound sidewalk curiosity. They were just going through the motions on a cold Sunday morning.

The short one hitched up his patent-leather police belt. The taller one took the initiative. "How about showing us some ID?"

I tugged my wallet out of my back pocket, flipped it open to display the driver's license, and held it out for the two to look at. At that moment the squawk box on their patrol car, which had been silent, began to broadcast. The cops looked at each other, and the shorter one began to move toward the car. "You have a good day, sir," the taller one said, and followed him. They never paid any attention to my driver's license, but even if they had, they wouldn't of learned anything. It was strictly legit.

"Sorry about what happened with the President," I called after them. Once they reached the car, they got in, the taillights blinked, and they departed in haste. I don't know if they even heard me.

Once they were out of sight, I went back into the building and down the hallway. "Truett. Come take a walk." Then I went back out on the sidewalk and waited for him. He showed up and we started walking east on Jackson Street. "You follow baseball?" I asked him.

"Follow it some. How about a cigarette?" He fetched me out a cigarette and we stopped while he lit it for me. (I was trying to cut down, and I thought it might help if I didn't carry my own.) There was a bit of movement in the air, and I thought about my jacket.

"Why you ast?"

"Just thinking about Rocky Colavito."

"I heard of 'im."

"Course you did. He's one of the best."

"He ain't no Mickey Mantle."

"What you mean is, he don't play in New York. If Mickey Mantle played in Cleveland or Detroit, it'd be a different story."

"What you got against Cleveland?"

"Not a damn thing. It's a great town." We had reached

the corner of Jackson and Lane Street. I turned north on Lane Street towards Commerce. I noticed that the plate glass windows that we passed all had grimy film on them, like they didn't get washed. Big city like that, you've got to wash the windows regular. "But it's still Cleveland."

"I dated a girl from Cleveland once," Truett recalled. "Some tits on her." He was a great free-association conversationalist.

"I'll bet." We walked on for a bit.

"You was askin' me about this Colavito guy," Truett prompted.

"Yeah. I met 'im once. In Miami."

"Now that's a wild town. Fuck in A."

"It was in a club. He had his girl with him. Or it coulda been his wife I guess."

"Nah. It was his girl," Truett said. "You know how come I know?"

"I got no idea." We were approaching Commerce. It was a big street, but there was still very little traffic. When we got to the corner we would turn back east, and go with the traffic.

"Dagos don't go to clubs with their wives, that's how I know." Truett was pleased with himself. "We got plenty Dagos in New Orleans. I grew up with 'em."

"This guy who shot the President, isn't he from New Orleans?"

"Why the fuck would you say that?" Truett wondered.

"Don't you read the papers?" I couldn't imagine that Truett had ever read a newspaper in his life.

We hadn't gone more than fifty feet on Commerce before we passed the first of the strip clubs. The Marquee, it was called. It was posted with bills advertising the dancers. They used the kinds of names that made you think of the girls you knew in high school: *Cindy Sue. Bubbles. Candy Kane. Paula Pounder.* A place where you could get even with all the girls who snubbed you back then.

"I heard this club was run by a Jew," Truett said.

"I think the Jews own the whole street if you want to

know the truth." Across Commerce in the same block there were another couple of clubs with the same kinds of cheesy posters. At least in New Jersey the girl's names were usually up in lights. Here, if the club was closed down, they could scoop up all their posters, disappear overnight, and rent another storefront somewhere the next day.

"That's the difference, see?" Truett told me. "Plenty of strip clubs in New Orleans, but it ain't the Jews. It's the Dagos. Like I's telling ya." We walked on. "That one there, I visited last month when I was passing through town." Truett pointed it out. It was called the Carousel. "Actually had some nice ladies. Kind of a classy joint."

"No doubt," I said.

"Most of the stiffs had ties on, but not me. I don't wear no tie for nobody."

"Man's gotta stand up for his rights," I agreed, although irony was lost on Truett. "We'll make this block and head back to the hotel," I told him.

Something about Dallas had me thinking. Thinking of Miami. Or Boston. Or Los Angeles, even though I'd never been. I'll say that for Dallas – it made you want to be someplace else. At least it had that effect on me. It had that cowboy stink on it, and if this was what bein' a cowboy came to, please keep me away from horses and six-shooters.

We reached the end of the block. The cross street was Prather, so we turned back south. Immediately on the right was a small diner. At first glance it appeared to be closed, but as we were passing in front of the grimy door, two fellows exited, one pocketing his wallet. I stopped. "I'll wait out here, why don't you run in and grab some coffees to go," I said to Truett. "I'll be down the block at the telephone."

"I got it." He opened the door and started in, then looked back at me. "Four coffees to go."

"Let's not forget your girlfriend."

He went in. By now it was seven thirty. Time to check in. There was a pay telephone further down the block, and I walked on ahead, went in the door of the cabin, and closed it behind me. I could see the entrance to the diner.

I fed six quarters into the phone and dialed the number. Three rings. "Talk to me," I said.

"How's our friend?"

"She's a little bored with the company, but she's keeping her cool," I said.

"That's good. Bored is good."

Up the block I could see Truett coming out of the diner. I opened the cabin door and stuck out my arm. He started my way.

"Well, then. Where do you want your package?"

"Be honest, I don't think Mr. D knows exactly what he wants to do. But he'll be by here in about 15 minutes. Can you call me back in half an hour?"

"Half an hour." I hung up.

Under his arm Truett was carrying a paper bag with the coffee. "I guess you heard about them train robbers," he commented. We walked on down Prather towards Jackson.

"Train robbers?" My mind was somewhere else. Almost to Oklahoma.

"The ones that held up the mail train over there in England last summer. Got away with a shitload of cash." He reached in the bag and handed me a Styrofoam cup.

"I remember. What about 'em?"

"Caught two more."

"Sorry to hear that," I said.

"No shit. Their payout was over $300 grand each." We had reached Jackson, and turned back East. The skies had lightened up some, but it wasn't going to be a sunny day. "I seen you was on the phone. What's the good word?"

"The word is your payout isn't gonna reach 300 grand."

"I heard that," Truett snorted.

After another five minutes we were in sight of the hotel. It was called the London Lodge, and it rented rooms by the hour. The bed in the room had a coin insert where you could put in a couple of quarters and get the bed to vibrate. For the sexually adventurous.

"I do believe I'm gonna nail me a piece of that poontang in there," Truett said jovially as we approached the side entrance.

I stopped on the sidewalk. "That girl is somebody's property, you got that? Paid for. When we're done here, if you wanna arrange to take over the payments, that's fine by me. But right now, we're just the help. So let's act like it." And without waiting for any further response from him, I went in.

Back in the room Eddie and Alphonse were eating hamburgers out of the bag. The woman had an emery board and was working on her nails. Truett passed out the coffees. "That's what I'm a- talkin' about," said Eddie. Alphonse looked up and caught my eye. After a moment I stepped back out of the room into the hallway and he followed. "This here a fuckin' mess," he said. "That lil' cracker keep workin' on the woman, sooner or later you gonna have a problem on your hand." The coffee was still hot, and he was blowing on it in the Styrofoam cup.

"You go on, get some fresh air. Come back in 15, and we'll be ready to move," I told him.

Back in the room Truett had sat down on the foot of the bed where the woman was. He had changed his tune, however. "Sure I can't get you a burger out the bag?" he asked her. "They're cold, but at least the coffee's hot."

"She ain't eatin' this morning. Her girlish figure an' all that," Eddie said. "Margo, I'm gonna buy you a nice breakfast after." Truett shot Eddie a look, and went back to his coffee.

I leaned against the small night table and drank my coffee. I thought about the Bonneville. I had her in a parking garage just three blocks away. It was going on eight o'clock. I could be the hell out of Texas by lunchtime if things went right. The job, whatever it was or was going to be, was losing my interest. Which of course is not healthy. Once your mind starts to wander, that's when your troubles begin.

The woman put her emery board back in her purse and rolled her legs off the bed. She got up and made her way to the bathroom, coffee cup in hand. She was taller than I remembered from the night before. And she was trim.

She closed the door behind her and then we heard water running in the sink. It was an interior bathroom.

"Eddie, you rode over with Truett from New Orleans, isn't that right?"

"No Siree, I did not. I got my own car, but it's in the shop."

"Eddie, how did you get to Dallas?"

"Come on the 'Hound."

"You and them fuckin' freedom riders," Truett commented.

I thought about this. "Well, when we leave, better you ride with Truett. The bus stations are likely gonna be real busy with cops. That okay with you, Truett?"

"If he pays for his gas," Truett said. He looked at Eddie. "Ride to New Orleans cost him about four bucks."

It was time to call in, but I wasn't going to do it from the room. Pay phones were safer. And private. But I wanted to wait until the woman came out of the bathroom. The water had stopped running. I crossed the room and tapped lightly on the door with the back of my knuckles. "Monica, you okay in there?" There was no immediate response.

"Thought her name was Margo," Eddie said.

Then the door opened and she was looking me in the eye. Just my height. She had taken the pins out of her hair and put on make-up. We took each other in for just a moment. This was going to inflame the boys' passions a bit, is what I was thinking. Something I didn't need. "I'm just going out for a minute. When I get back, I'll take you home. Just sit tight until then, okay?" When a woman is made up nice like that, you feel like you need to ask permission.

I left her with the crackers and went out. Alphonse was outside on the sidewalk. He was talking to another Negro, one who wore the uniform of a garage mechanic, blue gabardine pants and shirt with his name stenciled on the breast pocket. "Better go get the Bonneville," I told Al, and handed him the keys. "Bring it over here and park in the alley there. Then wait for me right where you are now. Ten minutes." Al nodded and left on his mission.

There was another pay phone just adjacent to the corner of Lane Street, half a block from the hotel. I strolled over, not in a big hurry. Again on the third ring. "It's me, pal," I said. "What have we got?"

"He thinks the lady needs to get out of town for awhile, starting now."

"Get out of town as in where?" I wanted to know.

"Just out of town. The further the better." There was a pause as he placed his hand over the receiver and consulted with somebody else. "Just bring her up here. We'll treat her right." Tommy was a heavy breather. Adenoids wheezing across the line at me.

"Send the boys home?"

"You're done there," he confirmed. "How long?"

"How long what?"

"How long it take you to get back up here?"

"Better part of two days, I would say." I had clocked the mileage on the way down. It was right at 1650 from the Triborough. Of course, I had been alone. Now I would have the girl with me.

"Two fuckin' days. This ain't a honeymoon, sport."

"Check your map. We're in the heart of goddamn Texas down here. There's cattle in the streets."

There was a pause as Adenoid Tommy considered this. "In the fuckin' streets?"

"See you in a couple," I said, and started to ring off.

"Check in with us tonight, why don'cha. Eight o'clock."

I rang off and walked back toward the hotel. As I approached, I saw the Bonneville coming down Jackson from the other direction, then swing into the alley. I waited beside the hotel until Al came around the corner and handed me the keys. "We're done here Al. I'm going to be leaving Dallas directly, and taking the girl with me. But I'm gonna need your help awhile longer." Being a Dallas native, Al could do the driving until we got clear of the city. That way, I would be free to keep the girl under control if she had serous objections to leaving the city. Which you never know.

While Al stayed on the sidewalk, I went into the alley, unlocked the Bonneville, removed the panel in the sidewall of the backseat, and took out the envelope. I counted out $1,000 in fifty dollar bills, replaced the envelope, and then replaced the panel. I slipped the bills into my pocket. They were clean and new and hardly caused a bulge. Then I left the alley, picked up Al, and together we went in. "Go on down to the room, Al. I'll be right behind you."

I went up front to the desk where the manager had come on duty after eight. "Ma'am, I need some envelopes, if you don't mind."

She was a wiry spinster with the face of permanent disapproval. "Envelopes?"

"Yes ma'am. Just some of those hotel envelopes you usually keep. The ones with the letterhead."As I spoke I carefully laid a five dollar bill on the glass countertop and pushed it in her direction. Hers to keep.

Without specifically looking at the bill, she slid open a drawer and pulled out a stack of the envelopes. "Just about five of 'em will do," I told her.

She counted out half a dozen and placed them deliberately on the counter in front of me.

"You're a dear," I said, picking them up. She in turn collected the $5 bill. "You boys have a nice day," she said. I've always had a way with spinsters.

"Yes ma'am. We'll be checking out shortly."

Back in the room I handed Eddie and Truett each an envelope. $250 apiece for less than two days' work was good solid wages. Plus their expenses had been covered. "Fellas, we're clearing out. Your job's done. Pick up the room real good, don't leave anything of a personal nature."

Eddie turned the envelope over in his hands without opening it. "That's it? You're saying we should take off outta here?"

"I believe that's what I'm saying. Truett, is that how you understand it?" I reached over to where the girl had been sitting on the bed and retrieved my windbreaker.

"You ain't said nothin' about her," Truett countered.

"The lady will be leaving with Al and me. In fact, the three of us will be going out first. Give us five minutes before you leave."

For a moment Truett said nothing. "We been talkin'. She kind of agreed to let me take her."

"That's a negative, pal. The three of us are actually still assigned to the job. You'll notice that Al didn't get an envelope like you did. Sweetheart, are you ready to go?" There was not going to be any letting Truett get traction with his troublesome urges.

"What if I was to say I ain't buyin' it?"

"Then I guess you'll be buyin' somma this," Al said from the other side of the room. He had his .38 out, cradled in his hand.

Truett looked at Al and then at me. "You gonna let this nigger hold a gun on me?" he asked.

"Al's not just any nigger," I pointed out. "If you're in the mood for romance, there are plenty more where she came from. Don't make your life any more complicated than you have to." As I read it, Truett didn't really need the woman, he needed to be respected, that was all.

"She's a cold one anyway," Eddie piped up. Bless your heart, Eddie.

I took the woman by the arm like a boyfriend might. "See you in the car, Al. Don't be long." And out we went.

When we got into the alley I opened the door of the Bonneville for her without ever turning loose of her arm. She was beginning to figure something out. "Where are you taking me?"

"Sunday drive," I said, and planted myself there by the passenger door while I waited for Al. He wasn't long in coming. I tossed him the keys. "You drive, man." Once Al slid behind the wheel, I got in on the passenger side. Miss Monica, or Margo, or whoever she was, was sitting nicely between us. "Drive real polite, Al. Just like we're going to grandmother's for Sunday brunch."

"Surprise the hell outta grandmother, I tell you that," Al said, and he pulled out of the alley and headed east on

Jackson. He didn't stay on Jackson long, however, executing a number of turns as we made our way north and east from Commerce Street. Al was shaking off any tail we might have attracted.

"I could use a cigarette," the woman said. I had my arm across the back of the seat behind her as a precaution. I liked feeling the heft of her against me. Al tossed me a pack of Pall Mall's. I took out a cigarette for her and once she had it between her lips, I lit it with the Bonneville's electric cigarette lighter, all with my free hand. She took a long pull and let the smoke escape from her lips very deliberately. "So I'm not going home after all," she said, without looking at either of us.

"Not right away. Things might not be so safe for you right now in Dallas."

She smoked in silence. We had reached a divided four-lane thruway, very nearly abandoned early on this Sunday morning. Al was driving north at 40 miles per hour. Polite, like I'd told him. Not hurrying, but making good time. On the other side of the grassy median, coming from the other direction, three State Patrol cars went by at a good clip, their lights flashing. With all the distractions which they were facing, law enforcement in the Dallas area was wonderfully preoccupied, and had no time for a late-model dove-grey Bonneville driven by a Negro, with a white man and woman riding beside him, a phenomenon that might, in quieter times, have caused a mild ripple of attention.

"Why do you want to lie to me?" the woman asked, this time directing her attention to me. I turned to face her. Wide set hazel eyes and that turned-down mouth. Nostrils that flared. "All this talk about taking me home. Nothing but bullshit, isn't that it?"

I looked back at the road ahead. A sign indicated that we were entering Richardson, Texas. The thruway had disappeared, and we were once again in what appeared to be local traffic, complete with the occasional stoplight. "Al, does this mean we're out of Dallas?"

"Suburb," Al said. "We got some miles to go to get clear

of Dallas."

Again I turned to face the woman. "I work for some people who get confused some of the time," I explained. "So if the story changed, I apologize. Don't take it personal or anything."

"You probably don't even know why I'm riding in this car with you," she said. "Why you came to the club last night and took me away. Did your people tell you anything about that?"

"As a matter of fact, they didn't tell me much," I acknowledged. "Not even your name. Any chance I could get that much from you?" I didn't really care so much about her name, but I didn't feel comfortable being on the wrong end of an inquisition.

"I tell the Negro," she said, and leaning, she put her lips close to Al's ear and whispered. Al was watching the road, and listened without any change of expression. "He at least is a gentleman. And you can give me another cigarette."

This I did, and we drove some more.

Now we were passing through Plano, and were no longer in the city. Farmland, some housing developments, a few shopping centers, municipal water tanks. Dallas seemed long gone already. I thought briefly about dropping Al so he could catch a bus back to the city at this point, but I wasn't sure of the woman, and other than handcuff her to me, I had no way of keeping her from bolting from the Bonneville if it were just the two of us. "What time it getting to be, Al?"

"Your dashboard clock got it about right, minus one hour." Five to ten, then.

"The lady would like to use a rest room," the lady announced.

"Look for a Mobil service station, Al. We'll top it off."

"You like that Mobil?"

"I like the big flying red horse."

Another fifteen minutes elapsed before the big red Mobil horse came into view. Al eased off the track and pulled up beside the pumps. The ladies' restroom door was near the corner of the building. "Wait in the car," I said. I got out, closed the car door, and walked to the restroom. I tapped on the door a couple of times, and turned the handle. The restroom was unlocked and vacant. I walked back to the passenger side of the Bonneville and opened the door. "C'mon, sweetheart, it's open for you."

I took her by the elbow as we made our way back to the restroom, and waited by the door until she was inside. Then I went over to the driver's side of the Bonneville. "I need you maybe another hour, Al. By that time I don't think she'll want to bolt from the car. Plenty in here for your bus fare back to Dallas." I reached in my jacket pocket and passed him his $250 envelope. In most instances a Negro would only get paid about half what a white man would. I never operated that way.

Al pocketed his envelope without examining the contents. "I like this here Pontiac," he said, running his hands around the steering wheel. "Like to get me one sometime."

"Runnin' mo-sheen," I agreed. "Four fifty four with a four-barrel." The attendant had come out of his cabin. He was wearing white coveralls with the flying red horse on the breast pocket. A nice touch.

"Fill 'er up?" He reached for the pump handle.

"'Preciate it," I said. "You got any cold drinks?"

"Co-colas there in the machine. It takes quarters."

"Al, reach me some quarters from the console there."

I was plugging the quarters into the Coke machine when over my shoulder I glimpsed a car pulling into the station. A police cruiser. I shot Al a quick look. He put both his hands on the wheel in plain sight and kept his eyes straight ahead. The two officers pulled to a stop on the other side of the pumps, but neither immediately exited the vehicle. The attendant looked up from where he was pumping and acknowledged the two with a nod of his head.

At this very moment I heard the door of the restroom open, and the girl came out. She had put on her dark glasses, freshened her makeup, and reapplied her lipstick. With her hair down she looked younger, less like her mother. I watched her as she took in the scene, including the police car. It was one of those times where events were beyond my control, and in our business, that's usually not a good thing. If she made for the cops it was going to be a challenge.

Instead, she walked right up next to me beside the Coke machine, took my arm, drew me against her, and very deliberately bussed me on the cheek. Then she whispered in my ear. "My name is Maggie, and I would like very much if we could get something to eat. Some breakfast, maybe."

"All the breakfast you want," I told her, and with two cold bottles of Coke in my free hand, I held her close to me and moved towards the Bonneville. Al caught my look, and turned the key in the ignition. After Maggie had gotten in the passenger side, I peeled off a ten-dollar bill and pushed it into the top pocket of the attendant's coveralls. "That's good enough," I told him. "We're on our way." He straightened up, withdrew the nozzle, and screwed on the gas cap. I slipped in and pulled the door shut and we eased away from the pumps deliberately keeping our eyes to the front. In the side view mirror I could see that one of the cops was out of the car talking to the attendant, but by then we had accelerated smoothly and were leaving the station behind. Three law-abiding citizens, out for a Sunday drive.

We drove in silence for some time, which was fine by me. I did some thinking. Miss Maggie, if that's who she was, apparently had no more use for the cops than we did, which eased my mind to a considerable degree. I didn't know for certain why we had been instructed to pick her up in Dallas. All Tommy had told me was that she was a "woman who we might want to hold on to," and that she was "going to be popular with the Secret Service boys," if we didn't get to her first.

"You said about the breakfast," she said to me. Her posture had relaxed somewhat. At one point, when I had lit another cigarette for her, she allowed her hand to linger on my leg for a time. It was a nice gesture, but I didn't put much stock in it. She was hungry.

"I did, and we will. Just want to put a little distance between us and that stinkin' cowtown before we stop again.

If you don't mind. You good, Al?"

"Been a while since them cold-ass burgers," Al pointed out.

"I like this black fellow," Maggie said to no one in particular. She lifted her hand and brushed the back of her knuckles against Al's cheek. "I never been with a black fellow, you know that?"

"That's what you done tol' me," Al said. "When you whisper to me back there."

"Be careful, he bites," I said. I didn't need her to get Al worked up.

"So do I," Maggie said, and removed her hand from Al's person. "What about you?" she asked, and turned to look at me. Behind her dark glasses I couldn't read her.

"No, I don't bite," I said. "If you know how to bark just right, you never have to." At this the corners of her downturned lips curled up. She was amused. Our little adventure was beginning to feel like a road trip.

Ahead of us the road, now a two lane, was going through stretches of rural. Fenced-in pastureland, barns, hay in the fields, tractors parked in driveways. Churches were letting out.

"What time do the churches let out down here, Al?"

"Long about noon, unless the preacher jus' can't quit." He slowed as we found ourselves snared by an orderly procession of churchgoing folk entering the roadway from the parking lot of a small wooden church. "Times I been trapped in church until after two in the afternoon," he said. "'Course on days like that, we usually had a pot luck."

"You go to church much, Maggie?" I asked her. Just conversation.

She didn't answer right away. "Now you know my name. I must know yours."

"You can call me Frank."

"Look, Frank. You see the sign? McKinney, Texas. 12 miles. Good place to stop for some food. How about it?" She gave me a look.

"Tell Al. He's your driver."

Twenty minutes later we hit the city limits of McKinney, and it was a sizeable little burg. We passed the red brick high school, a fire station, and a small shopping center. McKinney was certainly big enough to find a decent diner, and likely a bus station for Al. After that, it was going to be farm country all the way into Oklahoma. "Let's find someplace, Al."

We came to an intersection with a stoplight. On one side was a used car lot that was tented by lines of those little plastic pennants that would snap in the breeze, but they weren't snapping today. On the other side was a wooden building painted red and orange. *The Bar-B-Cue Pit* the sign said, and below it, *"Best ribs in Collin County."* The parking lot was paved and had a handful of automobiles snugged up to the building. When the light changed, Al pulled the Bonneville in, and parked her off to one side. "Let's get us some."

We pushed through the swinging door with Al going first, then Maggie. Al took a hard left and we planted ourselves in a booth in the corner, away from the tables and the lunch counter where a scattering of other diners were passing the time early on a Sunday afternoon eating that famous Texas barbecue. Nobody seemed to pay us any particular attention, and after a minute I slid out so Maggie, seated on the inside, could make her way to the restroom.

"I think the lady's going to behave herself," I observed.

"I notice that. She no friend of the po-lice, is she?"

"Think you can get a bus back to Dallas from here?"

"McKinney? The Hound run through here all the time."

"I appreciate you getting us up the road a 'ways. Don't mind sayin' that city gave me a dose of the heebie-jeebies."

"After Friday, Big D give the whole damn country the heebie-jeebie."

We were still waiting for table service when Maggie came back from the rest room. I watched her walk across the floor to where we sat. I hoped that none of the other diners were watching her the way I was. I stood up and she slid in next to me. She kept her dark glasses on, and for some reason I thought she might have been crying.

The waitress came. A bespectacled mousey blonde with a distracted look about her. "Y'all get a chance to take a look at the menu?" The menu was on the wall, grease pencil on a white board.

"Three rib plates'll do fine," I said. The waitress was looking back over her shoulder, and I noticed there was a small television going on the countertop near the kitchen.

"To drink?" Still looking over her shoulder at the TV.

"Ice tea all around. Thank you."

She turned back to face us. "Ain't that the damndest thing?"

"What thing is that?" Something she wanted to tell us.

"That boy they say done shot the President? Well, now they done shot him."

"You mean over there in Dallas?"

"Right there in the basement of the *po*-lice station," she said. "I don't know what-all this country is comin' to. Three rib plates," she confirmed, and off she went. Or wandered.

I looked at Al, Al looked at me. Maggie looked at me. I reached over and gave her thigh a squeeze. "Excuse me, sweetheart. Phone call."

Outside the front door I had noticed a phone booth, and out I went. This time, five rings, maybe six. "Tommy?"

"Frankie."

"Tommy, what the fuck?"

"Not our operation, Frankie. I don't know what to tell you. It was the damn Jew, matter of fact."

"Which Jew?"

"The Jew from the club. The club where you picked up the package."

"What the fuck."

"What the fuck is right. You still got the package?"

"Right here with me. Why don't you level with me, Tommy. What does she have to do with this business?"

"Nothing, as far as we know. Not a damn thing. She's just a party girl, that's all."

"Mr. D. don't have enough action as it is that I've got to come all the way down here to cowboy country to bring him another piece of tail? C'mon Tommy, is that the best you got?"

"You complainin' about the money or somethin' Frankie? Is that what this is?"

"I am not complaining about the money. But I've got the law up my ass down here, an' no good idea why." I paused. I was, as always, on a need-to-know basis. That was the strength of our business. That was the contract. "Just help me out a little here, Tommy."

"Well, in fact the package to which you refer is no longer considered an asset. The package is a liability. You got me?"

"I thought she was just a party girl."

"She is. It's just the people she parties with. Or partied with. The Feds may be lookin' for her, and if they find her, they'll be all over us. Trouble we don't need. Mr. D says she's got to go."

"Go as in send her home?"

"Go as in disappear, Frankie. Do I have to spell everything out for you?"

"Disappear."

"We will augment your fee, Frankie. If that's what's worrying you."

"I'm not worried, Tommy. But what the fuck. The Jew from the club?"

"Look, Frankie. If Mickey Mantle had not run into a goddamn storm drain in the '51 Series, we'd all be happier. Some things just can't be helped. Now please. Finish your job, and come on back. We'll see you then." I was still holding the receiver to my ear when the line went dead.

I went back inside. The food had been delivered to the booth. Al was gnawing on rib meat with gusto. Maggie had bought a pack of cigarettes for herself and was smoking one and looking at her plate. I slid back in beside her. "You were in such a hurry to eat."

"I was waiting for you."

I took the cigarette from her and had a puff. It was mentholated and surprisingly cool going down. I guess that was the idea. "Let's eat and get back on the road," I said.

In the end, Al did most of the eating. Maggie ate almost nothing, but she drank her ice tea and smoked another cigarette. I tried the rib meat, and it was actually not so bad. It wasn't like a Porterhouse or anything. In fact it could've been horsemeat. When you cook the hell out of it and slather it with all that sauce, who knows?

The potato salad had sweet pickles, so I ate it. The waitress came back to the table to leave the bill. I pulled out a $20 and pushed it into the little pocket where she kept her order pad. "Just keep it," I said. "What about that shooting? Did the fellow die?"

"He's over at the hospital right now. They don' know if he's gonna make it or not."

"He won't make it," I told her. "Just a hunch."

"You got a restroom, ma'am?" Al asked her.

"The coloreds' is around the side of the building." And she wandered back towards the television.

"Hand me those keys, Al. We'll be in the car."

Outside the sky remained overcast and the air was cool. I opened the passenger door for Maggie and she slid in. I went around, opened the other door, and slid in behind the wheel. Maggie had moved over to sit in the center of the seat, next to me. "You didn't eat a damned thing," I remarked. "You gonna be all right?"

She didn't answer, but stared straight ahead through those dark glasses. After another minute, Al reappeared and slid into the backseat. I looked over my shoulder at him. "Look more proper that way," he said.

I turned the key and the Bonneville rumbled nicely. I eased her out of the parking lot and headed north. "Any idea where that bus station is at, Al?"

"Jus' keep on straight. It's up here 'bout half a mile."

We went through two red lights, and on the left I spotted the familiar Greyhound sign, the lean running dog all stretched out in mid-stride. I pulled to the curb and slid the shifter into Park. Al got out and leaned in the passenger side window. "Goodbye pretty lady," he said. "You take care now." Maggie reached across and briefly clasped Al's hand, then let it go.

"Al, don't send me no postcard from Dallas, you hear me?"

"Next time, Uncle Frank," Al said to me. "You know how to find me."

"Stay loose, Al," I said, and he walked around the front of the automobile to the sidewalk. I slipped into drive and we eased away from the curb.

We drove north. Maggie had not moved, and sat close to me on the seat. My mind had been occupied back in the diner, but now had settled down. And I was behind the wheel of my Bonneville again. "Is Maggie your real name?"

"Magda. Is short for Magda. Americans like Maggie."

"Magda, I'm not sure what kind of trouble you're in, and it may be none of my business. But you know, I can't let you go back to Dallas."

"Maybe I don't even care. About Dallas, I mean."

"Well, that's good. I'm glad we got that settled." I had been mulling over Tommy's comments, and in fact, I did have an idea what kind of trouble she might be in. She was a party girl, and her last party had likely been with somebody important. Somebody who had a big appetite for party girls. Somebody who was now dead.

We drove on. After we got clear of McKinney, which didn't take long, I spotted a sign for Durant, Oklahoma. Fifty-eight miles. "How do you feel about Oklahoma?"

"Oklahoma is a place for Indians," she said. At this point she removed her dark glasses, reached into her purse, pulled out her compact and examined herself in the tiny mirror. The road was open enough and traffic was light enough that I could watch her looking at herself. She looked up to see me watching. "I'm looking old," she explained.

"You're looking like you could use a good night's sleep, that's all," I said. Where the road opened up, I had the Bonneville moving at a good clip, passing the occasional farm truck or Sunday driver before they ever saw us coming up. The gray ghost, from coast to coast. "Magda, I need to ask you something, and I want you to give me a serious answer."

"That's okay. I am a serious woman." She had placed her dark glasses on again, and reapplied her lipstick. I could see where she might be in demand as a high-class party girl.

"How would you like to go to California?" The Bonneville rocked along and for a moment the question hung in the air.

"Who will buy me the ticket for the bus?" she asked. A practical woman.

"I mean you come with me. In this car. To California."

"You don't have to do that," she said finally.

"Maybe I do, maybe I don't. How about you answer my question?"

"You want to go to California."

"With you, yes. Have you ever been to California? Because I haven't."

"It's a long way from Dallas."

"About as far as you can get in this country."

She rummaged in her purse and pulled out her menthols, lit one, took a pull, and placed it between my lips. "I don't know. What we will do in California?"

"Live near a beach. Swim in the ocean. Get a tan." She took back her menthol and smoked in silence. I could feel her shoulder against mine, and the speed of the car, the tires clipping the edge of the pavement when we flew past the trucks, didn't bother her at all.

"We could start something new, Magda," I said after a while. "That's what people do out there." If I was going to disregard Tommy's instructions, we would both need new lines of work, new identities even. Maybe I'd have to go so far as parting with the Bonneville, but I wasn't ready to think about that. "Los Angeles. The City of Angels. How does that sound?"

"Like a foolish American paradise," she answered. "A good place to wear my bikini."

"I can't wait to see that."

"I'll wear it to the supermarket," she said, and passed her menthol back to me.

Rough Romance

I waited for him at the top of the hill on the corner of Olivia St. He was coming up Whitehead from the direction of Joe Russell's place down on Greene. It was December and already dark when he came up the hill, head down, moving with a rolling gait like a fighter or a sailor. Some sailor.

"Hey Hem," I hailed him. I stepped out of the shadows. His big house was behind me and that's where he was going. He looked up. "Got a minute?"

He didn't arrest his forward progress in the least, and I could tell from the way he held his shoulders that he was probably drunk and feeling mildly unsociable. "Fuck off," he said.

"No, you fuck off, Hem," I countered. Just making sailor conversation.

He glanced up as he drew abreast of me. "My wife's got dinner on the table," he said, crossing Olivia, still moving up Whitehead.

"She got more on the table than dinner," I said. "And you're late."

He slowed and turned to get a better look at me. He was big across the chest and strongly built. Making up his mind, he came back in my direction, but I was watching his hands and I was ready for him. He threw the right first, a short hard right that came up from his waist. In Aikido we are well versed in neutralizing an aggressor's energy and, if need be, turning it against him. I neutralized it but didn't turn it.

After I released his wrist he followed up with a looping left that was born of his conviction that with his fists he could extract compliance out of anybody. I neutralized the left as well. Then I head-butted him politely in the chest and sat him down on the cracked and dirty pavement.

"You fight like a faggot," he said.

"Lucky for you," I said. I extended a hand to help him up and he came at me low, getting his arms around my upper thighs and driving me back into Olivia Street. I pivoted sideways and brought the heel of my hand sharply across his ear, using his momentum to break his hold and send him skidding on his hands and knees. This time he took a little longer to stand himself up and brush himself off. I knew what he was doing.

"One of those faggots who likes to beat up a man when he's drunk," he said.

"It's usually the other way around for you, isn't it Hem?"

"I repeat my original premise: fuck you," he said, and he adopted a boxer's crouch, bringing his hands up into a fighting position. He was, or had been, a boxing instructor, which usually affects a man's philosophy. Or stems from it.

"I'm here to talk about your wife, Hem. The one who has dinner on the table."

"Put up your dukes, pal. That's the only conversation I want out of you." He began advancing again, still drunk and beginning to enjoy himself.

"If I cut you and you bleed will you be willing to stop fighting and talk?"

This time he led with a straight jab, which is the easiest punch to neutralize. He followed it up with an overhand right. His wrists were thick and strong and I gathered all his body weight, rolled him up and pitched him face-first into Olivia Street with enough momentum to cut him and make him bleed. This time he didn't get up right away. He got himself into a sitting position and sat there clearing his head, doing some thinking.

"Take the mandatory eight," I told him. "Then I want you to listen to me."

"What division you fight in?" he wanted to know. "You punch like a girl."

"I'm not a boxer, Hem. I haven't even thrown a punch."

"Thompson sent you over here, didn't he?" He was still sitting in Olivia Street. In the dark I could see the blood on his forehead where he had hit the pavement.

"I don't know any Thompson," I said. "But I know your wife. And I know what you're about to do to her."

With his hands resting on his knees he shook his head as if trying to clear it. "You oughtn't talk about a man's wife like that," he said.

"Pauline deserves better. Why don't you get up out of the street?"

"Pauline's got her house. She's got her sons. She's got her friends. Everybody down here loves her."

"Everybody except her husband."

"You're going in circles, pal."

"Am I? You've been fucking the blonde, Hem. Right under Pauline's nose. And if you haven't, you might as well be."

He pushed himself up and stood facing me. He was built from the ground up with broad shoulders and a broad forehead, which was scraped and bloody. "I'll give you about one minute to knock it off with that kind of talk," he said.

"I'm only here to point out a few things to you, Hem. Things you'll never hear from the drunks you keep around yourself."

"Do you know the blonde?" he asked after a moment. The wheels were starting to turn.

"I know enough."

"What if I told you I was in love with her?"

"Sounds about right. You've been down this road before."

He considered. "If we're going to keep this up, we're going to need a bottle," he said. "I've got plenty in the house." He started to come up past me and I turned as he came, prepared for another assault, but it didn't come. He passed me going towards his big house. "Tell you what," I said. "You go on up to the house and bring the bottle outside. We can sit on your veranda. What I've got to say is not dinner-table conversation." He shrugged and went on up the hill towards his front gate. "Clean yourself up before your wife sees you," I called after him.

He went in. I crossed Whitehead and stood under the lighthouse and when he did not reappear after fifteen minutes, I went on back down Whitehead to Angela Street where I was staying in the Coco Plum Guest House for 75 cents a night with coffee and toasted flatbread in the mornings. There was a nice Guava jam you could spread on the bread. "Cuban breakfast," they called it, and unless you were doing heavy work it was all you needed until noon. It was the month of December and the temperature never got below 70 degrees. In the evenings a nice offshore breeze came through the Queen Palms and in the morning you woke up to the cries of the Bantam roosters. It was an easy town to get used to. A seductive place all right.

I gave him an extra night to make some mental adjustments and then I went back to my station at the top of the hill on the corner of Olivia and Whitehead. This time he came up the hill with a couple of his hangers-on. I stepped back into the shadows and let them pass. The next night he was with Josie Russell the saloonkeeper. The following night he didn't show at all. Maybe he was wary of being waylaid again. But as long as those Cuban Breakfasts held out I knew I'd get another chance. Any hunter of big game knows you have to be patient and learn the creature's habits on order to get close.

On the following night he was alone again. I made sure he could see me from half-a-block away so he could decide how to handle himself. "Thought you went back to the mainland," he said as he came up, a false conviviality in his demeanor.

"I wanted a chance to finish our conversation."

He pulled up short of me and kept his hands in the pockets of his dirty canvas fishing shorts. He had strong, well-developed calves and balanced himself nicely like the deepwater sportsman he was. "It's finished as far as I'm concerned."

"You're a writer. You know better than that."

He didn't like to be crowded, and I was crowding him plenty. He wanted to come after me, but I had put him down three times in the first round, and he was determined to be more careful. "If this is about my wife again, maybe you'd be better off talking to her lawyers. She's got some fine lawyers."

"With a character like you for a husband she's going to need them, isn't she?"

"You keep pushing me, boy," he said. His hands were still in his pockets.

"I'm not the one who's pushing you, Hem. You know who's doing the pushing."

"Who's pushing and who's not is my private business."

"Bullshit, Hem. It's all over the island. And it's getting into your work. Right where she wants it."

"She's a pushy broad, all right."

"She's just getting started. Before this is over she's going to push you out of your house and out of your marriage. She's going to push you right off the island."

"You're talking crazy. You don't even know the girl."

"I know enough. I know she fights like a girl. Which means it's not a fair fight as far as you're concerned."

"Not a fair fight?"

"She makes use of her vagina."

"No point in getting vulgar."

"Let me put it another way. She's got more guts than you, and probably more stamina. A better reach and more mobility. You think you're landing all the punches, and when it's over she's outpointed you on all three scorecards. Unanimous decision."

"She's treating me pretty goddamn well at the moment."

"Sure she is. Once she gets you off the island those kisses you love so much are gonna be scarce. And those long legs you like to talk about, she's not gonna be spreading 'em like she does now. Your bed, which is where you like to make your stand, is gonna get cold and lonely. How do you like it now, gentlemen?"

We stood there, maybe eight feet apart, in the shadows of the large tamarind tree next to his house. Two men went by on bicycles, heading down the hill. One rang the bell. "My wife's got dinner on the table," he said finally. He didn't look so much like the world-renowned sportsman anymore, and he didn't sound like one either.

"I guess you think I've been pretty hard on you. America's number one purveyor of rough romance."

"I've taken harder punches from my two wives," he said.

"Nobody punches harder than a wife," I agreed. "I just hate to see you get used to it."

"I'm used to it all right." He still hadn't moved from where he stood.

"The stuff you've been writing lately is shite, Hem. That's what bothers me."

"I still cash the checks," he said. I thought I saw a smirk. I wondered when he had developed the habit.

"No point in getting vulgar," I said. "You've got a great life down here. Between the blonde, the boat and the boozehounds I'm afraid it's going to cost you your title, that's all."

He seemed to consider this rather dark observation, and then brightened up. "We're taking *Pilar* over to the Tortugas tomorrow for bonefish. Four day run, out and back. Water out there is clear as gin. Maybe you'd like to ship with us." He was looking for a sportsman's way out of a bareknuckle confrontation.

"I didn't show up down here to be your pal, Hem. I know what happens to your pals. They wind up in your books."

"You're one character who doesn't have to concern himself with that," he said in a level-voiced snarl.

"Maybe while you're out of town I'll concern myself with the blonde." We were in it now.

"You're wasting your time. I've already boated that one."

"You surely are one miserable prick, Hem. They may love you in Montparnasse, but here on the island you're just about worthless."

For the first time he removed his hands from the pockets of his shorts. It looked like he might want to defend himself against the charges. Then he shrugged. "Guilty as charged, your honor. Guilty on all counts. The writer will petition the court for clemency, and suggest that a bottle is procured before advancing to the sentencing phase."

I stepped out into Whitehead Street. "What the hell. I've said my piece. Go on up to the house, Hem, and get that drink. You sure need it."

"I'm no damn rummy," he said, and he began moving up the street again towards the property that Uncle Gus had purchased for him and Pauline. He was living under the roof which his good Catholic wife provided, fucking the daylights out of another woman, and not troubling to hide it.

"Go ahead, Hem. You're a souse and a louse, but not a rummy. Never a rummy."

"I'll see you around, boy-o," he said over his shoulder as he moved on up the hill. I let him go. I saw him turn in the gate and a moment later the big front door opened and shut with finality. The house had been built by slaves before the American Civil War. It was a solid work of construction that had fallen into disrepair but they had brought it back and now it looked like a government building in French Equatorial Africa that appeared to be sound but was under siege to jungle rot and intemperate living.

I walked back down Whitehead Street to Fleming and kept going, past the La Concha hotel where the swells down from Miami or up from Havana sat at the bar with their beautiful mulatto whores and drank *Ron Varadero* over ice, which is as smooth as any rum you can pour. They got agreeably drunk every night, sometimes disagreeably drunk, but there wasn't a rummy among them. You had to be a poor working man or a moral derelict to be classified as a rummy.

Halfway down the block I turned north into the darkened alley. Up ahead was a single light over the hand-lettered sign for Virgilio's. Two people were smoking cheroots under the sign. I went in. Augustine the black boy was behind the bar. He was a good-looking boy who could play the piano and he knew everybody that came and went. There were three or four boys on the barstools, and one good-looking dark-haired white girl who wore culottes or toreador pants that she filled out beautifully. She was there for the music, which usually began after 10:00 PM unless the musicians felt otherwise.

I saw Sandy in the back room and went over to him. He was talking to a fellow I hadn't seen before, and the fellow shoved off as I approached. "You're intact, thank God," Sandy said and he slipped his arm around my waist. Christmas was only two weeks away. "I thought he might knock your block off."

"He wanted to," I said. "But I fight pretty good for a faggot." We laughed. "Poor Pauline," I said.

"I don't know. Didn't you tell me that she stole him in the first place? What goes around."

"She won't be able to compete with the blonde, will she?"

"Not if the blonde really wants him."

"Well, she came all the way down here. People who come this far usually know what they want." I was looking at Sandy when I said it.

"Or they're ready to settle for what they find," Sandy said. He was not above scooping my insides out a little. In 1937 people were having their insides scooped out all over the country. This period was later called the Great Depression, primarily by people who understood very little of depression.

"Let's go up to the roof bar at Chicha's," Sandy said. "I'll buy you an expensive rum drink."

"He actually invited us to go out on his boat tomorrow.

Over to Tortuga."

"That's where the old prison used to be. It's like the end of the world out there. God-awful."

"I don't really think he meant it. Just trying to make amends somehow." I thought of him in the big house up on the hill with his short-haired, stern-faced, well-moneyed Catholic wife. He was trying to make amends all right. "I'd rather go over to Front Street and eat the *gambas al ajillo*," I said.

We walked the few short blocks to Front Street, past the rum shacks and the gambling houses. The sea-smell came up strong after dark and people sat on their stoops and smoked and drank. Even when times were tough on the island, and times were tough then, people had something to smoke and drink. Front Street was right on the docks and the fishermen brought their catches up and sold them for cash or sometimes credit to the proprietors of the many fish shacks along the street. The Conch style, which had come up from Cuba, was to pan-fry the shrimp with plenty of garlic and butter if you had it or oil if you didn't. Salt and pepper to taste. You ate the shrimp like that and dipped your bread in the juices. Conchs didn't favor the heavy cream sauces or the tomato-based concoctions that came down from Miami where people liked to abuse the shrimp by displaying their culinary talents. After pink shrimp come out of the Gulf Waters you wanted to interfere with them as little as possible. They were best consumed with cold beer to keep your palate fresh and your appetite sharp.

The last time I left Key West it was from the steamship docks at Trumbo Point aboard the *Governor Ross*, bound for Havana. It was the first week of 1942, as I recall. It was just a few weeks after the Pearl Harbor business, and the mood on the island had shifted. The Navy was taking over the docks and much of the available housing. The great author of Whitehead Street was long gone by then. He had departed by 1940. As I had foreseen, the blonde had cost him his house, his marriage, and his island. But he was one crazy lucky character. She installed him on a bigger island in a better house and dragged him off to Spain where he hatched the plot for his last big book, maybe his best book. The one that enabled him to keep his title, at any rate. Most of the stuff that came later, the critics agreed, was shite. But I was wrong about the boat, the blonde, and the boozehounds robbing him of his talent. For a time at least they had sustained it. And the myth of his invincibility with it.

Flat and low-lying though it is, it was always surprising how quickly Key West faded from view when you sailed away. By the time the water under the keel had turned from the inshore aquamarine shades to the deep cobalt of the Gulf Stream, the island was no more than a narrow gray-green strip on the horizon. At ten miles out it was almost gone from view, and so you went up to the main salon on the second deck and ordered a smooth rum drink and consumed it standing at the rail while you tried to identify, before it escaped you entirely, what you had acquired during your time on the island, and having departed, what you'd left behind.

The Havana Treatment

Eddie had to laugh.

It was not an out-loud laugh. Not a laugh of hilarity. More of a side-of-your-mouth laugh, the kind you don't care to share because nobody else in the room would get it the way you get it.

He was sitting in an airport lounge in Dallas. Overpriced drinks, desultory conversation. Killing the time, as if it won't die of its own accord quickly enough. The kind of situation you avoid, if you've got any sense. But the length of the flight delay was perfectly tailored to a cold beer, so it made sense.

Eddie had been conversing with a fellow passenger, a fit-looking fellow wearing aviator glasses, with close-cropped hair just going gray, and an earnest air about him. Like Eddie, he was on the backside of forty. They were talking about travel, places they'd visited, or might want to, and the fellow leaned over the white Formica tabletop and told Eddie how he'd read recently that Cuba had become, as he put it, "the new sex destination." He delivered this information in the kind of tone that they used to call "confidential." Privileged information for privileged characters.

Eddie just shrugged. But on the inside, he had to laugh. A new sex destination? Eddie knew that the only time that description might have fit Cuba was when Columbus landed 500 years ago. Ever since, the island had been renowned for the frequency and the enthusiasm of the exotic sexual couplings available to the casual visitor on the so-called "Pearl of the Antilles." For the past five centuries, sailors, soldiers, adventurers, bully boys out to see the empire, corporate junketers, banana barons on expense accounts and finally, starting in about 1920, American tourists from the United States, all got off the boat, or the plane or the ferry knowing full well that they would have the opportunity, practically the obligation to discharge themselves agreeably between the legs of a local lady (or a local boy) before leaving the golden shores of Cuba.

Nice to know, Eddie reflected, that his fellow traveler had stumbled onto their "secret," probably gleaned from the pages of one of his "men's magazines" on a page titled *Confidentially Yours.*

As for Eddie, he had learned of Cuba's seductive allure firsthand twenty years earlier. Christmas, 1956 to be precise. The season for visiting Cuba typically began in October once the threat of hurricanes was past, and extended about six months until the unbearable heat and humidity began to creep back into the picture. In the Fifties, if you were a somewhat footloose or unattached fellow and had a tolerance for good pussy and top-shelf liquor in an ambience of exotic splendor, you headed south: New Orleans, Miami, Havana. And of the three, Havana was the standout. Not only did you get more bang for your buck (and that's a deliberate pun), you got an entirely different world in the bargain. The damned restraints of Midwestern morality, not to mention the puritanical mores and the meddling laws and statutes of the Motherland, were absent. You were right back on the beach where Columbus' men had cavorted with uninhibited tribal lovelies five centuries earlier.

What Eddie knew was that most of the Caribbean was a "sex destination" for the Europeans during those centuries of exploration and development. It wasn't until the Twentieth century that Cuba really began to separate itself from the crowd. Nearness to the United States, corrupt politics, unstable governments, and the heavy hand of United Fruit Company all played a part in the evolution of this splendid R&R property. (Not to be overlooked, the feminine pulchritude, present all over the region, seemed to be especially in abundance on this largest island.) But let's be honest, once the Mob came in and set up shop in the late Forties, Cuba went over the top. Over the top with hotels, with casinos, with high-end brothels, with all the touches of home and none of the inconveniences. Bourbon Street? South Beach? Ybor City? *Fuggedaboutit.* The food wasn't as good, the liquor was overpriced, and the ambience was an artificial reproduction of the tropics. As far as the sex goes, you were probably gonna be banging some runaway from Minnesota who was on drugs and was barely able to pay attention, and you were spending five times what it was worth.

Please.

"Down Havana way" was the place to go.

The flight from Miami was 55 minutes and could be purchased on weekend getaway rates for 36 bucks. If you were inclined to the more leisurely route, you could take the car ferry *City of Havana* from Port Everglades Florida, the crossing was twelve hours, cost you $45 bucks along with your car. And the trunk of your Buick was a handy place to stash contraband liquor, tobacco, or weapons, if you wanted to run the risk.

Screw all that. If you were a player, you flew.

Which is what Eddie had done.

He made the trip with two pals. One was Brant Ryan, a big-shouldered, easy-going farm boy from St. Louis who Eddie had met a couple years earlier during a convention in New Orleans. Brant sold tractors for Caterpillar and had a number of serious business contacts in Cuba. He'd been encouraging Eddie to make the trip ever since they'd met. The other was Brian Rooney, a wisecracking college pal of Brant's from Philadelphia who was on the corporate law fast track in Newark, New Jersey. Ryan had been to the island a number of times before, but Rooney and Eddie were both rookies. Eddie came over from Biloxi, Mississippi, where he managed an agency that performed background checks on new corporate hires at hotels and casinos along the Gulf Coast. Rooney flew in from Philly. Brant had handled the travel and lodging arrangements, and was going to be the group's de-facto guide during the four-day, three night stay.

They touched down at Rancho-Boyeros airport outside Havana about midday on Christmas Eve. Brant had arranged for a car service to whisk them into the city in a big black Oldsmobile, along palm-lined avenues with Spanish Colonial architecture and a sense of freedom and anticipation that might or might not have had something to do with the rum cordials they'd been served from a tray by a white-jacketed waiter before they even cleared customs. "You boys're about to get busted out," Ryan chortled from the front passenger seat of the cab.

"Busted out or just busted?" Rooney cracked.

"Keep talking, smart guy. We'll see how well you hold up when the serious fun begins."

The Deauville was one of a line of showplace hotel/casino complexes overlooking the harbor, with a big, splashy lobby, a soaring atrium, plush carpeting, and well-trained legions of scarlet-jacketed bellhops eager to be of service. Eddie had heard of the "Havana Treatment" and it was apparent from the beginning that it was no mere figment of the travel writers' imagination. You could lay your burdens down with your bags at the reception desk, and not worry about picking up either for the duration of your stay.

"Fellas, lunch and drinks poolside in thirty," Ryan said as he passed out room keys. He eyed Rooney. "Unless you're going to require room service right away?" Rooney had served notice that he was eager to have his sexual needs serviced early and often, and the query was not meant to be ironic. Eddie laughed out loud.

"How about you, Eddie?" Brant asked him. "You diving into the oysters right away?"

"I can hold out fine, Brant," Eddie told him. "I'll see you for lunch." They were standing in front of the bank of elevators.

"I'll be there," Rooney chimed in. The elevator arrived,

manned by a comely *mulatta* girl in a tight skirt and snug white blouse that nicely accented her lace brassiere. "Num-num," Rooney commented as they slid into the elevator.

The three of them watched the girl's trim backside as the elevator rose. They reached the fifth floor and the door slid open. "The hotel help is not included in your package price, fellas," Ryan laughed.

It was easy to see why so much of the daytime action in Havana took place around hotel swimming pools. The Deauville's pool area was a rambling paradise of tropical foliage, miniature waterfalls, reclining beach chairs and glass-topped tables. White-jacketed stewards weaved their way through the bathers bearing trays of food and drink. The biggest draw, however, was the company. This was not your suburban American country club crowd. Sure, there were a few pasty-looking gringos, but they were far outnumbered by the lean and tanned bodies, the firm flesh, and the superior genes of people who could afford to make a habit out of frequenting the international pool scene. It was a smorgasbord of earthly delights, and as the three of them wolfed their club sandwiches and guzzled their vodka-laced orange squashes, even Rooney was speechless except for the occasionally low wolf whistle or the muttered imprecation.

"Brian, my man. You realize that lots of these ladies are professionals plying their trade. If you want to make a bid, just send a waiter over with a couple of drinks and a note," Ryan instructed.

"You mean a bank note?" Rooney honestly wanted to know.

"A hand-written note, you dope. The bank note comes later."

"Oh brother. This is the candy store I've always wanted to visit."

As Ryan had explained earlier in the airport lounge back in Miami, the sex trade in Havana was tailored to suit all tastes and all budgets. Everything from a one-dollar throwdown for five minutes of friction to a three-day all-perks-included full-time female companion could be arranged. For Eddie's part, he was less preoccupied than Rooney with getting himself serviced, although it was something that he had in mind to do at some point. After lunch he went out by himself and walked through the city's Vedado neighborhood taking in the easy tropical air and the graceful Caribbean bustle of the city. There would be gifts to buy for some of the folks back home, but Eddie was content to find a small park and sit for a while to take in the passing parade of humanity. They were all aware that the island was run by the dictatorial government of Batista, but here in the center of Havana the citizenry seemed anything but oppressed. Seasonal lights were strung from lampposts, music sounded from car radios, the stores were full of high-end goods, the streets and parks were immaculately clean, and the people Eddie observed had, for the most part, a well-scrubbed and contented air. Once he doubled back towards the hotel he found himself going through an area that was a little seedy, with bordellos clustered along a street that also had pawnshops, adult bookstores, and bars populated with locals. A number of the women chatted Eddie up in what can best be described as an overly familiar style, but it was all in good fun, and nobody's feelings were hurt when Eddie just grinned and kept walking.

When he got back to *porte cochere* of the hotel, Rooney was just walking out with a girl on his arm. She was young, probably not yet 20, and she was a looker in a short skirt with an off-the shoulder blouse and the flawless skin of radiant youth. She would've turned heads in New York City. "Eddie, say hello to my new friend Vicky," he said, obviously very pleased with himself. Vicky held out a hand, palm down, in Eddie's direction and he gallantly lifted it to his lips.

"You've very lovely, Vicky. Brian is a very lucky fellow."

"Eddie, this ain't true romance, pal. We've been busy up in my room," Rooney grinned . "I found her at the hotel bar. You oughta stop in and get yourself some company." Rooney was right. He had found his candy store. As the two of them sailed off into the street, Rooney shouted back over his shoulder, "I'm taking her out to buy some jewelry. She's earned it!"

As it developed, Eddie did swing by the bar. He told himself it was worth a look-see. He lied to himself. He should've known better. He could never resist a thoughtful, well-timed sales pitch. Backed up by a captivating perfume and a deadly pair of eyes, caramel-colored skin and luscious lips, one of the choicest girls in the bar singled him out and attached herself to him right away. "Buy you a drink?" Eddie asked her, a little redundantly.

"Manhattan," she said. And that was about it for her English.

She carried her own condoms, and their roll upstairs in Eddie's room was brief and decidedly mechanical. Of course there was no kissing, which Eddie missed, and while she didn't mind him fondling her breasts, she wasn't in favor of receiving kisses there either. She deftly rolled Eddie into the missionary position, and as he plunged in an out of her, his attention wandered to the view out of his windows towards the harbor. He found himself wondering how many other gringos fresh off the plane had found themselves in the exact same room, maybe even with the same girl. The thought didn't disturb his erection, but it did prompt him to finish up his business in a timely fashion. She wasn't in the room for more than thirty minutes, took the three $10 bills Eddie had placed on the dresser, blew him a kiss from those unavailable lips, and slipped out the door. Brian had found himself a wonderful lover and Eddie had gotten a mere service call, both out of the same bar. If he had just handed her his credit card, it might've been different Eddie thought briefly, and then he snoozed.

There was no question about the evening's activity. The Tropicana was the place to be, Brant had made that clear from the beginning. "Nothing ya'll have ever seen can prepare you for the Trop," he had told them. "Best floor show in the world. Probably see a movie star or two while we're at it. Frank fuckin' Sinatra hangs out there when he's in town. I saw Gary Cooper at the bar the last time I was in." They met in the lobby at 9:30, dressed, as Brant had instructed them, in loose-fitting white linen shirts and dressy slacks with a high shine on their black dress shoes. ("Set us apart from the boat crowd, but we'll still be comfortable...") They caught a taxi out to the club, which was on the perimeters of the city, about a fifteen-minute ride. "You boys made any friends in the hotel yet?" Brant asked them as they rode.

"I think Rooney's gettin' married in the morning matter of fact," Eddie announced. "He's already bought the ring."

"That was for sexual favors," Brian countered. "You never want to get married to a girl from the candy store."

"Hell, you'd be surprised," Brant said from the front seat. "This is Cuba, remember?"

Shortly after that, the taxi swept up the winding drive with all the palm trees backlit by spotlights and the big neon *Tropicana* sign beckoning seductively in the distance. "Ho-ly *shit*," Rooney exclaimed. It was impressive, to be sure, and as the cab negotiated the big circular drive and pulled up next to the main entrance, they could already hear the syncopated rhythms lighting up the night from within the club. Standing at the curb amongst the blue-jacketed valets and the bright glare of multicolored floodlights highlighting the immaculate landscaping, Eddie felt in his chest a sense of infinite expansion as he contemplated a night of magical proportions. If this was part of the "Havana Treatment" he was ready for it.

At the reception area Brant passed a couple of bank notes to one of the hostesses with a few words, and she took them in tow and steered them through the maze of lights into the main patio. Completely open under the stars, this patio was enclosed by a number of stages at varying heights, and on each stage swirled, pumped, and bounced troupes of dancers in impossibly bright multicolored costumes. The patio itself was enormous, must've been nearly 200 feet in diameter Eddie reckoned, with patrons dining and drinking at sixty to eighty tables, each one with an immaculate white tablecloth and fine silverware. The whole scene was so preposterously, outlandishly embracing that Eddie didn't bother to hide the dumb rube's grin that stole across his features. The thought crossed his mind that it was just like a circus, except a circus for adults.

But there was no time to linger. Their hostess was determined to get them through the main patio and into another area. The owners of the club had laid it out in such a way that you got the sense of being outdoors under the stars, which in fact the main patio was. The dining room and the adjoining cabaret into which they were ushered were enclosed in soaring glass pavilions that even included tropical plants and palm trees, thus reinforcing the atmosphere of being outside in a perfectly natural setting. "When I'm in Havana of an evening, you'll find me at the Trop," purred Susan Hayward in one of the popular stateside ads for the Club, and at first blush, Eddie had to agree with her assessment entirely. The whole universe seemed to fit into the place. What would be the point of going anywhere else?

Once inside the glassed-in pavilion, they were guided to a small, more intimate dining area and shown to a circular table already occupied by two American couples. Brant made cursory introductions. The two men were both in-country sales reps for Caterpillar. The women, one of whom was a Latin, were their wives, and Eddie briefly recalled Brant's earlier comment about the likelihood of marrying a local. "This is Cuba, remember?"

In short order large colorful drinks were placed in front of them. "Rum punch, house specialty," said one of the Caterpillar guys. Eddie drank. The drink reminded him of nothing so much as the famous Pat O'Brien's "Hurricane" drinks in New Orleans, and was likely even more potent. Next to him Rooney pulled out the straw and drank directly from the tall glass. "Num-num," he said. "Let's keep these numbers a-comin'."

Brant leaned over and spoke into Eddie's ear. "This dining room is more upscale than the main patio, and the service is better," he explained. "Also, all the top-shelf showgirls work this room."

Eddie nodded, and as the rum punch swirled in his blood, he sat back and took in the colorful menagerie of exotic dancers performing on raised platforms on either side of the room. He had seen dancers, strippers and showgirls in a number of locales in the USA, and for the most part these girls, although young, were of a similar overworked and underpaid ilk. A number of them appeared to be not yet out of their teens. But he had to acknowledge that quite a few were so wonderfully proportioned and fine of feature that they took your breath away. Of course, when a girl dances the samba, or the mambo, or any one of a variety of dances practiced in the islands, she is able to present her assets in the most seductive light imaginable. Eddie had read somewhere that the origins of these island dances were found in African mating rituals, and if a man's blood is ever going to gather excitedly in his nether regions, those African mating rituals will usually do the trick.

Rib eye steaks came and were consumed. Potatoes baked in their jackets and topped with a savory seafood sauce. Served on the side was one of the Cuban staples, fried bananas (plantains they were called), which normally Eddie would have eschewed, but these were caramelized and of a crunchy texture that made them hard to resist. Aware of the alcohol they were consuming, Eddie deliberately tucked away as much of the fare as he could knowing that it would serve him later in the evening by keeping him steady on his feet and providing sufficient endurance to make a night of it. Brant seemed similarly focused on the kitchen's offerings, but Brian steadily pursued a liquid diet, his eyes wide as he took in their surroundings. The food and drinks flowed continuously, provided by a virtual ballet company of waiters who sailed effortlessly between and among the tables. Also circulating, passing out roses and taking photos, were shapely hostesses in skimpy outfits and fishnet stockings. Part of their allure was the Santa hats which they wore fetchingly cocked on their heads, and it was one of these Santa-hat-wearing cuties that would very shortly open the door on Eddie's real introduction to the

Havana Treatment.

Brant stood up. "Into the cabaret for a nightcap," he announced. Eddie glanced at his Omega Seamaster and was surprised to see that it was after 11:00 already. Not surprisingly, the married Caterpillar couples begged off and departed while Brant and his charges made their way into the cabaret. Here the lights were low, the dancers were absent, and the atmosphere had a surreal movie-star quality to it. "First one sees a bona fide movie star gets a free hotel night courtesy of Caterpillar," Brant laughed. "Let's sit at the bar, what do you say?"

Feeling good about being on his feet, Eddie remained standing while Brant and Brian sat, with their backs to the bar. They drank the famous *Cuba Libres*, dark rum, Coca-Cola, and a twist of lime. Eddie briefly surveyed the sharply dressed denizens of this inner sanctum. He spotted a couple of uniforms with lots of braid, several sharkskin suits worn by smooth operators, and a handful of high-maintenance females in expensive cocktail attire. Lost as he was in his reconnoitering, Eddie was completely taken aback when Rooney, who had been sliding more deeply under the influence of the demon rum throughout the evening, suddenly leaned forward on his leather-upholstered stool and gripped a passing hostess indelicately by the upper arm. Eddie's face was no more than eighteen inches from Rooney's when the latter announced to the girl in an uncomfortably loud voice, "Honey, I'll bet I could fuck that Santa hat right offa you." Under other circumstances, it might've been a comical and light-hearted moment, particularly on Christmas Eve. In Philadelphia maybe. Even in Chicago, possibly in Miami. But not at the Tropicana's *Cabaret Bajo Las Estrellas*, where, owing to a momentary lull in conversation in their immediate vicinity, it resounded loudly as the epitome of American ugliness abroad. Time ground momentarily to a halt. Unfortunately, Rooney did not.

"Whatta ya say, hot mama? How much moola to make it, you and me and the Santa Hat?"

The young lady, much to her credit, did not panic or overreact, but such was the bluntness and force of Rooney's advance that she was obliged to withdraw her arm forcibly with an cautionary flash of her eyes. Rejected, Rooney laughed but not with hilarity. "What the hell, bitch. I can buy cunts like you all day long right in my hotel..."

Brant had come to his senses and placed a heavy hand on Rooney's shoulder. He might have given the lad a timely lecture right then, but he never got the chance. The hostess had moved quickly away and another female appeared suddenly at Eddie's elbow, actually shouldering him partially aside to put herself squarely in front of Rooney. "Let's get something straight, you little prick," she said. "First of all, in your dreams you couldn't afford any of the women in this place. Who do you think you're dealing with here, one of your cute little American whores? These are real women, not suited for the likes of college boys like you." Eddie took his eyes off the female long enough to glance at Rooney's face, which had gone through a bit of a sobering-up phase in the last thirty seconds.

"Who's responsible for this little asshole? Are your mommy and daddy here with you, college boy?" Eddie looked at the woman, trying to place her origins. In spite of her fluency in colloquial American English, she spoke with a clipped accent that added additional force to her delivery.

Brant now stepped up to the plate. "Sweetheart, I completely apologize. He is an asshole, and he's completely out-of-line. I will remove him from the premises immediately and personally assure you that he'll never set foot in the Trop again."

While this was exchange was going on, Eddie, who was a full head taller than the girl, did what so many young men would likely have done under the circumstances, and briefly inventoried this particular female's assets. She wore a snug black cocktail dress with a scooped neckline that perfectly displayed the firm orbs of her breasts. Then there were the smooth, square, lightly freckled shoulders, and a glimpse below of wonderfully taut calves. The girl in black, as Eddie had come to think of her, relented in her tirade but stayed put, staring remorselessly into Rooney's face. "That would be the perfect thing for you to do, all right," she said. "But first he's going to reach into his wallet and pull out a hundred dollar bill which he's going to place on the bar. The barman will see that Rosa gets the cash. We'll call it your friend's apology money, since I really don't want to hear him open his mouth again."

Brant didn't hesitate. "Get out your wallet, bud, and do as the lady tells you." At this point it occurred to Eddie that Brant was going the extra mile to protect his own reputation at the Trop. Rooney managed to extricate the wallet from his trousers and passed it to Eddie. "I don't know what the hell I've even got in there," he said. With the girl standing at his side, Eddie opened the wallet and thumbed through the bills. As he did so, he became sharply aware of her presence, of the smell of her and the charge that went through him when their upper arms briefly touched. He glanced briefly at the crown of her head where her lustrous black hair was parted. He managed to find a $50 bill and added to it three $20's. He closed the wallet and held the bills out in her direction. "I don't want to touch anything of his," she said, not looking up. "Put it on the bar."

Brant took the bills from Eddie's hand and placed them behind him on the polished wood surface of the bar. "Done deal," he announced.

"Not quite," said the girl, and with a short, powerful movement her forearm flashed out and she caught Rooney full on the side of his face with an open palm. The crackerjack sound could be heard quite a ways down the bar, Eddie guessed. "Now march his ass out of here before one of these high-ranking officer friends of mine decides to make a pool boy out of him," she instructed, and just as abruptly as she had come she turned away and departed, the heels of her patent-leather black pumps ringing on the tile floor with a commanding finality.

Brant and Eddie exchanged glances. "I'm gonna have to bail out of here with him pronto," the big Missourian confirmed. "You don't necessarily have to come with us. If you think you're up for it, you can stick around. Hell, man, it's Christmas Eve."

Eddie had no intention of leaving just yet. After the two had gone, he ordered another *Cuba Libre*. He looked around for the beauty who had so aroused both his libido and his imagination. The bar was separated from the seating area by a low railing. He spotted her at a table on the other side of the railing. She was in the company of three or four men, dashing fellows in uniforms with lots of ribbons on their chests. When he caught her eye, he raised his glass in her direction. A moment later one of the officers from the table came in Eddie's direction. *"Bienvenido,"* he said by way of welcome, and taking Eddie by the elbow, steered him through the opening in the railing and over to the group. Eddie forced himself to keep his eyes off the girl while introductions were made. *"Me llamo Eddie,"* he told them, using about half of his workable Spanish. They made a place for him on the other side of the girl, and he sat, grateful for the fact that the food he had eaten was doing a good job of keeping the rum at bay. He already knew that this was a night he needed to be at his best.

Some women you don't notice at first and then they are all you notice. Eddie had experienced that phenomenon a couple of times in his life, but never like this night. He could not be troubled to hold back the waves of masculine admiration that he found himself beaming steadily in her direction. Even when he wasn't watching her, he couldn't keep his eyes off her. When she turned to him at last and said with a shrug, "I don't usually talk to people that way," Eddie barely heard her. There is a certain type of female born to wear a sleeveless black cocktail dress cut just above the knee with delicate silver sequins along the scooped neckline just as there is a certain type of man born to provide the greatest admiration for such a dress. That was the happy circumstance in which Eddie found himself. He realized after a moment that she was apologizing for her earlier chewing out of Rooney. "I thought it was pretty appealing myself," Eddie responded. She laughed cordially and Eddie felt himself going under her influence as quickly as a swimmer caught in a storm drain. He concentrated on her face and tried to keep his attention off the rest of her.

While the men at the table went on in the Spanish of that rapid-fire sing-song Cuban variety, Eddie caught his breath long enough to engage the girl in a passably interesting conversation. He had learned as a younger man that getting a girl talking about herself and her interests was the surest way of holding her attention, so that's what he tried to do. Her name was Natalie, she lived in Havana, her father was from Spain, her mother an American, she had grown up in Havana, had spent considerable time in the United States, and was presently occupied as the director of a charity for rural children who lacked proper medical care. Had she any children of her own? It seemed improper to ask. Her passion, her scorn, her sense of moral outrage, and her protective side he had seen displayed earlier. Her sexual proclivities, that kind of secretive information that clings to a female even more provocatively than a slinky black cocktail dress, were left to Eddie's imagination. He tried not to imagine too much.

The evening wore on, too rapidly. Christmas Eve became Christmas. The men at the table were hatching a plan that seemed to bore, or not to include, Natalie, and her attention began to wane. Eddie, who had kept drinking steadily because in this situation he knew he would have to rely upon rum for some type of guidance, had an inspiration. Adjacent to the cluster of tables was a small section of polished marble that seemed to serve as a dance floor. With the last of the floor shows having died away, the music was now provided by a small band on one of the risers, and when the band broke away from the usual diet of hyperactive salsa music and launched into a slow rhythmic ballad, Eddie stood up and held out his hand. "I'd really like to dance with you." Natalie looked up at him for a moment without expression and without moving. Her companions at the table were laughing. "It's Christmas," Eddie said, keeping his hand out there. "And you're not wearing a Santa hat."

She rose, led Eddie to the floor, and in one smooth move placed herself in his embrace. Any hesitation Eddie had about managing the rhythm was quickly erased when she took over and moved them both in a way that seemed entirely of Eddie's choosing. The inclined top of her head rested against Eddie's cheek and her scent filled his nostrils. Involuntarily he began to produce an erection that in vain he tried to conceal. She laughed. "Is that because of Christmas?"

"Sorry, it's not appropriate, I know."

"On the contrary," she said. "It's my tribute."

Once he heard that, Eddie let the tribute stand. As they moved together, Eddie was seized with the conviction that this dance on this evening with this girl would enable him to generate the momentum to live forever.

By the time the dance was finished, Eddie was weak in the knees but his resolution had doubled. Back at the table, he asked her, "What's going on after this? Is there another club we could visit or something?"

"They're talking about going to an *exibicion*," she told him. "A sex show." Brant had talked about the Havana sex shows. More risqué and less left to the imagination that any of the watered-down shows back in the USA.

"You going along with them?"

"Not me. Not this girl. I'm going to see my mother." Eddie watched her face. She had bold, beautifully formed eyebrows above dark, inviting eyes, a straight, slender nose, a strong jaw with a squared chin, and lips molded to break your heart. Taken as a whole, her features presented a vision of female allure that was both fluid and timeless, capable of hovering effortlessly between wanton disregard and polite interest. With looks like that, the power that she could exert over a man was both disturbing and captivating.

"Look, Natalie, I hope you don't mind my asking, but I'd really like to see you again at some point. Maybe I could take you to dinner. Or the beach. Or you could show me some of your Havana sights…" He was presenting a pitiful excuse of being a man, but he was not going to lose his sense of mission.

Natalie's countenance, up to now a little guarded, seemed to soften for a moment. Then it hardened again. "Eddie, you're a great guy and I've enjoyed talking with you. But let me save you a lot of trouble in your life and tell you that in a few minutes when I get up and leave, I want you to give me a nice kiss on the cheek and wave goodbye. Can you do that?"

"What if I don't mind trouble? In fact, what if I actually like it?"

At this, Natalie smiled indulgently and leaned in Eddie's direction, placing her hand lightly on his forearm. "You know, you're already kind of on the radar for that little incident earlier with your friend. Don't think that chatting with me is going to get you off the hook with everyone. If anything, it could even make you more of a target."

"You talking about your friends here at the table?"

She laughed dismissively. "These Batista cocksuckers? They're thinking about their sex show, they couldn't care less." Around the table her uniformed male companions were pushing back their chairs. "Look, if it means that much to you, wait five minutes after I leave before you come out. I'll see what I can arrange." And with that she leaned across, gave Eddie a dry peck on the cheek, and was on her feet and ready to go. *"Buenas noches,"* she said, and let herself be collected by the men as they made their way towards the exit. *"Buenas noches,"* Eddie said to the men as they departed. Then he went to the bar and asked for a drink of ice water.

Five minutes later, after confirming that the bill for himself and his companions had earlier been paid, and leaving another $50 in cash with the barman "for the young lady," Eddie left the bar and retraced his way across the main patio towards the entrance. It was after 1:00 AM and with the dancers having retired for the evening, the tables were beginning to empty. At the front portico there was a crush of automobiles as patrons pushed off into the night in search of other, perhaps more intimate entertainment. Eddie noted that there were more than a few glamorous-looking women being shepherded into polished sedans by hovering consorts. Wonderful way to wake up on Christmas morning, Eddie thought to himself. His Natalie was nowhere in evidence, however, and Eddie waited, his newfound faith unshaken, to see what arrangement she might have made.

He didn't wait long. After a moment one of the Tropicana's young, smooth-faced attendants, wearing a white tunic with a bright red *boutonniere* in the lapel, stepped to his side and took him by the elbow. "This way, sir." He led Eddie along the curved portico, past a number of automobiles jockeying for position at the curb as they picked up passengers. They reached a black sedan with the rear passenger door open. Reflexively Eddie thrust his hand into his pocket and pulled out a couple of bills that he passed to the attendant. At the same time he reached across and tugged the red boutonniere from the boy's lapel. Then he slipped into the sedan. The scent of her filled his nostrils before he even saw her on the other side of the backseat. All in one smooth motion he leaned into her and surprised her by finding her lips with his own for just a heartbeat before he drew back and affixed the *boutonniere* to her dress. "Sexier than the Santa hat," he pronounced. "Oh, for goodness sake," was all she said, and then the sedan was in motion and they were going back down the magnificent landscaped drive and into the night.

In the plush leather seat, Eddie took a deep breath and reached for her hand, which she yielded to him. "The night is young...I think," he said.

"Where are you staying?"

"At the magnificent Deauville," Eddie told her. The rum and Natalie, and probably Havana itself, were swirling in his blood.

Natalie spoke to the driver in Spanish. Eddie heard mention of the hotel. "Santa's not taking me home already?"

"There's a quiet place at your hotel where we can talk," she said. He hoped she would make herself more comfortable by moving in his direction, but she seemed content to maintain a polite distance between the two of them. Her hand was warm but inert.

"No clubs, then?"

"I'm not a clubbing kind of girl anymore, Eddie. Sorry."

"Sorry for what?"

"If you're disappointed."

"With you that could never happen," Eddie said. In the dim light of the car her skin was electric against the inky black of her dress. Her legs were crossed with the hem falling well above her knees. For the first time Eddie realized that she wore no nylons. Her legs were bare. He took a deep breath. "Deauville it is."

Natalie gave the driver further instructions, and when they swung into the graceful, curving drive of the hotel, he pulled the car to the curb before reaching the brightly lit *porte cochere*. She took him by the hand and they walked across the lawn to a garden path that led them to the pool area. It occurred to Eddie that she was not particularly wanting to be seen out in public with him. They came to a pergola with vines climbing over it. In the pergola was what Eddie's grandmother had used to call a glider, kind of a sofa on rails that had a back-and-forth movement to it if you swung your legs. He had come all the way to Havana to find himself back on his grandmother's front porch in Ocean Springs, Mississippi. With the girl of his dreams. Or beyond his dreams.

They sat. Eddie made a point of parking himself as cozily close to her as he could. Their upper arms touched, their thighs were partially conjoined, and their entwined hands now rested in Natalie's lap. It was as much heaven as Eddie could stand, for the moment. He turned to look at her. A certain glance from her and his life would never be his own again. "You mentioned that you're not a clubbing girl anymore. It sounds like you used to be."

"Once upon a time. If you're a pretty girl growing up in Havana and your family has a little money, that's part of your life."

"And if your family doesn't have money?"

She laughed mirthlessly and turned their hands over

in her lap. "You'll never be seen at the Tropicana, that's for sure. Or at the Deauville."

"What about those so-called cocksuckers at your table tonight? Do they have money?"

"When they're devoted to sucking cock they don't need it." Spoken flatly, her words carried an edge that made Eddie pause. Something told him that this was not the path he wanted to go down.

"Tell me about your boyfriend."

"What makes you think I have one?"

"I've seen enough of the Cuban guys. They're not going to overlook a girl like you." Eddie was watching the side of her face, but she kept her eyes trained on the pool, visible not far away through the decorative growth around the pergola.

"Well, he's been away for awhile. Not on the island."

"In the USA?"

Now she looked at him, and then looked back at the pool. She was no longer the self-assured, assertive girl that had dealt with Rooney at the bar a lifetime ago. She was somebody else, but Eddie didn't know who. "He just got back earlier this month."

"I would've thought you'd be with him on Christmas Eve."

"He's not in Havana. Look, Eddie, no offense, but let's talk about something else. How did you like the Tropicana, anyway?"

"Except for meeting you there, I can't remember a thing about it."

"It's just as well. That whole scene won't last much longer anyway."

Here came her private darkness again. Eddie squared his upper body in her direction. "Natalie, would you mind very much if we shared a kiss?" While it's true that in Eddie's overheated core he yearned to solder himself to this girl forever, he was at the same time cooling his jets, hoping just to prolong the bliss he was feeling in her presence.

"I thought we already did that."

"No, that was a kiss I stole. I'd rather you gave me one."

She turned her head in his direction and lifted her chin. Her eyes met Eddie's. "If that's really what you want, you'd better just take it."

Eddie reached up his right hand, placed his fingers at the base of her neck, and drew her towards him. When he placed his lips on hers, she drew her breath in sharply through her nostrils. The fresh tropical taste of her was like nothing Eddie had ever experienced. In spite of himself, his loins ticked urgently. He flicked his tongue in search of hers, but she was not forthcoming, although she seemed content to leave their mouths coupled together. When after an interval Eddie took his hand away from her neck and placed it on her bare knee, she slowly inhaled and pulled herself away. They regarded one another at close range. Time, which earlier had been racing, had now come to a halt. "Eddie, for me that's not what this evening's all about. I hope you'll understand."

Still reeling from her kiss, Eddie plunged ahead despite her protest. "Natalie, please come with me to my room. We could have a Christmas breakfast in bed."

"You're completely forgetting my mother. That's not very gentlemanly." A trace of a smile played at the corners of her mouth.

"There's a phone in the room. We could call her and wish her a Merry Christmas."

Breaking the contact of their upper bodies, Natalie drew back and regarded Eddie from a more circumspect distance. "I could do that." She reached across and brushed the side of Eddie's face with the back of her fingers, almost as one might calm a disturbed child. "And I'm sure you would be able to show me quite a good time. There's only one problem, which is that I actually like you."

"I don't quite get it. That's a problem?" At this point Eddie was beginning to believe he was being toyed with. The thought occurred to him that Natalie was actually a party girl, and was just setting the hook, setting it deep, before she reeled him in and made a play for his credit card. The thought further aroused him.

"Most of you who come from the US are here for the same thing: wild sex with a luscious Cuban showgirl. As far as I'm concerned, the whole picture is completely cynical, and I'd have to think very little of you to let that happen."

Eddie blinked. "Couldn't you find it in your heart to despise me just a bit, then? For the next hour or so?" At this they both laughed. As the laughter tapered off, Natalie leaned forward, cupped Eddie's head from behind, and kissed him fiercely, her tongue filling the void in him, the scent of her permeating his nostrils, the animal warmth of her drawing him into an ocean of wild and dangerous currents. Eddie had to struggle to keep his hands from diving beneath that cocktail dress as the kiss went on, and then it was finished and she released him. Her hair was in disarray and her mouth was momentarily slack. She breathed in deeply. "That's all I can offer you, Eddie. You'll have to be content."

Eddie toyed briefly with the idea of simply overwhelming her, right there in the pergola. It was a bad idea, and he knew it. But he couldn't conceal his disappointment, and didn't want to. "I guess I don't get it. Why did you wait for me at the club if you don't want to be with me?" He still held one of her hands, which, after a moment, she gently withdrew.

"Because I wanted to give you some important advice, that's why." From the clutch she held on her lap, Natalie withdrew a small brush and began restoring her appearance as she continued. "The Tropicana is a dangerous place. The whole island is getting to be a very dangerous place. And it's only going to get worse. Don't go back there, and tell your friends not to go either."

Eddie wasn't entirely buying it. "It sure didn't seem that dangerous. Unless you count getting taken for a ride to nowhere by a beautiful party girl."

Natalie was applying lip gloss, and shot him a look almost like the one she had earlier directed at Rooney. Eddie immediately regretted receiving a look like that. But her features softened quickly and she went on. "Officially the government will tell you there are no problems at all.

But everybody in the street knows different. Who are you gonna believe?" She closed her clutch and reaching across, took Eddie's hand to soften the finality of her next words. "There's a lot more at stake here than a night on the town, Eddie. I enjoy your company, but my main priority is to see that you and your friends get home safely. Don't come back to Cuba after this."

Eddie wasn't satisfied. Far from it. Instead of a stirring memory of an exhilarating romantic interlude he was going to go home with some kind of a crazy warning? "Is this about Batista? About the so-called cocksuckers?"

If the bluntness of Eddie's query put her off, Natalie didn't show it. She looked at him with a gaze of disarming tenderness. "It's more about my boyfriend. He's not in Havana tonight, but he's on his way, and when he gets here, Batista will be leaving. And then all hell will break loose. It won't be safe for anyone."

"Is your boyfriend a gangster or something?"

"The gangsters are all with Batista, Eddie. He's not a gangster. He's a patriot."

Eddie was in no mood for politics. He watched her. As his passions subsided, he was beginning to accept the fact that she might be completely sincere, and that a sexual encounter had never been on her mind, only on his. He ached for her still but was ready to withdraw his claim. "That boyfriend of yours is one lucky guy," he conceded. "I want you to know, at least, that I've never met a girl like you. And I get the feeling that I never will again."

"That's quite a tribute, Eddie. Which I'll accept." With one more squeeze of his hand, Natalie stood. "I need to get back now."

Eddie stood. Facing one another, they moved into a spontaneous embrace. They held on to one another for a string of heartbeats. Her face against his shoulder, her head tucked under his chin, Natalie folded herself fully into him, and at the same time, held herself somehow apart. It was not sexual by any means, and yet it communicated something of complete acceptance and understanding. Reflecting later,

Eddie realized it was the kind of an embrace you would never get from a party girl or even a girlfriend.

Natalie relaxed her embrace and came out of Eddie's arms. When he looked at her, it seemed that her eyes were momentarily full. She reached for his hand and together they walked out of the pergola and along the pathway towards the circular drive. Once they reached the perimeter of the bougainvillea bushes, she stopped and squeezed his hand. "This is as far as we go, Eddie. I'm going to leave alone. So please, don't follow me. Just stay here and watch me go. One last tribute. Can you do that?"

Eddie couldn't answer, but squeezed her hand in return before dropping it. Leaning in, she raised her lips and gave him a brief kiss. Squaring her shoulders she stepped out into the light coming from the hotel entrance and moved away, Eddie watching her go. He moved a few steps out into the light to keep her in sight as long as he could. Down the driveway he could see the lights come on and the car begin to move up along the curb to meet her. Then the restraint which had served him so well throughout the evening momentarily abandoned him and he jogged after her, catching up with her just as she reached the car. The look she gave him was not welcoming, but she didn't appear to be surprised either. She already had the door open when he drew up in front of her. Across the top of the open door he confronted her. "Before you get in that car, Natalie, answer me one question: will you marry me this morning and come and live by the ocean and have my children?"

"Merry Christmas, Eddie. Stay away from Cuba," she said, not unkindly, before ducking her head and sliding into the backseat of the car.

"I had to ask," Eddie said into the darkness of the backseat. Then he pushed the door shut and with the tires crunching on the gravel, the car moved off into the night.

On a Christmas morning in Havana when a man might reasonably expect to linger for a time in bed, with or without company, and watch the delicate play of tropical light on the high white ceilings of his lovely bayfront hotel room, Eddie was yanked indecorously from his slumber by an insistent rapping on the door. It was not a room service kind of summons. "Who the hell is it?" Eddie demanded to know without getting out of bed.

The rapping stopped, a key rattled in to door, and before Eddie knew it, two men in cheap suits had barged right into his room. While one parked himself in front of the door, the other approached and stood over the bed, where Eddie had swung himself up into a seated position with his feet on the floor. "Mr. Eddie Coyle. That's you, right?" The man was a skinny Cuban with Miami-accented English, dark jowls and the rumpled careless look of a government worker or a pawnshop owner. As he stood over Eddie his eyes scanned the room taking in as much of Eddie's life as they could. From where he sat, Eddie could smell him: stale sweat, cheap cologne, black tobacco.

"You've got some fucking manners," Eddie told him.

"You bet," the man said. "I've got a nice big gun too, right inside my coat. You wanna argue with me? Get up and get dressed, we're taking a ride." He spoke to the other man in that Cuban Spanish that Eddie couldn't follow. Eddie stood up. He was bigger than the guy, whoever he was.

"Maybe you'd better explain what the hell you're doing in my room. Or should I just call the desk and find out?"

"You ain't callin' nobody, Mr. Eddie," the fellow said matter-of-factly. He had backed away from Eddie slightly and now withdrew his wallet, opened it, and flashed a shiny gold badge for Eddie to see. "My name is Captain Cesar Quiroa, National Police. I'm here to escort you to the boat so you can get back to the USA without any more difficulties."

"I didn't come by boat," Eddie said. "I came on a plane and I've got a return ticket for day after tomorrow. And I haven't had any difficulties at all." Eddie was resisting the thought that these cartoonish characters had the power to throw a big wrench right in the middle of his Cuban Christmas vacation.

"Yeah, well, not until now, anyway," Quiroa said,

and turned away. In a flash, the other man came up on Eddie's side and landed a blow behind his ear with some kind of short billy or blackjack that put Eddie on his knees tumbling in the middle a hazy, swimming universe filled with strange lights and distorted sounds. As he struggled to catch his breath and reassert his grasp on his surroundings, he understood very clearly that his Christmas vacation in Cuba was ending early.

The two men pitched Eddie's belongings haphazardly into his suitcase, cleaned out the bathroom and swept his gear from the bedside table. Disoriented and hurting, Eddie got himself dressed, and hoped they weren't stealing from him as they went. Not more than twenty minutes after they had stormed into his room, the three men were in the elevator heading down to the lobby. "What about my friends? The fellows I came with?" Eddie wanted to know.

"Probably still sleeping in their beds," Quiroa said. "You gonna be traveling by yourself."

In the big black Mercury, Eddie sat in the backseat with the two men flanking him. The ride wasn't a long one, and Eddie tried to get additional information. Since the detainee had decided to behave himself, Quiroa was casual and forthcoming. "The reason you leaving on the ferry is that there ain't no more flights back to Yunay Estay until tomorrow. And you gotta be off the island today."

"You still haven't given me any explanation for all of this." He wasn't being combative, it was a simple statement of fact. "I don't even know which laws I may have broken."

Quiroa had his eyes averted, watching the neighborhood through which they were passing. "Look, you probably not a bad guy. Just call it bad associations, Chico. You made friends with the wrong people."

Eddie thought of Natalie's uniformed friends at the Tropicana. Then he thought of Natalie. Then he asked a stupid question. He was a mainland gringo, he had the right. "You guys work for Batista, right?"

"*Policia Nacional*," Quiroa reiterated. "You figure it out."

Within just a few more blocks the Mercury was down in

the port area where uniformed workers were just securing the boarding gates of the large car-ferry. The three men exited the car and Eddie was escorted rapidly through the terminal, his escorts flashing their badges and Eddie's passport as they went. At the foot of the gangway, Quiroa handed across to Eddie his suitcase and passport. "This is as far as we go with you, pal. Have a nice trip, and write us a postcard sometime." As they turned away, Eddie reached out and lightly grasped Quiroa by the upper arm. "Has this got anything to do with the female company I had last night?"

The detective's eyes widened in a parody of surprise. "Female company is the name of the game here in Havana, Senor Eddie. Everybody knows, in Cuba we got the bes'-lookin' ladies in the world." He tugged his arm free of Eddie's grasp. "But if I was you, I would not try coming back for more, you got me?" The two stood for a long moment at the foot of the gangway, Eddie trying to decipher Quiroa's irony. A screech from the ferry's whistle ended the moment. "Have a nice trip home, my friend."

Up the gangway Eddie went. He dropped his suitcase along the railing and watched a minute later from the lower deck as the sliver of green seawater between boat and dock began to widen. He could feel the engines rumbling as the boat gained headway. On the dock, Quiroa and his associate stood watching the vessel until it cleared the breakwater and made for the open sea beyond, just as they had been instructed. Eddie had moved aft and watched until the ferry slip had disappeared and the colonial spires of Old Havana stood out against a blue copula of Christmas sky. His head was throbbing. He picked up his suitcase and went in search of a *Cuba Libre* and a couple of aspirin.

Back in Biloxi, the whole affair took on an air of unreality for Eddie. He struggled with feelings of resentment and self-reproach. The memories of the glorious Tropicana, of the intoxication he had experienced in Natalie's presence, and of the passionate kiss she had bestowed upon him along with her dire warnings he tried to catalogue away, not wanting to discard them entirely, but not wanting to torture himself unnecessarily with them either. A week after his return, over the telephone he briefly sketched for Brant the circumstances of his untimely departure from Cuba, but he left out the part about Natalie. Brant wanted to believe that they had given Eddie the bum's rush because of the altercation, and Eddie was content for him to believe that. "The reason they didn't nab me and Rooney, I'm guessing, is that we never came back to the hotel that night. Ended up in one of those bordellos on Copas Street. It wasn't what I would call a great environment, but Rooney was bound and determined to fuck the daylights out of somebody, and I couldn't hardly turn him loose on his own." About that much, Eddie reflected, Natalie and Quiroa had been quite correct: for the gringos, it was all about the pussy. Eddie had no doubt, however, that if they wanted you, Quiroa and his people had the resources to find you at any hour in any location in Havana. And of the three companions, he was the only one they had wanted.

It wasn't until nearly two months later that a chance encounter with one of his Biloxi business associates shed new light on the events of Eddie's aborted Cuban vacation. Phil Boudreaux had been in Havana early in the New Year, looking forward to a visit to the world-famous Tropicana. "You guys probably went there, right?"

"We were there one night," Eddie allowed. "Christmas Eve, in fact."

"I guess you heard then."

"Maybe not. Heard what?"

"Shit, the place was closed down. All the reservations were cancelled. We ended up going to the Sans Souci instead. One of Trafficante's clubs." Phil kept up with the gangster business, know some of the bigger bosses by name.

"Closed for good you mean?"

"Probably not. Just closed because of the explosion. They blew the fuckin' place up."

"Blew it up?"

"New Year's eve, pal. Bomb went off in the nightclub. Made a big mess the way I heard it. Made a bunch of people mighty nervous too. You can imagine which people…"

That was it, then. Natalie had been perfectly on the level with him the whole time. About the danger, about the boyfriend. Probably even about the cocksuckers.

And about trying to protect him.

From a polite distance, then, Eddie and all his gringo countrymen watched as the Cuban situation deteriorated over the next year and a half. Despite Batista's assurances of maintaining civil peace and political continuity, to so-called *"barbudos"*, or "bearded ones" and their folk-hero leader Fidel Castro kept the pressure on, and on the second New Year's Eve after the Tropicana explosion they rolled into Havana and Batista abandoned the island, just like Natalie had told Eddie that he would. As Eddie watched the newsreel accounts of the tumultuous flag-waving crowds parading through the streets of Havana, he couldn't help himself, he looked for a glimpse of her. Her boyfriend would have been a *barbudo*, he guessed, just as he had by then guessed that despite their precautions on that Christmas morning, someone, probably her driver, had reported their tryst, which had resulted in Eddie's rapid departure. Even then the Batista people must have feared and respected her, likely because of her family connections as much as her unbridled tongue and outspoken nature. After the *barbudos* had settled in (and received almost overnight the recognition of the United States government), Eddie found himself caught up in the improbable fantasy that he would get a scratchy long-distance call from Havana, with Natalie professing her tender feelings for him and her willingness to have his children after all, could he fly down and whisk her away? It was a delusion that ultimately disrespected both he and Natalie, however, and in the interest of his own emotional maturity, after a time he forcibly shed himself of it.

Which is not to say that he overcame entirely the desire for romance in his life. He accepted it as a personality disorder that he would have to live with. Natalie had left a void that he was able to patch over for some years with sexual adventures, hard work, big-ticket purchases, travels to foreign climes (though of course not to Cuba), and eventually with a marriage, followed by divorce and a second marriage. At the time of his encounter in the airport lounge in Dallas with the knowledgeable expert on Havana sex tourism, his second divorce was nearly finalized. In fact, he had already encountered a new love interest, a compact little redhead with an hourglass figure, a terrific sense of humor, and a healthy appetite for the kind of carnal knowledge that so interested Eddie. Just the week before Eddie's trip, the one that routed him through Dallas, they had spent a long weekend at Eddie's timeshare in Nassau lollygagging on the beach, parasailing, dining out, dancing at a nightclub, and making love in the moonlight. On the second evening, as they stood watching the sun set from the balcony while drinking a nice Malbec, Sheila had pulled Eddie to her and snuggled her head against his chest in a touching display of trust, affection and contentment. For most men it would have been a sublime romantic moment, but for Eddie there was a familiar hollowness at the center of it. The embrace he had shared years earlier with Natalie in Havana had been something in a category by itself. It had been the kind of embrace that signaled a love that was both unfulfilled and unfulfillable. Which of course is the most durable and memorable love of all.

The treatment he had received in Havana, Eddie came to conclude, was something that a man doesn't receive very often in life.

But he had received it in Havana. And now, for better or worse, he had it for always.

The Rescuer

I've got my wife in the car with me.

Not just any car, either.

We're riding in the limo. You know the one, the big slate-blue Continental. Over twenty-one feet long, weighs nearly four tons. In the front seat, Greer and Kellerman, two solid citizens. (I know the names of the all the fellows in my detail.) On the jump seats are the Governor and his wife. He's one of Lyndon's show ponies, sharp and shiny, but in contrast to the woman I married, his wife is a dowdy southern matron. In the plush two-tone blue leather back seat my wife in her pink Chanel outfit is sitting next to me, a splash of red roses across her lap, her slender knees visible below the hem of her dress.

The red roses are hideous, but the pink is a real standout.

Contrary to rumors, I'm deeply in love with my wife. She's 34 years of age, firm and shapely even after four pregnancies. Small-busted, bedroom eyes, lovely wide mouth, great legs, very shapely behind, and possessing all the arts of seduction which she's had since the age of five or thereabouts. Most girls acquire those arts from their mothers, which is why none of my sisters was especially endowed in that regard. My wife, however, is a true concubine, born to seduce.

Yesterday afternoon, as we were taxiing out in San Antonio for the flight over to Houston, she'd flashed me a look. It was one of those shorthand looks that a married woman uses from time to time. "If we do, you'll have to have time to get dressed afterwards," I told her. She just smiled. Let's go ahead, that was her attitude. So we did. A quickie in that cozy little stateroom on the too-small bed in the private suite aboard Special Air Mission 26000. She held on to me tightly, and I gave her what I had. "Oh, Bunny," she said. When we were done she said, "I love you."

"I love you too," I told her, and changed my shirt. We were back on the ground less than ten minutes later.

But now, after a night in the Texas Hotel among the good citizens of Fort Worth and a fifteen- minute hop in the big 707 with the baby-blue trim over to Love Field, we're back in the limo. It's our fifth motorcade in the last two days. It's warm in the Continental, bright and warm with the sun coming off that leather. Without my Saratogas, which under the circumstances I can't wear, I have to squint against that big Texas sky. Voters are voters, you've got to respect them, no matter how damn bright it gets. My wife is squinting too, and at one point she slips on her sunglasses. With a look and a word I correct her. The fact is there are probably as many people out to see her as there are to see me, and you never want to distance yourself from the voters, even if it's only by slipping on a pair of sunglasses. It had been that way in San Antonio yesterday and Houston last night. She's bringing the full power of her seductive arts to bear. Not only am I madly in love with her, but I'm damn glad she agreed to come along on the trip.

This is the first road trip she has taken with me since we got to the White House. Two years and nine months. My sister Pat has come out with me numerous times. Pat's a trooper, through and through, a purebred political animal. My wife is not, and that is a large part of her appeal to the voters. They can sense that she's not out there trolling for votes. Retail politics goes against her grain, against her nature, against her breeding. And this Texas trip is brutal – five cities, six receptions, seven motorcades in two days. She's a private woman, a woman who likes to curl up in her sweater with her Newports and a good book. I don't mind her devotion to solitude. But I also know what a great political asset she is. Her sex appeal reels in the men, and her fashion sense enchants the women. (Her brief comments in Spanish last night at the Rice Hotel in Houston charmed the bejeesus out of the entire room while not incidentally arousing in me a strong desire to pin her down again on that small bed on the flight back to Fort Worth, an impulse that died with the lateness of the hour and the busyness of the next day's schedule looming.) When she agreed to make the Texas trip I accepted that as a positive omen not only for my presidency, but also for our marriage. Airplanes, cars, hotels, standing in receiving lines, shaking lots of hands and being utterly charming to people you don't know and frankly couldn't care less about – retail politics can be a terrible grind. Unless maybe you're Irish, then it has a certain inexorable rightness to it. Politics and funerals, that's where our Irish heritage really shines.

It's a seven-mile trip from Love Field to downtown. So I've been told. The first part of the route is on a highway. The crowds are sparse and we travel at a pretty good clip, 30 miles an hour or more. Once we get into the downtown area the crowds begin to build and we have to move at a progressively slower pace. At one point I ask Greer to stop the limo in response to a sign: *"Mr. President, stop and shake our hands."* Half a dozen ladies press close to the car and I am able to comply briefly with their request. After less than half-a-minute we move on. This isn't my first Dallas motorcade. Lyndon and I had visited the city in September of 1960, hoping to salvage a state that, quite frankly, nobody viewed as a winner for the Democrats. (Eisenhower had carried it easily in each of his wins.) We had come up through Dealey Plaza sitting in the back of a white Ford convertible without any Secret Service protection at all (we were only candidates at the time), the crowds had been large and enthusiastic and people had been able to approach the vehicle, particularly when the roadway ahead was thronged so badly that we came to a complete stop, which happened on numerous occasions. At one point a particularly bold female admirer reached out and tried to snatch my pocket square, but with a bit of sleight of hand I managed to reach across, pull Lyndon's from his pocket and pass it to her instead – one good Texan deserves another. As it developed, we managed to carry Texas that November by about two percentage points. Lyndon would of course claim to be responsible for this, but I was never convinced of anybody's affection for the big galoot. Lyndon could be an effectively intimidating presence in the backrooms of the Capitol where deals were hammered out and people were convinced to go along with ideas for which they had no enthusiasm. But Lyndon will never be mistaken for being a particularly lovable, inspiring or even trustworthy fellow. To his credit, he knows this. So in the hearts of the voters Lyndon appeals to the vindictive side, the petty side, the reactionary side. Can you win elections on that kind of an appeal? You bet you can. But not many of your supporters are going to spend time standing on a downtown street corner to cheer, applaud, or hold up signs when you drive by in your limousine. There has to be something else at work for that to happen.

And whatever that something is, my wife's got it. To be candid, after thirty years of *hausfraus* like Eleanor, Bess, and Mamie, parading my girl before the American public is like introducing a high-octane hooker to a randy schoolboy – the sparks are going to fly. The press likes to proclaim our "star quality" together. Like my father before me, I've spent time in Hollywood, and I've been around enough star quality to know how potent it can be. We're a star-loving people over here in the colonies, a nation of "starfuckers," and if it takes a dose of star quality to arouse the voters, rest assured, arousal is what they'll get.

As happy as it makes me to have her with me, getting my wife out of Washington was accomplished at a cost. She wouldn't be in Texas if there were a newborn infant in his bassinette in the second-floor family quarters of the White House needing her love and attention. But the infant, whom we had named Patrick and who had been born six weeks prematurely, lived less than two days before expiring.

Respiratory failure. My wife never even held him. When I brought her home from the base hospital two days later, she was as tender and sweet and lost as a schoolgirl. She turned to me to save her. Ironic, I know. After my not being there for her during most of the ten years of our married life together, that she would turn to me. But there was also a certain poetic balance to that equation. The child's birth had coincided with the day exactly twenty years earlier when my crew and I had been rescued after the sinking of our patrol boat in the Solomon Islands. We had survived for six days by swimming from one island to another and hiding in an area controlled by the Japanese. So I knew what it was to be rescued. And now it's my turn to be the rescuer.

But there's more. My darling girl had gone off to the Greek Islands with her sister for a little recuperation after the infant died. I wasn't happy about it - her sister is an unstable character, not a positive influence. By the time they got back, I felt pretty certain that I had become linked to that damned Greek in a most intimate, uncomfortable way: he'd already had a fling with her sister, and now he'd gotten my wife into his bed as well. A nasty business, but there were benefits. For one, it added a little *frisson* to our sex life, but more importantly, my wife's natural Catholic guilt over the incident helped me to leverage her into making this road trip with me. So in a sense I've already managed to rescue her from herself. Being out in this sunny Texas weather and being beloved by the voters is a marvelous tonic for each of us.

Hardware stores, finance companies, beauty salons, hat shops, banks, bars, hamburger joints – it's Main Street, USA, the usual mélange of small-town America passing by as we roll along. But in recent months Dallas has shown it isn't like Main Street America at all. General Edwin Walker and his people had sabotaged an appearance by my Ambassador to the U.N. (and our party's Presidential candidate in two elections), the very honorable (too honorable, I always thought) Adlai Stevenson. After having his speech destroyed in an auditorium overrun by Walker sympathizers, Adlai had been obliged to flee the premises after receiving a whack on the head and strands of saliva in his face. Adlai deserved better. This was just one month before my wife and I arrived. Partially as a result of that incident we're accompanied by an extra-large contingent of law-enforcement people, including a squadron of motorcycle cops, along with our own Secret Service detail on the running boards of the second limo, which follows closely on our bumper. I keep the Secret Service detail off the Presidential limo for the same reason I typically refuse the option of the Plexiglas bubble-top – I have no use for the trappings of officialdom that you see in places like Cairo, or Buenos Aires, or Moscow where the implied message is that rulers serve not at the pleasure of the populace but at the point of a gun. It goes against the fundamental nature of the American democratic experiment. *Of the people, by the people, for the people.* Although I've never done it, I'd like to believe that if we so desired, we could pull to a halt right here on Main Street and duck into one of those cafes for a grilled cheese sandwich and a Coke. Exchange some light banter with the fry cook and the waitresses before scooting back to the Continental and continuing on our way. At one point I briefly reach over and take my wife's hand, a gesture that catches her by surprise. Across her lap she's got that large bouquet of red roses and she knows as well as I do under the circumstances we need hands free to hail those voters. Living with a politician has taught her that much. I hold that white-gloved hand just for a moment before letting it go. We're almost like kids on a prom date. Well-dressed kids in a big damn car.

It was just a month after Patrick had died in his hyperbaric chamber that we celebrated our tenth anniversary. Ten years, four pregnancies, two children. Plenty of pain and heartache along the way, much of it self-imposed. She was just a girl when I met her and wooed her, with wide-set hazel eyes and a determined tuck at the corners of her lips that implied that something that had evaded the rest of us was for her, or in her, settled. She had been abroad more than I had, knew something of the world, and was also an accomplished horsewoman, used to mounting large animals and guiding them with nothing more that the pressure from the insides of her thighs. (As her mother had before her, however, she would find that the technique which controlled horses so well seemed not to work with men). She was a brave, disciplined Daddy's Girl with some Irish traits that were immediately endearing: ironic, witty, guarded, romantic. I, on the other hand, was every bit my father's son: jaded, callow, opportunistic, lazy to a fault. When we began seeing one another, I didn't audition for the role of Daddy, but early on I gave my girl some of that Daddy action, and in return she handed me the key to her heart. Initially a state of marriage worked well for each of us. She needed someone to bankroll her sophisticated tastes, and acquiring a young, well-bred, attractive wife just made good sense from my perspective. But then she went and fell in love with me, and that complicated things a good deal. She made up her mind to be a Good Wife, which is not something I was prepared to deal with. In our family good wives are not the norm. Battleaxes, baby-makers, bitches and boozehounds, that's who philanderers tend to marry. She didn't readily fit into any of those categories, and God knows touch football, our favorite outdoor family pastime, left her completely cold. Meanwhile, it took us five years to produce our first child. So on top of our personal struggles, she was something of an outcast among the larger family. More than once they urged me to dump her. That's not so easy when you're a Catholic and the plan is one day for you to become President. So we dug our respective trenches and settled in for the long haul. She stayed out of my wars and I stayed clear of hers. I went on seducing a lot of women, and she responded by living regally on my credit line. Which is not much of a basis for a thriving marriage. And you gather a lot of silent scars along the way. When it came to a tenth anniversary, it was a little surprising to each of us to reach that milestone. Surprising and gratifying, to discover finally that you deserve one another and that, contrary to what you have believed for so many years, this may actually be a good thing.

Coming down Main, three or four blocks ahead you can see open sky at Dealey Plaza. That signals the end of our parade route, after that it's a short hop up the Stemmons Freeway and over to the Trade Mart. Less than three miles to go. I see a clock on a drugstore: 12:25. Another ten minutes we'll be sitting down in the air-conditioning. At that point I see another handheld sign with my wife's name on it. That makes at least a dozen I've seen since we left the airport. She's a hot property in Texas, all right. A hot property in hot pink. And I'm the lucky guy who'll get those 25 electoral votes if enough of these people remember her on election day.

As soon as she was comfortably able after Patrick, I'd wanted to have sex with her. Happy indeed is the man who's happy to romp his wife. That hasn't always been the case with me, a fact that is generally known. I've got no elaborate excuses. The medications. The lower back problems. The undisciplined libido. The multitude of opportunities. Kennedy men have always been skirt-chasers. Isn't that what it was put here for? Especially on those road trips that are part of a politician's life, I've found the quickest and easiest way for me to wind down at the end of a day is to get myself between a woman's legs and let her take it out of me. It isn't love, it isn't making love, sometimes it isn't even intercourse. In many cases I just have the girl in question perform oral sex because I have a compulsive need to produce an erection and *express my potency*, and it works so much better with a girl helping out. (I am not devoid of affection, but that has never been essential to the process.) Now, with the sweet tender girl who came home from the hospital, I was discovering that I was just as happy to be with her (and in her) as she seemed to be to have me. This is something of a revelation. Even on our honeymoon it hadn't been this sweet. Not enough shared grief I suppose. No sense of endings or beginnings. No perception of time running ahead or running out. A full appreciation of the fragility of life is one of the greatest aphrodisiacs of all.

"Oh, Bunny." You're damn right.

Then the buildings end and we're making that ninety-degree turn on Houston Street. Seeing the sky open up like that is a lot like clearing the harbor at Narraganset or Hyannis aboard the *Honey Fitz* in the summertime. Or even better, late spring when the Atlantic breeze still has a bit of bite to it and there is a lovely chop on the water. Across the way the regatta is going on, and I'm parked in my chair on the fantail with one of those Petit Upmanns clamped in my teeth, enjoying the spectacle, the sails poignant against the deep blue, the sun glinting off the whitecaps. Beside me my wife is lost in a book, her smooth, tanned legs curled under her, smoking one of her Newports. Salt air, open horizon, sweater weather. A cold beer. Nothing to arouse the libido like a saltwater day. The *Honey Fitz* has a small stateroom below decks and I'd like nothing better after we clear the harbor than to lure my wife down there with me and give her a quick tumble. She'll like that, I tell myself. Whether it's true or not, the thought that she might is enough to bestir my libidinal urge as we turn the corner onto Elm.

I say "turn the corner" but it's a bit more complex than that: with those long cars and the phalanx of mounted officers in either side of us, it's more like nautical maneuver, shifting the flotilla. We have to virtually back our sails against the wind and pivot in place before we can resume our forward motion, easing down the incline toward the triple underpass where the shade awaits. We've entered an area of green, with grass and low trees bordering the route on either side. The crowds have thinned out considerably. In another moment we'll be able to relax our uplifted arms and sit back for the remainder of the ride. Suddenly, however, my back is bothering me - a sharp, confusing new sensation that I can't immediately identify. Out of the corner of my eye I catch a look from my wife. She's attuned to me so completely, how could I not have honored that loyalty better over the years? She clearly senses that I need her, although I can't quite understand why she has this impression. She leans solicitously in my direction, peering into my face as though she might want to dab something out of my eye. Then, just as we're clear of the harbor, the sky opens wide admitting a brilliant light. Even as I sail towards it, I feel suddenly exhausted. I want to lie down, to pillow my head in the roses on my wife's lap. I need that benediction, that acceptance. She receives me tenderly, the way she always has when I've come to her seeking absolution. She lowers my head onto her lap and puts a gloved hand over my eyes to shield me from the sun so I can go to sleep.

Rescued again.

On Van Ness Avenue

I'm over at Positano's on Van Ness Avenue. Not the dry cleaners, the lounge. It's just a couple of blocks up from Lombard. I've got somebody meeting me there at 5:00 PM. Early, I know, but it's just for cocktails, and I've got something to celebrate, right? After all, I got home again in one piece and I've got my future ahead of me. And that's something.

Positano's isn't one of those Dago joints like you find down in the Marina district, with all the mirrors, the swag carpet, and the red accent lighting. The heavyset guy in a sharkskin suit on a stool near the door. None of that. Positano's is modern, clean Italian, a bright, well-lit place with nice picture windows looking out towards the bay, with chrome and mahogany accents, with a sweeping black formica bar, and with cocktail hostesses in their tasteful white blouses and trim black pants. A gleaming black baby grand set in one corner. I had first visited Positano's with my mother when her health was good and she was able to enjoy a cocktail now and then, so it has some sentimental value to it as well. It's the kind of place where I spot Bill Holden when he comes in.

Bill's got something to celebrate himself. Two or three weekends ago Twentieth Century Fox released his new film *Love is a Many-Splendored Thing,* and it's doing terrific box office. Bill plays a war correspondent who falls in love with a beautiful Eurasian doctor in Hong Kong, and the title song from the film has been number one on the charts for over a month. The Four Aces sing it. You know the song: *"Once, on a high and windy hill, two lovers kissed in the morning mist, and the world stood still..."* You got a better song about romance than that one, pal, I'd sure like to hear it.

Anyway, it's not entirely by chance that Bill drops by, even though he's known to frequent Positano's when he's in town. We had spoken by phone when my ship got in from Honolulu three days earlier. Since Bill had somewhat patterned his character in the film after me, he wanted to touch base. And no, it didn't bother me one bit that Bill borrowed from me in his depiction of Mark Elliott, overseas correspondent. Anybody who looks as good in a cashmere sport coat as Bill Holden does can have anything from me that he wants. You want a snapshot of a true-blue American male, circa 1955, Bill Holden is your guy.

On this sunny afternoon in San Francisco Bill's not alone. How could he be? I mean, this is the guy who a year earlier had made back-to-back films with Grace Kelly. Of course she fell in love with him. How could she not? Since he's a married man, however, Bill's discreet about his female companionship, and doesn't talk out of school. With him in Positano's is a very young woman he introduces as Jean, using the French pronunciation *Jeanne*. She's extremely good-looking, although in a tomboyish sort of way with her close-cropped hair and her lack of makeup. She's wearing a simple sleeveless blouse and toreador pants and she looks to be scarcely out of her teens. "She's over from Paris, just getting started in the business," Bill explains without irony. "I told her you had just come back from Indochina and she wanted to meet you."

We order drinks. I'm happy with my beer, but Bill is strictly a highball guy with a preference for blended whiskey. Neat. Jeanne wants white wine. Underage? Never mind that underage business. If you can walk, you can get a drink in Positano's. I was in Spain during the Civil War, and typically they sent the children to the shop to pick up the day's supply. If you were old enough to carry the wine back from the shop, you were entitled to drink as much of it as you liked. Which always made sense to me. It's not like those Spanish kids had a supply of milk or soda-pop like our American kids.

"So. You saw the film?" Bill wants to know.

"I did see the film," I tell Bill. "You did good."

"So did you. What about that ending?" he asks me. In the film his character is dramatically, romantically killed in a strafing attack in Korea while typing a letter to his girlfriend the doctor. In *The Bridges at Toki Ri* the year earlier he had died by getting machine-gunned in a muddy ditch, also in Korea - making a widow out of Grace Kelley in the process. Two years after I saw him in Positano's, he would again die of gunshot wounds, this time in a river in Indochina. Our boy Bill was the indestructible American.

"That's one part that I'm glad is not true-to-life. At least not true to my life." I had been in a forward area in Korea, and again more recently in Indochina, but as a journalist I did my best to keep out line of fire, and had had pretty good success with this tactic.

"You said it there," says Bill, and we lift our drinks together. At Bill's invitation I had worked briefly as a script consultant on the film, but hadn't received a screen credit. I hadn't been in favor of the hero getting killed, but the other writers insisted the public would want it that way. Apparently they had been right.

Jean/Jeanne has something to say, but she says it in French which, in spite of the time I had recently spent in Saigon, is not one of the languages that I speak or follow very well. She looks at Bill with admiring eyes when she says it. "She says she liked the scene on the hill under the tree when the girl lies down in the grass and we kiss goodbye," Bill translates.

"An all-time classic," I agree.

"As far as I'm, concerned, you're the all-time classic, pal," Bill says. "I read your stuff as often as I can."

"Much obliged for the endorsement, Bill, but the thing is, I never get the girl." I look at the girl and grin when I say it. She gets my drift and flashes me a sweet look in return.

"Getting the girl is overrated in my book," Bill laughs.

"Easy for you to say," I tell him. And we laugh. Bill has on a nice pair of khaki slacks and a navy blue cashmere sweater. Those penetrating blue eyes. He's ruddy and tanned and looks ten years younger than he should. That's the thing about Bill. The thing that makes him big box-office. On the screen he gives the impression that things which might produce a lot of anxiety for most of us mortals – slipping in and out of war zones, romancing beautiful, headstrong women, straightening out rough characters, or for that matter, pushing forty years of age – are much more manageable for him. And he gives the same impression sitting across the table from me in Positano's.

"You gonna stick around for awhile?" Bill wants to know. "We're going up to Tahoe tomorrow for a couple of days at the Cal-Neva. Do some sunning and sailing. You should come up."

"Kinda rich for my blood, Bill," I tell him. The Cal-Neva is well-known as a swanky hangout for big shots – film stars, celebrities, mob types. It's right on the California-Nevada line, in fact the state line is painted right though the swimming pool. Now, if I had a girl to take along – and not necessarily a teen-ager either – it might be a pretty attractive proposition. "Besides, my mother's here in the city and her health hasn't been good. I probably need to spend some time."

We chat for maybe half an hour after that. Nothing of substance, really. If there is substance, it is the backdrop provided by Positano's. By Van Ness Avenue. By the city of my birth. By the fact that all these things are, for the moment, eternal and everlasting. As are Bill Holden, his young friend Jean, and myself. As a writer, I tend to frame things perhaps more dramatically than others, but that's where a writer's best stories come from anyway – from finding substance in the insubstantial details of everyday existence. Still, Bill has always been solicitous of my career, wants to know where I'll be going and what I'll be writing about next. "That business in Indochina's kind of winding down, at least that's what they're telling us."

"Well, the French are out for sure," I say, and look at Jean. *"Sa vas pas le Indochine,"* I tell her. She turns down her mouth at the corners and shrugs in that utterly dismissive way that the French have. Then she smiles at me, the untroubled smile of youth. She has the charmingly fluid mannerisms of an actress already. "But I'm not sure about things winding down over there." I don't know it then, and I'm not sure if Bill does, that his next film will be set in Indochina and will prove to be a huge success. I won't be invited to work on the script, however.

Over Bill's shoulder the light is softening as it will do at a certain hour in San Francisco. One of my favorite things about my city is that late afternoon light, which has travelled across the country and is now setting out to traverse the mighty Pacific. You realize that once it's gone, the whole country will be in darkness.

We order another round. I think it's Jean's idea. Or *Jeanne's*. Not that you have to twist Bill's arm when it comes to booze. About the time the drinks arrive the pianist shows up, and probably owing to the fact that the manager cues him, as soon as he sits down at the baby grand, he goes into the theme song from Bill's movie. Bill doesn't catch it right away but Jean does, and she runs her finger along the side of Bill's cheek to get his attention. *"Ta chaisson,"* she tells him. He grins at her and she leans across and presses her forehead affectionately against his shoulder. You can't blame her – it is, as I say, a seductive melody, and Positano's is that kind of place. In that neighborhood Van Ness is not what you'd call a romantic destination. It's more of a working neighborhood: dry cleaners, furniture shops, a hardware store, savings and loan institutions, even a car dealership or two. A street like you might find in Joplin, Missouri, or Ashtabula, Ohio. Except for the light which I mentioned. You won't find that in the Midwest. And you probably won't find Bill Holden with an up-and-coming French starlet on his arm, either.

"So you're sure I can't talk you into running up to Tahoe

with us? Those people never get to hear war stories about real wars. You might be able to educate 'em." This time I catch the irony in his tone.

"Sound likes a good time, Bill." I glance at Jean and wonder if she is going to be part of it. I decide she is. "The truth is, I'm hoping to stick around the city for a few months, catch up on other parts of my life," That is the God's truth. Ninety days out of pocket can leave you with truncated relationships, unpaid bills, unfinished projects, and friends wondering where you disappeared to. Unless they read your byline, which they usually don't. There will be time for the Cal-Neva someday, when I have a little more disposable income, maybe. And a girl who brushes the side of my cheek with her fingers, that would be nice. When you're on the road as much as I've been, you're I probably not getting your cheek brushed a great deal.

Bill has finished his highball and now shifts in his seat and looks at Jean, then back at me. "We're gonna take off, sport," he says, stubbing out his cigarette. "Some people have put together a dinner for us down at Jack's. We've got a car service. Can we drop you anywhere?"

"Much obliged, Bill, but I've got a couple of my cohorts on their way over, so I'll stick around and nurse my beer. But it's always a treat to catch up with you."

They slide out of the booth on their side and I slide out on mine. Jean comes to me, places her hands on my shoulders, and gives me the lovely French send-off, a breathy kiss on each cheek accompanied by the press of her upper body against mine. Bill's handshake is robust, his gaze penetrating and direct. As they make their way towards the entrance, a number of patrons are watching them and even the pianist briefly lifts one hand in tribute. Bill brings a couple of fingers up to his brow, a casual salute to acknowledge their acknowledgement. He has his other hand resting on the back of Jean's neck when they hit the door. Through the windows I see the two of them sliding into the backseat of a big black Buick. The patrons of Positano's return to their private lives and conversations. I slip back into the booth where my half-finished beer awaits. It feels for a moment as if the whole world has just walked out the door, and things will have to start all over again if we're going to have any future at all.

Part IV

What A Girl Has To Do

"She reminded me of well-bred girls
I had seen during my brief college
days, her fine features infused with
the healthy glow of higher education,
proper grooming, and a guiding
ambition. I could tell at once that
she was the type of gal who insisted
on getting down to business, but I
couldn't tell what the business might
be."

Penance in Par'Bo

The Empty Bench

After he had finished paying for the ticket at the counter next to the gun rack and the soda case, he turned around, and she wasn't there. His first thought was that maybe she had gone to the rest room, but before he could act on it, he caught sight of the top of her head under the dusty light filtering through the plate glass window in front of the building. He folded the envelope and tucked it into the pocket of his denim jacket while he was walking across the room. Then he pushed open the glass door, and found her sitting on the bench next to the generator pump on the sidewalk in front of the bus station.

"You ain't cold out here?" He stood above her, not sure what to do with himself. After she didn't answer, he moved closer and seated himself on the bench next to her. He sat on the edge of the bench as though he might have to get up at any minute.

She wasn't talking. He'd pretty much expected that. But her silence wasn't a scolding silence, or the kind of silence that invited him to find a way to talk to her. It was a breakaway silence. The kind that gets deeper and more final the longer it goes on.

"Babe, I got your envelope right here," he said, withdrawing it from his jacket pocket. He realized that he could see his breath in the early spring air. "You got a safe place where you want to keep it?"

After a moment the girl reached over, took the envelope

from between his hands, undid the clasp of her purse, thrust the envelope inside, and re-fastened the clasp. It was all done in one efficient maneuver, accomplished without conscious thought. It was the business of the day at hand, which must be done when the need arises, not sooner and not later.

"It's got two hundred and twenty dollar," he said, looking straight ahead towards the dim light from the street. There was a street light overhead, but one of the bulbs was busted and the light was tired. There was no traffic moving on the street. "I got rid of a heifer at the auction barn last weekend," he explained. He snuck a glance at her face, hoping he would not find her looking all tore up. In fact, she looked pretty calm. Tired maybe. Tired and a little put out. "I wished to hell you'd let me come," he said truthfully.

At this point, she dug back into her purse and pulled out a pack of Marlboro Lights and a disposable lighter. She withdrew one, lit it, replaced the lighter and cigarettes in her purse, took a deep drag, and sat back looking out into the street. Business of the day.

"I could still get a ticket," he said.

"We talked about this already, Steve." Her voice was level, but lacking in interest. Since she had spoken to him, he felt at liberty to turn and look at her. Looking at her was the one thing that had come easy in their relationship. Most of the rest of it - the getting together, the romancing, the talking, the planning, and now the separation - had been hard, difficult, time-consuming, beset with problems. She had even taken to jokingly referring to herself in conversation with him as "your problem child." But looking at her was the easy part. It was also the part that had eventually created their problems.

"How come you feel like you need to go through this all on your own, anyway?"

At this question, she looked at him for the first time. It was a look that answered his question and then some. He went back to staring out at the street.

"I don't want you callin' my momma while I'm gone," she said.

"I never was in the habit of callin' your momma, Laura."

"Well, don't get started now." The cigarette had opened her up somehow. She took another long pull. "I swear to God."

He glanced at her and found her face tugged into a tight smile. "Beth wanted to come with me, you know. I told her no, just like I told you."

"How about I call Beth then?" he asked, and they both grinned a little. He reached across and felt for her hand. She let him take it. It was limp and very cool to the touch. "You know I love you, don't you babe?"

"In your own way," she said. "Mostly you loved bein' in my panties."

It was a flat statement, spoken without rancor, but close enough to the truth to make him flinch. "I'll confess to that," Steve said. "But I never had no doubt that I wanted to take care of you."

"Well, you bought me the bus ticket, and you got me the money for the clinic. That makes us just about even. What time is it?" Steve didn't wear a watch, but looking over his shoulder back into the building, he could make out the red and white-faced Nehi clock above the ticket counter.

"Twenty past," he said. "If you're cold, we can just as well wait in the truck."

Her hand had warmed up, and she squeezed his hand a little bit. "Seem like waiting in the truck is where we got in trouble in the first place."

"Not parked on Main St. we didn't." They had parked near the quarry, in one of the river overlooks, and sometimes on Steve's family's property. They really had had no other place to go.

From down south, Steve thought he could sense the approach of the Greyhound. "If anything happens, you will call the house, right? Leave me a message?"

"I ain't calling, Steve. I'll be back by Thursday. If you still feel like you've got to know everything, we can talk then." He wished she hadn't called him by his name, but by one of the endearments she had formerly used. Those private names he hadn't always cared for at the time, but now he would have welcomed.

Steve's hearing had always been keen. They heard the bus downshifting as it climbed up the alley between the post office and Tootie's Bar, and watched as the headlights flashed off the side of the Dollar Store as it swung onto Main Street. Its engine and tires blew up a faint film of dust from the pavement as it approached. Laura dropped the butt on the pavement and briefly ground it with the toe of her boot. The Hound stopped practically in front of them. Where they had been looking out onto the quiet street, now they looked at the side of the bus. "Laura, I'm gonna get me a ticket and ride up there with you." He meant it. But when he went to stand, she gripped his hand firmly and pulled him back into a seated position.

"You'll do no such a thing. I need the time to myself anyway." The door to the bus gushed open, and the driver in his grey uniform swung down. He was middle-aged, lean-faced, and wore wire-rimmed glasses. "Three minutes, folks," he said in the direction of Steve and Laura, and then tugged open the door to the station and disappeared inside.

For the first time Steve let himself go a little slack and reclined against the back of the bench beside Laura. "I guess that's it, then," he said. He wasn't trying to start anything, he just wanted to make dead sure that she was dead sure. He guessed that she was. Laura was dead sure about most of the things in her life. Even though this was a new thing to her, she still acted dead-sure of it.

"My poor Stevie. He don't know what to do with his problem child. Probably just as soon take her to the truck for old time's sake." She was looking at him, and a bit of her old coyness had slipped into her tone. In fact it had occurred to him earlier that she might invite him for a quickie before she got on the bus. I mean, the damage was done. What would it hurt? But now it was too late. And they had too much clothing on anyway.

"One thing is for sure," he told her. "Waiting for a Greyhound bus after dark on Main St. is not what I had in mind back when we got started."

"Near as I could tell, you pretty much had a one-track mind when we got started," she said. Not angry or anything. Just said it.

"As I recall, your mind was pretty much on the same track." He looked over at her. He had been a fumbling, inexperienced lover when they had started out. The first couple of times, she'd had to disrobe herself. And do most of the rest of the work as well.

"Live and learn," she said. "I never blamed you for any of this, did I?"

"You never had to. I blamed myself plenty."

"Well, you can stop now. And I got to go." She turned loose his hand, and they got up together. She had her valise in her hand. The driver came back out the door, and shot them a glance. "Any luggage, folks?"

"It's just me," Laura said. "And just this," indicating her valise.

"All right then," he said, and boarded the bus ahead of her. Probably to let the boyfriend say goodbye.

"On Thursday, then," she said to Steve, and began angling her body away from his toward the bus. She gripped her valise with both hands in front of her, like a little girl on a scout trip.

Steve put his arms around her shoulders and pulled her into an awkward embrace. "Problem child," he said into her ear. "My beautiful problem child." When they separated, her cheeks were damp. Behind them the bus sighed heavily. It was her signal.

She went up the steps into the bus with deliberation, and without a backward glance. Once she was inside the door sighed shut. What with the darkness and the tint on the windows, Steve knew he'd seen the last of her. Still, he stood there with his hands in his pockets. The bus let out three little gasps and began to move forward. Steve watched the windows as they slid by, but didn't see her.

Quickly then, he jogged across the street, got into his pick-up, cranked the engine and executed a quick U-turn.

Ahead of him, the taillights of the Greyhound grew closer as he closed the distance. The bus slowed, turned right at the blinking light, and accelerated towards the north. Steve stayed with it for a good half mile until he reached the Harrison Road crossing. Then he slowed, eased off on the shoulder and stopped. Out ahead of him the Greyhound hit its stride, and the taillights were soon only pinpoints. They dimmed, winked once, and then were swallowed up entirely by the darkness.

Steve drove back through town towards the farm, but not on Main St. He didn't think he wanted to pass by the bus station with that empty bench out in front.

Penance in Par'bo

They say that whiskey will wreck a man. Enough whiskey. Over enough time. (Neither the quantity of whiskey nor the time required to accomplish the wrecking have ever been established with reliability.)

They say this in many places. I have heard it in Kansas City, Missouri. I have heard it in Chicago, Illinois. (Midwesterners speak with certainty when they speak at all). I have even heard it in San Francisco, the city where I was born, although there it is put forth with less conviction. In New York it not an uncommon sentiment, and in the far-flung cowtowns of Houston and Dallas there are numerous adherents to that dictum.

Once you cross the ocean, however, (any ocean will do), that kind of anti-whiskey talk dies out in a hurry. Lisbon, Madrid, Paris, Rome, Berlin – their citizens all have long-standing and amicable relationships with hard drink, and will not pretend otherwise. On the other hand, looking to your Middle and Far Eastern territories, whiskey is roundly condemned and religiously avoided. If a man has a hankering for the hard stuff, he is expected to come to terms with his demons, whatever they might be, and not inflict his unwary peers with the particulars of his struggles, or the wisdom he feels he has achieved as a result of them.

When you go to the southern latitudes, however, to the sunny, humid climes which we call the tropics, you'll soon detect a different response to "demon rum." It has been my observation that in the tropics, owing to a combination of factors including topographical, latitudinal, denominational, and the always-important disposition of the Beaufort-Scale, not only is grain alcohol regarded as benign presence, by tropical citizens it is openly and fervently embraced as a bearer of glad tidings, a bringer of succor, and a necessary aid to getting a day's worth of work done, even if it takes a week to accomplish that.

Given this kind of permissive atmosphere, readers may wonder: will a life in the tropics be more likely to make a wreck of a man? Smart bettors will take the odds. A certain type of man, in fact, is drawn to this clime perhaps for that very reason. Spend any time in the tropics and you'll come to appreciate the fact that wrecks are a natural part of the landscape, a feature of daily life. So much so that they are frequently considered treasures, and are pointed out with pride and wonder by the more experienced tour guides listed in *Frommers*. Shipwrecks. Plane wrecks. Wrecks of old schools or churchs. Picture-postcard relics of the Colonial era. Depending on the circumstances of the event, wreckage of any sort, whether it consists of the bleached skeletal remains of a PBY Catalina on the side of a hill overlooking San Juan harbor or the dimly-seen figure of a man at one end of the long bar in Jimmy's El Dorado in Rum Cay, Belize, tropical wrecks often possess a certain restrained elegance, hinting at stories left untold, dreams left unrealized. Or perhaps just an abundance of carelessness.

Whatever the case, in the summer of 1942, at the advanced age of 29, I was the act of politely becoming one of those wrecks.

I was by no means alone in my endeavors. In 1942 in Surinam the wreckage was piling up. The war of course had contributed to that, but the chronic primitivism of the local economy, one hundred years of heavy-handed colonial rule, the high humidity, the prohibitive interest rates of the Dutch-owned banks, and the sensation that time was mired in an immovable state – these were also factors. Getting through the day at hand was a full task, requiring, as Mr.

Lincoln would say, a man's last full measure of devotion. And once you got through that, there was the night. And night in the tropics is all the reason you need to hope for another day.

After two decades in these climes, I have concluded that what the nay-sayers and reformers fail to take into account is that, while whiskey is performing its insidious chore of wrecking a man, it will also provide him with an interesting education. Not necessarily the kind of education that will entitle him to a top-floor office and his name engraved on a brass plaque on the door, but an education with a number of utilitarian features nonetheless. Sorting out truth from fiction is one of those features. Recognizing true grit when it makes a chance appearance is another. And understanding underlying human motives may be the most utilitarian of all. Most of these lessons will be transmitted in barrooms, of course, for that is where whiskey's graduate studies are conducted, especially in the tropics, where not everybody in a barroom is a drinker, but all the real drinkers are in barrooms.

Paramaribo was no exception. In the evenings, when the daytime heat had abated, the bars along Waterkant St. were thronged with in-country wartime personnel. You had your American Army officers, they commanded the forces whose job it was to guard the Bauxite mines just a short ways up the Marowijne River. There were Army Air Force and British pilots, most of them in transit and glad of it, and your civilian contractors, who had the most money to spend and knew where to spend it. There were the ever-present Red Cross people, your local Dutch functionaries, and a smattering of Aussies, who always seem to turn up when a fight is in the offing. Then there were those few sweaty, corpulent Germans, who had legitimate business interests in the region along with their nefarious designs on intercepting Allied shipping in the Caribbean and reducing the flow of bauxite coming out the Guyanas to American East Coast ports. Later that year, when the Bogart film "Casablanca" was released, one wondered whether the wartime intrigue in an exotic locale couldn't have been more accurately filmed in Paramaribo.

In the many drinking establishments clustered along Waterkant Street, improbable war stories and fabricated personal histories were the currency of choice. True gen, or as the Army boys liked to say, "solid intel," was in short supply. Throughout the Caribbean basin -- Puerto La Cruz, Port-of-Spain, Belize City, Port-au-Prince, Montego Bay -- the War Shipping Administration had posted agents such as myself in an effort to expedite Allied shipping schedules. Being sure that our ships were fully bunkered, provisioned, and dispatched in a timely fashion, along with providing their skippers with the benefit of our best local knowledge, such were our assigned tasks. Any information we could glean on other particulars - how many U-boats had the German navy actually mobilized to the region, what was their disposition, and where were the submarine tenders that were dispatched to fuel and sustain them during their operations - was also of considerable value to the WSA. For the price of a bottle of Cuban rum, British Gin, or blended Scotch whiskey, you could get the real story, and with each glass the teller would become more certain of the facts and more assertive in his presentation of them. As for any success the Germans might truthfully be having, due to wartime censorship and the sprawling, disconnected nature of the Caribbean itself, this was entirely speculative. On successive evenings I had personally witnessed at least two sinkings in the Gulf of Paria from a lovely rooftop verandah in the hills above Port-of-Spain. This turn of events had caused the WSA to pull me from the lights of Trinidad and dispatch me to the comparatively primitive and remote environs of Paramaribo the following week. *"A slip of the lip can sink a ship"* went the old wartime admonition, and it was deemed that the slip which caused the fiery ends of the two oil tankers in question was likely mine, a judgment which I disputed in vain. Par'bo, as the Americans had familiarly labeled it, was to be my penance. In a way in was a penance for every foreign national in-country, and we all served our time, separately and together.

Several of the bars on Waterkant St. had outdoor decks that overlooked the sluggish waters of the Saramcoca river. After dark, when the overhead fans stirred the thick air and the city lights glimmered on the water, it became a perfectly natural environment for wrecking oneself. One evening, while applying myself to the task, I chanced to observe a knot of loose and loud American officers in uniform spilling into the establishment. At the center of the cluster I soon glimpsed the reason for their high spirits. She was slender, blonde and wearing white, a beacon of sensuality improbably descended into our collective darkness. Her laughter, throaty and silver, regularly soared above the self-satisfied barking of male approval that surrounded her. I was in the company of Andrew Goldsworthy, an attaché to the British embassy and a man worthy of his gin, as we looked on at the happy scene. "Methinks the lady doth not protest at all," he remarked. Goldsworthy was a Brit, he was entitled to his Shakespeare. We watched the group's carrying on for a time and then returned to our conversation, which may have had something to do with Goldsworthy's assertion that a Dutch associate of his was deliberately sowing misinformation on behalf of the Germans.

The evening passed without further incident, and in the morning was thought about no more. Lovely lady or no, signs, omens and sightings were quite the norm in these far-flung outposts during the war. Drink up and move along, folks, show's over.

Except that it wasn't. It was just beginning.

I was bellied up to the bar several nights later when I felt a tap on my shoulder. It was one of the American lads, a short friendly Lieutenant with whom I had a passing acquaintance. He reintroduced himself and placed a comradely hand on my shoulder. "Skipper, I wonder if I might borrow you for just one moment. I've got someone who would like to meet you."

I glanced over his shoulder. "Not just here," he said. "Down at the other end."

I followed him towards the back of the establishment to a cluster of small glass-topped wicker tables. I saw the blonde sitting by herself. "Ma'am, the Captain is here," he said, stepping aside in a fine gesture of manliness. I nodded and parked myself on a chair opposite the woman as the Lieutenant touched my shoulder briefly and departed.

She was tall and sat up straight, her blonde hair tumbling loosely down the sides of her head. She had lively eyes and a well-formed mouth, with something of a girl-scout earnestness about her. She reminded me of well-bred girls I had seen during my brief college days, her fine features infused with the healthy glow of higher education, proper grooming, and a guiding ambition. No wreckage here, by God. She had a tall drink in front of her and a look of bemused anticipation in her eyes. I could tell at once that she was the type of gal who insisted on getting down to business, but I couldn't tell what the business might be.

"Marty Gellhorn." She extended her hand across the table. The name didn't ring any bells right away.

"Andy Cochran."

"Captain Cochran, isn't it? The man of the hour, at any rate?"

"I could make an exception in your case." She seemed like the bantering type, or maybe I was just in the mood.

"I'd much rather you didn't. I'm quite the unexceptional type."

"Sure you are. I believe I caught a glimpse of you the other night in Freddy's behaving unexceptionally with a group of your American officer friends."

She laughed charmingly. "In that case, let me correct any first impressions that you might have had."

"I'd much rather you didn't. I like them the way they are." That made her laugh again, a thing for which I instantly admired myself.

"I'm glad you're in agreement. *Viva la Republica*," she pronounced, lifting her tall drink in my direction. I raised my Dewars in return. Then I caught it. "Wait a minute. You mean you're Martha Gellhorn?"

"I mean it every bit that I'm able." The "Marty" business had thrown me, that and the easy familiarity of her approach. But the unmistakable reference to the recently-concluded Spanish Civil War brought back at once the name that had become a familiar byline in the reporting of that conflict. She had written primarily for *Collier's*, the pre-eminent weekly newsmagazine of the era.

"I'm sorry I missed it the first time around. First impressions stand corrected." I raised my glass in her direction. "You're one hell of a writer."

She peered at me over the rim of her glass. "Well, I never have gotten caught up in all that objectivity shit, at least."

"Your politics are fine with me, sister. I read all your stuff from Spain." The three-year piecemeal death of the Spanish Republic at the hands of the Fascist rebels had been nothing less than a Twentieth-century passion play, and Martha Gellhorn had chronicled the passion of it. And not from the boardrooms, command posts, or parlors where the bleeding hearts gathered, either. From the streets, ditches, and fields mostly. The places where the real bleeding was going on.

"Seems a long time ago, but thanks for your compliment, Dear Reader."

"Think nothing of it. More to the point is, now you're here in Surinam. I must be missing something." What I wasn't missing, I now recalled, was that this was a woman who had been hired personally by Harry Hopkins to report on the nationwide impact of the depression and had been so angered by the graft and corruption she had witnessed in the administration of the various relief funds that she had barged into the White House to tell Eleanor about it and was invited to stay for dinner and discuss her findings with Franklin – the beginnings of a lasting friendship. This was a woman who had inspired the country's greatest novelist to produce his greatest war novel, *For Whom the Bell Tolls*, and dedicate it to her. Not only that, she had written two or three novels of her own, and established a reputation as a war correspondent that few men could equal. She had the status of legend, and the legend was sitting across the table from me. A damned goodlooking legend at that.

"Oh, Surinam." Again her gay laugh. "I came for the beaches."

The discharges of Surinam's sluggish rivers into the sparkling Caribbean produced a fan of flat brown waters that hugged the coastline and extended twenty miles out to sea. "I'm afraid you've been misinformed on that count," I told her, and even as I did, I could see from her eyes that the joke was on me.

"No, I'm actually on assignment again, probably here for the same reason you are."

"I seriously doubt that. I'm here because they ran out of places to put me. Surinam is the last place that I would expect to see a reporter. Especially one like you, who has something to say."

"Well, *Collier's* at least thought it was worth a look. The Germans seem to think so as well. The whole Caribbean has become a pretty intriguing story." 1942 was a year in which the future of the United States was very much in play, and the bold German incursions into the region underscored the fact that the country was in a fight for its life – a fight which might be won or lost in the sea-lanes traversing the Caribbean basin and skirting the various coasts which bordered it.

"Well, Miss Gellhorn, if I can help you with your assignment, I'll do my damndest."

"Well, one thing you can do is to knock off that Miss Gellhorn stuff. First of all, as you probably know, I'm an old married gal, and secondly, I am and always have been just plain Marty." She raised her glass again, by now empty except for the remnants of the ice cubes. "And if this conversation is going to go anywhere, a bottle is probably required. May I do the honors?"

"Not in my bar, you may not. Anyway, there's a war on. The Government's buying."

A bottle of Jameson's Irish Whisky was never so well spent as it was that evening. Marty was a spirited storyteller and loved a good laugh. She regaled me with tales of her travels of the past month, which had seen her island-hopping through the Caribbean in small boats. (One, as I recall, a ancient, leaky, thirty-foot diesel, was called, without irony, the *Queen Mary*.) Becalmed at sea, practically devoured by ants, marooned twice, tossed about by storms, she found herself bathing on remote beaches, picnicking in the jungle, and once or twice hallucinating the presence of German submarines. From San Juan to Tortola, then on to Anguilla, St. Martin, St. Barts, and Antigua, she had made her way with no travel companion save a rescued cat and the native fishermen whose boats she hired. "It was a true horror journey," she said. "Of course, those are the kind you remember best." The previous year, she informed, she had spent three months in China: hours of tedium in the company of inscrutable Chinese Generals, death-defying plane rides through storms over Japanese lines, numerous physical maladies that eventually reduced her to "a rather constant state of whimpering. It was not for the faint of heart, at any rate."

I wondered why a person would voluntarily submit to these kinds of privations.

"I'm a born peripatetic." She had been on the move since the age of 21, she told me, when she dropped out of Bryn Mawr and took off for Paris with a typewriter and $75 bucks.

"Must've been quite an adventure for a girl on her own."

"Huh," she scoffed, eyeing me. "That's male code for 'you probably slept with a lot of fellows.'"

"You understand male code?" I asked, mocking.

"My husband taught me. He said it would come in handy in certain places." She laughed. "And brother, he knew what he was talking about."

By "husband" she was referring of course to the world-renowned novelist Ernest Hemingway, a man who cast a long shadow among men of my generation as a writer, adventurer, two-fisted drinker, hunter, fighter, and bedder of beautiful dames. (Sitting here before me was certainly proof of the latter.) I poured each of us another generous portion of Jameson's and hoped that his shadow was not going to put a damper on our evening. "Men," she said, raising her glass. "You're all shits. And I love you to death."

What had gotten her started, she explained, was a fascination with place names. "I look at maps the way some people stand on the sidewalk and read restaurant menus. I want to taste everything, the more exotic the better. Especially the things I've never tasted before."

"Surinam falls into that category?"

"Sounds like a delightful treat. A excursion of the primitive sort, which is my favorite."

"You did mention an assignment."

"Well, there is that." She paused while I lit her cigarette. One of life's pleasures is that of first lighting the cigarette of a woman you would very much like to burn down. She exhaled through wonderfully pursed lips. "Haven't you heard? You fellows are all the news."

I made a show of scanning the bar behind us. "Must be a damn slow news cycle."

"Captain, don't pretend you don't know what I'm talking about. The wolf-packs are rampaging in the Atlantic, they're shredding our Murmansk convoys, and now they've decided to pick us clean in the Caribbean as well. Surinam's bauxite mines, the oil in Venezuela and all that. Isn't that why you're here?"

At this point, despite the Jameson's, I urged upon myself a sense of caution. Alcohol-fueled, rambling conversation with a captivating female had possibly been my undoing in Trinidad. I couldn't afford to repeat that letdown. "The Bauxite mines are the army's business, not mine."

Sensing my sudden reserve, she laughed disarmingly. "Oh, don't I know it? And very proud of it they are, too. In fact, tomorrow I'm scheduled to ride up the river in one of their crash boats to take a look. Your business, if my sources are reliable, is more in the shipping department."

"Look, Marty, you're a great lovely gal, but if we're going to be pals, let's change the subject. I've got nothing to say to you about shipping."

She hesitated for a moment, and then reached across the small table and placed her hand on mine, looking me in the eyes. "I'm sorry, Skipper, that came out a bit snide and snippy, and I don't mean it at all. All I mean is, I need a favor, and they assured me that you were the one man in Surinam who could accommodate me. I'm not after state secrets, for God's sake. I just need a boat."

I considered this briefly. "A slow boat, no doubt. Back to China maybe?" We laughed together, and our boozy cordiality was restored.

"Allow me to be precise: Saramcoca." She said the word deliciously, as if it were an aphrodisiac. Under the circumstances, it may as well have been.

"You mean the river?"

"Captain Cochran, it may be just a river to you. It's one of those irresistible place names to me."

"Marty, it's slow-moving, it's muddy, and it goes nowhere. Hell, you look at the maps there aren't even any navigational aids. Except for people wearing loin-cloths, nobody's ever traveled it."

"Precisely the appeal, Skipper. But I have no boat. You're the boat-man. How about it?"

The boat-man. That was me, all right. And viewing her through a filter of Jameson's and the stagnation of his own life, the boat-man was drifting close to the shoals of infatuation with the endlessly fascinating female in his company. The fortunes of war. Or the misfortunes. "You're serious about this boat-business?"

"Try me, mister."

"Don't think the thought hasn't occurred to me."

To her great credit Mrs. Hemingway, having demonstrated her formidable skills of persuasion with the opposite gender, gently pulled back. "I hope you won't think me overly bold, dear Captain, but under the circumstances I think I'm entitled to ask: how did you come by your skills as a mariner?"

"Legitimately, I can assure you." Briefly I ran though my *bona fides*: for one thing, leaving home at the age of 18, I had been in ships for as long as she had been hunched over her typewriter. I had become a Master at the tender age of 26, and I had sailed three times to Murmansk and back before accepting a position with the WSA. I didn't include the tale of my troubles in Trinidad.

"I was in Puerto Rico just a few weeks back talking to some of the shipwrecked lads. We're taking quite a beating out here, aren't we?"

"We're keeping up." I knew damn well that wasn't true in the Caribbean in 1942, but I had an official position to uphold.

"You poor thing." Again she reached for my hand. "And now you've got this absolute shrew of a woman pestering you about the kind of folly that has absolutely nothing to do with our grand war effort." Although I seemed to remember that she had Midwestern origins, she had either legitimately gained or artfully contrived a passably British way of expressing herself. In the international circles in which she moved, I suspected it was a distinct asset. Along with being the wife of Ernest Hemingway.

Around us the bar crowd had thinned and the room was becoming subdued. "Where are you staying?"

"At the lovely Paramaribo Grand, of course."

I glanced at my watch. Past midnight. "They're going to want to close the doors here shortly. Let me walk you back."

Before we departed she excused herself briefly and walked between the small tables to the lady's room. I watched her go. She was wearing a pair of khaki-colored linen shorts and a trim-fitting white blouse, and watching her cross that small room was one of my greatest wartime pleasures.

We left Vandy's and made our way along Waterkant St. under the hanging branches of the trees for a couple of blocks before turning away from the river and going another two blocks, past the stately Dutch-colonial house fronts to the hotel. She was nearly as tall as me and steady on her feet. I walked with my arm cocked so she could thread her wrist through it. I had the remnants of our Jameson's in the other hand. Across the way we could hear the strains of a scratchy gramophone playing in the lobby of the hotel. "Good God," Marty remarked. "Big-band music at this hour."

"All part of our tropical charm, dear girl."

"I absolutely adore it."

We sat at a small table near one of the hotel's columns, just outside the ring of potted palms that was strung around the lobby. A boy in a white coat brought us glasses and asked if we desired ice. "And a bottle of water," I told him. Another boy followed in his wake discharging small bursts of FLIT from his spray canister into the muggy air to disperse the bold Surinamese mosquitoes.

"Surinam," she pronounced. She lit a cigarette and sat with her back to the column. "It's everything I imagined it might be."

For a man who viewed it as a damnable banishment from the civilized world, I wondered aloud what she might have imagined it would be.

She reflected briefly. "Unformed. Expectant. Welcoming. A place to immerse oneself in the small rituals of daily life and to rely upon the charity of new friends." She took a draw on her cigarette and exhaled in the direction of the lobby. "Perhaps a place to find something of yourself you didn't know you'd lost."

"Not exactly like being in a hotel in Madrid in the summer of '38, then? The one where you were being shelled every day?"

"We were hit a few times, but I suspect most of that was incidental. The artillery in Spain was very much a random affair. The lads were not good shooters at all. Or not good aimers, at any rate." She seemed not greatly interested in war stories of her own.

Out near the potted palms, with the faint scratchy music of the gramophone to accompany us, an air of romantic unreality, rather common in wartime, was pressing in upon us, or certainly upon me. I tried to remind myself that that I was in the company not so much of an alluring female as a bold, accomplished American war correspondent. I struggled to separate the two, but the Jameson's and the hour were making it difficult. "And when you're not gallivanting around in remote corners of the world like this, where do you make your home?"

"In Cuba, with my husband."

"He's there now?"

"When he's not out in the Gulf hunting submarines." Judging from her tone she did not seem to believe in the worth of that particular cause. At least, not so far as her husband was concerned.

"Two writers in the same house," I ventured. "That's got to be something of a challenge."

"Sometimes you need a big house, I can tell you that." She laughed dryly.

"I wonder what it was about Marty Gellhorn from St. Louis that attracted the mighty world-traveler Hemingway." I hoped this would not be interpreted as male code, even though I knew it was.

"Oh God," she said, and crushed her cigarette out in the white porcelain ashtray. "If you must know, it was my backside."

"And Cuba isn't fascinating enough to keep you at home?"

"More male code, dear Captain: isn't your husband able to satisfy you? " Her eyes grew hard across the table, and then relaxed again. "Well, I'm not cut out to be a domestic, I'm afraid. Too many place names on the map." She upended her glass of Jamesons and looked across at me with a smile. "Let's talk about my boat trip, shall we? As I've said, I'm scheduled to go up to the mines for a look-see tomorrow – or today – with the Army boys, but I could be ready to leave after that."

"Hell, I'll have your boat, Marty. And if you like, I'll go along with you just to be sure you get back to Cuba in one lovely piece." It was a promise I was entitled to make, so I made it.

"I can pay, you know. Well, *Collier's* can pay, at any rate." A new melody had made its way onto the turntable of the gramophone. After hearing the first few bars, I stood up. "We can take care of that right now. It'll cost you a dance." I extended a hand in her direction. She met my eyes briefly and rose without hesitation. I guided her by the elbow towards the center of the lobby, nearer to the music. The tune was *"Begin the Beguine"* by Artie Shaw, and if there ever was a better tune for a romantic interlude, I've never heard it. Its haunting melody and Shaw's bittersweet clarinet assured great popular success in every wartime theater.

We danced. She allowed herself to come against me with familiarity, but not suggestively. And she moved easily in my arms. I've always been a pretty good fox-trot man. The fox-trot was designed for polite wreckage like me, a simple repetitive motion with a hint of elegance to it. Hemingway's wife was in my arms, but I was able to relax and dance with Marty.

Neither of us could find any reason for further conversation. The dance was conversation enough.

When the tune ended, we walked back to the table to collect our belongings. "And I shall see you…?"

"Unless you'd rather brave the crowd at Vandy's again, I'll just come by the hotel this evening. The travel arrangements should be in order by then, but if not, they won't be long in coming."

"You're a lovely sport, Captain, and I will be forever in your debt." She came around the table to where I was and leaning into me, kissed me briefly on the mouth. Her lips were warm, dry, and distant.

"Just tell Eleanor that I can't hold off the krauts much longer all by myself." I grinned jauntily and then turned and made my way down the front steps of the hotel and onto the sidewalk. I would like to have waited and watched her walk back across the lobby to the stairs, but I guessed I'd have another chance before long.

I guessed wrong.

That afternoon I found myself in the company of the District Manager of WSA and one of his associates who'd flown down on the regular Pan-Am flight out of Miami, which stopped briefly in Paramaribo for refueling on its way to Rio. (That's how Marty had arrived as well). Their visit was unexpected (the movements of military personnel in an active war zone were always conducted under a shroud of secrecy) and of course I was expected to perform the yeoman's task of rendering their brief stopover in Paramaribo as delightfully colonial and wonderfully exotic as possible under the circumstances. As my yeoman's chores didn't end until well past midnight, I didn't trouble to return to Marty's hotel until the following evening. The proprietress, Gertie, an agreeable, matronly Dutch national in her thirties with the slightly pallid air about her which seemed to cling to the Dutch despite their long years in the region. "Oh yes, Miss Gellhorn, " she nodded. "A lovely girl, but not with us at the moment, I'm afraid."

"Not with you?"

"Well, she's kept her room, but has gone off exploring, or some such thing. Upriver, I believe. Didn't give much in the way of detail." She looked up at me worriedly. "Not in any trouble, is she?"

"None that she can't handle, I'm sure," I responded, not trying to disguise my disappointment. Apparently Marty had gotten a better offer. Or at least, a quicker one. "No word on when she would be returning, then?"

"She's a girl who keeps her business to herself, I'm afraid," said Gertie, commiserating for the both of us.

"I guess we'll just have to read about it in the dispatches, then," I said, and left the hotel feeling suddenly adrift. Wreckage. It seemed to be my lot.

The days passed. Three or four days, maybe more. I plunged back into my work and tried not to think too much about her, where she might be, and under what circumstances she might be operating upriver in the Saramcoca. It was inhabited by local tribespeople, and I didn't think she'd find herself in harm's way, but the woman seemed to have a capacity for attracting adventure, for converting the mundane details of life into sound and fury of some sort. In her sudden and unexplained absence, the details of my life seemed suddenly mundane.

Before returning to her hotel, I had in fact found a boat for us to use, and contracted with its owner/operator for a modest day-rate. The boat was large for a river-going *panga*, sturdy and stable with a five and one-half horsepower outboard that would have enabled us to cover quite a bit of river in just a few days. I had even laid the groundwork for our excursion with our District Manager during my night out by explaining to my visitors that I was planning a Saramcoca excursion to investigate rumors of an upriver settlement of Dutch nationals that might or might not be involved in providing sanctuary to certain shipwreck survivors. "Wouldn't that be the Army's business?" one of them had wanted to know.

"The Army is here to babysit the mines," I explained. "When it comes to shipping affairs, we're pretty much on our own." As implausible as it may have sounded, in the end they both thought it was a capital idea, and my head swam at the thought of three or four days on the river with long-legged Miss Gellhorn, going so far as to imagine how she might choose to express her gratitude to me for services rendered. Those kinds of thoughts will make a wreck of a man quicker than whiskey, but they can also make the days more tolerable, and the nights positively enchanting, even in Godforsaken Surinam.

After a four or five days, when there was no sign of Marty either in the bars or at the hotel, my tender thoughts had hardened, and I began to regard her as an interloper, a tourist, an un-necessary distraction to men focused on the hard and dangerous business of war. Damnable, in a word. And damnably distracting.

I allowed another day to pass before I went back to the hotel. "Oh, my goodness, you've missed her," Gertie exclaimed. "The poor thing has come and gone."

"Come and gone?" It was a pronouncement I couldn't bring myself to accept.

"The poor, wretched thing." Gertie briefly recounted how Marty had suddenly reappeared in her room two mornings earlier, a much different person from the outgoing, confident woman who had swept through our lives a week earlier. Her features were puffy and drawn, her skin a welter of burns from the sun and sores from insect bites. Sporting a broken wrist and too weak to walk, she had barely been able to consume the tea which Gertie had brewed for her, and had remained pitifully ensconced in her room, having lost all interest in further exposure to Paramaribo or its charms.

"She explained to me that she had had a terrible attack of allergies and hoped to be feeling better when her fever went down," Gertie said, and shrugged.

"And did it? Did her fever go down?"

"Oh, I can't say, Captain. Just this morning she insisted on being helped into a taxi and went off to the airport for her Pan Am." She watched my face apologetically. "The poor, wretched thing."

I left the hotel and made my way back to Waterkant St, where I followed the curve around the harbor to Vandy's. I walked to the back of the long narrow room and sat at the table where I had first fallen under Mrs. Hemingway's spell, and there I drank highballs alone until late in the evening. Then I walked back to my rooms and went to sleep.

Weeks passed, and the episode slowly released its grasp on my waking consciousness. Initially I made polite inquiries in an effort to discover who had provided the boat and accompanied the journalist during her Saramcoca adventure. I was able to confirm that the Americans had taken her to the Bauxite mines but had seen no more of her after that. I also learned that the U.S. Army arranged for polite upriver outings for families of its officers, which led to an unexpected revelation from a certain Army Lieutenant whose wife had been part of such an excursion just two or three days after Marty had been to the mines. "My wife commented that she had seen the lady upriver in one of the villages where they stopped to take some photos."

"How'd she know it was her?"

"Let's see. Sexy, long-legged blonde gal traveling by herself. Kind of fits the profile, don't'cha think?"

"Who was she with?"

"Bunch of nigger locals, near as my wife could tell. You could probably find them if you tried. One of 'em apparently owns a boat, at any rate."

For the sake of my own mental health, I made no effort to find the boat owner. I had to let the story go. Thinking back to the anecdotes Marty had recounted to me of her travels in the Caribbean prior to arriving in Paramaribo, her impulsive decision to make the trip up the uncharted river in the company of local men of unknown reputation was completely in character for her. She had an almost male fearlessness about her, trusted her intuition implicitly, and threw herself at the mercy of strangers without hesitation. It was the only way she could have ever gotten to the unmapped or off-limits places she reached to be able to deliver the stories which she did. With my barely-disguised romantic fantasies, and being a fellow Yank to boot, I might have represented an unnecessary complication to her itinerary. *Steer clear of local wreckage.* That was probably one of her rules of the road. In time, I came to regard her decision to go ahead upriver without me as a wise choice.

I had limited access to current American newsmagazines or newspapers during my stay in Paramaribo, which lasted another 6 months after Marty had come and gone. It wasn't until late in the summer of '44, more than two years after our meeting, that she resurfaced in my life, or at least her byline did. Having determined to reverse the course of my life from shore-bound stagnation and willful self-destruction, I was back at sea and back in command, sailing in Liberties that were part of the large convoys steaming west out of Oakland, San Pedro, and Port Chicago, ferrying fuel and weapons to the Pacific theater as the Allied forces made their big push toward Japan. During a layover in Guam, in the wardroom of one of our escort destroyers I came across a worn and slightly tattered three-week-old copy of the *San Francisco Examiner*. Her by-line leaped out at me, and I read her eyewitness account of the D-Day landings at Normandy. As it would later be revealed, she had been denied a press credential to accompany the invading armada (such credentials were routinely denied female correspondents; apparently the American High Command thought that war was just too damn serious, or maybe too damn scary, for girls to be admitted). So while her world-famous war-novelist husband watched it all unfold from the bridge of a warship located comfortably three miles off the beach, Marty, who had stowed away on a hospital ship to cross the channel, bluffed her way into one of the boats heading for Omaha Beach and spent the afternoon on the bloody sand with machine-gun rounds whistling overhead. Knowing what I knew of her, she probably never flinched, and her account of that day was one of the first and most genuine pieces of the flood of invasion reportage that came later.

It came as no surprise either to learn that by then she had had enough of being Mrs. Hemingway. The much-celebrated couple parted company shortly afterward.

As for me, my love life was going in the other direction. I had, after a comparatively brief romance, gotten married in San Francisco to a terrific girl that I met in a record store. Like Marty, she was a Midwestern girl, from Missouri. Like Marty, she had terrific legs and a well-developed sense of humor. Our first child, a daughter, was born in May of '45, while I was at sea. My wife dutifully signed the birth certificate using the name upon which we had already agreed.

We called her Martha.

Got What We Came For

For the first six months of our romance we really didn't have any place to do it. We ended up a couple of times in cars, and there were one or two motels, which didn't work for me at all since they fulfilled every one of my dread fantasies of a dirty, cheap affair. I remember that at least once we did it in a park under some bushes near a pond. That was kind of interesting. I guess I was turned on as much by the idea of being seen as I was aroused by his hands on me, or my skirt hiked up around my waist. Finally, when he split up from his wife and got himself an apartment, we went at it like crazy for the first two weeks. He didn't even have a bed at that point, so we satisfied one another's appetites on a mattress on the floor. I've been through some therapy since then, given up drinking and smoking, and I understand much better the desperate need we each had for coitus. I came to realize that my need was really not for coitus, but for the resolution of other issues, and coitus was just my preferred method for dealing with that lack of resolution.

Not the healthiest start for a relationship, exactly.

For one thing, in my case it simply allowed me to defer getting in touch with my real needs, and healing myself.

And for him, it convinced him that he had stumbled onto every man's fantasy: a hot babe who loves wild sex, and simply can't get enough of it.

Well, after my husband and had I split and I also left my house and rented my own apartment, there came a time that we would spend alternate weekends at one another's places. More gross irresponsibility, of course, but the sex was pretty good, all things considered. By this I mean considering that it was only sex, and contributed nothing really to the sum of us, pointed in no future direction, and left us, at the end of the weekend, going back to our respective lives with nothing more memorable than the orgasms we had gotten out of each other. (And I'll say this about orgasm – when it's happening, it's fabulous, delightful, and all that, but in the end all orgasms are pretty much the same, you can't distinguish one from the other. Think about it.) In time we moved in together, and then there began the inevitable decline of our sexual marathons. We got to be a pretty predictable couple, and I think it freaked us out a little bit. Our early attraction had been based on the fact that we saw ourselves (and each other) as dangerous, unpredictable people who would never settle for lives of plodding normalcy. (In fact, he used to call me his "dangerous woman.") So, like any couple who watches the nightly news together and brushes their teeth before slipping politely under the covers, we started looking for a way to keep our love (or at least our carnal interest in each other) alive. It was probably more of an issue for him than it was for me, because I had learned during my first marriage how to use liquor, grass or pills to get myself ready for sex. I had nearly fifteen years of practice in this area, and I'm pretty certain my ex-husband enjoyed every minute. As for me, it's surprising how much of the time I wasn't even there.

Anyway, we came up with a remedy for this trend towards normalcy - I think he may have first hit on the idea - and that was to take weekend or overnight trips out of town and stay in one of those great little southern institutions, the Bed & Breakfast. (Yes, in fact, it is a Southern institution, started after the Civil War, when housing was at a premium, the land was full of vagrants, itinerants, and wayfarers and the landlords were broke and looking for ways to make ends meet. In case you were wondering...) We wouldn't travel that far, usually not more than two to three hours from home, but it was a nice little break, and while we were driving I could just feel him beside me getting excited about the whole thing. He would be glancing over at me, or at my legs actually (he was convinced I had the greatest legs of any woman alive), and we'd make small talk, we'd laugh and carry on, and it wasn't until later in the relationship that I found myself beginning to resent his arousal, because it was all based on the expectation that once we arrived at the B&B I would be ready and willing to perform. Never mind that I might be tired, or stressed, or even have a sinus headache. I had selfishly and stupidly conditioned him to expect a find a sex-pot in his bed, especially when there was added time and expense involved. So once the time came, I'd better be ready. And to tell you the truth, I can't remember a single time when I didn't rise to the occasion.

There was the beautiful little place in Daphne, Alabama, with the raised four-poster, where he could stand beside the bed and take me from behind. That was different. The high-ceilinged cabin in the woods in Mississippi where we went at it on the floor in front of the fireplace, and he got so excitable that he was actually hurting me, and I had to make him take a time-out. There was also a one-night stay in an attic room in Bay St. Louis, where, as I recall, we were both kind of tired and snappish and I honestly can't say whether we actually got it on, although with my track record, I probably gave in to him at some point. The thing that made the B&B's special was that the other guests were almost always couples, so there was a kind of sexy energy around the place anyway, in case you needed it. And the other thing, besides the cute decor and the really nice mattresses, was the fact that the owners were always very discreet, they didn't know or care anything about your background, your motives, your issues, their simple concern was to see that you were undisturbed, well-fed, and could feel as uninhibited as possible under the circumstances.

My favorite was the Tolle House (one of the few B & B's the name of which I actually remember) in Mobile. We stayed two nights as I recall, and the place had a real

Confederate atmosphere to it. Elegant, kind of restrained, with a big four-poster bed, and the biggest dining area of any of the B&B's we ever stayed in. The owners, an elderly couple, lived in the house, which meant that it was a very well-run, orderly establishment, meticulously kept, with period furniture in the public areas and a faint smell of furniture polish throughout. We were there sometime in the spring, I think. He had been traveling quite a bit, and it was one of those weekends he was home. We hadn't been able to spend much quiet time together, and this was a get-away that he especially looked forward to with his hot-blooded girlfriend. The trouble was, his hot-blooded girlfriend was already moving on. I had warned him more than once during our time together, "You better not leave me alone too long." I didn't say that because I have a wandering attention span or anything. It's just that I have a strong need for reassurance, for touching, for being held, feeling protected. So when he gets this job that requires overseas travel for weeks at a time, I know we're on shaky ground, but I had given my warnings. I wasn't going to drum it in. I left him in his own little world. As long as I was ready and willing on these weekends, that was the whole story as far as he was concerned. If he was ignorant, it was because he wanted to be.

I had recently been in touch with a guy whose acquaintance I had originally made four or five years earlier. He was crazy about me from the beginning, and didn't bother to hide it. But he was also quite the gentleman, and would never have taken liberties with our friendship just to get me into bed. He actually wanted to marry me all along. But our relationship was completely proper. At the same time, with my live-in traveling so much, this friend and I began to spend more time together than we should have, and we both knew where it was going. By the time the Tolle House weekend came up, I had already accepted the fact that I was going to go with my new suitor sooner or later. But I still had to get through the B&B weekend.

It was easier than I thought. I maintained an air of

quiet civility with my guy, tolerated his horsing around, his eccentric sense of humor, his unintentionally cruel little comments. We ate out both nights in nice restaurants, once right on the bay, where the fried seafood was really excellent. He was in some ways a complete fool. I'm sure some men would have been more receptive to the distress signals I had been sending out over the previous months. By that weekend, I was done with those signals. No more distress signals. At the same time, no more lovey-dovey cuddling, hand-holding, or casual touching. We were at the B&B for a reason, and true to my standard, I was going to give him what he came for. In the big four-poster. Oh, it would take a couple of drinks (I didn't bring any smoke with me, because I was concerned about smoke detectors in the house), and maybe a Zanex, but by the time we would slip between the sheets, my mind would be a blank, and when he reached for me, I would be as ready as a party girl could be. I would even become wet after a couple of minutes, and once I got him in me, it was as good as over. It hardly required any active participation on my part. Oh sure, he liked it when I came, and early in our relationship I would insist on coming, but by this point, I'm not sure I even bothered to fake it. I could make some polite noises, which I did, and flick my tongue at him because I knew how much that flipped him out, and after just fifteen minutes, he wouldn't be able to contain himself any longer, and bang, that would be the end of that. Knowing how good-looking and sexy he thought I was actually helped me to get through it. I mean, what women doesn't want to be ardently desired by her lover? But then there was also the knowing of how little he really cared about me as a person, and the realization of how much in denial he was about the true nature of our relationship. Well, no point in starting up about all that. Fucking is what had brought us together, and what had kept us together, plain and simple. And I had been every bit as responsible for that fact as he had.

On our second night at the Tolle House, we had gone down to the living room for complimentary drinks before going out for dinner. I don't remember exactly what I was wearing. Something he liked, I'm sure. Maybe a dress. He liked me to wear dresses, wanted to see my legs, and liked to fantasize about lifting up the dress and taking me from behind. That kind of stuff was never far from his mind. But on this particular occasion he was behaving well, and we were looking forward to dining out. There was another couple in the living room when we came downstairs, a younger couple, very Southern and very proper. The guy was wearing some kind of preppy garb, and the girl had her blonde cheerleader hair going on. Once we had been served our drinks, my Tony raises his glass and proposes a toast. He was always doing that kind of thing, he liked being the center of attention. But he had a way of doing it, I will admit, that entertained and even inspired people, most of the time. "Here's to the true home of the Confederacy," he said, meaning Mobile I suppose. Or maybe the Tolle House itself. "And here's to you Confederate women (meaning me and the cheerleader), who took your broken men and your broken land, and made them whole again."

Well, right out of the blue, I completely teared up. I don't know where it came from, it took me by surprise. I think, looking back, that it was because I felt sad that I wasn't in love with him anymore, and he didn't know it yet, or worse, that he knew but simply wasn't going to react to it. We all lifted our glasses and shared that elegant little moment, it said something wonderful about all of us, and about the Tolle House as well.

Later that night, after he'd gotten his fill (or given me my fill) of what we'd come for, he slept like a baby, spooning against me. I slept too, eventually.

What a Girl Has to Do

They have chosen seats at a table well out of the center of bustle, near the large windows overlooking the tarmac and the aircraft coming and going outside. At first glance she could pass for a Latina, a blonde Latina. She has the high cheekbones, the inviting hazel eyes, and wears her hair in the swept-back style. She has on a nice calf-length strapless sun-dress that looks breezy and comfortable. A good dress to wear when traveling in the tropics.

Across from her, however, her husband is unmistakably American in his plaid shirt, his Dockers khakis, and his L.L. Bean deck shoes. He is about 45, and his facial features bear that brand of obtuse openness often seen in Americans traveling abroad, as if they know and understand much, but nothing which will help them in their present situation. With unswerving attention he peruses his copy of the *International Herald Tribune*. She is reading a paperback novel by a writer who is known to write for the purpose of giving people something to occupy their minds when they are on vacation.

I purposely elect to sit at a table adjoining theirs, not because they are Americans, but because, like me, they value their privacy. I sip coffee and watch the early morning sun reflect brightly off the fuselages of jets nosed into the terminal. From where I sit, I can see several garishly-colored regional carriers, and also a large American Airlines wide-body, looking in its red, white and silver livery very staid and conservative in this hip-hop-flavored Central American airport. That is probably the aircraft in which the couple will be flying, I think. Flying home on American Airlines.

She asks her husband a question. She has to ask it again before he looks up from his newspaper and acknowledges her. He squints involuntarily, as if she is speaking a foreign language. Then, obediently, he pushes away from the table and walks toward the cafeteria. More coffee, perhaps. I don't blame him. I would obey her in a heartbeat. Her Blonde Eminence.

"You like him?" I ask, indicating with a nod the book in her hands. "I read his last book," I say. That's a lie, but the coffee has me feeling sociable.

"Oh," she says, understanding my question after a moment's hesitation. "No, this one isn't very good." As she turns to address me, her face is more mature than I had thought. There is a bit of fleshy fullness beginning to appear beneath her chin, signaling satisfaction, or perhaps the acceptance of choices not pursued. She's well educated and well groomed. Practices good hygiene. Applies makeup with practiced ease in appropriate amounts. Doesn't visit much with strangers in airports. "I usually look for more in his books, I'm a little disappointed."

"You look like the kind of a person who would like D.L," I say, naming another author whose books can probably be found in Wal-Mart by now. "Have you tried anything of his?"

She regards me for a moment before responding. I think she likes being referred to as a "person," as opposed to "woman," or "lady," or certainly "gal." I cut my eyes in the direction of the cafeteria to see whether we'll get a chance to socialize a little before Sparky comes trudging back from his errand. "Actually, I haven't," she says finally, smiling broadly and quite out of context. "But I will next time." She turns slightly in her seat to better accommodate our conversation. Her crossed legs, tanned and firm, are a splendid presence between us.

"How did you all like Costa Rica?"

"We've been here before. Not long after we were married.

I still like it, but my husband is a little bored, I think. Ready to get home." I like the way she shields her husband from the impertinent questions of strangers. He's a husband, and that's all I get to know. Which means, of course, that she's a wife. Which, apparently, I need to know, if I haven't figured it out already. But she's also told me, a little apologetically, that he's bored. Bored with her, possibly, and her air of certainty, her perfect grooming, her developing second chin.

From the corner of my eye, I can see the husband working his way towards us between the tables, a Styrofoam coffee cup in each hand. I have no enthusiasm for digging around in Sparky's brain this morning, even if his wife does look as good as an ice cream cone. "Well," I say, "I hope you get a chance to finish your book on the plane." Dismissing myself. She smiles a little stiffly, and accepts my dismissal.

"Nice talking to you." She turns away to greet Sparky.

I go back to my newspaper, and within a couple of minutes, they gather their belongings, and depart their table. Her book, I notice, remains behind. Sparky is already ahead of her, making for the gate.

"Hey, you forgot your book," I say, and snatch it up to extend it in her direction.

"That's okay. I actually finished it." Just like that, she discards the author and his story on a Formica tabletop in a foreign airport. She probably guesses that I'll rescue him.

"Have a good flight."

"You too," she says with what I take to be genuine good will, and then she hurries after her husband.

A quarter of an hour later I'm standing in the passport control line when I see them hurrying back in the opposite direction. Apparently, in spite of their early arrival and their careful timing, they have gotten steered into the wrong area, and are now late for their flight. He plunges ahead, grim-faced and angry. Somebody will be held accountable for this. She's digging urgently in her purse, pulling out passports and tickets, handing them across. She understands accountability. Been managing it for years. All that, plus some cooking and sexual services too. Quite a contract Sparky has there.

She doesn't see me as she hurries by, a few strands of her blonde hair trailing by the side of her face. Soon enough she'll be comfortably seated on the American Airlines wide-body sipping a scotch and water, heading home from her tropical vacation. And in spite of the presence of many people banging about to and fro in the gate area and circulating in the lounge where we wait and watch the jetliners trundle down the runway and heave themselves into the hazy morning skies of San Jose, in her absence I find myself discomfited. Beauty makes choices, I know that. Choices I can never understand. Choices to stay, choices to go, choices to live with a husband, or without. This beauty seemed so certain that the choices she had made were the best choices under the circumstances, I guess it made me wish we could have spent time together, and she could have explained to me why, looking back, a girl has to do what she has to do.

American Love Story

I'm not stupid. I'm her husband.

People think that talk of a woman's "virtue" means that her body is the last of the secrets that she will allow to be revealed. In my experience, it's usually one of the first. There are plenty of secrets after that.

I do know what it's like to get out of bed before daylight, leave a woman lying there soft and warm, put on my pants and shoes and go out to catch a bus or take a ride in a taxi. To go down to the yards or the docks, down to where the Dispatcher is picking z-cards randomly out of a pile, deciding a man's fate with his stubby tobacco-stained fingers.

Done it plenty of times. Like I said, I'm not stupid.

Some men will stay in the bed at a time like that. Not me. One last whiff of her scent, and when my feet hit the floor, I'm as good as gone. The city is dark, the only people out and about are the ones like me who've got business somewhere, are on their way to an assignment, maybe a meeting, or a job. Maybe even a war.

The Dispatcher doesn't know me from Adam. That's better for both of us. If my card comes up, it comes up, and I'm on my way. If not, I get to spend another night in my bed with my wife. Whatever the troubles are at home, when a man faces eternity before he's even had breakfast, in bed with his wife is where he's wishing he could be. Crawl back under the covers, snuggle up against her, and drift in a light sleep until she reaches for him.

San Francisco. Kansas City. Houston. New Orleans. Uptown or down. Mid-city or out in the 'burbs. Doesn't matter. If you're on the move before daylight, making your way between the uneven haloes of the streetlights, hearing the streetcars clanking and screeching, you might as well be on a different planet. Your life is no longer your own. You're on the way to the Dispatcher. Abandon hope all ye who enter here. Ha.

The Judge speaks: *"We have determined guilt. Punishment must be administered."*

"Oh goody," she says.

A tube of lipstick. A bottle of aspirin. Your face in the mirror - the last person you wanted to see when you looked there. Try to explain this to the judge, you tell yourself. "There's a big difference between a war zone and a combat zone, your honor."

"Take some codeine, watch three Doris Day movies, and call me in the morning," says the judge.

So you can call me stupid, but I've had fun I can't even talk about. And that's sayin' something.

This I remember: that she once affixed me with what I would call a cool, appraising look. Here's what she said: "Wade, you're going to have to come up with a better story than that.. I need a better story."

You get the drift. There were too many of those early morning departures on my part. Too much time to think on hers. In the end, it was a damn carpenter. He came to the house to put in some screws for her, and it wasn't long before he stopped using a screwdriver and began to use a different tool. My wife is the kind of woman who is not overly inclined to dispense information but early on, maybe just to get my reaction, she mentioned that he had come around once or twice. "Jeez," I said. "He's not a stalker, is he?"

"Christ, I hope so," she tells me.

Later, when she acknowledged that she was having a fling, and I didn't react strongly enough, she complained,

"You're doing this so that you can place most of the blame on me."

"Well, you're giving me a lot of help in the direction, don't you think?"

Once, when it appeared that we might be headed to divorce court, she blurted out her strategy: "I'll tell them I married a war criminal," she said.

"You do that," I told her. I thought that was a rap I could beat.

But that was later. When the carpenter had first starting doing her, I couldn't tell the difference. Looking back, I had a lot of things on my mind. Now *that* you could call stupid. Wash the dog. Tidy up the shed. Get the oil changed in the lawnmower. Have Julio come in and cut down the weeds. You see what I mean? Nothing. My mind was going blank from lack of better options. Once in a while when we were making love, I would be reviewing the standings in the American League. That didn't happen often, but once is probably too much.

She came to me on our third anniversary and asked me if I would take her downtown to buy some fishnet stockings. "Hell, for fish-net stockings I would take you clear across the state line," I told her. We were getting ready to go out. One of those "Original Sin" parties that were fashionable in certain circles at the time. You know the type -- Bourbon and Chicago blues. She displayed for me her newly-polished fingernails and I all I could think of was how they would feel being dragged across my back. Despite our status as "old marrieds" we had our fun.

Heavenly shades of night are falling... It would be damn hard to write a song with a better opening line than that one.

At night we cuddled. Those upstate nights can be like that. "I don't know what the future holds, but we'll find out before the rest of 'em do," I said in my post-coital glow. It cracked her up. She sat up in bed and laughed out loud. Maybe the happiest moment in my life up to that time.

From there, it was only a couple of short years before I would be going out to sit by myself on the stoop at night fighting off the dark and the cold with a cigarette. And I wasn't a smoker.

Stupid, right?

When I first met her, I thought I had her pegged right away. She was a Frankie Laine kind of girl. *"To go where gypsies play, down in that small café, and dance 'till break of day..."* "D'you like what you see?" she'd asked me. "I'm not surprised. You look like the type who would." The first time we kissed she had a spasm of delight that came very close to being a bite.

If you're one of those people who thinks he can get through life without groveling for sex, all I can say is you've missed out, pal.

After we'd been shacking up for about a month, she decided to take me to meet her mother. (Her father had been an abuser, and was out of the picture, lost in South America somewhere). Her mother had remarried well and lived in The Heights. Great view of the ocean, or the bay, I never knew for certain. Big rambling ranch-style house with a tile roof and a gardener or two to keep up the curb appeal. Before we went in, she cautioned me. "Now listen, Wade. This ain't a country club or any other kind of club, so please check yourself before you go talking any kind of club talk."

I loved that "ain't" business about her. It was simple and direct. Some would say it showed a lack of education. What do those motherfuckers know, anyway? This was a woman who loved Chinese food and English period tapestries. She positively adored French films. Thought Jean Paul Belmondo was the sexist man alive. Told me I had lips like his. "Lizard-lips" she called me. She had certain reptilian features of her own, I don't mind saying.

Call me stupid if you like, but she figured out my wooly-headed romantic outlook early on. I had known her less than a month before we spent the weekend together in her apartment. Wood floors, wall hangings, political posters, and that teapot of hers. Big tea drinker. And big on orgasms. She clocked three of 'em in our first session. (Yes, as a matter of fact, I was counting. Always do.) Later, we lay in bed and watched the play of light on the ceiling. She smoked a cigarette. "Wade, I want to ask you just one favor – let's not have any conversation about what this might mean, to either of us. You write your history and I'll write mine."

What's a fellow supposed to think about an ultimatum like that? I knew from that moment that I had to marry this woman.

There was a war on. Even if it was only a Cold War, it was there. I tried to use that as leverage. She knew one day I would have to go. "Whatever you do, just don't leave me alone, Wade. I'm no good on my own."

I should have listened more carefully, but would it have made any difference? I loved the Cold War. Couldn't keep away from it. I loved the certainty of it. You knew who your friends were. And your enemies. There were plenty of secrets to go around, and a whole variety of topics that were *verboten*. Like a Republican cocktail party. The first time, I just went for the weekend. Later, I began lingering for a week, even two weeks at a time. It was on one of these absences that the carpenter made his play. It wasn't like she hadn't warned me.

And no, I have never been to a Republican cocktail party. It was just a figure of speech. Like "our national heritage," or "In God we trust." Stupid stuff like that.

But I never badmouthed God when I was with her. She felt like she had a relationship going there. "What kind of relationship?" I wondered. She thought for a moment. "If what I know of the Bible is true, then I'm probably going straight to Hell," she said, taking some comfort there. Like many women, she was wise in protecting the things she loved, but she did not always include herself among them.

So I thought the answer would be to take her with me on one of my visits to a Cold War site. This I did. It was a four-hour drive from where we were living. By the time we arrived, my left arm was sunburned from where it had been resting on the window frame, ready to make turn signals – straight out for a left turn, with the elbow bent and the palm raised for a right. Our destination was an elementary school, preserved exactly as it had been on the day the children had been evacuated. Through the grimy windowpanes you could still see books and toys scattered around in the classrooms. Lunch snacks on some of the desks. Cocksuggin' Commies. To be honest, I never thought the Rosenbergs were at fault. We had opened Pandora's box and then couldn't understand how the stuff inside got dispersed so quickly. (Come to think of it, who'd put the stuff in the box to begin with?) *Put the bunny back in the box.* Wasn't going to happen, and frying two New York Jews wasn't going to change that. Playgrounds all over the world would never be the same. Not with the kids indoors hiding under their desks.

But that wasn't what got me. What got me were the monkey bars. Unpainted steel they were, worn smooth by the touch of all those small arms, legs, hands. They held a strong magnetic appeal. Your skin felt like it was glowing with youth just being near them. "Come sit," I said to her. Naturally she was depressed by the whole scene, which had more to do with her own childhood than with the abandoned look of the playground. She finally managed to sidle up and sit herself down on one of the wooden swings, placing her hands on the chain risers from which it was suspended. "Let me push you. Like kids," I offered. When she didn't object, I started her off slow, and gradually increased her arc. She became a girl again. Pretty soon I had her going almost at full tilt, her hair flying off her shoulders, her sundress riding up above her knees.

I felt like a 12-year old with his first boner all over again.

We had rented a room in a boarding house so we wouldn't have to make the long drive back that same day. We had a bite to eat at a small diner, and I played it cool, hoping to coax her into performing a sex act. Any act would do. After the scene at the playground, I was wound up pretty good. Even though I got a couple of vodka and Sevens into her using a flask I always carried, she was slow to come around. But sooner or later we all say yes. I told her I wanted to show her my favorite sex position. She gave me a faint grin finally and said, "Okay, what is it?" I showed her.

"Know what I call it?" I asked her. She didn't know. "I call it Two Out in the Bottom of the Ninth." She let me practice it on her again before we went to sleep.

I thought moving to New York might be a good idea. We rented a house upstate, in Newburgh. It was on a quiet street with big broad-leaf trees that provided plenty of summertime shade. I got her to a shrink who gave her a prescription for pills. She calmed down somewhat after that. Listened to Arthur Godfrey on the radio. When I was home I fiddled around in the basement. We went to card parties, our knees snugged up against one another's under the table. To tell you the truth it was like being in a witness protection program – the life you're living ain't bad, but it ain't yours either. One night we were listening to a program describing the efforts of missionaries off in darkest Africa or some such place. She had a save-the-world streak in her that would come out from time to time, so I had to be careful. "Could you see me as a missionary, Wade?" she asked. "Why not, you already know the position," I answered. But she didn't laugh like she might have at one time.

I got home after one of my absences and found out about the carpenter. "It's nobody you know," she told me. After they've been doling it out to another man, why do they always think that'll ease the blow? "Is it the pills?" I asked her. "Pour yourself a drink, Wade, and leave it alone." That night in bed she tried to make it up to me. The Yankees were five games up in the American League, what did I care? I let her try.

There was a disturbance in our neighborhood. The problem was at the candy store, which was down on Beacon Road where the kids lined up to catch the school bus in the mornings. Apparently the old fellow who ran the store had had "improper relations" with a couple of the kids who frequented the store. Boys or girls? Details were never provided, you had to use your imagination. Which most of us were happy to do. The store was closed down. That was about the time that Charlie Chaplin left the country. The government claimed he'd been a Communist, said if he ever came back they'd get him but good. Again, I'm not stupid. You cut off the candy supply and boot the clown from the big top, you're going down a different road, aren't you? All the Arthur Godfreys in the world ain't gonna change that. Something is disappearing right before your eyes. Something you didn't even know you had.

I took up beer drinking. Most of us do, if we know what's good for us. I would've been just as happy watching my wife in her white short-shorts move around the backyard pouring lemonade while I wagered the shape of her ass against eternal life. In those shorts, I bet on her ass and won every time. My neighbor Ralph was a big beer-drinker, he's the one who got me started. Here's what I discovered: beer is best drunk in a convivial environment, like a bar. Beer drinkers are happy to devote themselves to passing the time entertaining one another. Drink beer at home alone, on the other hand, you just get stupid. You can always recognize that peculiar brand of beer-fueled backyard suburban laughter. It comes out too loud, too often, and with too much forced jocularity to be tolerated with a great deal of frequency. I also found that the best marriage or relationship counseling was found in bars. Ralph was kind of a blowhard, but he had no doubts about the worthiness of our gender. "You wanna know what women are there for, I'll tell you. They are put on this earth to *get the message*. And whenever I meet one who looks like she needs or wants to *get the message*, she'll damn well be able to get it from me."

He also told me that if I never had to beg for sex, I was missing the best part.

I was missing something, I know that much. The thing about the Cold War is that it was going nowhere, and after awhile you just couldn't stay interested. John Foster Dulles could put you to sleep with just a look. I had a pal, one of the fellows I'd sailed with during the actual shooting war, who was flying with the SAC – Strategic Air Command. I know, it sounds like something you'd read about on a box of cereal, but it was serious stuff. They were headquartered out there in Oklahoma of all places, and they flew around-the-clock missions all over the world with their new bird, the B-47 Stratojet. I know, it sounds like something out of Tom Swift. But they had a mission patch that was the envy of every one of us so-called red-blooded American males, a white star on a blue background with two golden wings outspread. (In the middle of the star was a big red circle, just like the Japs had used during the war. That part I never figured out). I actually made inquiries of my friend, to see if he could get me on with a SAC outfit. I didn't care so much for the idea of getting cramped up for hours at a time in one of those Stratojets, but I did like the patch. I know it could've helped my libido. God knows, John Foster Dulles wasn't doing it much good.

The last words a man ever wants to hear from a woman, unless it's his mother: "grow up."

How about we take a vacation, sweetheart? We're a little money ahead, I'll put in for some down time. The baby blue Nash Rambler I bought on a whim is running like a top. Where do you want to go? The inspiration for a motor trip actually came to me from watching Dinah Shore doing those Chevy commercials: *"See the USA in your Chevrolet."* (Most of us would've been quite content to see the USA with Dinah in a Chevrolet or any other automobile). My wife and I got out the Texaco road maps and pored over them. What could be simpler? You get in your car and drive. We've got thousands of miles of public roads, most of them paved, with gas stations at regular intervals. At night, you stop at one of the "motor courts" that are proliferating all over the landscape, many of them have neon signs you can see for several miles off. And they feature some mighty appealing amenities - color TV's, air conditioning, swimming pools. Staying at these motor courts ($5.50 per night double occupancy was about the going rate for the better ones) might be the whole point of the vacation. What did I know? Maybe we'll go up to Niagara Falls. Or travel through the Amish country down in Pennsylvania, eat some shoe-fly pie at a roadside stand. Drink Old-Fashioneds overlooking a lake somewhere. Possibly search for arrowheads in a pine forest. The main thing is to get out of our confining little orbit here before we do something stupid like burn the patio furniture. There's a resting place and there's a staying place, and the key is to know the difference.

That's how our Western trip came about. We loaded up the Rambler and lit out like a couple of Okies. We burned through the East pretty quick, both of us a little tense and preoccupied, in a hurry to get away from our history. (We did manage to try out the shoe-fly pie on our way). Through Ohio, Indiana, and Illinois we drove, the land getting progressively more open, pastures of Herefords grazing, grain silos against the sky, rambling farms with picket fences, rolling green hills. I figured that this is where they got the inspiration for those lovely pastoral drawings in our grammar school books. Then at Missouri we hit the hardscrabble Midwest, all those landlocked people with their guns and mules, their Harry Truman, their Old Testament, their stone fences, that squinty-eyed look of Civil War survivors. The pace of our journey slowed, we covered on average about 35 miles in an hour on those two-lane blacktops with frequent stops for sandwiches, soft drinks, gasoline, souvenirs. We became sightseers, which is about as useless a breed of person as you could ever hope to meet. Amoco, Mobil, Gulf, Texaco. *Trust Your Car to the Man Who Wears the Star.* Ding-ding goes the bell when your car rolls over the cable, and out the door comes the local farm lad who's manning the pumps. Gap-toothed grin and oil rag in his back pocket, just like the brochures. On one occasion, when I'm returning from a piss-call, I catch my wife and the local farm lad lost in an intimate conversation. She seems happier than she has at any time on the trip. He sees me coming, straightens up and steps away from the car. "Like to tap that, sir," he says, or maybe he says, "Hurry back, sir." I have no idea what the immigrants were thinking about when they bought into the American Dream, but this did not seem like it.

On the long stretches I make sure my wife is on her meds. She has a sketchpad which she keeps on her lap and she'll go for long periods working with her colored pencils, wetting her forefinger and making strokes on the page to get the shading right. She's wearing a skirt and when she concentrates she has a habit of letting her knees separate and poking her tongue out between her lips, which of course gets me to concentrating as well. Once into Oklahoma our rhythm changes, our horizons expand, and we stop listening to the news on the car radio. One morning she tells me she feels like driving, and although I'm reluctant (don't know how those meds might affect her depth perception, which was not good to begin with), I yield the chore to her. That night in the motor court she's insatiable. We perform Old Testament sex, which is where you're equally hot for one another, nobody's on the clock, the pleasure is entirely of the flesh and time has no end. After that I frequently ask her if she wants to drive, but the mood has evidently left her, and she goes back to sketching and peering out at the passing scenery for long periods. "I wanna have as many orgasms as I can before I die," she had told me after our first time together. I doubt that is still her goal, but I was still willing to do my part.

It was outside of Gallup, New Mexico that she started crying. I sensed it at first, glanced over at her, and there were the tears rolling down her face. I'm not stupid. My first thought was, what have I done now? I ran down a quick mental checklist - a worthless exercise. Most of the time you didn't know what you were doing wrong even as you did it. (*If she sees what I did with that washrag, we probably won't have sex for a month…*) After a decent interval, I asked her, "You okay, hon?" She went on crying, didn't say anything. Here's the deal: I was at the Battle of Midway, a nineteen year old kid, Ordnance Mate 2nd class, aboard the *U.S.S. Yorktown.* Famous battle, famous ship. (Which sank on the last day of the fight after Kamikaze and torpedo hits left her dead in the water with all hands having by then abandoned ship.) The fact is I never was scared, not even for one minute. We knew who the enemy was, we knew what he was trying to accomplish, and we knew what we had at our disposal to meet the threat. When my wife's tears started flowing, I didn't have any of that data available, and those tears put the fear in me, they really did. My heart's sinking like the *Yorktown*, but I keep my eyes on the road ahead and remind myself that I'm married to a movie star, and this just comes with the territory. She's been mistaken for Myrna Loy more times than I care to remember. They both have those bedroom eyes, perfect noses, and fine English mouths. That air of sexual fragility. Myrna is taller, I guess, but my wife is built better. And that scene from *The Best Years of Our Lives* when Frederick March, coming back from the war, walks in the doorway of his house somewhere in the bosom of middle America, drops his bags, and Myrna's in the kitchen with an apron on washing dishes when she looks up and sees him -- that had us both tearing up, swear to God. As much as I love the woman (everybody in America loves her), life with Myrna is probably no picnic. But I doubt she's ever burst into tears for no reason outside of Gallup, New Mexico. I'm as lost as Frederick March in his pajamas with a hangover.

In the end it turned out to be the Indian thing. Remember I mentioned about her wanting to save the world? We were going through an area that was part of the Navaho nation and it wasn't pretty. Tumbledown dusty storefronts with hand-lettered signs, shambling drunks in clothing stiff with dried sweat, lopsided vehicles without shock absorbers. Even the roads meandered like they were lost. After we had eaten breakfast and I was paying the bill, she went outside first, and when I came out she was petting a dog in the back of a beat-up pick-up truck. The dog's owner was a young Navaho guy, wide cheekbones and the noble brow of his race, and he was watching her stroke the dog. You could read his mind. Who could blame him? And after we started back down the road, the sadness of the whole Indian thing caught up with her. Who could blame her? I couldn't look that deep into the sorry mess, I didn't even want to. I wanted nothing more at that moment than to be back in the East Village drinking a Schaeffer on tap (*"Schaefer is the one beer to have when you're having more than one"*) with one of my old Communist pals from the pre-war days.

Even when it was no longer fashionable to be a Communist you could always count on them for conversation that went well with beer.

"*May I ask direct question, Your Honor?*"

"*I'll allow it.*"

"*When I first met my wife, she wanted nothing more than to dance around the pool table with me. Is that such a bad thing?*"

"*Son, let me caution you that your testimony in this court constitutes a permanent record of your depravity, mild as it may be.*"

We never got as far as Flagstaff. The roadway had become remote and deserted, and I was able to run at 55, 60 for long stretches. As soon as I could, I turned the Rambler north, hoping to escape the gravitational pull of my wife's Indian Sadness. We went up through some good-looking high country - landscapes, buttes, mesas, outcroppings - but she left her sketchpad untouched on the seat. It was a bench seat, and I eventually put the sketchpad in the backseat hoping that my wife would slide over next to me. Eventually she did. Came a moment she just slid over, hooked her arm through mine, and gave me one of those dazzling smiles that she'd worn back in the days when I was courting her. Didn't fool me for a minute. I hoped it would. Fool me, I mean. At a certain point in his life a man wants nothing as much as he wants be fooled – irrevocably, completely and everlastingly fooled. And for me this was one of those times. I don't have an analytical mind, but I do have a talent for daydreaming.

Night was coming on, and the only place to sleep was going to be on the ground somewhere. It was after dark by the time I pulled off the road into a sandy area adjoining a field, far enough from the roadway so that we wouldn't be disturbed by other motorists passing in the night. We had a pup tent and some bedrolls in the trunk, and I had us set up in no time while my wife rummaged in the car and performed her toilette in a sandy area nearby. "Some Enchanted Evening" from South Pacific began running through my brain, and I hummed the melody while I worked. "*Some enchanted evening, you may see a stranger, you may see a stranger, across a crowded room..."* Once she was ready, she slipped silently into the tent, and I followed her with my flask, which had been in the cooler sloshing in the ice water. "Nightcap?" I offered. She tilted the flask and took a pull. She had on a pair of long johns and a simple mesh top, and we drank the ice-cold vodka. Afterwards she was nicely compliant as I peeled the long johns off her. Her nipples were hard as nuggets through the mesh top and once I was inside her, I did my best to get her full attention, but I could tell that she was off somewhere. I lay on my side and she lay on her back with her leg over my pelvis, affording herself relaxed comfort and permitting me easy access. The floor of the desert supported my slow thrusts. Looking up at the roof of the tent, she asked me, "Are we making love, or is this a negotiation?" Since she didn't laugh like she should have, I wisely ignored the question. When I was finished she went to sleep almost at once while I lay there nursing a leftover hard-on, missing her already.

I determined that our westward movement could not go on. It was time to turn back east. I didn't make any kind of formal announcement. On the map I spotted a likely sounding attraction called "Monument Valley," which was not far off our route. Hoping that it might be a fitting capstone to our Western odyssey, I made my calculations on the Texaco map, and we set out. (She was never any good at reading a map. Intuitive was her nature, linear never suited her much.) As we rode I stole glances at her to try to determine what kind of weather she was having. Much to my relief, she took up with her sketchpad again and not for the first time I pondered a man's ability, when in the throes of passion, to offer up promises to himself that by morning's light have no more substance than a light ground fog.

Far from the main roads, from the comforts of supermarkets, hot showers, and freshly brewed coffee, we motored through the vast openness, each lost our own thoughts, which is noticeably different from being lost together. I got to doing some thinking, and we all know where that can lead. Not too long ago, I thought, when the country had been at war, we didn't need this introspection business. What we needed, and what we got, was a bunch of guys walking around with their dicks hanging out looking to fuck the daylights out of something. Compatibly wounded, you might say. And we did our jobs, accomplished our mission, for what it was worth. The buffalo, the Indians, they didn't make it. Like the Communists like to say, it was all in the historical dialectic.

"Your Honor, if it please the court, my client is, I think, fond of ejaculating. Making love would be quite foreign to him. He has a tendency to indulge in self-gratification and other behaviors that are, at this present time, unrepented."

It was after noon by the time we reached the Kayenta turnoff and came up into the valley. The big sandstone buttes loomed ahead like Spanish galleons, and a passing thunderstorm created fast-moving patterns of light and shade on the red surfaces. Our simple two-lane road was swallowed up in this vastness until it seemed like we were traversing the surface of another planet. Beside me on the seat I could feel her stiffening herself against this big-sky panorama, refusing to be absorbed by it while I gawked and exclaimed like a dumbstruck tourist. I know silence can be golden, but timing is everything. Up against the base of the buttes I saw the long low form of a building, and I navigated in that direction. It turned out to be a trading post built back in the Twenties. Post cards, soft drinks, burro rides, overnight camping. We used the toilets and I got her a large glass of iced tea. While I watched hopefully from the corner of my eye, she drank it down. Then we got back in the Rambler and drove down into the valley, past the roadside Navaho vendors hawking pottery and handicrafts. Some bright storm was passing by, and I remembered a snatch of rhyme from a poem I had read in a seventh-grade textbook:

"With gilded fury it tumbles low, to bend the sage's withered bow, and dash the dying sunlight's hope, upon the mesa's saintly brow..."

The afternoon was slipping away but I managed to get her to sit for a photo with the buttes as a backdrop before we picked up the road heading east into New Mexico. She moved closer to me on the bench seat and together we came down the long sloping road with the land spread out before us. I know that if a woman isn't free, she won't be able to be unashamed in bed, and I wasn't going to risk anything at this stage. "What you need is a wife during the day, and a mistress when the sun goes down," she had told me early in our relationship. That's not too much to hope for, is it? Well, I'm not stupid. I'm her husband. And the sun was going down. So I drove on and kept my thoughts to myself. Once, on our second date, she had told me the sad story of how, when she was eight years old, her mother had fallen in the bathroom, hit her head on the edge of the tub, and never been right after that, an event that had affected the family from that time on. I had gone ahead and fucked her anyway, so she knew what she was signing up for. I'm not the first man who thought that by using his wife's tits and her mouth, her tongue, her thighs, her legs, down to her toes, he could build a fortress to protect himself against old age or death. If she was thinking of cancelling my mortgage, I wasn't going to give her any help at this stage.

"Your honor, I will concede that during our relationship, my wife never held nothin' back."

"Really? And what about you?"

"Oh, me, I held back plenty."

I didn't want to put us in a tent again, and by the time we found a little motor court in Shiprock, New Mexico, it was pushing midnight. During the night, as my wife tossed restlessly with her back to me and her sex buttoned up as tight as a maiden aunt's, I had experienced some erosion of my mental resolve. When we woke up in the morning I was ready to commit to the following: 1) *Go for rides in the new car whenever she wanted* 2) *Have dinner parties at home* 3)*"Eat out" on a Saturday night* 4) *Have "get togethers" with friends of her choosing* 5) *Go shopping together at least once a month, and* 6) *Visit an Indian reservation and talk to the elders so that we could get to the bottom of the whole sad Indian story.* As a reserve clause, I toyed with the idea of telling her we could adopt an

Indian child if that would help, although I fervently hoped it wouldn't get quite that far. We found a "cattleman's café" and ordered *huevos rancheros* in green chile sauce, and when she went to the restroom, I wrote on a napkin something that I hoped would ease the strain and introduce a bit of levity back into our lives:

I'm best at "bring" and "take." "Sit" I can handle. "Stay" gives me problems. "Get up," well, that's one I'm really good at. "Good boy" is what I live for.

After we ate the eggs and got some coffee in us, I pushed the napkin across to her, noting with hope that she hadn't slept well herself. She read it and smiled wanly. "Wade, the way I'm feeling I'm probably going to cry, and you can't stop me," was all she said. It sounded like a good starting point, and I thought that when the time came it might be a good idea if I joined her.

The Player

"Wanna fool around?" Mitchell tried to make it sound as casual as he could. He reached up and placed his hand on the back of Carla's neck. She lay, as usual, with her back to him.

"Let's just go to sleep," she said over her shoulder.

"Let's fool around." Mitchell curled his arm around his wife and cupped his hand over her breast. They lay like that for a time, and when his wife did not remove the hand, Mitchell began to have thoughts. He carefully snugged his pelvis in closer to her backside. She lay still, but was not asleep. He spooned against her, letting her feel his developing erection. "C'mon, for God's sake," he said, and his voice had gotten a little husky. "C'mon, Honey. Please."

Her voice came over her shoulder again, without rancor. "Jerk yourself off."

"You jerk me off." And he began to massage her nipple through her the sheer fabric of her nightgown. His body was becoming rigid with anticipation. "Let me eat you."

Carla shifted, removing her husband's hand from her breast and rolling onto her back. In the dim light of the room Mitchell saw that she was staring up at the ceiling. "What in the hell is the matter with you?" she asked finally.

"What's the matter with *me*? What's the matter with *you*?" he wanted to know. "Is the idea of a man wanting to make love to his wife so difficult for you to grasp?" He left his hand lying on her stomach to show that he was not being hostile.

"You've never learned to make love to me. Why is it so important to start now?"

At this blow, Mitchell removed his hand. A gulf now separated them. "Seems like there was a time when you clocked orgasms pretty regular," he said, not allowing maudlin sentiment to creep into his voice. Just stating the facts.

Now she turned her head to look at her husband. "It might surprise you to know that I still do. I just don't need you to be part of the process."

"What's that supposed to mean?" This was one of Mitchell's favorite phrases, but he hadn't meant to use it on his wife. It just popped out because it fit the occasion perfectly.

"It means I've learned to take care of my own needs, and no, in case your little brain is working overtime, I don't need the services of another man any more than I need yours."

Mitchell too had now rolled on his back and was watching the ceiling. They seemed like two people in a movie. A romantic comedy. Except that it wasn't funny. "Carla, why am I so unappealing to you? I mean, what is it about me that turns you off so much that I can't touch you in public, let alone get into your pants in the privacy of our own bedroom?"

"You don't want to go in that direction, mister. You really don't."

"Sure I do. Why not? What's left for us? You keep on making money until you're satisfied, and then maybe you boot me in the ass and find a guy who complements your upgraded lifestyle? I mean, I've reached the point where I don't really care anymore. This is bullshit."

For a time nothing more was said, and the longer the silence lasted, the more Mitchell feared what his wife might say, or do. His last sentence hung in the room like a curse. But he waited, longer than he was accustomed to waiting. His body was tense, and what he wanted at that moment was to fondle himself, take a few whacks, and go to sleep.

Too late for any of that now.

"Where's your wallet?" she asked him, lying unmoving, staring at the ceiling.

"What do you mean, where is my wallet?"

"Pretty simple question. Get out of bed, and go find your wallet. Go on."

It was an unusual request, but considering the kind of peril in which he had placed himself, it could have been worse. Mitchell slipped out of bed and made his way down the corridor off the master bedroom, went into the den, and from the top drawer of his credenza recovered his cowhide wallet, the one with the silver inlay that he'd bought the year before in Dallas. Then he went back to the bedroom. He sat on the edge of the bed in the semi-darkness. He still hadn't figured it out.

"Check and see if you've got any folding money."

"I've got some."

"Good." Carla rolled onto the blade of her body and pushed herself up on her elbow, letting the sheet slip down and expose her breasts. "Here's the deal: you can feel me up for $100. You want to kiss and make out, that's $150. You want me to masturbate you, $200. You want penetration, that's $300. If I come, that's $500 dollars."

Mitchell immediately began to produce an erection, in spite of his confusion. "I've got to pay money to make love to my wife?"

"You're in the wrong movie, Shorty. We're talking strictly business here. Pony up, or the lady goes back to sleep."

Mitchell, feeling like a fool but now fully erect and wildly desirous of banging the daylights out of his wife, opened his wallet and drew out all the bills. "Gonna have to turn on the light, can't see what I've got here."

"No light," Carla insisted. "How many bills you got there?"

"Seven, it feels like," he said after a moment.

"Well, be a sport. Take your chances. You give me all seven bills, and you can French kiss me and play with my tits while I give you a hand job. You may be getting a real bargain."

His brain clouded with passion, Mitchell for the life of him couldn't remember what he was carrying. Sawbucks were pretty common in his wallet. Ones and fives he usually carried apart, folded in his pocket. And he seemed to remember at least one hundred dollar bill. There had to be better than $300 in all. Maybe enough for the full ride. "There's more here than that," he insisted. "I want the whole works."

"No deal." Carla reached across and slipped her hand inside Mitchell's boxer shorts. Her fingers were long, tapered, and cool. She flicked her fingernails against his scrotum. "C'mon, big boy. Hand Mommy the money." At the mention of Mommy, Mitchell sucked in his breath. He handed Carla the bills, and she reached behind her, not ceasing her ministrations, and slid them under her pillow.

"I want the whole thing. You've got over $300 there."

"Maybe, but it's still not a good investment on your part. C'mon, move over this way. I'll take care of you."

Mitchell groaned involuntarily, and knelt next to his wife. She was stroking him, slowly and firmly. She had terrific hand pressure.

"The whole works, Mommy. Please."

"Forget it, Mitchell." Carla's voice too had gotten a little husky. "This way, we'll both know you at least got your rocks off. The other way, I'd probably just fake the orgasm, and you'd be throwing away your money. C'mon. Move over here. You can come on my chest."

Mitchell swayed above Carla in the darkness, his loins tight as a drum, and in spite of himself he concentrated on trying to remember what bills he'd been carrying in his wallet.

The Arrangement

I don't suppose that my story – our story, really – is terribly unique.

It's the story of a wartime romance, after all. I'm English, he was American. Yank, as we invariably knew them. "Overpaid, oversexed, and over here," went the popular refrain, and with good reason. As an officer and a member of a combat aircrew, he was better paid than most of the lads who visited the canteen on a daily basis. He was a bombardier, and his rank was Lieutenant. He was 22 years of age, he came from Detroit. And while I had always thought of myself as romantically reticent, he lacked for nothing in the libido department, I can assure you.

Or maybe it was just the effect I had on him.

The Stage Door Canteen was located in Piccadilly Circus, and for servicemen on weekend passes it was the most well-known and conveniently situated dance and entertainment club in London. Open six to midnight, admission free to servicemen (although there was a ticketed shift system in place so as not to exceed the building's maximum allowable capacity), coffee, tea, sandwiches, milk, juice and cigarettes served, and of course, band music throughout the evening. No alcohol, of course. That, the lads could readily find in a number of other locales. But what they could not find, at least not on such short notice, was the female companionship available at the Canteen.

The dance hostesses were all volunteers, mostly quite

young (at 25 they would be considered long in the tooth), and strictly forbidden to fraternize with servicemen outside of the club. The rate at which they fell in love, got pregnant, got married (sometimes both), and eventually followed their soldier-boys home would indicate that a considerable degree of this fraternizing occurred notwithstanding, but the club officially discouraged the practice, and considering the whirlwind nature of those weekends and the volume of soldiery that flowed through the place, boys and girls were, by and large, limited to just dancing and holding shouted conversations in an overcrowded, poorly ventilated room overlaid with the cloying aromas of perfume, perspiration, and stale tobacco.

And of course all of it was fueled with the constant anticipatory buzz that only a war can provide.

"I don't hate the war or anything. Just so you know." My bombardier pursuer felt compelled to confess this to me the first time we were alone together. It was a moment I had not anticipated nor hoped for. I was not a hostess, and except for bumping into one another quite by chance, there was no reason for us ever to have met. My friend Priscilla had recruited me to "sort of pitch in and lend a hand," and as I had evenings free and was perhaps chafing a bit at the predictable nature of my existence when so much in the world was uncertain and hence invigorating, I agreed to come aboard as a kitchen manager. "It's really just a matter of watching the kitchen staff and making sure they have everything they need on hand to keep up with the crowds," she assured me. "You'll be safe back there in the kitchen – all the wolves are out on the floor."

And I was. Safe in the kitchen, that is. Or, would have been had I stayed there. But I periodically dispatched myself on errands to recover empty trays, discarded cigarette packs and the like, and on this occasion I was on such a mission and was skirting the edge of the main ballroom, anonymously I thought, when I was intercepted. "Say, I didn't know I'd find you here tonight," he said, almost as if we'd been dating for months or something.

"And so you haven't. I'm not here at all, really." And I pushed along my route.

"Then we've got something in common, 'cause I'm not either. We're actually ghosts of our former selves." He was moving laterally, keeping up.

This was a novel approach, I thought to myself. Kind of literary. I kept going.

"You know what one ghost said to the other, don't you?" He had come in closer, only an arm's length away. I spotted one of the trays I was after and stopped to retrieve it. With it safely in hand, I turned back towards the kitchen but not before he caught my eye and held it. "What one ghost says to another is: when can I see you again?"

He showed up again on the following evening and parked himself against a column near the serving area, lingering there with no interest in dancing or carousing. No interest in anything or anybody but me, apparently. When he showed up for a third night, a Sunday, the pace of the Canteen was much less frantic. During a band break he leaned in and said over the hum of animated conversation, "Might I buy you a cup of tea?"

"I'm actually on duty here," I told him.

"You're right," he said. "We have not been properly introduced."

This came about one month after my boyfriend Peter had finally convinced me to hang my stockings at his tiny coldwater flat off Bayswater Road. It had not been a casual decision on my part, and I was completely closed off to the attentions of other men. Peter was a decent man, and our relationship was safe and reliable, and I wanted to keep it that way.

He showed up again the following weekend. Max, his name was. Pale skin, dark eyebrows, a strong chin, lips that were forever mocking and inviting. And of course, there was the officer's uniform. Don't count that out.

We went for tea that evening after I got off. It was after midnight. "Don't you have a plane to fly or something somewhere?" I was still hoping to evade the trite story of a wartime fling, but his dedicated lingering had worn down some of my reserve. If other girls could briefly experience the heady thrills of wartime London, why not me? Who knew what tomorrow would bring besides the slogging inevitability of more shortages, more duty, more drear?

"It flies just fine without me," he said. He was holding me lightly by the elbow as we crossed Piccadilly and walked toward Regent Street where I knew of a proper tea shop. "I've been watching you, and you look like you might be a Pauline."

This caught me up a bit short. "Claudine, actually. Whatever gave me away?"

"Your false modesty, of course. Not as prim as you pretend to be, I'm guessing."

"You just jump right in, don't you?"

This was in the spring of 1944. The nighttime bombings of the Luftwaffe had been silenced some time ago, but the city center was nothing like its pre-war self. It was still poorly lit, with barricades set up around weak and tumbledown buildings, piles of brick where other buildings had fallen or been demolished. The heat and light of the conflict had moved on, but the stamp of war was everywhere evident, and it seemed that it would remain that way for some time to come.

Across the small table from one another we sat, so close that our knees brushed. "I've come to realize the difference between tea and coffee," he told me. "When you drink coffee, you think about where you're going. With tea, it's more about where you've been."

"Not many tea drinkers among you Yanks, are there?"

"We're a very forward-looking people."

He wasn't much for the kind of getting-to-know-you conversation, and he discouraged my polite efforts to find out more about him. Which, to be honest, were a bore anyway. The pressure of his knees against mine was a lot more to the point. "What is it that you do in your aeroplane by the way?"

"Your English countryside is a lot more interesting."

"You mean, '*Oh, to be in England, now that April's there.*'" The glories of an English spring were a staple of English poets and writers.

"I mean *Taverham, Rackheath, Attlebridge, Stratton. Old times there are not soon forgotten.*" He was toying with me in a way that an Englishman could not have dreamed. Yet there was something utterly sincere in his prattle.

"Those are towns around Norwich. You must be with a Flying Fortress squadron." I had picked up a smattering of tactical information from snippets of conversation overheard at the Canteen.

He eyed me appraisingly over the rim of his teacup. "Not exactly. I'm with a Flying Coffin outfit. And if you purse your lovely English lips at me again that way, I may lose all my manly restraint."

I wish I could relate that I fought the good fight for English womanhood everywhere, but that line more or less did me in. I was surprised to discover that my resistance was so scant, if you want to know the truth. I could imagine him undressing me.

Unless she's going to allow herself to be taken on a spot of damp earth behind a collapsed flat, however, (and there were more than a few who did) a girl's got to mind her manners at a time like that, and I managed to convince him that yes, we could see each other again in five days hence and I would take some time off to show him a bit of the city. Which we both understood to mean I would also arrange a site for a romantic tryst. Or at least I imagined that he imagined it that way.

He was staying at a servicemen's club near Charing Cross Road, bunking in a room with three other officers. We walked in that direction looking for a cab.

"A Flying Coffin. I'm assuming that's a morbid figure of speech, and not an actual aircraft designation."

"It's a designation, all right. Goes by the official name of Liberator, but what do the officials know?" He went on to inform me rather tersely that his B-24 aeroplane was inherently unsafe in battle, prone to losing its wings, catching on fire, rolling upside down, or creating a flaming pit in the face of the earth, virtually any of which spelled death for its occupants.

"But they do provide you with parachutes, I would imagine."

"Yes they do. Parachutes and condoms. If you can't save your life one way, maybe you can save it another."

I'm certain I blushed. Up ahead we could see Nelson on his pillar faintly highlighted against the London skyline. Max stopped on the sidewalk. "Sorry, Claudine. I didn't mean to be forward. That's just the way we Yanks express ourselves."

"Does that mean you're looking for someone to save your life, then?" And he took me by the elbows and drew me towards him, fitting his mouth over mine like an airtight seal, so that my breath could not escape without his receiving it. I could smell his aeroplane as we kissed. That and his aftershave, which had a scent that contained hints of tall pines and distant mountains. Drives in the countryside with children in the backseat. The wide-open spaces of America. After four years of war and bombardment, we English lived in comparative squalor.

"You express yourself quite freely, I should say."

The following weekend Max did not get down to London, but it seemed as if everybody else did. This was in May and our emerald isle was overflowing with a million or more troops who were gearing up for what would come to be known as D-Day. It was said later that the Germans knew the invasion was coming. And how could they not? Not only The Stage Door but The Paramount, the Strand, the Trocadero, the Windmill, the Boomerang, the Brevet, all were overflowing during the month with troops of the allied nations. Aussies, Yanks, Poles, Czechs, Canadians, the New Zealanders, all in uniform and all eager to consort with our female population. The music blared out until all hours, the tea and soda flowed, the conversation swirled, and the war, which had already destroyed so much and terrorized so many, now gave license to a wide range of behaviors that just a few short years earlier would have been roundly condemned in so-called polite society. Many of our girls handled themselves rather poorly, allowing themselves to be swept up in the general frenzy at the expense of their dignity, if not their maidenhood. Others resisted. As we have seen, I was somewhere in the middle ground, but I carried on with a semblance of life as one half of a couple, although what degree of passion Peter and I shared had largely ebbed away (if it had truly ever existed) and we lived politely, considerately, in a pat-on-the-back fashion more suited to a brother and sister.

Diligent girl that I am, I proceeded with the plan for a romantic weekend with my bombardier, knowing of course that at any point I might receive notice of his untimely demise. (In fact, because of the tight security in place regarding the status or movement of all military personnel, it might be weeks before a girl would learn, usually from his comrades, that he was no longer among the living, or mangled in some hospital somewhere.) Through my friend Millie I managed to secure a room for us at a guest house in Ipswich, a well-scrubbed Romanesque town situated about halfway between London and Norwich on the River Orwell. Known for its sleepy pace and it picturesque docks, it was a ninety-minute train ride for each of us. I relayed word of the plan through the lads of Max's squadron that I knew from the Canteen ("Mind very much if we tag along?" was the common refrain when they heard of our upcoming tryst) and on the appointed Friday evening I made my way to Euston Station clutching my overnight bag and doing my best to convince myself that I was not being selfish, but performing a duty on behalf of God and King, although neither one of those august personages seemed to be very much in evidence as we rumbled northward towards the bonny grounds of East Anglia.

I had furnished Max with the address, (and Peter with a story about a getaway with girls from the Canteen) so my plan was to go straightaway to the guesthouse and wait until he arrived. No need. As I waited on the station platform near the cab stand an arm encircled me from behind, snugged up tightly under my bosom, and held me fast. I smelled the pines, and reaching back patted the top of his head affectionately, a favor for which he bit me rather forcefully on the neck before turning me around for a proper hug. "Now you're a marked woman," he said. About that he was completely right, although not perhaps in the way he suspected.

We did not rush off to our little aerie all at once, but at his insistence went in search of a restaurant. "Tablecloths and china," he said when I asked him for his dining preferences. "Silverware."

Our taxi driver obliged by dropping us off at the Last Anchorage Pub near Bridge Street. ("You'll find a bit of life there, at least...") We parked our bags in the foyer and were shown to a booth with a window looking out over the river. Owing to the restraints of my upbringing I have never been one to frequent pubs, but they are the best window imaginable onto English life, embracing all the possibilities and the peculiarities of our culture. Even in provincial Ipswich a Yank in uniform and his English dolly fit right in. "Pity you lot don't have pubs in your country," I said. "They provide quite a civilizing influence."

"We have neighborhood bars," he responded. "Good for fighting." He gave me that crooked, hopeful and utterly devastating grin of his, which made it impossible to guess where the facts ended or the irony began.

The fare was substantial and filling: a nice Sunday roast of beef with potatoes and veggies on the side. A bottle of Italian wine, probably procured before the war, gave the meal the continental flare for which Max had probably been hoping. Absent the tablecloth and china, it would have to do. I did prevail upon our server to bring us a long tapered candle in a silver candleholder. In one corner a few lads were tossing darts while others at the bar provided an ongoing commentary. We held up our glasses in a toast. "To the magnificent Claudine and her lovely island. And to the bloody war which brings us together."

"To the bloody magnificent Yanks and their lovely flying machines," I countered. A shadow flew across Max's features, but he said nothing and we were thankfully able to carry on with our fragile charade of a honeymooning couple on holiday.

Outside we walked towards the Bridge Guest House, only a few blocks distant. The air had an open and scrubbed feel to it, owing to the nearness of the North Sea. There were no blackened or collapsed buildings nor the pockmarked roadways that were so prevalent in London. It might have been appealing to walk near the docks but predictably there were police barricades up to keep civilians out of the area. Max had taken my free hand in his and I cast a sidelong glance at his face. We were, I judged, not too far from the very coast over which he and his comrades flew on their missions to and from the continent. I imagined the agony of war that began just on the other side of the waters. "How long does it take your aeroplane to actually fly across the North Sea?" I asked. It was an incautious question but my father always called me his curious girl.

"Forty five minutes to cross the water," Max said. Then, after a moment: "And the bombs. Claudine, don't you wanna ask me any questions about the bombs? I'm the man who has his hand on the switch, you know."

"No thank you. I'm a Londoner, Max. I understand something about the bombs."

We covered the remaining distance to our place of lodging without speaking, which is not the same as silence. Whatever it was in London that had made this kind of a getaway between two people who were essentially strangers seem like such a good idea was suddenly absent from my mind, but I was content to walk on at his side, determined to enjoy getting away from London regardless.

The Bridge Guest House was a slightly worn yet venerable two-storey red-brick structure standing all by herself on a corner next to a copse of elm trees which were just in the act of leafing out. The old manse had a lovely abandoned country look to it, and I felt the anxieties of wartime London slipping away like a worn overcoat. We were met at the door by a sharp-eyed dowager who gave us quite the once-over as we were signing the register, a process required by law during the war, particularly in the coastal areas where saboteurs were always thought to be a threat. I'm quite certain she knew that our visit was likely of a connubial sort, with me looking quite smashing in my nylons and flowered skirt and Max the gallant savior of our island in his trim-fitting olive dress uniform with the silver wings on the lapels. Ask any woman and she'll readily be able to relate the physical features of herself with which she's less than pleased (in my case I would like to have been a little longer in the thighs, a little fuller in the bosom), but when she's on the arm of an ardent suitor she'll have few complaints. Handing over our room key the proprietress could not resist a disproving glance in my direction as we moved away toward the stairs. "We serve tea in the parlor from 4:00 to 6:00," she informed us primly. "What we'd like please is a bottle of water and a couple of glasses, if it wouldn't be too much trouble," Max responded, squeezing my hand. I did love that bit, coming from my Yank.

The room was quite small, and though lacking a great deal of charm, was serviceable and accommodating. A slightly sagging four-poster bed with a floral coverlet occupied most of the floor space, and gauzy drapes filtered the light through a small window that looked out over the treetops. Best of all was the attached bathroom. No need for trips down the hall. We parked our grips and Max promptly zippered open his kit and pulled out a bottle of American whiskey. There was a tap-tap on the door when the young man brought up the water and the glasses. I had gone into the bathroom, where I examined myself briefly in the small mirror and reflexively freshened my lipstick. A small brave smile. A wink. An arch of the eyebrows. Once that bit of self-encouragement was done, I went back into the bedroom. Max had shed his shoes and draped his jacket and tie over the bedpost. He poured whiskey into the two glasses and added water, passing one to me. Lifting our glasses and touching the rims together, we drank. The whiskey was fierce going down and then kindled a slow fire. I sat on the edge of the bed. Max lowered himself into a cross-legged sitting position on the floor in front of me. "Are you quite comfortable there on the floor?" I asked him.

"I do my best work in this position," he said, and we lifted our glasses and drank again. "In case you were wondering, this is something I've never done before. I mean, I don't run off with English girls into cabins in the woods or anything."

I glanced at my watch. "That's all very well, Lieutenant, but I must tell you to get on with it. Your time is running out, and I've got three lads downstairs who are waiting their turn." I was marvelously straight-faced, letting the whiskey do its work. On the collar of his shirt his bars gleamed in the low light, and I kept my eyes on them, not yet entirely entirely trusting myself to look into his face.

"I don't want to disrespect you, Claudine." He was watching me carefully and also letting the whiskey perform. "How does this work, anyway?"

"I'm going to remove my nylons, at the very least." I placed my glass on the floor next to Max and rolled the hem of my skirt up my thighs to unsnap the stockings from my garter belt. Resolute British girl.

"They're quite intoxicating," Max observed. His voice had gotten thick.

"From Paris, actually. I obviously save them for special occasions." We were, I assumed, still taking about the nylons. At least, I was.

"Get many special occasions?"

"This is the first, if you really must know."

Placing his glass next to mine he got to his knees and leaned over to kiss me. I parted my lips to receive him, but it was a curiously chaste kiss. Almost like a first kiss. "That's quite intoxicating," I said when it was over. Watching his eyes, I began to unbutton the top of my blouse. He reached up to stay my hand. "Don't take off your clothing, Claudine. Please." I gave him a look, I suppose. "That's my job," he explained.

But not yet. Once I had rolled my nylons down my legs, removed them and set them aside on the bed, he placed his hands on my knees and gently separated them. A more experienced girl, or maybe an American girl, might have known what was coming next, but I was blissfully unaware. Sliding his hands under my skirt, he grasped my panties and tugged them down my legs, whirling them away to the corner of the room before lowering his head and making his way up the insides of my thighs. Having no immediate purpose at hand, I let myself fall back on the bed and arched myself to meet him, reflexively hoping that my standards of female hygiene were going to be up to this unanticipated exploration. I could dimly hear voices on the second-floor landing and from the window came the sound of a small plane making its way through the skies above. I felt myself relaxing, and let my fingers rest on Max's shoulders as he worked. With his hands under my buttocks he unhurriedly devoted himself to pleasuring me, and after awhile I moved my hands to the back of his head so that I could unashamedly direct him in his efforts.

"I don't hate the war or anything. Just so you know." That came later as we were lying, our appetites, or at least our curiosity, momentarily abated, under the coverlet.

"How could you not?" I wondered. To me, hating the war was axiomatic. It gave me a place to register my emotions. To balance my view of the world. To identify myself. On the other hand, the act of his prolonged cunnilingus on me seemed to speak of the need to exorcise some inner turmoil. It was not an ordinary sexual impulse at any rate. Was it?

"I understand the arrangement. Once you've got that, what's the point of wasting energy thinking about the rest?" We were side by side. I had shed my skirt but Max still had his uniform blouse on, one hand resting proprietarily between my legs. Like old lovers.

I rolled onto my side so I could watch his face. The room was becoming dim and lemony in the spring dusk. "What is the arrangement, pray tell? Perhaps we could all benefit from knowing." With my fingers I traced patterns on his chin and throat. When he had kissed me after, I had tasted myself on his chin and his mouth.

"It doesn't work like that," he said. "I just know it goes for me. I'm scheduled to die in my aeroplane. Join the magnificent list of the Glorious Dead. Get my name up on a monument somewhere. Like that big one you have down in Trafalgar Square." He turned his head and grinned. So as not to scare me, I suppose.

"Is that why you spent three nights picking me up in Piccadilly? Bringing me to his lovely spot? Absolutely burying yourself that way in my muff? So you could tell me about how you're going to get yourself killed?"

"And a lovely muff it is, too."

"I'm serious." Trying to be, at any rate.

"There's no call for that, now, is there?" He began unbuttoning my blouse. "We never got to explore this lovely terrain, did we?"

"Take off your bloody uniform, Lieutenant, if you're going to talk to a girl like that."

It was not so much that he was a "fatalist," he explained. He had identified something in him, something that, despite his best efforts, was seeking a death, a dutiful one, or maybe, with luck, even a heroic one. "And considering the numbers of people that are out there every day trying to oblige me, it seems like a pretty likely match-up." We were back at the Last Anchorage where we had walked after leaving the trysting bed in search of evening sustenance. We were just mopping up the last of our fish and chips when the barkeep announced Last Call. Max glanced at his watch. "Nine o'clock, and there's a war on. There should be some leeway here." He excused himself and went to the bar, returning a moment later with two glasses of whiskey. "Johnnie Walker okay for you?"

"I usually insist on Johnnie Walker with my fish and chips."

It didn't trouble him, his rendezvous with death, he said, because had had "made an arrangement."

"What sort of arrangement?"

"I've agreed not to resist in exchange for certain considerations."

"I didn't know one could make deals with death that way."

"Once you agree not to resist, things are different. It's not for everybody."

"What about your mates? The fellows you fly with? Do they make deals like that?"

"I wouldn't have any idea." He had thoroughly cleaned his plate and took a drink of his whiskey. "It's not exactly a topic for discussion in the dayroom, Claudine."

His point was well taken. "And how has it worked out for you, this arrangement?"

"On balance, and after today, I'd say it's working out fine." He gave me an earnest look, and shrugged. I suddenly wanted more than anything else to be near him, have him near me. At this point we were interrupted by a stocky fellow in workingman's rough garb who deferentially approached our booth. "Beggin' your pardon, Captain. Me and the lads just want to express our thanks to ye, and to say, when you're up there, happy bloody hunting! " He lifted his glass at the last and took a healthy pull at his whiskey. Max and I followed suit. "No offense to the Missus of course," said our friend, and offering up a casual salute, he moved away to rejoin his mates at the bar, all of whom, I realized, were drinking whiskeys. A result of a certain gallant Lieutenant's errand at the bar, no doubt. All part of the arrangement, as it were.

We strolled back to the Guest House under a lowering sky, the air swimming with a fine mist. A proper English spring evening. Up in our room I slipped into the bathroom to dry my hair and change into the cream-colored floor-length negligee that Priscilla had loaned me for the occasion. When I came out he had poured us whiskeys from his bottle. He was sitting in the small Queen Anne Chair in the corner of the room. I went and stood in front of him and he held out a glass. I drank, and the whiskey went down more smoothly than it had earlier in the day. He reached out and took my wrist and had me sit across his lap. I feared for the Queen Anne. "Have we been properly introduced?" he teased.

"You're not in the habit of snogging strangers, are you?"

"Snogging? Is that what you call it?" He was watching my lips, a habit of his that was alternately disconcerting and arousing.

"And what do you call it in Detroit?"

"I'd rather not say." He laughed and drew me close to him for a kiss. The whiskey tasted better on his lips that it did in my glass. "I could eat you with a spoon," he told me.

"Actually, I'm rather fond of penetration, myself." It was not like me to tell a person what I wanted in an intimate situation, but the whiskey and the hour had emboldened me and I heard the words as if they had come out of the mouth of another. After a moment I could feel his sex stirring restively beneath me. For a time we stayed in the Queen Anne wrapped in one another's embrace. Then I disengaged myself and got into bed.

Once he came along, I reached for him and urged him to mount me, which he had not yet done. Having him on top of me had been my inclination, my hope, from the beginning, to have his hard chest crushing my breasts, to be able to use my knees and pelvis to manage the force and direction of his thrusts. The so-called missionary position was, I'm afraid, culturally embedded in my psyche, the natural habitat of this rather unimaginative English girl, and I thrived in it. The phrase that rang through my brain as the bombardier was performing his manly labor was the one which I'd heard so often from the girls at the Canteen, East London girls who were largely beneath my station and whose libidos were marvelously untroubled by concerns of conscience, class, or gender. "Fucked proper" is what they expected and strove for in their liaisons, and by the time Max heaved a shuddering sigh and gone limp in my arms I covetously felt I had experienced at least a measure of what the East London girls meant. I'd been fucked proper. It was something I'd had no hope of achieving with Peter.

"What is it like, Max? Tell me about the place where you

work."

"I live in a small metal building like a rabbit hole with the other rabbits."

"No, I mean your aeroplane. Your "Liberator" as they call it."

"That's a real rabbit hole." Prompted by my curiosity, he went on to describe the tight crew confines of the big bomber which carried a crew of ten fellows. He was "jammed up," as he put it, in the nose section with a gunner and a navigator. "It's cold, tight and noisy as hell. There's no reasonable chance of escape. It's a death sentence. You sign your own death sentence every time you go up."

"A flying coffin I believe you said."

"Designed by people who view our lives as expendable. Once you're in, you can't get out, except through the bomb bay. We have other names, not so damn polite."

"Which must be why you made your arrangement, as you call it."

"Clever girl."

But it wasn't cleverness that prompted my curiosity. I don't know what to call it. I wanted to understand, I suppose. To know what occurred at the intersection of a man's love of life and his sense of duty. Over the many nights that we Londoners had cowered under the droning Heinkels of the Luftwaffe we had developed a cold, implacable hatred of the machines and of the men who flew them. We did not distinguish one from the other. The men were machines, the machines were men. But now I was beginning to grasp that the men were in the machines, but were not themselves the machines. Like Max, the German fliers themselves undoubtedly experienced fear, desolation, resignation, prayed their own prayers, made their own arrangements. We English had another turn of phrase that aptly described such a plight: "Proper fucked," we called it. It was for when you got yourself into a situation from which there was no immediate relief, maybe no relief ever. "Fucked" might be a passing inconvenience, a momentary interruption in an otherwise decent life. "Proper fucked" meant that normalcy was suddenly a long way off, and that life might never be truly decent again. It was what Max felt when he crawled into his rabbit hole and went into the sky.

Side by side we lay on our backs, not touching. I could tell by his breathing that Max had drifted into slumber. Selfishly I hoped that he might reach for me, touch me, bury himself in me again. But I was still an English girl, and war or no war, I had my natural sense of reticence, my pride. Outside I could hear a light rain brushing the treetops. Eventually I too slept.

Accustomed to rising well before dawn as he was, Max was up and out, shaved and dressed before I ever stirred. I was awakened by the aroma of coffee. When I opened my eyes he was sitting on the edge of the bed holding a cup. I recalled his comment about coffee in the tea shop. "Looking forward this morning, are we?" I asked.

"It's the instant variety. Hope you don't mind. I brought along a couple of packets."

I fluffed up the pillows underneath my shoulders and sat up, sipping the slightly chalky, bitter brew. It was rejuvenating, if not savory. Max watched me. "You look a lot like the singer," he said. "You know the one."

"Vera Lynn. So I've heard." Just a few years older than me, she was the enormously popular sweetheart of the Allied troops for her touching renditions of the classic wartime songs "White Cliffs of Dover," and "We'll Meet Again." Vera had the slightly horsey features and the inbred composure which we British had long associated with female beauty, though I'd always thought of her rather severe looks as something that might look appropriate on the bow of a clipper ship. Still, it was by no means a disadvantage to be compared with her, especially coming from a Yank. Between Peter and me it was a sort of standing joke. "I'm with Vera," he would tell new friends when we were out and about.

"You're much lovelier, though," Max added, and leaning in kissed me lightly on the forehead. Ever the gallant one.

I sipped from my cup. "I'm curious about one thing, Max." I suppose my vain female ego was seeking some understanding for the manner in which I had abandoned the safety of my life and fallen into such a predictable fling with an awkwardly dashing airman. "When you first spotted me at the Canteen, and you sort of began stalking me - did you want me because you thought you could have me?"

He looked at me as though taken aback by the idea. "That's not the way it works, Claudine," he said. "I thought I could have you because I wanted you."

That broke me a bit. Tears squeezed out, unbidden. I drew up my knees and placed my forehead upon them. Reaching out, Max took the coffee cup from me. He stroked my hair. "Your virtue is unattainable to the likes of me, Claudine. It could only come as a gift." He leaned in and drawing back my hair, pressed his lips briefly to my ear.

After a moment I looked up and met his gaze. "Because you agreed not to resist."

He shrugged and grinned crookedly. "And here we are."

There was to be no second night in our honeymoon bed. As Max had informed me at the station on the previous afternoon, all leaves had been cut short. He was due to report back to his squadron at Halesworth by 3:00 PM on Saturday.

"I thought they weren't flying as many missions," I said by way of complaint.

"Invasion stuff," he'd explained tersely. "When we're not flying actual missions, we're training." And that had been the extent of the conversation. Girls who persisted in asking questions about military matters were not popular on anybody's dance card. And so, after I pulled myself together and made myself presentable (the precious nylon stockings were safely tucked away in my grip) we toddled downstairs with our bags all packed up. On the sideboard in the parlor of the guesthouse tea and scones were being served, but neither of us was in any mood to make polite chitchat with other guests. Max collected a couple of scones and after making arrangements with the proprietress to leave our bags until later, we slipped out-of-doors to find that the rain had passed and the skies had a nicely scrubbed look to them. A watery sun warmed the air considerably. It was getting on towards the end of May, and our English spring was beginning to take hold at last. It was an open invitation to go for a stroll.

As we munched our scones our route initially took us away from the river but after we had covered just a few hundred yards we turned onto a smaller road that carried us back to the east and soon we were just a hundred yards or so from the river and walking parallel to it. Except for the occasional workingman's lorry, the road was marvelously abandoned. Max held my hand loosely as we walked. "I'm sorry we didn't get to spend time in your London," he remarked.

"Pooh. I'm damned glad to be out of it for awhile." Then I thought perhaps I had caught an ulterior meaning to his comment. "Which is not to say there won't be other opportunities, is it?"

"Who's to say, Claudine? Fortunes of war and all that." He squeezed my hand and grinned at me, squinting in the bright hazy air. He wore his dark brown officer's cap cocked at an angle over one eye. His khaki tie matched his trousers. For the first time I noticed that the bronze-colored wings that he wore on his lapel were adorned with a tiny bomb. Sometime later, in a conversation with another American flier, I learned that the bombardiers were considered the most important members of the combat crews because they were the ones who were trained to drop the bombs on the target - which was of course the entire purpose of the mission. Without a qualified bombardier on board the whole exercise became rather pointless. The same officer told me that in shoot-downs of Libertors the bombardiers, navigators, and nose gunners rarely survived because they couldn't crawl out of their assigned spaces quickly enough to don their parachutes. Flying Coffins indeed. But on this day that conversation was thankfully yet to take place.

Nonetheless, the "fortunes of war" was not likely to be a cheering theme, so I smoothly switched gears. "Detroit is where you Americans build your motor-cars, isn't it?"

"Sure is. They don't call us the "Motor City" for nothing." His boyish pride was shining through.

"And how would you say our English motor-cars compare?"

"Other than putting the steering wheel on the wrong side, they're all right. Except that it seems like they're all black. We paint ours different colors – blue, green, red."

"And you build so many of them."

"When we're not building bombers." His expression suddenly changed. Dropping my hand, he lifted his and shaded his eyes, scanning the sky to the west. "Speaking of which."

After just a moment I too became aware of that change in the atmosphere that signaled the approach of a fleet of airships. It was an event well known to us Londoners, to say nothing of civilian populations all over Europe. First there would be a slight shading of sound as the vibration of the heavens would drop into a lower register. The vibration would begin to spread and the register to drop even further. Depending on the time of day or the weather you couldn't necessarily see the bombers yet, but by then you would be scuttling down the stairs into the Tube or looking for a basement somewhere if you knew what was good for you. Since the Germans had bombed almost exclusively at night, we seldom saw much of the machines themselves. But we knew the sound well enough. Too well, in fact.

Like children interrupted at play we stood with our faces tilted expectantly upward as they materialized against the hazy horizon. Wingtip to wingtip, black and ominous, with that thrumming sound building, inexorably they came. "Are they your Liberators?" I asked him.

"The Forts don't make a sound like that, Claudine. Nothing does." As the leading edge of the formation drew near their amassed engines thundered with a deep-seated intensity that seemed to reach right down into your very soul. It entered and lodged itself there both as a promise and a threat. "Heading for the pens at Le Havre," Max concluded, his face still turned upward. For a long moment

I watched him watching them. His attitude seemed almost prayer-like.

Being in the roadway with the planes approaching overhead was reflexively causing me to feel unsettled, in need of sanctuary. Reaching out I took his hand and tugged him toward a gentle berm that separated the roadway from the fields beyond. Once across the berm we walked out into the wild grasses. They were knee-high and caressed our legs as we moved. Accented with small explosions of color from the volunteer marigolds, primroses and hollyhocks, the field was as fragrant and inviting as the plush garden of a hidden country cottage. The steady din from above was still increasing when I sank to my knees and pulled Max down beside me. He seemed uncertain of himself and of me, so I spelled it out more clearly by lying on my stomach with my face thrust into the grasses, breathing in the aroma of my England. I released Max's hand and I'm afraid to say that I arched my body invitingly.

Once his fixation on the sight of the B-24's overhead was broken, Max wasn't long in accepting. Straddling me he drew my skirt up over my bottom and tugged my panties down my thighs. Quickly he was inside me, grasping my waist and drawing me up to improve his angle of penetration. This was not the measured and loving cadence of the previous evening. This was a splendidly brutish animal act between two people whose cravings for the moment overrode any considerations of dignity or propriety. Their civilized behaviors, their delicate emotional needs belonged to another time. The sky above was now filled end to end with the oddly liberating choir of mechanical certainty and as Max's strokes became more feverish I braced my knees under me and hurried to keep up. As he approached his climax he pounded into me with an urgency that gave me an exhilarating, focused identity quite apart from any I'd ever felt. In exquisite agony I worked my bare feet into the grasses and dug the rich earth with my toes, biting my lips until they bruised. As suddenly as it had begun, it subsided, and Max lay spent on top of me, the two of us still except for the heaving of our chests. Soon the armada of Liberators dwindled, passed away, and the heavens were returned to a state of Spring quietude. Lifting himself off me, Max arranged my undergarments and smoothed my skirt down over my legs. I rolled over and our eyes met. Finding each other intact and unrepentant, we stood up, brushed one another off, and made our way through the grasses, across the berm, and back to the roadway where we resumed strolling as any civilized couple might.

That is our story. The rest is postscript, *denouement*. After an hour Max caught his train to return to his base, and I embarked for London just a short while later. That evening I was back at Peter's flat in the comfort of his familiar dry embrace, and the next evening I returned to my station at the Canteen, thankful for the distraction of the work and the busyness that accompanied it. Max did not come down the next weekend, and when the club went virtually dead the weekend following, we all knew what that meant. The invasion was launched in the early hours of that first Tuesday of June, and for a time we were all drawn out of our selfish private concerns as the mighty armies wrestled for control of the continent, and ultimately the civilization which had flourished upon it. Then as the weeks went by and there was no call, telegram, or letter I girded myself emotionally to accept the obvious conclusion.

"Miss Simmons?" He had the twin bars of a Captain on his lapel and his tone was polite and official, not one for banter. "I'm Captain Brashears of the Second Combat Group, 458th Squadron. We're based up in Halesworth." He had come into the Canteen early in the evening in the latter part of June and asked one of the hostesses to fetch me. I met him in a quiet corner near the kitchen. When I replied, "I know," to his introduction, he gave me a quizzical look. "I know you're based in Halesworth," I explained. Get on with it, I thought.

"I've been asked by one of our squadron commanders to make a point of informing you. It's not good news, Miss Simmons, but it may not be bad news either. *The Barnstormer* has gone missing over France. Down by enemy fire we presume. As far as the crew goes, there has been no word. They very well may have become prisoners, we've no reason to believe otherwise."

I had every reason to believe otherwise, but I saw no point in inflicting the good Captain with my female misgivings. Compassion was what was called for. "May I invite you to drink a cup of tea, Captain?"

Grateful I suppose not to find himself in the presence of an angry, distraught shrew, the Captain readily accepted my invitation. Over the span of the next half-hour he somewhat reluctantly confirmed what Max had told me about the low survival rate of Liberator crews. But I didn't need statistics nor actuarial tables, not even the aviator's methods of celestial navigation to confirm for me the fate which had awaited my Max over the skies of France. If the night of lovemaking in the Bridge Guesthouse in lovely Ipswich had not sufficed to satisfy the terms of his "arrangement," the spontaneous trip over the berm and into the fields the following morning certainly had. When we had parted company on the station platform at Ipswich, he had hinted as much.

"It would be nice to plan on seeing one another again, don't you think?" I had ventured.

His smile was untroubled but not very convincing. "More than I could ever ask for, I'm afraid. But I will. Just in case." Taking me by the shoulders he had kissed me rather sweetly and then boarded his train. There was no leaning out the car window for a jaunty wave or a last longing look. Once aboard, he did not reappear.

He had wanted, I suppose, to accustom himself as quickly as possible to the remainder of a brief life without me.